OBLIVION

Also by Kelly Creagh

NEVERMORE

ENSHADOWED

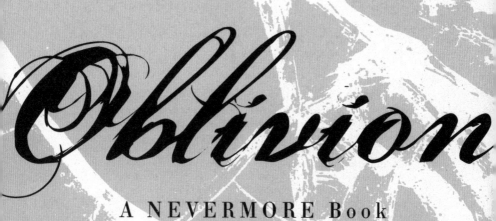

Oblivion

A NEVERMORE Book

KELLY CREAGH

A Atheneum Books for Young Readers
atheneum NEW YORK LONDON TORONTO SYDNEY NEW DELHI

ATHENEUM BOOKS FOR YOUNG READERS
An imprint of Simon & Schuster Children's Publishing Division
1230 Avenue of the Americas, New York, New York 10020

For information about special discounts for bulk purchases,
please contact Simon & Schuster Special Sales at
1-866-506-1949 or business@simonandschuster.com.
The Simon & Schuster Speakers Bureau can bring authors to your live event.
For more information or to book an event, contact the Simon & Schuster Speakers
Bureau at 1-866-248-3049 or visit our website at www.simonspeakers.com.
The text for this book is set in Stempel Garamond LT.
Manufactured in the United States of America

2 4 6 8 10 9 7 5 3
Library of Congress Cataloging-in-Publication Data
Creagh, Kelly.
Oblivion / Kelly Creagh.
pages cm — (A Nevermore book)
Summary: Isobel Lanley is terrified to return to the desolate and dangerous
dreamworld where she had a deadly confrontation with Varen, but when her
nightmares resume, bleeding into reality, she is left with no choice, and to make
matters worse, the ghostly demon Lilith will do anything to get Varen for her own.
ISBN 978-1-4424-3627-5 (hardcover)
ISBN 978-1-4424-3629-9 (eBook)
[1. Horror stories. 2. Poe, Edgar Allan, 1809–1849—Fiction. 3. Demonology—
Fiction. 4. High schools—Fiction. 5. Schools—Fiction.] I. Title.
PZ7.C85983Obl 2015
[Fic]—dc23 2014015820

FOR MY DEAR
FRIENDS AND FELLOW
DREAMWORLD DWELLERS

April Joye Cannon, Nick Passafiume, and Bill Wolfe

Contents

Prologue 1

1. A Valentine 5

2. Missing Pieces 20

3. Disillusions 34

4. Dust to Dust 41

5. Loss of Breath 46

6. The Grey Tombstone 62

7. Echoes 69

8. Approaching Darkness 78

9. Beyond the Veil 91

10. Cobwebs of the Mind 100

11. Noc Noc 111

12. Phantom Chased 119

13. Within the Distant Aidenn 127

14. Emergence 133

15. Images 138

16. Perils Parallel 153

17. Back into the Tempest 160

18. Ashes, Ashes 172

19. Double Exposure 177

20. Twixt and Twain 189

21. Head Games 198

22. Checkmate 206

23. In the Hearts of the Most Reckless 213

24. Mummer 223

25. Disturbances 228

26. Crisscrossed   237

27. Amid the Mimic Rout   244

28. The Assignation   252

29. Time Out of Time   265

30. By Horror Haunted   272

31. Reversion   279

32. Dissever   292

33. Yet Unbroken   300

34. Darkness and Decay   308

35. Deadlocked   319

36. Out All   326

37. Neither of Ingress or Egress   331

38. Shrapnel   337

39. Redoubled   341

40. Dual   346

41. Relics   357

42. Unbinding   364

43. The Heart Whose Woes Are Legion   372

44. White-Robed Forms   376

45. Nameless Here for Evermore   380

46. In a Mad Rushing Descent as of the Soul into Hades   389

47. Nepenthe   398

48. Dreams No Mortal Ever Dared to Dream   410

49. Only This and Nothing More   427

Epilogue   431

Acknowledgments   435

⁎   *⁎*   *⁎*

The boundaries which divide Life from Death are at best shadowy and vague. Who shall say where the one ends, and where the other begins?

— Edgar Allan Poe, "The Premature Burial"

There is no passion in nature so demoniacally impatient, as that of him, who shuddering upon the edge of a precipice, thus meditates a plunge. To indulge for a moment, in any attempt at thought, is to be inevitably lost; for reflection but urges us to forbear, and therefore it is, I say, that we cannot. If there be no friendly arm to check us, or if we fail in sudden effort to prostrate ourselves backward from the abyss, we plunge, and are destroyed.

— Edgar Allan Poe, "The Imp of the Perverse"

⁎   *⁎*   *⁎*

Prologue
Providence, Rhode Island
The home of the widow
Mrs. Sarah Helen Whitman
November 9, 1848

"I beg of you to hear me, Helen!"

His voice rang shrill through the house, funneling up the narrow stairwell and down the hall, muffled little by the barrier of her bedroom door.

Pen in hand, Helen stared at the blank sheet of paper that waited on her writing desk. In her other hand, she clutched her white, lace-trimmed handkerchief, and the saccharine aroma of the ether contained within the cloth enticed her to breathe from its folds again.

She resisted, her focus remaining on the parchment.

But the promise of an empty page did little to ease the poetess's mind the way it might have on a quieter morning. Even the ether, with its power to lull her senses, could do nothing to slow the palpitations of her agitated heart. Not with her ears attuned to the beseeching roars of the man whose recent behavior both confused and terrified her.

"Helen, without you I am lost. *Lost!*" he shouted, the anguished plea like a cry from hell itself.

It was true that she was hiding from him, firm in her decision to wait him out as she would a storm. She told herself, again, that she *could not* see him like this, fearful less of what words might pass between them—even of what answer she might give him—than of what she would find if she dared to look too closely into those eyes.

"A single word! *One!* That is all I ask."

"That is *enough*, Mr. Poe."

At the sound of her mother's sharpened tone, Helen glanced toward the door, the tight ringlets of her dark-brown hair bouncing against her cheeks.

"You should be ashamed of yourself," her mother went on. "There is simply no excuse for this beastly conduct."

Helen could tell her mother's patience had fled. Her indignation had at last morphed into fury, and it would not be long now until one of them would bend to the breaking point.

Goodness knew what would happen then. . . .

Clearly something had to give. Someone.

Despite her trepidation, Helen knew that if any semblance of peace was to be restored to her home—to her *spirit*—that someone would have to be her.

"Helen! I pray that you are listening," he railed, continuing to ignore her mother's upbraiding. "Hear me in this—in what is certain to be my final plea. My life, my very *soul* depends upon you!"

Helen dropped her pen to the desk, rising. She pressed her handkerchief to her lips, closed her eyes, and inhaled. Then she made her way to the door and, opening it, frowned at finding her sister, Anna, standing just outside with her back pressed to the wall.

"You're not going down there," Anna said, her expression stern. "Ignore him as you have been. Let him crow on like his damnable raven until he has no voice left with which to squawk."

Helen's name rose once again from the first-floor foyer, this time in a ragged scream.

Anna sneered. "Lord in heaven, have you ever heard anything so awful in your life?"

"Has he made any mention of what might have prompted this . . . visit?" Helen asked in a murmur, not wanting him to hear her, to know his howling had succeeded in drawing her from her seclusion.

"I think impropriety is the word you are searching for," Anna replied in a hiss. "And yes. He did attempt to explain to Mother that after sitting for a daguerreotype this morning, he saw a white face in the studio's light-reflecting mirror. It stared straight at him, he said, with eyes black as night."

"Those were his words exactly?"

"He is mad, Helen. Do not go to him."

Helen made no reply but took her first steps toward the stairwell, skirts rustling.

"Do you care this little for me?" she heard him wail. "Do you doubt me? Or suspect I have not told you the truth entirely?"

"It is no use shouting these delirious inquiries, Mr. Poe,"

her mother said. "It should be beyond clear to you that my daughter has no wish to entertain your call."

"I am doomed, Helen! Doomed! In time and eternity. All I ask is for one word. Say yes, Helen. Say yes and save this poor wretch. Say what you have not yet said. That you *do* love me!"

"Edgar." Helen spoke his name as she stepped onto the topmost stair. At the sound of her voice, his head jerked up.

Dressed in his shirtsleeves, his dark hair wild, his eyes crazed, he looked, to Helen, the very portrait of insanity.

She drew in a sharp breath. Clutching tightly to the banister, she steeled herself and began to descend, closing the distance between them one tremulous step at a time.

"*Helen.*" He held a quivering hand out to her. "You *have* heard me. And now at last you've come. An angel sent to save me from perdition."

"Edgar, what is the meaning—?"

"My fate rests with you." He fell to his knees and clutched the skirts of her dress, peering up at her. For a moment, Helen lost her ability to speak, wondering if what she saw could be attributed to the heightening effects of the ether.

Gone were the ghost-gray eyes of the man who'd proposed to her in the cemetery less than two months before, and she now wondered if the spectral gaze he'd claimed to have seen in the mirror that morning could have belonged to his own reflection.

For the eyes that stared up at her now, imploring and full of dread, were indeed as black as night.

Blacker.

1
A Valentine

Dear Varen,

    After putting your name on paper, it seems I can hardly hold my pen steady. So this won't be neat. I'm not good with words like you are, so it won't be eloquent, either.

    Valentine's Day is this weekend. I'm in English class, and Mr. Swanson wants us to work on composing romantic sonnets. He's gone over the format twice, but thinking about iambic pentameter and quatrains makes me feel like I'm trying to solve a math word problem. At least, I'm pretty sure my poetry reads like one.

    If you were here, I know you'd already be done with yours. I also know it would be beautiful.

    I can see your desk from where I'm sitting. I won't find you there even if I look, but part of me is always afraid that I will.

    Sometimes I wonder if that's what you wanted. For me to be afraid of you. For everyone to be afraid, so no one would try to get close.

    They tell me that I died. They say that I was dead, and I want to tell them I still am. At least that's how I feel. Because I know where you are and what's become of you. Because

I couldn't stop it and I couldn't bring you back. Because Reynolds was right when he told me I couldn't reach you.

Everything's broken.

And yet here I am, writing you what must be a Valentine.

Because even though I know I shouldn't still love you, even though I know that is the last thing I should have room to feel for you, more than anything, I want to tell you I do.

Isobel lifted her shaking pen from the vein-blue lines of her notebook, wondering how the confession had managed to escape her.

She'd never written like that before, where the words just poured out, unstoppable.

The final line burned into her retinas, echoing a truth that she'd hoped to keep hidden away, locked inside with everything else.

She smacked a hand on the paper, crumpling it.

What was *wrong* with her? Why couldn't she let go?

Why, when he had let *her* go?

The lunch bell rang, the noise shredding her already frayed nerves.

"Okay, folks," Mr. Swanson said, standing from behind his desk, his wooden rolling chair sliding back to bump against the chalk tray. "I'd like to go ahead and collect these today, even if you're not finished. I'll hand them back tomorrow, so you'll have the first few minutes of class to do some revising, and then I'll grade them over the weekend."

Everyone got up, papers flapping, and the unanimous

flutter in the room reminded Isobel of a flock of birds taking wing.

Tekeli-li . . .

Afraid someone might catch sight of Varen's name, Isobel ripped her own rumpled paper free and stuffed it into the middle of the notebook.

Glancing up, she saw that Mr. Swanson had moved to the door. Like a ticket taker, he collected papers as her classmates filed into the hall.

"Another reason I should gather these now," he said, "is the simple fact that many a great work of literature has been lost by remaining tucked haphazardly into the pockets and knapsacks of young, carefree scribes such as yourselves. Wanderlust wayfarers, cavalier bards, wistful wordsmiths — "

"And phat rappers," Bobby Bailey said as he handed Mr. Swanson his sonnet.

"And portly rappers, why not?" Mr. Swanson conceded with a nod, adding Bobby's paper to the accumulating stack.

Isobel rose. She tore off the top sheet of her notebook and, gathering her things, kept her head down as she approached the door and its guardian. Handing in the blank paper, she ducked past him into the hall.

"Ah, Miss Lanley," he called after her, his voice carrying over the rising chatter and banging of lockers.

Flinching, Isobel stopped.

"I see thou hast submitted parchment free of words, and thus error. How very avant-garde," Mr. Swanson said, talking in that way he sometimes did, like a Shakespeare character who had somehow clawed his way out from the press of musty book pages.

The power of words . . .

"Fear not, fair leader of cheers," he went on, "I both recognize and appreciate the temperament of the artist who feels her work is, as yet, unfit for the scrutiny of another's eye. So how about I grant thou till the morrow to turn in yon magnum opus I saw thou scribbling on mere moments ago?"

She clutched her books tighter.

"No offense, Mr. Swanson," Isobel heard Katlyn Binkly interject, "but I think you read too much."

Grateful for the momentary distraction, Isobel slid alongside Bobby and his basketball friends. Hiding herself between their lumbering forms and the wall, she used them for cover while they headed for the cafeteria.

"Alas," she heard Mr. Swanson sigh as she moved down the hall, "'tis entirely possible. But would you have me forfeit my adoration of the written word for such folly as reality TV?"

Isobel steered herself away from Bobby's group and past a senior couple kissing behind an open locker door meant to hide their PDA from Mr. Nott, the hall-slash-lunchroom monitor. The girl had her arms thrown around the boy's neck. In one hand, she clutched a small bouquet, bundled together with baby's breath and wrapped in clear plastic.

Isobel halted when she caught sight of crimson buds through the glossy film.

Three red roses.

Taking notice of Isobel, the girl broke the kiss. Following

his girlfriend's gaze, the boy turned his head to see what had interrupted their embrace.

"What are you staring at?" he asked.

An infamous question, Isobel thought. One she'd been asked before.

"Taking notes?" the girl chimed in.

Notes.

Isobel moved on without responding.

"Freaking head case," she heard the boy mutter.

The whispers didn't bother her anymore, though. Not like they used to.

Bypassing the entrance to the lunchroom, she made her way to the side door that led to the courtyard. She wanted to avoid the displays of cardboard-cutout arrow-pierced hearts, dart-shooting cupids, and dangling red-and-white streamers. That meant steering clear of the cafeteria and the gym, both of which had been festooned in decorations.

Isobel shoved open the door, and February greeted her with icy breath.

As she walked to one of the courtyard's empty stone benches, gathering the escaping wisps of her hair and tucking them behind one ear, her fingertips brushed the cheek that bore a slanted, needle-thin scar.

Though the wound had healed, and though she took care to mask it every morning with concealer and powder, Isobel still felt the scar's presence. It carried with it a constant, low-grade pain she could never be certain was real or imagined: a by-product of lingering nerve damage, or a sensation produced from the lasting memory of how she'd received the gash.

We are ever and always home now.

Pinfeathers's final words bubbled up through the mire of haunting echoes in her mind. In spite of herself, she checked the oak tree limbs and scanned the school's roof ledge, searching for any sign of ebony feathers, or the black stare that longed for . . . what? She doubted even *he* knew.

Had known.

Isobel set her things down on the bench, unsure of what to do with herself. Wanting to avoid Gwen, she hadn't stopped by their adjacent lockers to pick up her parka or the sack lunch she'd made that morning.

Since today was Trenton's annual Valentine's Day luncheon, she had told Gwen the previous afternoon that she wanted to spend the lunch break on her own. She'd done so as a favor to both of them. So Gwen could be with Mikey without feeling guilty about leaving her alone, and so that Isobel wouldn't have to endure Gwen's sympathetic glances and well-meaning attempts at condolence.

Even though Gwen still knew nothing about what had happened after Isobel disappeared through the open tomb door and into the dreamworld, there was one thing her friend could deduce through observation alone.

Isobel had failed to return with Varen.

As far as Gwen knew—as far as anyone knew—Isobel remembered nothing. And whether or not Gwen bought the amnesia act, Isobel didn't think her friend had any real inkling as to what had actually occurred. She must have assumed that Varen had been determined to stay. Or worse, that Isobel had found him dead.

In a way, it felt like she had.

Whatever conclusion Gwen had drawn this time, though, she wasn't asking questions or pushing for answers.

Maybe she had learned her lesson in that regard.

Maybe now that Gwen had her own losses to take into account—a fractured arm and a shattered sense of reality, perhaps even her own nightmares to contend with—she would simply give Isobel the slow fade. Like Isobel's crew—Stevie, Nikki, and Alyssa—Gwen would find a way to bow out and extract herself from Isobel's life. Or, like Brad, she might even convince her family to move to another state.

"Special delivery," came a voice from behind her, its clipped and all-too-familiar Brooklyn accent instantly negating all of Isobel's theories.

Turning, she found Gwen standing a few yards away, her left arm free of its cast but still supported by a navy-blue sling. In her other hand, she held up a small paper basket of food.

"Mummified cucumbers and petrified potatoes," Gwen said. "I hear pickles and Tater Tots are good for what ails you. Of course, I hope you don't mind that I took the liberty of implementing the friend tax by eating the crispy Tots off the top."

"Where's Mikey?" Isobel asked.

With a small, chagrined smirk, Gwen jerked her head over her good shoulder toward the cafeteria, where Mikey stood behind one of the wide windows, the side of his face and both palms smashed against the glass. Dressed in a black-and-white checkered hoodie and a pair of sunglasses that sat slanted across his mashed nose, he reminded Isobel of a giant swatted fly.

"Wow," Isobel said.

"He makes up in skill what he lacks in couth, if you catch my drift," said Gwen with a wink.

"Won't Mr. Nott catch him doing that?"

Gwen shrugged, then set the paper basket down on the bench next to Isobel's things. "I think he's trying to cheer you up. You gotta cut him a break, though. He doesn't know anything about, y'know . . . anything."

Isobel knew Gwen meant Baltimore. And Varen. And her.

Even though Isobel didn't quite get Mikey's allure, she was glad he and Gwen had started dating. Or pseudo-dating or . . . whatever was up with them. Mikey's added presence to Isobel and Gwen's locker run-ins and lunch breaks gave Isobel an excuse not to talk about things that fell into the "anything" category Gwen had mentioned. And a reason for Gwen to continue keeping her questions to herself. Aside from that, though, and perhaps most important of all, Isobel could tell Gwen was falling for the guy.

The tipping point, she knew, had been the morning Mikey had flown up to Baltimore to get Gwen—January nineteenth, the same morning an anonymous stranger had dropped Isobel off, soaking wet and half-dead, at the city's university hospital.

The same morning she'd flat-lined.

Edgar Allan Poe's birthday.

A week later Isobel had come home with her family. A week after that, she'd returned to school to learn through Gwen, during their initial and only private locker visit since Isobel's literal reintegration into reality, that Mikey had used money from a pizza delivery job to buy his plane ticket. Since Gwen had suffered a fractured arm at the hands of Reynolds while trying to help Isobel in the cemetery, the task of making the eleven-hour return drive in her Cadillac had fallen to Mikey as well. According to Gwen, however, he'd made the trek in under eight. Having ridden with him the night of the Grim Facade, Isobel didn't find that hard to believe. At all.

In addition to filling Isobel in on the details of her return, Gwen had also recounted how Reynolds had run from the police after Isobel had shut him out of the dreamworld. The responding officers, Gwen had said, had seemed determined to detain anyone involved in the scuffle, even if that someone happened to be the Poe Toaster himself.

No one had caught him, though. He'd vanished, like he did every year, and Gwen had used the distraction of his flight to take refuge behind the headstone he'd flung her against. After that, she'd made her own escape by slipping into the crowd of onlookers.

Because of the overshadowing story that the Baltimore Ravens had lost the finals, missing out on their Super Bowl ticket, the only mention of the Poe Toaster ordeal in the press had been how a few spectators had scaled the cemetery walls. Again.

And while Gwen's parents (who thought Gwen had headed to New York to meet up with her cousins for a concert) had bought their daughter's carefully constructed story—one that included a mosh-pit mishap—Isobel's parents had perceived much more of the truth.

Though they knew nothing of Isobel's trip to the graveyard, Gwen's involvement, or how everything tied to Poe, Isobel's mom and dad knew enough to guess that she had gone to the city looking for Varen.

Her mother and father had interrogated her a thousand times over as a result. In each instance, Isobel had regurgitated the lie that she remembered nothing past the point of sitting down to dinner at a restaurant with her father.

No, she didn't know whose car their Baltimore waitress had seen her climb into. No, she didn't remember where the driver had taken her or why. No, she didn't know who had dropped her off at the hospital. No, she wasn't faking, and no, she wasn't lying. No. No. No.

Thankfully, Isobel's psychologist, Dr. Robinson, had instructed her parents to stop the barrage of questions, to carry on with day-to-day life and wait for the memories to resurface on their own.

In truth, Isobel would never forget what had happened. Ever.

Bloodred rose petals, falling ash, broken shards. Destruction and ruin—everything reversed. A beautiful monster and a monstrous beauty. Voices in the corridor. Varen. The cliff . . .

Her ribbon floating up and away, a fluttering line of pale pink blotted with her own blood.

"Pretty bad if you're trying to cheer up a cheerleader, huh?" Gwen asked.

Isobel blinked from her reverie. "I'm not a cheerleader anymore."

"Ehh." Gwen waved her off. "You're just on sabbatical. You and I both know your feet won't stay fixed to the ground for long."

Isobel winced but tried to hide it by glancing at Mikey, who had since started to mime walking up and down an imaginary flight of stairs, his lower body hidden by the school's brick siding. He switched to mimicking rowing a boat just as Mr. Nott appeared behind him, his lined face fixed in a glower.

"So . . . you two are going to the Valentine's Day dance tomorrow, right?" Isobel asked.

Shifting her weight, Gwen gave her a hooded glare. "Like you weren't standing right there when he asked me. Hey, how about I see your obnoxious bid for a subject change and raise you one swift kick in the spankies?"

Isobel tried for a smile, but it didn't stick.

Frowning, Gwen tucked her good hand inside her patchwork purse and withdrew a folded newspaper, holding it out to her. "Listen, I know you said you wanted to be alone or whatever, but I saw this in today's paper and thought you should know."

Isobel took the paper. Reading the first line of the short block of text circled in red, she felt her heart stammer a beat.

Nobit, Bruce Albert, 69, passed away Monday, February ninth, at his residence.

She looked up, dumbstruck, a sharp pit-of-the-stomach pang shattering her numbness.

"He said March," she breathed, her voice catching as she recalled the ominous warning Bruce had given her the last time she'd been inside Nobit's Nook, the bookshop he'd owned—the same place where she and Varen had once met to work on their Poe project.

Assuming she'd know where Varen had gone—that she was still in contact with him—Bruce had wanted Isobel to tell Varen how long he had to collect his vintage black Cougar, which he'd left parked outside the bookshop. *That's what the doctors said,* Bruce had added, betraying the fact that the March deadline had little to do with the car.

Along with so much else she'd wanted to say to Varen, she'd never gotten the chance.

Isobel scanned the obituary, searching for an answer to Bruce's death. It mentioned his military service as a Green Beret and the two local businesses he'd owned. Below that, Isobel skimmed over the names of a deceased wife and son and a surviving nephew who lived in New York. There were no other details.

Isobel shook her head, still not comprehending. "It says the funeral is tomorrow morning."

Gwen shrugged her good shoulder. "Yeah. I, uh, didn't know if you . . . I dunno . . . wanted to go or something."

Go? To the funeral?

"You mean skip school," Isobel said.

"I can take us."

"I can't." Isobel held the paper out to Gwen.

How could she risk it? One more step beyond her parents' boundaries, one more instance of sneaking off, and her mom and dad would have her shipped off to reform school for sure. Or more likely, locked away in some mental facility.

Besides that, Bruce had never been shy about letting Isobel know he blamed her for everything that had happened to Varen, including his disappearance. *Especially* his disappearance. She doubted he would have even wanted her there.

Still, the old man had been Varen's best friend. Quite possibly his only true friend.

"So," Gwen said with a sigh, "I know you're out here to get away and process and all that. I just figured this was important. I know I'm not supposed to call your house or cell, so if there's a possibility you might change your mind, you should let me know before last bell. Or if you want, I can just leave."

Isobel looked down at the paper again, which Gwen had yet to take back. Tomorrow would be Friday the thirteenth. *Ironic,* she thought.

Then she had a new thought—one that drove the ache for Bruce's passing straight out of her, replacing it with a sickening stab of hope-laced fear.

Would Varen be there?

Isobel tightened her hold on the paper.

In the past, Varen had been able to astral project, to

appear or even be invisible in places other than wherever his body slept. The first time he'd done so had been the day of their presentation for the Poe project. Halloween. Though everyone had been able to see and hear him then, he'd vanished after leaving class.

Did Varen still hold the power to project into this world? If he did, and if he somehow knew about Bruce's death, if he came to the funeral and saw *her* there—saw that after everything, she still—

"Yes," Isobel said, before she could stop herself.

Gwen's face fell.

"I mean, no," Isobel corrected, "I don't want you to leave, but yes, I change my mind. I want to go . . . to the funeral. Please."

Gwen's expression softened. "Meet me by the door next to the gym right after second period. The one behind the stairs. No one's over there that early."

Turning, Gwen began to walk away.

Through the cafeteria windows, Isobel saw Mikey using a rag to wipe away the smudge marks he'd made on the glass while Mr. Nott stood to one side, hands on hips.

"Wait," Isobel called after her. "What about your arm? I thought you couldn't drive."

Gwen stopped and spun to face her again. With her good hand, she pinched the fabric of her sling at the elbow and, straightening her fractured arm, wiggled her fingers.

"Drove myself here every morning this week," she said, winking. "Arm's good. I'm just milking it."

With that, Gwen nestled her elbow back into its cradle, whirled, and hurried to the cafeteria, skirt swishing.

Dropping the rag, Mikey scuttled to meet Gwen as she entered through the glass doors. They shared a kiss, and Isobel felt her insides ice over again.

She turned her back on the scene, folded her arms, and shivered against the cold.

Now that she was alone, Isobel's momentary hope of seeing Varen began to dim and fade.

Since her return from Baltimore, she had neither dreamed of him during the nights, nor seen him—or anything from the other side—during her waking hours. Not even through the mirrors that had once acted as windows between worlds.

Perhaps, she consoled herself, it would be best to think of attending Bruce's funeral as a way to move on. To bury not just a man, but the memories that surrounded him.

Her way of saying good-bye to Varen, instead of writing him notes he'd never read.

Her turn to let go.

She thought she could do that if she didn't see him.

And maybe . . . maybe even if she did.

2
Missing Pieces

Isobel wasn't allowed to catch a ride home from school with Gwen anymore—or with anyone, for that matter. Taking the bus was out of the question, but her father no longer picked her up either.

That task now fell to her mother.

Every afternoon Isobel met her mom in front of the school and climbed into the rear seat of the car as it idled in the line of waiting vehicles.

Muttering a quick "Hey," she would then fork over her cell phone, which she wouldn't see until the following morning when her mom dropped her off again.

The only day her mother did not drive her straight home was Thursday, and although Isobel hated the weekly appointments, a part of her felt grateful for them too.

Her meetings with Dr. Robinson provided a barricade between her and her parents, a protective yellow tape barring them access to the evidence she held within. Because as long as Isobel kept her appointments, her mom and dad couldn't press her for answers. They had to back off, doctor's orders. All Isobel had to do in return was endure one hour every week of a stranger's tiptoeing inquiries.

During today's appointment, Dr. Robinson carried a clipboard to the black leather swivel chair across from Isobel. Her face still held that same kind-yet-uneasy smile. Isobel wanted to tell Dr. Robinson not to worry about keeping that expression in place, not to pull a cheek muscle over it. She knew the woman didn't know what to do with her, or what to tell her parents.

But Isobel said nothing. So far she'd done a good job of keeping her answers to various questions at a maximum of one to two sentences, well aware that anything she uttered in this woman's presence would end up on the doctor's word processor or yellow steno pad and, consequently, in her file.

Isobel's parents would undoubtedly be allowed to see her file at some point. And even though today was only her third session, she knew her mom and dad had to be petitioning for the reveal to happen sooner rather than later.

Three windows lined the wall behind the doctor's chair, their shades pulled snug to the sills. Sunlight peeked in around the edges, and its white glow ricocheted off Dr. Robinson's carefully arranged chestnut curls, giving her the ironic illusion of having a halo. A pair of floor lamps stood in opposite corners of the room, the light they offered far colder than that of the smothered sun, as unfeeling as the pavement-colored walls and the stiff, comfortless furniture.

"Your mom and I spoke on the phone yesterday about last week's appointment," Dr. Robinson began. "Did she tell you?"

"No," Isobel said. "But I didn't ask."

"So I'm gathering that you and your mom don't often talk. Would you say that's pretty normal, or is this a recent development?"

"Recent," Isobel said. "She and I know why we don't. Talk, that is."

"Because of what happened in Baltimore," Dr. Robinson said.

Isobel glanced up, wishing she had a stopwatch. She'd love to start clocking the amount of time it took during each session for the doctor's plaster smile to fade without her realizing. Today felt like some kind of record.

"Are we ready to discuss that?" Dr. Robinson asked. "You could start from whatever point feels most vivid."

Isobel knotted her hands in her lap, fingers twisting together. *Everything* felt vivid. Knife sharp—as potent and cutting as if she'd only just awoken from those moments that had almost been her last.

"I told you," Isobel said, dropping her gaze again. "I don't remember anything."

"On the phone, your mother mentioned that you were involved with the boy who went missing last Halloween. She said you two were paired up for a project and that you—"

"You already knew all of that," Isobel said.

"I'm sorry?"

"My mom told you to start asking about him, didn't she? I know she must have. So you can stop pretending that you didn't know about all of that from the very beginning. Before you ever started seeing me."

"Okay," Dr. Robinson said. "So let's assume for the moment that I *did* know from the onset of our sessions."

"You did," Isobel said, not sure why she wanted to do things this way today, why she wanted to challenge this person who was only trying to help her.

Maybe, she thought bleakly, the reason she wanted to push back was because she knew this woman *couldn't* help her, no matter how many framed degrees she had nailed to her wall.

Dr. Robinson tapped her pen against her chin. "So should I take this unusually strong approach of yours as an indication that you are ready to discuss his involvement?"

Isobel stiffened, scolding herself for not sticking to her usual formula of keeping her mouth shut. She wanted to backtrack, but now, thanks to her apparent need to be combative, she couldn't.

"He—doesn't have anything to do with what happened," Isobel said.

Dr. Robinson pinched her lips, a clear sign that she wasn't buying it.

"As long as we're airing things out, eliminating pretenses here," the doctor said, speaking more softly now, "if you truly don't remember anything that happened—like how you got that scar on your cheek, for instance—then how can you be so certain he *wasn't* involved? Your surety seems to suggest that you do know *something*. And . . . well, that's more than you've been letting on, wouldn't you agree?"

Isobel resisted the urge to look toward the door—to rise

and run. She gripped her knees instead, forcing herself to sit tight. "Are you calling me a liar?"

"I think you're afraid."

You don't know afraid, Isobel thought, glaring straight at her.

"Listen," Dr. Robinson said, "I know what happened had to have been bad. That's why you're here. I can help you cope. I understand that you might not feel ready to tell your parents what you've been through, and that's—"

"You would never believe me," Isobel said, shocking herself with her own words because she knew that, essentially, she'd just admitted to hiding the truth. That she had been hiding it the whole time.

Dr. Robinson blinked and raised her eyebrows, seeming equally surprised. Given that the doctor never reacted to anything Isobel said, she knew she'd crossed a line. From this point on, she could forget about trying to retrace her steps. Or covering her tracks.

But then, how long had she hoped to hold out? How long could she stand to keep everything hidden? Like with the letter she'd written that morning, the pain, confusion, and chaos that consumed her seemed determined to eat its way out regardless. If she kept it in, tried to drown it, what would stop it from rising again? From becoming something she could no longer control? Her very own Noc.

"Isobel, do you know where Varen Nethers is?" Dr. Robinson asked, hand tightening around her pen, apparently deciding to go for broke.

Isobel's eyes welled. His name still had the power to do that to her, to summon tears. Her body, still awake, still breathing, seemed to remember how to interpret pain. Yet she didn't feel the emotion that should accompany the prickling sting, not while her soul remained vacuum-sealed.

One tear slipped free and trailed hot down her cheek, dividing in two the warning scar Pinfeathers had given her.

"Isobel?" she heard the doctor ask, her voice dropping to a whisper. "Where is Varen?"

Isobel had asked the question once herself.

And what had Reynolds told her?

She looked up to meet the doctor's gaze, knowing that he'd been right.

"Lost," she said.

"Mom and Dad are going on a date tomorrow. Did you know that?"

Isobel's eyes flicked up from her algebra worksheet to her little brother, Danny, who sat across the kitchen table from her. He didn't meet her gaze but remained fixated on the shoe-box diorama in front of him, one plump hand shooting out to grab the glue stick at his side before vanishing behind the cardboard barrier again.

"It *is* Valentine's Day weekend," Isobel replied, returning to the quadratic equation before her, searching for where she'd left off. She frowned, unable to concentrate on the numbers. She *hadn't* known about the outing.

Probably because their mom and dad hadn't wanted her to.

Since she'd come home from Baltimore, at least one of her parents had always been present in the house with Isobel. So if Danny was telling the truth about the date, then tomorrow would mark the first time both her mother and father would be together somewhere other than home. And a date on the Friday night before Valentine's Day meant that the two of them must have made plans and reservations in advance.

She already knew that there would be zero chance of their leaving her in charge of Danny like they used to. Most likely, their mom had arranged for one of her single friends to come over.

"First of all, it's gross," Danny said, using scissors to cut out a large pyramid from a sheet of yellow construction paper. "Second of all, since when do Mom and Dad go on dates?"

Isobel shrugged. "They used to go out all the time." She drew her calculator close, not willing to admit to Danny that it *did* seem strange for their parents to make things sound so official. "Remember all those babysitters you used to torment? I think Mom and Dad only stopped going out when they ran out of cash-strapped high schoolers they could bribe to watch us. Then I became a freshman and, lucky me, I got to watch you for free."

Danny tossed the scissors onto the table. "Yeah, but they never called it a *date* before. Dating is what you do when you're getting to know someone. Or like, when you're trying to impress them. Not when you're married."

"Okay, Dr. Phil," she said, "is there some point you're trying to make?"

"Yeah. I don't like it."

"Because you're twelve and you think it's gross."

"I'll be thirteen in five months, it *is* gross, and no, that's not why I don't like it. I don't like it because it's weird."

"Yeah, well, you're weird but . . . I still like you."

Danny went silent, staring hard into the open recess of the shoe box. She watched him pick up the glue stick again, and when he went to work slathering the paper pyramid with it, she gave up waiting for a response and tried to refocus on the still-unsolved equation.

From somewhere upstairs, the vacuum kicked on, breaking her concentration a third time. Glancing to the clock on the stove, she saw that the digital numbers read 5:42, and her shoulders tensed. It had gotten late without her realizing. Their dad would be home soon—within the next ten or fifteen minutes, probably with pizza or some other kind of take-out in hand, since their mom hadn't been cooking much.

"You're not going to try to go anywhere while they're gone, are you?"

Isobel's attention snapped back to Danny, who peered at her intently through his mop of black bangs.

"Where would I go?" she replied in a quiet voice, because it was the quickest response she could think of. Because she didn't know if cutting school to attend the funeral tomorrow counted, since that would be in the morning. And because she didn't want to lie to him anymore in case it did.

Danny jutted his bottom lip out, somehow managing

to sneer at the same time. "Oh, I don't know. Another state, maybe. Some cult party. Bike-trashing event."

Isobel ducked her head as heat rushed to her cheeks. "I'm not going anywhere."

"Promise."

She tapped the pencil's eraser on the table, taking her turn to say nothing. She glared hard at the equation before her, willing the stupid thing to factor itself.

Above them, the vacuum droned on, creeping across the top landing toward Isobel's bedroom, where Isobel knew her mom would stop and let it run as a sound cover while she riffled through her things.

"Promise," Danny pressed. "Or I'll tell Mom and Dad not to leave."

"Jeez, Danny." Isobel smacked her pencil down. "I said I wouldn't."

"They keep fighting," he blurted. "Not when you're around. But they yell at each other over the phone when Dad picks me up from Scouts. I guess they don't think they have to hide it from me. Because I'm not the one who went crazy."

Isobel's mouth fell open, but it wasn't Danny's comment about her sanity that surprised her. She knew their parents had been fighting, and that the rift she'd caused between them wasn't something that could be healed with her dad's usual trick of flowers, or even a date. What she hadn't been aware of, though, was how much Danny had picked up on. Or that things had degraded to the point of yelling.

"Look, they're going to work it out," she said, because

she wanted to believe it too. And because saying so helped to assuage the guilt that crushed her a little more each day.

Because any other outcome seemed too impossible to consider.

"*I'm* going to work it out," she added, a vocal reminder for herself as much as for him. "So we're all just going to work it out. Okay?"

"Yeah well," Danny mumbled, nodding to her papers, "I hope you're better at solving mental issues than you are at math problems."

Flinching inwardly at the shot, Isobel tried not to let the hurt show on her face.

"You really think I'm crazy?"

"Um, *yes*," he said. "No," he amended quickly, hands ducking into the diorama again.

Isobel leaned back in her chair, the sting in her heart easing by a fraction.

She folded her arms. "That sounds suspiciously like something a crazy person would say. I dunno, maybe it's contagious. Or maybe it runs in the family. Ever consider that? You could probably start coming to my sessions with me if you wanted. The worst part is when they hook you up to the electrodes. But I haven't lost any hair yet, so the voltage they're using can't be *too* high."

"Izzy, I'm scared," he said, not taking the bait. "I'm scared they're not going to be okay. I'm scared something is going to happen to you again. I keep . . . having bad dreams."

Isobel sat up. "What do you mean? What kind of—"

"I don't want to talk about it."

Isobel nervously flicked a corner of her paper, hoping that Danny's dreams were his own, products of internal stress. Memories replaying. But just in case they weren't . . .

"Dreams aren't real," she said. "You know that, right? They only feel real when . . . when you let them."

"You die in every single one," he said. "So you tell me how that's not supposed to feel real."

Isobel opened her mouth, ready to spew more false comfort. That well had run dry, though, and all she had left was the idea for a stupid distraction.

"Hey." Leaning over the table, she grabbed the partially shrink-wrapped stack of construction paper sitting by his elbow. Pinching the edge of one pink sheet, she drew it free and folded it on the diagonal. "Check this out. You can use it to impress your girlfriend tomorrow."

"I don't have a girlfriend, stupid," he snapped.

Isobel stopped. Abandoning the sheet of paper, she found her pencil and returned the lead tip to the equation she knew she had no hope of answering now.

"Sorry," she murmured. "Just forget it. I'll go back to solving my mental—excuse me—*math* problems."

A beat of silence passed. Then Danny straightened in his seat.

"I have *girlfriends*," he corrected, and placing a palm on the pink paper, he pushed it toward her. "Duh."

Again, Isobel laid her pencil down, slowly this time, a slight and unexpected smile teasing one corner of her mouth.

As she took up the scissors, Danny went quiet, his glower softening into a concentrated frown while he watched her clip off the bottom strip, making a square. She spun the square on the tabletop and continued folding, pressing a finger hard along each edge to get a crisp line.

Even though she hadn't made any origami since she was Danny's age, Isobel found that her hands still remembered every fold, and the final product took less than a minute.

"There," she said, scooting the paper butterfly across the table to him. "Hand me another piece and I'll show you ho — "

"Dad's home."

Despite the warning, she still jumped when she heard the motor for the garage door kick on.

Swallowing hard against the familiar lump that lodged in her throat like a stone every time her father came within twenty feet of her, she leaned down and hefted her book bag into the empty seat beside her. Hurriedly she began pulling out more books, surrounding herself with binders and anything else that would make her appear too absorbed to interact.

"You lost your watch, didn't you?" Danny asked. Picking up the paper butterfly, he twirled it between his fingers. "The one I got you for Christmas. You used to keep it clipped to your backpack."

Isobel spared a quick glance at her bag, knowing better than to act surprised he'd noticed. What *didn't* he notice?

"I . . . didn't mean to."

He shrugged like it was no big deal, though she could tell by the knitting of his brow that it was.

"I dropped it by accident," Isobel said, remembering how the trinket had slipped from her fingers while she'd been in the rose garden of the dreamworld. "I needed to run and . . . it fell out of my hand."

Danny looked up, eyes narrowing.

Footsteps on the wooden stairs and the muffled sound of their father's voice on the phone sent Isobel's heart skipping. She forced her head down and her gaze squarely on her papers.

"She *said* that?" her dad asked whoever was on the other line as he approached the door.

"I knew you still remembered everything," Danny whispered, still twirling the butterfly. "I'm not as dumb as the adults."

I know you're not, Isobel mouthed as their dad entered the room, a cold breeze wafting in from the garage.

"Hey, listen. I just got home," he said, his volume dropping. "I'll . . . have to call you back after I discuss this with my wife. Just . . . don't do anything until then, okay?"

Isobel heard the snap of her dad's cell, followed by the sound of the door shutting.

She frowned at the unusually abrupt way he'd ended the call, then blinked as her father set a plastic bag of Chinese food on the table between her and Danny.

"Hey, you two," he said, actually giving Isobel's shoulder a squeeze. "I need you both to stay here while I talk to Mom. Just . . . go ahead and eat."

Isobel's hand twitched, and she wanted so badly to place

it over his. But her father didn't stay long enough for that to happen. He swept from the room, dropping his keys on the long hallway table and trudging up the steps.

"Jeannine?" he called. Upstairs, the vacuum went silent.

"Wanna take bets?" Danny asked, extracting an egg roll from the yellow, smiley-face-stamped bag and aiming the fried cylinder at her.

"Bets?" Isobel murmured, wishing the fading sensation of her father's warm, forgiving, *protective* squeeze could remain on her shoulder forever.

"My vote is that they're making plans to donate you to a government study."

Isobel scowled at her brother as he bit into his egg roll, but she knew that on some level he was right. Even if Danny *had* been teasing, the phone call definitely pertained to her.

3
Disillusions

Midday sunlight streamed through Trenton's tall hall windows.

All around, lockers slammed. Girls laughed, and sneakers screeched against linoleum. Two boys shared a fist bump before splitting off in separate directions.

Isobel recognized faces and voices. Even the sensation of her own breathing.

But she knew she was in a dream. She knew it the moment she saw *him*.

Because she saw him.

With his back to her, he walked down the center of the crowded hall, his gait even and slow, as graceful as ever.

Unable to move or look away, she watched him while her mind scrambled to come up with an answer as to how she'd gotten here, and how real "here" actually was.

The dusty hem of his long coat swayed at his ankles. His once-black combat boots, now white with ash—as white as the crow emblazoned on the back of the coat she'd come to hate—left tread marks of soot on the floor.

Ahead of him, the other kids stepped out of his path, most without daring to give him more than a sidelong glance. Then the crowd folded around him.

Isobel started forward, keeping her sights on the still-visible line of his angular shoulders. Sleek and jaggedly cut, his jet hair caught a gleam from the fluorescent light fixtures as he passed beneath them. That detail, so minute, so *real*, prompted her to second-guess herself.

Sparing a quick glance at the walls, she checked for the hallway clock that would confirm what she already knew—that she *had* to be asleep.

That there wasn't one at all gave her the last shred of evidence she no longer needed.

When her eyes found him again, however, she saw that he'd traveled twice as far down the corridor as before, as if time had skipped while her gaze had been diverted.

A jolt of terror spurred Isobel to stumble after him on shaky legs. Then her mind caught up to her actions, commanding her to stop, to slip into the crowd so he wouldn't see her.

Wake up, wake up, wake up, she told herself, even while her feet kept moving, following the thrumming command of her heart.

A deep ache pulsed inside of her, urging her to yell out to him. To repeat the words she'd written that morning, and make him hear what he'd already proven he couldn't.

But then he vanished around the next corner, into the stairwell.

Isobel stopped, her chest constricting with a debilitating mixture of sorrow and fear. Sorrow that he'd once again evaporated. That this glimpse of him had happened within the realm of her imagination, and not in that midregion where she knew he truly dwelled.

The sensation of fear welled higher. It consumed her longing and warned her not to let him discover her here—in *his* world.

Wake up, she told herself again, *before he finds you.*

Her body didn't want to listen, though, and her soul, the part of her that dreamed, moved forward again.

She wove her way between tall basketball players, dodging their book bags. She sidled past girls with rose bouquets who threw their arms around their boyfriends' necks, past teachers collecting papers. The bodies began to squeeze in tighter, closer and closer with every step until she felt herself getting crowded out. Blocked. Shoved back.

Then the bell rang, shrill as a scream, and still more students poured out of classroom doors. Kids carrying books and holding hands bumped into her from every angle, knocking her from side to side.

Isobel squeezed between one of the kissing couples, forcing them apart.

The boy rounded on her with a glare. "What are you staring at?" he asked. But neither he nor the girl had any eyes. Just peeling, burned-out holes, as if their faces were made of paper.

Isobel shrank from the couple and collided with one of the teachers, who thrust a stack of blank pages at her.

"You forgot to sign our name," said a girl's voice.

Looking up, Isobel found herself staring into her twin's

expectant gaze, the likeness between them complete, right down to the slanted scar on her cheek.

Again, Isobel scrambled backward, bumping into yet another version of herself, this one almost doll-like in her pink party dress from the Grim Facade.

"I found you," the double whispered, words she'd once uttered to Varen.

A hush fell over the hallway.

Isobel spun—and saw that her classmates had all disappeared. In their stead, a dozen of her own faces watched her with unblinking stares.

She saw herself dressed in the ebony version of the party dress, her features shell-shocked. A stream of crimson ran down the duplicate's arm to soak the satin ribbon tied to her wrist.

Another replica had on her blue-and-gold cheer uniform. Yet another wore a pink robe and pajama pants—the same haphazard outfit she'd worn the night she'd climbed onto the ledge outside her window to meet with . . .

The truth, more disquieting than the clones themselves, struck her with stomach-twisting alarm. The versions of herself before her represented each different way Varen had seen her. Each way he remembered her.

"Go away," she ordered. "All of you. *Now.*"

The face of the Isobel who held the stack of papers crumpled first, collapsing inward. The double's arm fell as it disintegrated, and the white leaflets slipped free, spilling across the floor. Then the edges of the duplicate's body curled in, collapsing like the remains of a burnt offering.

Pink Party Dress Isobel went next, bursting to cinders. One at a time, the others followed suit, and her legion of look-alikes dissipated to dust. Ash floated to the floor, coating the spotless linoleum and powdering the lockers in the leftover gray-white grime of whatever essence had allowed them to exist in the first place.

Freed from their stares, Isobel turned in a circle—wondering, as the sun-filled windows dimmed, if being alone wasn't a thousand times worse.

Glancing down at her feet, she caught sight of her name scrawled across the scattered papers, written in an unmistakable hand.

She wrapped her arms around herself, gripping her sides when she saw that the ink wasn't violet but red.

Bloodred.

Close by, one of the fluorescent lights popped, going dark. Then the intercom system cut on with a shriek of feedback.

"-ode red," a man's voice echoed through a blast of static. "I repeat. Th-s is a -ode r-d."

In unison, the classroom doors slammed shut with a resounding bang.

Another light popped, echoed by the tinkle of glass. Then another, and another—getting closer.

She shut her eyes just before the final light, the one right above her, snapped off with a smash.

"Wake up," she told herself out loud, wanting to open her eyes and be in the real world—her world. Someplace where she could hide from this person she didn't know anymore. Who had forgotten who she was. And who he was too.

Lost. Lost. Lost. The word echoed in her head.

Then the far-off sound of door hinges creaking long and low startled her, and Isobel's eyes flew wide again. She wasn't at home, though, and she wasn't back in her bed. She was still in that awful hall, facing windows filled with black tree trunks back-lit by a violet glow.

"Cheerleader."

She felt his breath stir the hair by her ear and, whirling, suppressed the urge to scream, covering her mouth with a quaking hand.

Varen's black eyes bored into her.

He took a step toward her, forcing her back. Her heels crunched over the shriveling papers bearing her name, and they crushed to powder.

As he advanced on her, Isobel continued to retreat, hypnotized by that all-consuming stare, yet still aware that the walls surrounding them had begun to transform, drawing in tighter, shooting taller.

The floor beneath their feet became carpet and the ceiling smoke.

One after the other, clinking chandeliers dropped through the murk, falling to hover just overhead. Their dim violet flames cast Varen's wan face in an alien glow, rendering him unrecognizable.

On either side of them, a thousand golden frames bled through purple-papered walls that might have belonged to a Gothic palace, each filling with the liquescent surfaces of shining mirrors.

Isobel's gaze darted from left to right, to that angry face the glass multiplied to infinity.

But *she* wasn't in any frame. Not a single one.

Snick. Pop. Crack.

The mirrors began to fracture, each sprouting its own spiderweb pattern, splintering Varen's repeated image into countless more.

"Paper girl," he whispered, and she flinched when he touched her cheek, "in a paper play."

She placed her trembling hand on his sleeve, but no sooner did she touch him than her fingers disintegrated, flaking away to nothing in the same way the false versions of herself had.

Isobel tried to speak, but she felt her throat cave in.

His lips came close to hers, almost touching.

"I thought I wrote you out," he whispered.

Then, like a reel of old film eaten through by heat, his face, the mirrors, the smoke, and everything else dissolved into the bright white glare of her bedroom's ceiling light.

4
Dust to Dust

Sitting up, Isobel clamped her hands around her throat. She gasped while her fingers climbed the contours of her face. Even though she could see the walls around her and the shadowy tips of her searching fingers, she still half expected to find her eye sockets empty, hollow as broken eggshells.

Releasing the breath she'd sucked in, she pushed off from her bed, retreating from the warmth of her covers as if that would help her escape the images that clung to her like cobwebs.

She snatched her alarm clock, hands fumbling as she read the blue numbers. The time twitched to read 6:30, and the sudden drone of her alarm sliced through her escalating panic.

She was awake now. She knew for sure because the digital numbers weren't scrolling. The interior of her room wasn't in reverse, and she didn't see her own body lying in her bed.

Isobel clicked the off button, silencing the alarm—but the rhythm of her heart still echoed its urgent bleating.

She glanced over her shoulder at her dresser and the dark-blue sheet she'd thrown over the mirror to hide it from view. And to shield herself from anything—*anyone*—who might be watching from the other side.

Setting her alarm down again, she kept her fingers on its casing, allowing the coolness of the hard plastic to ground her while the voltage of the dream ran its course through her system.

Pins and needles prickled her cheek in the place where he'd touched her—the scar.

She brushed her fingers over her lips where the sensation of his breath lingered.

Slowly, Isobel twisted to survey her room, her focus trailing upward to the light she *knew* she hadn't left on.

She got to school early that morning.

Once inside, Isobel didn't bother waiting to watch her mother drive off.

They hadn't spoken during the ride, and Isobel hadn't been able to bring herself to ask about the light—to see if one of her parents had come into her room during the night to check on her, turned it on, and then forgot to switch it off again. She decided she preferred to think that it *had* been her mother's or father's doing. Or even Danny making sure she was still there, still breathing, after another nightmare of his own.

Hurrying through the empty central foyer, she passed the velvet ropes sectioning off the school crest and then the trophy cases. She veered left, moving past the main office's wide windows, wanting to get to the next hall over—to the scene of last night's dream.

She didn't know what she hoped that would accomplish, or how being there could clarify or change anything. Varen hadn't left something in the dream for her to find in reality, as he'd done with the pink ribbon in the bookshop.

Even if he had, did she really need proof the vision had been true?

Dreams aren't real, she'd told her brother the previous night, delivering the worst of lies moments after she'd resolved not to tell him any more.

Isobel stopped when something in the main office caught her attention: There was a man standing at the front desk. A man she knew.

He leaned against the counter, one hand propped at his hip, curtaining back his duster-style coat to reveal a holster and gun. He drummed the fingers of his other hand on the countertop, waiting, it seemed, for Mrs. Tanager, the secretary, to finish her phone call.

Too late, Isobel realized she shouldn't have stopped. Catching sight of her, the man did a double take; she could tell he recognized her, too.

Detective Scott, she thought, plucking his name from the recesses of her brain, remembering him as one of the two officers who had knocked on her door the night after the Grim Facade. The night after Varen disappeared.

Isobel's cheeks flamed as he continued to stare, and snapping her head forward, she started power walking to where the hall split in two directions. She hooked a right at the corner and stayed close to the lockers, her heart galloping in her chest. Her ears perked for the sound of pursuing footsteps while her own feet sped faster, the cogs in her head beginning to whir.

After yesterday's session, Dr. Robinson must have called the police. There was no other explanation. After what Isobel had said, all that she'd alluded to knowing, she should have expected as much to happen.

There was probably some mandate somewhere that obligated doctors to contact the authorities in certain circumstances—like when a patient divulges information pertaining to a missing person.

Isobel gritted her teeth and wondered if *this* was what her father's cell phone call had been about last night. She thought back to the shoulder squeeze he'd given her and wished he was there with her now.

Ducking into the alcove of a darkened classroom doorway, she pulled her phone from her coat pocket. She flipped it open and dialed her father's cell, then hesitated, her thumb hovering over the send button.

A gnawing dread scraped at her spine. That same sickening sense of being followed.

Lowering the phone, she leaned out, peered down the hall . . . and felt her stomach bottom out.

She didn't see any adults. Detective Scott had not come after her.

Worse.

Strips of yellow caution tape roped off the opposite end of the hall, halting the group of freshmen who trickled in from the side entrance, their chatter ceasing the moment they took in the ominous scene.

Beyond the tape barrier, ash dusted the floor and lockers.

Isobel folded her fingers around her phone and clamped it shut again.

Because the darkened light fixtures and the trail of boot prints cutting a path through the grime told her that calling for help couldn't stop what was coming for her now.

And neither could the police.

5
Loss of Breath

"So I guess you heard about Lesley Groveston," Gwen said, breaking the long silence that had stretched between them since leaving school.

Isobel offered no answer. She continued, instead, to stare out her window at the passing storefronts, their displays filled with kitschy hipster dresses, used guitars, and artfully arranged antiques.

Peace and calmness reigned in the cold and cloudless morning sky. Like there was nothing the matter. Like this world was the only one there was.

"She got dumped by Alex Trimble right after first bell," Gwen continued, but Isobel tuned her out, turning her thoughts to their destination: Bruce's funeral. Her last and only chance to confront Varen on neutral ground. On ground she *hoped* would be neutral.

After discovering that last night's dream had leaked into reality, that Varen could not only re-enter the real world, but could affect it physically—and that he apparently still sought to finish what he'd begun in shoving her from the cliff—Isobel had finally come to understand that there could be no peaceful parting of ways. No escaping the dark world he'd embraced. No escaping him.

Not as long as he continued to buy into the twisted version of the truth Lilith had shown him.

By astral projecting from the dreamworld into reality, Varen had overheard Isobel say horrible things on more than one occasion. That she wished she'd never met him, that she'd never had feelings for him, that she was the last person who would know anything about what had happened to him. That she was the last person who would care.

All lies. Part of the front Isobel had donned to convince everyone that she'd moved on.

But Lilith had been one step ahead of her, using Isobel's own words against her in order to distort Varen's perception—just as she had his heart and mind. And now the demon would use him to gain access to this world, to carry out her plans to destroy reality.

Unless Isobel could convince Varen to listen, to hear her.

"Of course, Alex Trimble has another girlfriend anyway." Gwen laughed. "One of the St. Bernadette girls. So I want to tell Lesley good riddance, but then again, the truth usually never cheers anyone up. Does it?"

"Mm," Isobel said, thinking back to how she'd sat waiting for something to happen during first period. How her stomach had churned with nauseating anticipation. Any second she had expected Mrs. Tanager to call for her over the intercom. Or for someone to echo the horrible static warning of "code red."

Over and over again, she'd imagined Varen appearing as

he had in Mr. Swanson's room that day of the project. Like in last night's dream, he would stalk down the hall in full view, a damning specter in that awful black coat. Everyone would pull away in shock and fear, but he wouldn't care. This time he'd do more than just shatter the lights in their fixtures. He'd bring the school down, flooding it with nightmares, loosing the demons of Poe's stories—and of his own mind—into this reality that no longer held a place for him.

And he wouldn't stop. Not until he found her. And maybe not even then . . .

That's why Isobel had to head him off at the pass. To intercept him at the only opportunity she would have to reach him. The funeral of his best friend.

"In other news," Gwen prattled on, "Marcus Tomes asked Candice Weiss to tomorrow's dance. She said no. Felicia Rowen is out with the chicken pox, aaaand there's a ceiling leak in Mrs. Lory's classroom. Also, huge mess in the first-floor north hall this morning. Busted lights. Weird dust all over the walls. But . . . you knew about *that* already."

Isobel's eyelids fluttered. "What?"

"I said you knew about that." Gwen's hands tightened on the wheel, her shoulders going rigid. "'Cause *everybody* knows about that. Per your usual way of dealing with things these days, however, you just weren't going to say anything."

Isobel locked her jaw. Swallowing, she forced her focus forward.

Given that Gwen never missed even the tiniest blip on the radar of Trenton's day-to-day grind, Isobel figured she would have known about the ash. But it surprised Isobel that Gwen had linked *her* to the incident, especially when Gwen knew so little about the dreamworld itself. But since she had made the connection, why hadn't she brought it up first thing, before they'd left?

Isobel frowned, realizing now that if she'd been thinking, she'd have guessed Gwen's plan to corner her in a moving car—where walking away wasn't an option—ahead of time.

"Of course, the admins think someone broke in last night," Gwen explained, her voice adopting a mock-casual tone. "Did it all as a bad prank. That's why they called the police. Did I forget to mention they called the police?"

Isobel grasped the cuffs of her coat, fidgeting with the fabric.

Straight ahead, an enormous clock tower loomed into view. It stood like a sentry over Cave Hill Cemetery's main entrance, casting its slanted shadow over them. An angel, her wings unfurled, stood at the pinnacle of the tower, an arm raised in proclamation of some unnamed triumph.

The clock's golden hour hand pointed at the roman numeral nine, the minute hand slightly beyond twelve, making them officially late. But at least the clock's hands weren't spinning. At least she knew for sure that she was awake.

"Everybody else seems to think it was the work of a ghost," Gwen scoffed. "But oh, those sad, silly, superstitious schnooks."

Refusing to look away from the clock, Isobel watched its

hands until the Cadillac crossed the last street, bumping up the short drive that led through the cemetery's iron gates.

"You and I," Gwen said, flashing her a tight smile, "weeeee know better."

To their left, a white-haired cemetery guard sat on an iron bench. Gwen offered him a wave as they drove past. Rising to his feet, he nodded in response, though his expression remained stern; Isobel had no doubt he could tell they were too young to be college kids on a photography excursion.

Gwen stiffened her arms as she maneuvered the car down the long, tree-lined lane, the crooked shadows of twisted limbs skimming the interior of the car, sliding over Isobel's lap, up her arms and behind her. She envisioned them gathering there, transforming into creatures with clawed hands and jagged-toothed grins.

Impulsively, she grasped the rearview mirror and, tilting it toward her, eyed the backseat.

Empty . . .

"He went inside," Gwen said.

Isobel froze for an instant, then pushed back the mirror.

"Or wait. Let me guess." Gwen slapped the dashboard, as if pressing a game-show buzzer. "You weren't checking for the guard, were you? Please, if we're about to get pelted with mutilated pigeons, I'd appreciate a warning this time. Given that I forgot to pack my inhaler and that defibrillator stations would be totally beside the point in a place like this—not to mention vaguely insulting to the residents."

"It's nothing," Isobel mumbled. "There's nothing."

Reaching up, Gwen fixed the mirror. "Riiiight. Of course it's nothing. That makes total sense. What else would any of this be adding up to besides a big fat steaming pile of nothing?"

Isobel gripped the seat beneath her. She waited, and as she'd hoped, the quiet quickly settled into place again. Yet the tension radiating from Gwen refused to fade. Anger rolled off her in invisible waves while, outside, the ticking of a rock stuck in the tread of one tire grew louder. *Tick tick tick tick tick tick tick.*

They rounded the first bend in the road and wound farther into the sprawling and seemingly endless cemetery.

Another stone angel emerged on the right. Draped in flowing robes, the statue stood atop a rectangular gravestone, the first of too many to count. Isobel waited for the moment when the figure would turn its head to look at her. The statue remained a statue, though, and soon it was behind them along with the guard and the tower and the clock hands she'd sworn hadn't been spinning.

Awake, Isobel told herself, *you are awake.*

"You know everyone thinks the boot prints are Varen's, don't you?"

Isobel's grip on her seat tightened, fingernails digging into the vinyl.

She hadn't heard *that* rumor. Of course, there had been the usual stares and whispers that morning, but she'd gotten out of the habit of paying attention. She had been preoccupied with the dream itself, replaying it again and again in her head. And then she'd been waiting for Detective Scott to appear in the doorway of her first class. He'd never shown up to question her, though, and neither had Mr. Nott or any of the other administrators. And maybe that was because they'd been preoccupied themselves—not with *her*, she now grasped, but with the possibility that Varen had been in the building.

"I know hearing his name bothers you," Gwen said. "Actually, I can tell it does worse. I can tell that it rips your heart out and crushes it every time. You know that's why I don't talk about him or ask what happened, don't you? Not because I believe you when you tell me you don't remember. And it's not because I think you need space, either. It's because I can tell it kills—literally kills you to remember. And because until this morning, I thought the truth could wait until you were ready. Because I thought it was all over. Clearly, though, it's not. Is it?"

Isobel sucked in a sharp breath and held it. Prying one hand free from the seat, she latched onto her door handle and squeezed hard, wishing she'd decided not to come after all. Really, what did she think she was doing? Hurrying the inevitable?

If talking to Varen hadn't worked before, why had she thought it would do any good now?

"I know you think you can wait me out," Gwen said. "I know you think you can keep giving me the silent treatment just like you do everybody else. But I promise you, I am the bad haircut photos you wish you could delete from the Internet. I am the dumb cheer-mixed pop-song mash-up beat-boxing in your head. I'm not going to go away. We've been through too much. 'We' as in 'me too.' That crap in the hall, Izzy. What the hell was it?"

"Please," Isobel said, "don't ask me." She tried to release the sharp breath she'd taken moments before, but it stuck in her lungs, lodged inside of her along with everything she wasn't saying.

"Listen to me, Isobel," Gwen began again, "I am tired of tiptoeing and I'm tired of being shut out. This involves me, too."

"I don't want it to," Isobel said. "Not anymore. I'm sorry. We—we shouldn't have come. We need to go back."

"Errrh. Wrong answer. Sorry, but you don't get to be sorry. And I think we both know it's waaaay too late to turn back now."

Open this door, Pinfeathers had once told Isobel, *and no matter what, you'll never close it.*

"Isobel." Gwen snapped her fingers. "Wake up!"

"I *am* awake."

"Then start talking."

"I don't know what you want me to say."

"Try the truth this time," Gwen said. "You might feel better. I know *I* will. But then, this isn't about me, is it? I mean, I only risked my life. I only hauled my ass across three states to help you find him. I only had my arm cracked on a tombstone. I listened when no one else would. I believed you. I believed *in* you. For what? For you to ignore me like I was never a part of it? I want you to tell me why Varen isn't here. Why he didn't come back. There. That's a good place to start. One, two, three—go."

"I—he—" Isobel jerked her head in the direction of a passing mausoleum, her eyes meeting for an instant those of the alabaster angel who watched from within, clutching the hilt of a sword between her hands.

"Yeah, I don't think that's summing it up enough for me," Gwen said. "You're gonna have to do a little better."

Isobel squeezed the door handle harder, resisting the urge to pull. Her other hand went to her seat-belt latch, her thumb pausing on the release button.

This all felt wrong. Her surroundings felt wrong. The conversation felt wrong.

She wasn't dreaming, though. She couldn't be.

"You found him," Gwen said. "You talked to him. I *know* you did."

Feeling suddenly too warm in her coat, Isobel pressed her forehead to the cold window, wanting out—out of the car, out of this cemetery, out of her own skin.

"Fine," Gwen snapped. "Let's skip that one and come back. Moving on to the more immediate question. Whose boot prints were those in the hall?"

Nausea crept over her, causing her head to swim. Saliva rushed into her mouth.

"Stop the car," Isobel said, but Gwen sped up, taking the twisting turns harder.

On either side of the winding blacktop, endless granite

markers and squat tombstones dotted the hilly landscape, crowding all the way to where pavement met with grass. No cemetery could be *this* big, could it? And that obelisk . . . Hadn't they passed it already?

"Tell me what happened," Gwen demanded, her voice trembling with equal parts hurt and fear. "I deserve to know."

In the distance, Isobel spotted an awning tent. Beneath it, an open pit. A pile of fresh red earth waited to one side and, next to that, rolls of fake green turf meant to make things appear more natural. The scene flew by and dizziness slammed into her, bringing with it the memory of being buried alive in just such a trench, dirt pouring over her in heavy clods, pressing her down, crushing her chest and filling her mouth.

The cemetery around her became a rolling sea of stone and grass. Craggy trees cropped up with more frequency, blurry black skeletons between the markers that seemed to creep ever closer. Or was the lane growing narrower?

Robed statues sprang up everywhere, some with wings, others without, some holding rings of flowers, others clinging to crosses, all of them looking straight at her.

She *was* awake. She *knew* she was.

Wasn't she?

"Isobel!"

"Stop. Please. I need to get out."

"Not until—"

"I said stop the car!" Isobel screeched.

Gwen hit the brakes, causing the tires to scream. The

sound, combined with the lurching halt of the Cadillac, prompted Isobel to inhale at last. She gasped for air, and then she gasped again. And again.

All this time, she hadn't been able to take a single breath. She'd forgotten to try, but now she was breathing too much, too fast.

The cab of the car seemed to squeeze inward, the roof threatening to collapse.

Isobel pulled on the sweat-slicked handle still in her fist and the door swung open. She unlatched her seat belt and stumbled out into the winter air.

Her feet found the lawn, but her cold surroundings continued to orbit her. Names and dates swirled in her vision. Bile rose in the back of her throat and she staggered to one side, afraid she might hurl right there on Eloise McClain's name plaque.

Instead she started running, bolting headlong through the rows of graves, the wind licking sweat from her skin.

"Isobel!" she heard Gwen shout.

Isobel dodged headstone after headstone. Then the terrain dipped. She felt her ankle twist. Faltering, she cried out before dropping, nearly tumbling into the stump of a stone topped by a tiny, acid-rain-eaten lamb — an infant's grave.

She gripped the grass beneath her, crawling away from the distorted marker until her back met with the cold side of another.

Unable to look away from the child's stone, Isobel covered her eyes.

"Isobel!" The sound of feet rushing over grass grew louder, and Isobel heard Gwen fall to her knees at her side, her bracelets clanging. Isobel dared not lower her hands to look, however, too fearful that Gwen would be like the paper people she'd seen in the hall—that her friend's face would erode right before her, another nightmare she couldn't escape.

"What," Gwen huffed, "are you doing? Why . . . did you run . . . like that?"

"I should be dead," Isobel gasped, her thoughts leaping out of her mouth as the memory of awakening on that hospital table ripped into her with chain-saw teeth. "I was, and I should have stayed that way."

"No!" Gwen pulled Isobel's hands from her face, forcing her to look into her frantic brown eyes. "Why would you say that?"

"He—he tried to kill me," Isobel whispered.

Saying it out loud for the first time felt like pulling a knife out of her soul. She was able to draw breath again, and gradually, the world stopped swirling.

Grabbing Isobel by the shoulders, Gwen pulled her away from the plinth. Isobel swayed, falling to lean against her warm friend.

Gwen's wiry arms wrapped around her, pulling her in tight, and the scent of lavender caught Isobel off guard, because she'd never noticed it before. The aroma was one detail her brain could latch onto, though, something that testified to the realness of this embrace, which had to be the first she and Gwen had ever shared.

"I'm sorry," Gwen said. "Isobel, I'm so sorry I brought you here. And I'm sorry I said those things in the car. I—I didn't know. I just wanted to—I thought he—"

"She won." Isobel sobbed the words against Gwen's shoulder, though her eyes remained dry; the storm raging within her took place inside a wasteland, where there could be nothing as cleansing as rain. "Gwen, she won. He hates me. She made him hate me."

"He hates himself," Gwen said. "You just got caught in the cross fire."

She pulled Isobel tighter. But the comfort of arms around her could not shield her from the memory of his eyes. Like a pair of black holes, they threatened to devour her, to inciner-ate her like they had in the dream, leaving no trace of her former self behind. Not even this shell she now occupied.

"He can find me," Isobel murmured. "Anywhere I am. He can find me. The ash in the hall . . . That—that happened in a dream. He was there. He . . ."

Gwen hushed her.

"I wanted to come here today," Isobel went on, "because—because I thought I might see him. Like before. Now, though, I'm afraid that I won't ever *stop* seeing him. He scares me so much. I don't know what he wants anymore."

Humming, Gwen began to rock her gently back and forth. Then, out of nowhere, she began to sing.

The sound of Gwen's singing voice, smooth and melodic—so different from the brash, cut-and-dried voice Isobel thought she knew so well—shocked her into stillness. Isobel blinked, her focus shifting at once to the strange syllables climbing and falling through their haunting phrase.

> *"Lyulinke, mayn feygele*
> *lyulinke, mayn kind*
> *kh'hob ongevoyrn aza libe*
> *vey iz mir un vind."*

As Gwen's song unwound with a slow, sad melody, Varen's face—angry, vengeful, hollow—dissolved from her imagination, dissipating like smoke cleared by a gentle breeze.

Cool air gusted past them, stirring Gwen's hair, intensifying the scent of lavender, and with each silky note, the world around Isobel grew clearer, its lines sharper, the colors more vibrant, until she was fully present in the moment, not split between two places, two worlds.

She'd never known Gwen could sing like this. She'd never have guessed, either. Before this moment, Gwen had always been wry wit and blunt truths. Gwen was sound advice and rationality. Her kindness had always been the sandpaper sort, as abrasive as it was smoothing. Apparently, though, Gwen had a softness, too, a gentleness she kept hidden. A gentleness Isobel found herself all too grateful for.

"That word," Isobel said as the song looped to its chorus. "*Lyul—lyul—*"

"*Lyulinke,*" Gwen said, pausing. "It means hush-a-bye."

Isobel shivered at the meaning, recalling how Varen's mother had once composed a lullaby for him. Isobel had seen his memory of that moment multiple times, both in reality and in the dreamworld.

Like Gwen's, Varen's lullaby had been unbearably sad. Sorrow distilled into sound. And though Isobel could not understand the lyrics of Gwen's song, the music helped her to feel less alone. Because it captured how she felt. Bereaved. Forsaken. Held hostage by the past.

As Gwen's singing turned again to humming, Isobel's clenched muscles began to relax. Her body slackened in Gwen's grip, and she rested her head into the crook of her friend's arm, content to feel like a child again. Content to be reminded that, despite everything she'd lost, she was still here, still alive.

The song ended before Isobel was ready for silence, and though the ache inside of her returned with the pulsing noise-lessness of the graveyard, the fear that had nearly consumed her moments before remained at bay.

"That was beautiful," Isobel said at last, staring into the bright blue of the clear sky. "Where did you—?"

"My grandmother," Gwen said. "Lullabies are kind of an old tradition in our family. In many families, I guess. They're said to have the power to protect. The word 'lullaby' itself means, 'Lilith, begone.'"

Isobel frowned, remembering how Pinfeathers had once said something about lullabies. About how they never worked . . .

Then her fingers rushed to her collar, burrowing through the layers of material to find the hand-shaped pendant Gwen had given her, the amulet that *had* worked to save her life. "You mean like the hamsa?"

"Like the hamsa," Gwen said.

The wind whipped past Isobel's ears with a white-noise rush, mixing with the chirping of birds. She listened, doing her best to sync her breathing with Gwen's, to slow the rhythm of her heart before trying to move.

Huddled there in the grass with the best friend she'd ever had, Isobel tried to limit her thoughts to the here and now, absorbing the calmness she would need to prepare her for whatever came next.

But then a loud crack boomed through the cemetery, causing the birds to disperse in a flutter.

Starting, Isobel sat up.

Gunshots, she thought as the blasts came twice more, their echoes ricocheting through the air like claps of thunder.

6

The Grey Tombstone

Peeking around the corner of an enormous mausoleum, Isobel saw another tent erected several yards away, its burgundy canvas shielding a gathering of about a dozen from the weak winter sun.

The cluster of mourners, dressed in somber suits, skirts, and heavy winter coats, stood with their backs to her and Gwen, facing what Isobel knew must be a grave site.

To one side of the small assembly, a trio of military officers waited at attention, each armed with his own rifle—the source of the gunshot blasts.

"Green Berets," Gwen whispered, peering over Isobel's shoulder. "This must be the bookshop guy."

Recalling how Bruce's obituary had mentioned his service in the army, Isobel realized Gwen had to be right. The shots they'd heard moments before must have been meant as a final salute.

Isobel scanned the ranks of mourners, searching for Varen's familiar form.

"Do you see him?" Gwen asked as the first notes of "Taps," played by a lone bugler, floated forth to fill the reverent quiet.

Slipping out from behind the tomb, Isobel glanced left

and right but saw no one among the other graves, no sign of that black coat or jet hair.

"No," she said.

Just because she couldn't see him, though, didn't mean Varen wasn't there. Watching.

Strengthened by Gwen's lullaby, by the reminder of the hamsa's presence around her neck, and by the knowledge that she had already survived Varen's worst, she pressed toward the memorial, Gwen behind her. Together, they crossed the grassy alley between plots and entered the shade of the tent, joining the group at the rear.

Gwen stayed close and pressed one shoulder into Isobel's, like she thought doing so would help to keep her strong, grounded. The contact did better, reassuring her more than any timepiece could have.

As the bugler's mournful serenade wore on, the tension in her shoulders eased, and her anxiety over the question of Varen's presence faded. For it suddenly occurred to her that by standing at this grave site, she'd already accomplished what she'd set out to do. Her presence communicated what Varen had refused to let her convey with words. That she cared more than he knew. That despite what he'd been led to believe, that wasn't something she could turn off, or shove aside. Or fake.

Isobel lifted her chin with new resolve and stared forward, through the spaces between shoulders, at the elevated casket. A flash of red, white, and blue fluttered as two soldiers lifted the American flag from the coffin's silver lid. The officers

then began to fold the banner in a series of clipped and practiced movements, and Isobel concentrated hard on the sharp,
choreographed motions, working to clear her head.

Though she had attended only two funerals in her life,
she had learned through both experiences that observances
like this were intended for the living, not the dead. Burying
someone meant sealing that person away for good, surrender-
ing everything that wasn't a memory. Anything that couldn't
be kept in an album or a box.

When the bugler's song ended, the crowd shifted as if
everyone had been holding their breath. Blinking, Isobel
turned her attention to the wavy-haired man and little girl at
the head of the group, the only two people to take seats.

When one of the soldiers stepped forward to kneel before
the man, offering him the folded flag, Isobel realized the man
had to be Bruce's surviving nephew, mentioned in the obituary. And the girl must be the man's daughter.

After presenting the flag, the soldier saluted and backed
away. Then another man in a black suit and green tie, a bible
tucked under one arm, stepped forth to address the crowd.
He thanked everyone for coming and announced the conclusion of the service.

Low conversation broke out among the group. People
angled toward one another and then away, breaking off in
ones and pairs.

Isobel remained in place, stunned at the ceremony's
abrupt conclusion.

Whole minutes ticked by until only Isobel and Gwen

were left standing under the awning. But Gwen, as if she was able to sense Isobel's inner turmoil, stayed put, continuing to lend the pressure of her shoulder.

Car doors slammed in the distance. Somewhere close by, an engine turned.

Resisting the urge to crane her neck and check their surroundings one last time, Isobel turned toward Gwen instead. She started to speak, to tell her that she was ready to go even though she wasn't. She stopped, however, when she noticed Gwen staring off at a pair of previously obscured metal tripods set up just outside the tent, each supporting a large photo.

The first tripod displayed a yellow-tinted portrait of a young, clean-shaven, and virtually unrecognizable Bruce in a Green Beret uniform, a strip of multicolored service ribbons pinned to his chest. The second photo showed an older and more familiar version of the bookshop owner, his face bearing an uncharacteristic grin. Seated next to him, a black-haired woman in a floral-print blouse beamed her own bright smile.

While Isobel assumed the woman must have been Bruce's wife, she wasn't immediately certain about the third and final person in the portrait—a boy who couldn't have been much older than her at the time the picture had been taken.

Lanky and tall, clad in a white dress shirt and tie, the boy stood behind Bruce and the woman, a hand resting on one of her shoulders. His fair hair, not quite chin length, hung straight and limp around his face.

Isobel stepped toward the tripods, her curiosity piqued.

She sensed Gwen following on her heels, but when Isobel stopped to study the photo, Gwen wandered ahead to the grave site and the casket that had yet to be lowered.

Squinting at the photo, Isobel noticed that unlike Bruce and his wife, the boy wasn't smiling. But she thought he didn't need to. He had kind and soft features, his bright steel-colored eyes lit from within by a spark of secret mirth, like he was wrestling with the urge to make a face or hold up a pair of bunny ears.

"Oh my gosh," Isobel heard Gwen say, and she saw her friend crouch in front of the flat slab embedded in the earth next to the empty space reserved for Bruce's. Gwen waved her over.

"Look at the dates," Gwen said. "His kid died only a year older than us. Couldn't have been too long after that picture was taken."

Isobel stooped next to Gwen and read the name engraved on the marker.

WILLIAM GREY NOBIT

Remembering that Bruce's obituary had cited a deceased son, Isobel frowned at the short dash separating the birth date from the death date. Letting her fingertips trail over the numbers, she wondered what could have ended the boy's life at just seventeen.

Though there was an epitaph inscribed below, the sad message held no answer.

Isobel mouthed the words silently to herself.

BARELY A MAN, YET SCARCELY A LAD,
OUR DEAR BOY, GREY, HAS GONE AWAY.

Recalling the heated argument she'd overheard little more than a month ago between the bookshop owner and Varen's father, Isobel tilted her head at the stone, and she began to grasp that there had been a deeper layer to the friendship Varen and Bruce had shared than she had originally perceived. One she could never have fully appreciated until that moment.

Suddenly the term "best friends" no longer seemed like a fitting label for the unlikely pair. *Family*. The two had been family.

A makeshift father to a stand-in son.

That thought brought with it sharp pang of remorse, and a cavernous sense of pity for Varen.

Despite the pain he had caused her, the fear he now instilled within her, Isobel also knew he'd suffered enough loss already. Enough to make him choose darkness.

Enough for that darkness to feel like a sanctuary. A home.

Wherever he was, whether he was there watching her right that instant, or somewhere wandering the woodlands alone, she hoped this final blow wouldn't drive him further into the despair that had already stolen him from her reach. But considering what she'd found in the hall that morning, Isobel feared it was too late—that Bruce's passing had done exactly that.

"Uh, Isobel," Gwen said, shooting to her feet. "We've got some stranger danger bringing up the rear here."

"What?" Isobel turned her head quickly—and then wished she hadn't.

Standing at the foot of Bruce's coffin, a familiar blond woman watched them from behind an enormous pair of sunglasses. Dressed in a neat black pantsuit and a wide-brim feathered hat, she seemed to be waiting for them to notice her.

For Isobel to notice her . . .

Isobel rose and took an instinctive step back, already aware that it was too late to make a break for it without causing a scene.

Especially since running was exactly what she'd done the last time she'd encountered Darcy Nethers—Varen's stepmother—face-to-face.

7
Echoes

"Do you know her?" Gwen leaned in to mutter. "Oooooor, does Funeral Barbie just have a staring problem?"

Glancing away from them, Darcy placed one hand on the side of Bruce's casket. "Don't worry," she said, "I won't try to chase you this time."

Gwen aimed a thumb at Darcy. "Is she talking to us? Or the dead guy? I know grief does funny things to people, buuuut—"

"She's talking to me," Isobel said. "I . . . know her. Sort of."

"Actually, we've never formally met," Darcy said. She took two slow steps toward them but stopped again, her shielded gaze returning to Isobel. "You know who I am, that is, but . . . I still don't really know who you are."

Isobel folded her arms, uncertain of how to respond.

Ever since Varen's stepmom had seen her in his car the night before Halloween, the night before he'd disappeared, Isobel had known the woman wanted to speak with her—to find out who she was to Varen and what she knew. Darcy must suspect, Isobel thought, that she knew everything.

"Just an FYI," Gwen leaned in to mutter. "I do carry pepper spray. Though the Lady Gaga goggles kinda pose a problem if that's the route you want to go."

"Gwen, it's . . . okay," Isobel whispered.

"The offer stands," Gwen said, clutching her patchwork purse.

"You know, I saw you there," Darcy said, gripping one elbow as though discomfited by her own words. She glanced to the coffin again. "On the other side."

Isobel stiffened, already knowing what Darcy was referring to.

While searching for Varen in the dreamworld, Isobel had entered a distorted duplicate of his family's old Victorian house. In the parlor, she'd discovered an oval-framed portrait of Varen's birth mother, Madeline. The image within the frame had been the same as the photo from the jewelry box Isobel had found hidden beneath the stairs in the bookshop. When she had picked up the portrait, however, the picture had transformed, shimmering into a mirror, her reflection bleeding through until her own face replaced Madeline's. Startled, Isobel had dropped the frame and the glass had shattered. In one of the scattered shards, for a single instant, she'd seen Varen's stepmom looking up at her in shock, each viewing the other from separate realities.

"I can tell you know what I'm talking about," Darcy went on when Isobel didn't reply. "And I know you saw me, too."

"Excuse me, Darcy?"

The man with the wavy hair—Bruce's nephew—stepped out from beneath the tent. As he made his approach, hands stuffed in the pockets of his dress slacks, he gave Isobel and Gwen a quizzical half glance.

"Our flight leaves in just a few hours," he said, stopping to check his wristwatch. "I hope you don't mind my interrupting, but is it okay if we go ahead and take care of those papers while I've got you here? For the car . . . ?"

"Cue optimum bail time," Gwen rasped, tugging hard on Isobel's arm.

Isobel stayed put, fixated on Darcy.

"Now is fine," Darcy said to the man, and just like that, she started away with him.

Isobel fought the urge to rush after them, knowing the car they were talking about had to be Varen's Cougar.

Bruce must have left the Cougar to Varen in his will when Varen never returned for it. Without Varen here to claim it, however, she could only assume the car would transfer to his parents instead.

If Darcy had agreed to accept the car on Varen's behalf, did that mean Varen's father and stepmom were still waiting for him, expecting that he might stroll through the front door any day?

"Mrs. Nethers?" Isobel said.

Darcy stopped, peering at Isobel from over her shoulder.

Hurrying forward, Isobel started to speak again but stalled, at a loss for what to say when there wasn't any feasible way to explain all that had happened. Even if Darcy did suspect otherworldly forces, Isobel didn't know how to affirm her suspicions with a stranger waiting and watching, listening in. She wasn't sure how to tell Darcy who *she* was either. That she and Varen had been . . .

Her shoulders sank, the impulse to speak withering under that expectant stare.

But then Gwen bumped one of her arms, her bangles clinking as she handed Isobel a folded slip of well-worn paper that she would have recognized anywhere. It was the final note Varen had written her, the one Isobel had found secreted away in the pocket of his green mechanic's jacket the night she'd learned that she'd left him behind, in the dreamworld.

Isobel had entrusted the note to Gwen just before Baltimore. And the small scrap of paper still remained her only tangible evidence that Varen had loved her.

Except . . . he didn't anymore.

The scars she now bore, both the inner *and* outer, were her proof of that.

Isobel took the note, recalling the instructions she'd given Gwen along with it: that if Isobel failed to return from the dreamworld, Gwen should give the note to Varen's stepmom.

Isobel *had* come home, but she'd done so alone. And that made the suggestion Gwen seemed to be offering, in producing the note at this moment, feel right.

So Isobel extended the paper to Darcy, who took it with slow, hesitant fingers. Isobel backed away again, pain squeezing the ruins of her heart.

"C'mon," Gwen said. Slinging an arm around Isobel's shoulders, she angled her away.

And as the sight of Darcy, the casket, and the white square of paper left her vision, Isobel felt the sudden lifting of an inward pressure she hadn't realized was there.

Because giving up the note forced Isobel to accept the most difficult truth of all.

That the quiet, strange, brooding goth boy she'd fallen in love with over the span of a beautiful and terrifying October no longer existed. Just as Lilith had said.

That Varen would have been here, at the grave site. That Varen would have cared that she was too. He would have heard her out.

But he wasn't there.

The boy who had composed the words written on that slip of paper was gone.

And he wasn't ever coming back.

To avoid being seen pulling into Trenton's main lot, Gwen chose a parking spot on the side street closest to the door they'd used to sneak out.

A pair of senior boys lounged against the building, the smoke from their cigarettes rising in coils. Their presence there meant the bell ending third period had already rung. Before Isobel could let herself out, however, the car door's lock slid down with a harsh *clack*.

"Confession."

Isobel turned her head and saw Gwen watching her with furrowed brow, one hand poised on her door's lock panel.

"I totally read the note," Gwen blurted.

Leaning back, Isobel let her head thud against her seat. Heat crawled up her neck and cheeks. "C'mon, Gwen. I mean, I sort of knew you would."

"I . . . have to admit," Gwen said, her words turning solemn, "it made me think for sure that you would come back. With him. That you had to."

"Yeah," Isobel murmured, watching the two boys stamp out their half-smoked cigarettes. "That was the plan."

"Your dream last night. About Varen . . . all that stuff in the hall. Do you think . . . I mean . . . is there any way that he could be—"

"I think that you were right," Isobel said, and felt the flush leave her cheeks.

"A favorite pastime of mine but . . . about what specifically?"

Isobel's hand went to the hamsa charm at her neck, her fingers running it back forth on its chain as she recalled how, on the same morning Gwen had given her the amulet, she had also related to Isobel all the known lore surrounding Lilith. That demons operated by luring their victims with false promises, but that Lilith's treachery and deceit could only accomplish so much on its own. In the end, Gwen had said, a demon's victim—at least to some extent—had to be willing.

"I think," Isobel murmured, "Varen is where—and what— he wants to be."

An uncomfortable tenseness spiked the air. Quiet buzzed.

Isobel couldn't meet Gwen's gaze, so she glanced to the door again and saw the two boys slide inside, one of them giving her and Gwen a fleeting backward glance.

Seconds later the cry of the bell came, muffled through the school's redbrick walls.

Isobel gathered her things into her lap and peeled her

winter coat from her shoulders, planning to leave it in Gwen's car, since, as she'd feared might be the case, they no longer had time to stop by their lockers.

"We should go," Isobel said, and pulling up the lock tab, she climbed out.

Wordlessly Gwen shed her own coat, tucked a notebook under her arm, and exited her side. Huddling against the cold, they hurried to the doors.

Inside, the warm stairwell had already cleared of students. A faint odor of mildew hung in the air, commingling with the quiet to give the enclosed space, Isobel thought, a tomblike feel.

"So," Gwen said, "what happens now?"

Isobel shrugged. "Maybe nothing."

"Except you don't really believe that."

Isobel could hear Gwen's keys clinking in her fidgeting hands. "No," she admitted, "I don't."

Gwen started to speak again, but for both of their sakes, Isobel interjected.

"If we get caught cutting together—"

"—your dad will have me extradited to Canada," Gwen finished for her. "I know."

"And that's if he's in a *good* mood," Isobel said, and she forced a small smile, figuring she owed Gwen that much at least.

"Lunch in an hour?" Gwen asked, tucking her keys in her purse, clearly trying to reestablish some sense of normalcy. Nodding slowly, Isobel took a retreating step, hoping now

that she'd done what she could to stitch her wounds closed—
to move on—normal was within their grasp.

Gwen mirrored her movement, backing in the direction
of the hall.

Then they pivoted to go their separate ways, and Isobel
started up the stairs. Alone now, she let her smile fall away
as she swung herself up one flight to the next, feet slamming
hard and fast, heading to the last place she wanted to go. Mr.
Swanson's class.

Despite her conviction to release Varen, to release *herself*,
the pounding beat of her sneakers could not drown out the
lines of the note she'd surrendered at the cemetery. Lines that,
after an infinite number of readings, she would never be able
to expunge from her memory.

> *In the shadows of the dreamland, he waits.*
> *He watches the gaping window to the world*
> *he had so longed to open. Now flown wide,*
> *bleak and empty, ravaged—like him—it*
> *grants his wish. He belongs.*
>   *It cannot compare to the memory of her*
> *eyes. Blue azure, warm as a summer sky.*
>   *If he could but fall into their world.*
> *Would that he had.*
>   *Now he writes the end to the story that*
> *past its Midnight Dreary—that too late*
> *an hour—has its own without him. It was*
> *always, he knows now, meant to end this way.*

Like that circle that "ever returneth into
the selfsame spot."
My beautiful, my Isobel, My Love. You
Ask me to wait. And so I wait.

Isobel imagined Varen speaking the words to her in her head, his voice low and even. But as she rounded the final stretch of steps to the third floor, his tone grew icy in her inner ear, mocking, and then—with the final line—threatening.

For all of this, I know, is but a dream.
And when, in sleep, at last we wake,
I will see you agai—

Isobel halted with a gasp, arrested by the two ash-caked boots positioned at the top of the landing.

Her hand tightened around the banister and she looked up, eyes meeting with the black gaze of the dark figure blocking her path.

8

Approaching Darkness

Roses, Isobel thought. Not mildew.

The stairwell smelled of roses—dead and decaying. She hadn't been able to place the odor, musty and all at once too sweet, until that precise moment. When it was too late.

Ash coated his clothing, smudging his gloves and dusting his slicked-back hair.

Even without his trademark cloak, fedora, and white-scarf mask, Reynolds was instantly recognizable. He glared down at her, his cold, penetrating eyes far more familiar than the sharp and weatherworn planes of the rest of his wax-white face.

Adrenaline flooded Isobel's veins, urging her to *do* something, even though there was nothing she could do. Nothing except run.

So why didn't she?

Perhaps the real question, she thought, was why Reynolds had not yet drawn one or both of the cutlasses he wore at his belt—especially given that he'd tried to slash her to bits during their last encounter, and on Lilith's orders, no less.

"The dream," Reynolds said, his low voice reverberating in the confined space. "It was my hand that took you there."

An image of her ceiling light flashed in her mind, and she had her answer as to who had entered her room the previous night.

"What do you want?" she demanded, because, as always when it came to Reynolds, it wasn't remotely clear. If he'd come to complete the assignment of killing her, couldn't the task have been carried out while she slept?

"We can't speak here," Reynolds said. "They're looking for you."

Before she could determine what he meant by "they," Reynolds stepped toward her.

Dropping her things, Isobel backpedaled to the landing below, her notepads and binders sliding after her. When her spine met with the wall, her hands formed into automatic fists.

But Reynolds brushed past her. "This way," he said, descending to the second-floor landing, that moldering floral essence trailing him. "Quickly." He rounded the corner below, slipping out of sight.

Dazed, still stunned by Reynolds's sudden appearance, and even more baffled by his breeze-by exit, she could only gape after him.

Did he seriously expect her to *follow* him? Weren't they past the whole Simon Says thing? He *knew* she knew he worked for Lilith—that he'd been under the demon's command from the very beginning.

And yet, since learning the truth about his allegiance, Isobel had puzzled repeatedly over why he had ignored all the opportune moments he'd had to kill her, and why he'd continually intervened on Isobel's behalf. Like when he'd pulled her from that collapsed grave in the dreamworld. Or when, in a surprising act of seeming compassion, he'd carried her home after she'd nearly died following his orders to destroy the link between worlds, Varen's sketchbook.

At the time, of course, she'd believed Reynolds had returned Varen home safely too. Like he'd told her he had. But if he'd truly been against her from the start, why would he have wanted that link severed in the first place?

Pushing off from the wall, Isobel ran a hand through her hair, and her thoughts returned to last night's dream. If Reynolds *had* transported her to the other side, stealing her astral self from her sleeping body as he'd done the night he'd first introduced her to the woodlands, then he must have known Varen would find her there.

Had Reynolds been counting on that? Perhaps he'd even staged the whole thing.

Drawn by the possibility of answers, Isobel took a step toward the descending stairway but paused again, unsure whether she was willing—or ready—to hear what he'd come to say.

Reynolds lied like it was his hobby.

And she had promised herself to let go of her part in all this.

I keep having bad dreams, Danny had said last night.

This involves me, too, Gwen had reminded her less than an hour ago.

And then there was the problem of the entire school witnessing the effects of last night's dreamworld encounter with Varen.

His abilities were expanding, that much had become evident. And if he could shatter lights and bring the other world with him when he came, then what more would he soon be capable of?

The nightmare had to stop. Varen had to *be* stopped.

Terror bubbled up inside of her as she spurred herself forward, each step taking her closer to her greatest fear. Toward the darkness that continued to prove it would catch up with her no matter what. As she neared the ground floor, though, she slowed at the sound of muffled voices.

"How should *I* know?" Isobel heard Gwen say. "She and I aren't even friends anymore."

Isobel ducked below the stair railing. Balancing on her haunches, she rose up just enough to peek over the low wall.

Catching sight of Mr. Nott's salt-and-pepper hair and Principal Finch's gleaming bald head, she realized that the administrators must be the "they" Reynolds had been referring to. She was a little relieved, seeing as the other option possessed claws and smiles filled with jagged teeth.

How long had the school known she was missing?

Had someone contacted her parents?

Her dad was going to go nuclear.

"Of course," Gwen went on while she glowered at the two men, "you might have known that if you cared to tune into more than this school's paltry sports channel. Vocab word of the day: 'paltry.' Adjective meaning measly, lackluster, or otherwise disappointing. There. Proof I'll make you guys look good with my ACT scores. Everybody wins. For once. Can I go to class now?"

Scanning the area, Isobel searched for Reynolds but saw no sign of him anywhere. The propped door leading into the darkened gym, however, told her where he must have gone.

Isobel frowned, wondering how he'd managed to pass through the corridor unnoticed.

His pasty complexion and grim-reaper wardrobe didn't exactly scream "substitute teacher."

"That's enough, Miss Daniels," she heard Principal Finch say, his words echoed by a scratch of fuzz from his walkie-talkie.

"—not in class," Isobel heard a woman's voice utter through static.

More walkie-talkie fuzz. Then Finch's reply of, "Thank you, Mrs. Tanager."

Mr. Nott spoke next. "We have two witnesses who say they saw both of you sitting in your car just now. Right outside those doors." He turned to point, and Isobel ducked low.

"Oh!" Gwen blurted, the exclamation letting Isobel know that Gwen, at least, had seen her. Isobel cringed.

"What?" Mr. Nott asked. "What is it?"

"What do you mean, 'what is it'?" Gwen snapped, recovering quickly. "You just called the two kids with the rolling papers in their pockets 'witnesses.' And if that's the terminology we're gonna use, then I think it's high time I give my legal adviser a ring. Let's just hope he's not in the middle of performing a laser procedure. Thank you, speed-dial and—"

"Stop that. Put your phone away—"

"Daddy?" Isobel heard Gwen say. "Yeah, listen, I know you're probably with a patient right now, but the school Feds wanna talk to you. Do me a favor and tell them who our lawyer is."

One of the two men growled in frustration. Rising again, Isobel saw Principal Finch snatch Gwen's glowing cell from her. Pivoting, he pressed the phone to one ear.

"Hello," he said, while Mr. Nott watched, hands at his hips. "Hello?"

Gwen shot Isobel a pointed glare. *Go home,* she said, mouthing the words, eyes round, brow furrowed.

Isobel tilted her head, unsure if she had misread the lip-synched message. But when Gwen kicked a foot at her, skirt flaring, Isobel moved.

"There's no one on the line," Isobel heard Finch say as she scuttled down the stairs and darted to the gym. Kicking up the metal stopper, she ducked into the darkness, guiding the heavy door behind her until it closed.

Isobel whirled around to scan the wide room.

Shadows blanketed the space, casting the decorations for that night's Valentine's dance in tones of gray and black. Opposite Isobel, the red exit sign emitted an eerie glow that mixed with the sunlight peeking through the closed doors.

Against the far wall, beyond the basketball hoop, a balloon arch waited in front of a backdrop set up for photo taking. A disco ball hung motionless from the center of the ceiling. Small cloth-covered tables lined the bases of the bleachers, which had been folded away to turn Isobel's old cheerleading practice grounds into a dance floor.

Isobel could no longer make out what Gwen or the administrators were saying, though she had no doubt her friend was already en route with them to the main office. With her cell still in the pocket of her coat—which she'd left in Gwen's car—Isobel suddenly felt very alone.

Noticing tiny piles of ash blotting the floor, she moved forward with careful steps, following the dust to the center of the room, where the trail abruptly ended. Halting atop the emblem of Henry the Hawk's scowling head, she turned in a slow circle.

"I did not expect to see you in that churchyard."

Reynolds's voice, deep and gruff, came from the empty space directly behind her.

The shadows shifted to her left, and fighting the urge to dart, Isobel forced herself to stand her ground as his hawkish profile entered her periphery.

"I thought for certain you would forget him," he said, and Isobel knew he was talking about Varen.

"Yeah," Isobel said, "and I didn't expect you to be a liar, a murderer, *and* an evil henchman. I'd say in terms of trumping first impressions, you've got me beat."

"You have mistaken me," Reynolds said, "and I freely admit that I have mistaken you."

"You sent me to die," she said. "The only mistake I might

have made was agreeing to listen to anything else you have to say."

"The fate I lured you to was one I thought would befall you regardless," he said. "And because of your willingness to do as I instructed, your world, unlike my own, remains intact. Forgive me if I chose to cut your losses for you."

Isobel folded her arms. "Yeah, you're good at doing that for other people, aren't you?"

He stayed silent, and lifting her chin an inch, Isobel awarded herself a secret victory check mark. But her smugness didn't last.

"You have already proven you would die for the boy by doing it," Reynolds snapped. "Now, you will listen to what I have come to tell you or you won't, but decide. Our time wanes."

Isobel blinked, startled less by this rare outburst than by what his words revealed.

There was only one way for Reynolds to know that she had actually died.

After waking in the hospital in Baltimore, she'd been questioned by the police about the stranger who had brought her to the ER and then disappeared moments after the medical staff took over. The conflicting reports and scrambled security footage had failed to offer any leads, however.

Though Isobel had not lied when she'd told the officers and her parents that she didn't know who the man had been, she'd kept her suspicions to herself along with everything else. In a practical way, it made sense that Reynolds had been the one to return her to reality. After all, he had displayed the ability to pass from one world to the other at will. But given all that Isobel had discovered about Reynolds's true moral code—or lack thereof—she couldn't figure out the deeper reason he'd bothered to rescue her once again.

That reason, she knew, would have everything to do with why he was here now.

Looking down, she focused on Reynolds's dust-encrusted boots. However he'd gotten here, it hadn't been without a struggle.

"The blending of the worlds," Isobel whispered. "It's happening again, isn't it?"

"Do you remember what transpired here, in this room?" Reynolds asked, ignoring the question, his eyes searching the gloom. "The day you fell in front of that crowd."

"I didn't fall," she corrected him. "I was pulled."

He was referring to the Halloween day pep rally. After she had climbed to the top of her squad's pyramid, one of the Nocs had yanked her base Nikki's wrist, causing Isobel to plummet straight to the floor. Just before she'd hit, though, she'd entered a twilight consciousness. The people around her became fuzzy silhouettes, and the world a blur of muddled shapes, muffled noise, and static. While she'd been in that between state, caught halfway in the dreamworld and halfway in reality, the Nocs had attacked her, attempting to draw her spirit out of her body and into the woodlands. Reynolds had appeared from nowhere to come to her defense.

"You fell regardless," Reynolds replied. "And then you entered the veil. I asked if you remembered."

"And I asked you what the hell you wanted," Isobel said, her anger flaring anew. He needed to get it straight right now that she wasn't interested in being his puppet anymore.

"He thinks you're dead." Reynolds locked gazes with her. "The boy. He thinks he killed you."

Isobel's lips parted in shock. Of all the things she'd expected Reynolds to say, this was not on the list. Her mouth went dry, and trapped again by those two black, coin-size holes, she found herself unable to look away or reply.

He was lying. He had to be. Varen had sought her out in last night's dream. He'd zeroed in on her. He'd made his intentions clear.

They were enemies now.

"Your disbelief is a factor I have already accounted for," Reynolds said, interrupting her thoughts. "That is why I risked crossing you through the veil while you slept. So you could witness the truth for yourself."

"Witness *what* exactly?" She shook her head. "That he—"

"—sees you everywhere," Reynolds finished for her. "You haunt him at every step. The guilt for what he believes he has done has all but devoured his sanity. His subconscious conjures your image without end. In short, your memory has become his everlasting nightmare."

Isobel swallowed hard. Reynolds's words sent a seismic tremor through her, shaking the dirt from all she'd attempted to bury that day.

Taking a leaf from Reynolds's own book, though, Isobel did her best to keep her face smooth, impassive. She'd learned through experience that she couldn't afford to let him see he'd struck a chord, to allow him to believe he still had the power to manipulate her. Not when he held so much power already. *Power he should not possess,* Pinfeathers had once told her.

"You're telling me that he didn't think I was real," Isobel replied in a monotone.

"No more, I suspect, than he did that night you approached him on the cliff."

Reynolds stepped away from her, making his way toward the double doors that lead to the world outside.

More dust fell from his frame as he moved, tumbling from his boots and shoulders.

The room seemed to tilt as Isobel watched him. Her arms fell limp to her sides, and her mind, trying to grasp the full weight of that statement, threatened to collapse. She took an involuntary step after him.

"Wh-what did you just say?"

"Tell me, Isobel," he said, glancing at her over one shoulder, the crimson glow from the exit sign casting his pale face in a wash of warning red. His ash-caked, gloved hand delved into his waistcoat pocket and retrieved his watch. "Did the boy assume you were real when you first gave him your word that you would return for him?"

He clicked the watch's little door open, but Isobel knew he wasn't checking the time.

No, Isobel thought, her heart hammering. In fact, when Isobel had found Varen in the dreamworld the first time and had spoken to him through the narrow stained-glass window in the purple chamber of Poe's masquerade story, she'd done her best to convince him that she *wasn't* an illusion. Varen hadn't believed she was real at all. Not until she handed him the ribbon from her dress, proving it with something tangible. Something from reality.

Something he couldn't bend or dispel or change . . .

"Did you yourself not carry a timepiece with you into the rose garden?" Reynolds pressed, snapping the watch closed. Tucking it away again, he turned to face the doors once more. "Do you suppose I have not learned the same trick? That I, who have dwelled on the other side so long, do not still require an instrument to tell me in which realm I stand?"

On that morning after Halloween, Isobel had pulled the very watch Reynolds had just checked from his waistcoat pocket as he'd carried her home. There was a name engraved on the inside. When she'd asked Reynolds who "Augustus" was, though, he'd simply told her that he was dead, long since.

"Last night," Reynolds continued. "The hallway of mirrors— he transported you to that corridor for a reason. Why else except to ensure that you were just another torturous figment? Another eidolon with no reflection?"

Scowling at his back, Isobel tried to keep up with his words, wondering, at the same time, how Reynolds knew about the pink butterfly watch Danny had given her. And why was he staring at the doors like that, as if he expected them to fling wide at any moment?

"What about before?" Isobel asked. "When he used the

mirrors to find me. You did too. He would know. He'd be able to see—"

"He isn't looking, Isobel. Because *she* isn't. They *both* think you're dead. And that is the best chance we now have."

"Chance for *what*?" Isobel demanded. "Who are you *really*?"

"If you still hold any love for the boy," he said, glancing at her over his shoulder again, "then you need only rely on the fact that I am not, nor have I ever been, your enemy. On some level, you must already know that. Otherwise, would you have followed me here?"

The halo of light surrounding the door flickered. Flitting shadows slid to and fro along the base, gathering there.

"What's happening?" Isobel asked, but she didn't have to guess to know who—*what*—lurked on the other side.

"I am being hunted," Reynolds replied, drawing both of his swords with a single, spine-freezing scrape. "Although I cannot return to the woodlands without facing certain capture, I can still travel within the veil. What yet remains of it. You, however, could pass through, undetected, to the other side. Provided you were so willing."

"You mean astral proj—?"

The doors flung wide with a deafening crack.

Midday sunlight flooded the gym.

Swinging one of his swords upward, Reynolds spun into an attack against an unseen assailant—and vanished midstrike.

9
Beyond the Veil

Isobel staggered forward. Then she ran.

Skidding to a halt at the spot where Reynolds had disappeared, she turned in place, but she didn't see him or his attackers.

Listening hard, she heard only the chatter of birds, the distant swish and hush of nearby traffic.

He was gone. Into the veil.

The veil.

He'd asked her if she remembered being there, in that hazy space between worlds. She did, but that didn't mean she knew how to *get* there. Not on her own.

She shut her eyes and scowled in concentration, willing her limbs to relax.

Varen had done this multiple times over, she reminded herself, separating himself in two with ease, leaving his body behind as he crossed over the threshold that stood between dimensions.

Now she needed to do the same.

Focusing on the rapid thudding of her own heart, Isobel waited for the disconnecting sensation she'd felt before, when Pinfeathers had drawn her out of herself and into a haunting vision of the past.

She recalled in a flood of images the events the Noc had shown her in that memory.

That old hospital. Poe on his deathbed—screaming repeatedly for Reynolds—writhing in agony as Lilith and the Nocs tortured his captured soul.

When Reynolds had finally appeared, however, instead of answering his friend's cries for help, he'd done the unthinkable. Drawing one of his twin blades, Reynolds had severed the silver cord that tethered Poe's astral form—his spirit—to his body, killing him instantly.

But the doctor at Poe's bedside had seen nothing. Not Reynolds's betrayal, not Lilith descending through the black chasm in the ceiling, not the Nocs as they spiraled through the walls in thick smoke tendrils.

The dreamworld demons had all been in the veil, Isobel realized. Reynolds, too. As they were right now.

And not only that—even in the veil, Reynolds had performed Poe's murder cloaked and masked. Lilith hadn't known him then; in fact, she had shrieked in protest.

Isobel had unmasked Reynolds herself after tackling him in Baltimore. Had she not seen his face then, she would never have known him in the dreamworld, when he'd stepped out to face her on Lilith's orders. When Lilith had called him . . . *Gordon.*

And then today, even as he was being hunted—today he had appeared to Isobel without his usual disguise. But then, why hide if he no longer had a reason to? If he'd been found out . . .

Suddenly Isobel knew she could be sure of at least one thing: that even if she couldn't bring herself to trust Reynolds completely, or to believe he'd told her all that he knew, he was still her enemy's enemy.

So for now, if there was even one kernel of truth to what Reynolds had said—that a modicum of the boy she loved still existed behind those black eyes—then sharing a mutual opponent indeed counted for something. And seeing that Reynolds was her only way to the other side, that something would have to be enough.

Isobel drew in a deep breath, picturing herself in the veil. Tuning her senses inward, she released her breath in a slow exhale, and as she did, the noise of the birds and the passing cars and the brush of the wind outside faded.

Her skin tingled. Electricity crawled up her arms, wrapping her body in numbness until she felt only the faint, everywhere prickle of pins and needles.

When she opened her eyes, she found herself within that white and nebulous world of shapes and muted sound.

A muffled shout drew her attention to one side. Then something came crashing to her feet, where it splintered into pieces.

Isobel backpedaled, and in doing so, parted from her body.

Her vision went double for an instant, and she felt a surge of panic. Then, focusing on the blurred outline of the person in front of her—on the sleek sheet of her own hair— Isobel rejoined her body with a jolt. She peered around to find herself alone again, still facing those gaping doors to the school's rear parking lot.

Hissing a curse, she straightened, determined. Again she shut her eyes, released her clenched hands, breathed, and tried letting go a second time.

Fading under, Isobel resisted the temptation to open her eyes as the sounds surrounding her dialed down to a low hum. Holding on to her calm, she allowed the buzzing numbness to overtake her. Then she stepped forward.

Blurred shapes and shadows seeped into view despite her closed eyelids.

Another stifled screech, followed by a muted crunch.

Isobel turned her head, and at her feet, a felled Noc peered up at her, his form shimmering between shadow and clarity. He tilted his head at her in a motion that suggested curiosity. But it was also a motion that caused the creature's neck to fracture. Sputtering out, his inkwell eyes went hollow.

The indistinct image of his empty, cracked face recalled the bittersweet memory of Pinfeathers's final moments in the rose garden. So much so that she could almost have knelt beside him, brushed his cheek—until, with a high-pitched shriek, the Noc at her feet burst into life again and sent a clawed hand straight into her chest.

Isobel stiffened in shock, locked in place by the clutching sensation of the hand that held her steady, as if its claws wrapped her very heart.

She gripped the Noc's arm but could not pull herself

away. She tried to scream for help, but her voice had become lodged in her throat.

Then, from nowhere, a flash of silver sailed between Isobel and the Noc, severing the creature's arm at the elbow with a crash.

Released, Isobel collapsed onto the gym floor in unison with the arm—and with the Noc, who hissed, bearing teeth at her until an ash-covered boot came down to crush his head.

"The creature that defended you," she heard Reynolds say while she clasped at her chest, checking for the hole that wasn't there. "He was not like the others. Do not make the mistake of assuming otherwise."

Reynolds's dark form sank to crouch beside her. In one hand he grasped the hilt of a cutlass. His other clutched his shoulder, where ash tumbled through a tear in his shirt.

"They will attack you if they suspect you're not a dream. You cannot fight them as you are now." As he spoke, his focus shifted to something straight ahead.

Isobel followed his stare, and her fear ratcheted higher.

A ragged, pitch-black hole marred the place where the gym doors and red exit sign should have been. Like the papery faces from last night's dream, its edges peeled back, crumpling into the familiar form of ash. The floor, too, began to erode as if being eaten by invisible flame, its jagged perimeters creeping toward them.

Reynolds rose, and Isobel rose with him. Together they backtracked several steps.

Isobel glanced to where she'd left her body. It stood just

a few feet away, the shining silver cord wavering between the two versions of herself with a luminous radiance she'd seen before—in the ethereal glow of Lilith's veils.

Before Isobel could contemplate what that might mean, Reynolds spoke again.

"I have told you before that the ghouls of the woodlands are the darkest shards of the self. A visceral manifestation of the boy's capacity for evil. That one of them defended you— perished for your sake—serves as my best evidence that his heart, at its core, remains pure toward you. Knowing that, will you put aside your mistrust and do as I tell you?"

"You want me to go in there," Isobel said, nodding to the open crater, which had expanded to envelop part of the wall. It wasn't a question.

Reynolds lowered his hand from his closing wound and stooped to reclaim his second sword, dropped during battle.

"The darkness within him is building," he said. "His rage gathers. His self-hatred is fueled by what he believes he has done. You and I already know that he is unlike anyone else. He should not be able to traverse realms, but we have seen that he is capable of that and more. Through him, I believe she has found a means to fulfill her desire for destruction. Somehow, he has *become* the link. His wrath is eroding the veil. If he sees you, though, if he discovers that you are alive, that you still—"

"When you and I were here before," Isobel said, cutting him off, "you told me Varen was lost. You said that there was no way to—"

"There *is* one way to sever the bond that holds him," Reynolds said. "Edgar knew what it was. And though I doubted him before, I now believe my friend might have found his freedom had the Nocs not dragged his spirit back into the woodlands."

Isobel scowled at him.

"Care to share?" she asked, figuring that it would be beyond the point to question why he hadn't bothered to relate this tidbit to her before now—why he hadn't explained it instead, say, that one time he sent her into the woodlands to die.

"When it becomes an option, I will tell you. First, we must return the boy to this world."

"Pinfeathers showed me what you did," Isobel said. "What happened to Poe."

"What you saw," Reynolds said, his voice gaining strength, "was indeed accurate. A memory stolen and replayed for your protection. Yes, I ended Edgar's life. But the task fell to me because of my ability to do it, *not* because I betrayed him."

Isobel thought suddenly of Brad. After Varen's Nocs had attacked him on the football field, they'd dragged his spirit into the dreamworld. There the creatures had tormented him in the same way Poe had been tortured by his own Nocs.

After Isobel had tried and failed to rescue Brad, Reynolds told her that Brad's spirit was being held hostage by the Nocs. A "torturous link," he'd called it, one severable only by death.

Poe hadn't been calling for Reynolds to save him. He'd been begging for just the opposite.

"He *wanted* you to kill him," Isobel murmured.

Reynolds made no reply, but the solemn expression on his sunken features provided confirmation enough.

"Interact with no one," he said. "If you encounter the boy, do not engage. Do you understand?"

"But—"

"He won't believe you're real. No one will as long as you assume the role of a dream. You cannot bring him back yet. That we must do together, when we are better prepared. For now, you need only sift through his darkness. Find the light in him that has been extinguished. Go now. More Nocs will come looking for the others, and they will find the rift. I can only fight off so many, and only for so long."

"What happens if *I* get stuck? What if the same thing that happened to Edgar happens to me?"

"Your world cannot afford your death," Reynolds replied. His eyes flitted to the silver cord, and back to her. "So see that it doesn't happen."

Isobel swallowed, deciding not to ask if that meant what she thought it did. This was Reynolds, after all. King of do-what-you-gotta-do. He was telling her, in his usual charming way, that if push came to shove, he'd do her the same kind of favor as he had his ol' pal Poe.

And who said chivalry was dead?

"Got it," Isobel said, and, resolving *not* to get caught on the other side, she turned toward the black gap.

As she stepped forward, moving through the static membrane of darkness that separated the gym from the dreamworld, Isobel thought that—for now—she could suspend her distrust of Reynolds. She could believe that he needed her enough not to lie about this.

About Varen.

Of course, one way or another, she knew she would soon find out.

10
Cobwebs of the Mind

The Woodlands of Weir stretched before her, the purple backdrop beyond glowing with a new and fiercer intensity, as if the horizon had been set ablaze with violet fire.

Glancing behind, Isobel found the black chasm open at her back, a flat screen of nothingness.

Dreaming, she told herself as she looked ahead again. Real or not, this was still officially a dream.

With that thought, Isobel fixed her mind on Varen and, spurring herself onward, made her way farther into the forest.

Prison-bar trees slid by on either side of her while ahead, their ranks seemed to march on into infinity. But as Isobel continued to hold Varen in the forefront of her mind, the scenery slowly began to shift, black trees peeling away from her path to form two lines.

Though Isobel no longer had her butterfly watch to act as a guiding compass, she hoped that this time, all she would need was the strength of her intent.

And her thoughts, it would seem, *had* triggered the woodlands to yield to her. To unveil the path that would lead her to what she sought. Who.

At least, she hoped that was the case as charred trunks

paled to gray, becoming pillars, the soft, ash-covered ground beneath her feet going solid.

Deeper shadows encroached on her from above as, overhead, skeletal branches bowed inward. Limbs locking like twining tentacles, they formed a dense canopy that then melded into the crisscrossing arches of a vaulted ceiling—like that of a Gothic cathedral. Or, Isobel thought, remembering Varen's mirrored hall, a palace . . .

Tall walls filtered into view, their contours trickling down to erase the woodlands and the rift before fading from sight behind shadows thick as ink. Low purple light poured through the netted panes of sparsely stationed stained-glass windows—the only sources of illumination within the corridor where Isobel now stood.

The scent of incense, familiar and luring, drew her attention to the far end of the hall, where tendrils of white smoke swirled up from the center of a carved dais. On either side of the marble altar, a pair of identical stone angels stood guard, hands wrapping the hilts of massive, downward-aimed swords.

Curious, Isobel started toward them.

Tap, tap, tap. The echo of her steps ricocheted from wall to wall, giving her the eerie sense of being followed.

She stopped, turning sharply, but there was no one there. Nothing.

Silence resettled, and swallowing the fear that at any second *something* would discover her, Isobel recalled Reynolds's words of reassurance. Even in the open like this, he'd said she would still be hidden. Just one dream—one ghost—among many.

Something stirred in the darkness to her right. Her head jerked in that direction, and out from between a pair of pillars stepped a black-cloaked figure.

"There she is again," the figure said, his face hidden in the shadows of his hood.

"The boy," answered another rasping voice from the gloom, and Isobel's gaze flitted to a second hooded form as it emerged. "He must be near."

"This one sees us," the first figure said.

"So it would seem," answered the second as he removed his hood, the dim light casting his hollow face in sharp lines of lavender and black. His eyes, deep-set and onyx, like Reynolds's—like Varen's—watched Isobel with guarded interest.

Too late, Isobel recalled Reynolds's warning not to interact. Figuring that staring probably counted as "interacting," she turned her head slowly back toward the altar.

"That scar," whispered the first figure. "There on her face. Did she have that before?"

Resisting the urge to touch her cheek—or to start running—Isobel began to move again. Keeping her stride even, as unhurried as she could, she pretended not to see the pair anymore.

"Only ever in the black dress," the second figure whispered, "and always bleeding. This one . . . she's new."

An involuntary wince touched Isobel's face. She smoothed her expression again, hoping the men had not noticed. Though she didn't know who the two were, she suspected they could be figments of a dream. From whose mind they might have sprung, though, she had no way of knowing.

Perhaps they were characters from one of Poe's stories. More residue left by the poet's time here.

Then again, maybe not, if they had the cognizance to assume *she* was a dream.

As the altar with its angelic sentries loomed nearer, Isobel wondered if, like Reynolds, the cloaked duo could be Lost Souls. Lilith had mentioned that there were others. . . .

"Where is she going?" one of the men whispered.

"Where she always goes," the other hissed. "To him."

Though Isobel softened her steps to better hear them, she didn't dare slow down and risk revealing that she wasn't the mirage they believed her to be. Instead she walked on, straining to make sense of the susurrant sibilants that, like the smoke rising from the altar, dissipated into the cavernous ceiling.

Then the voices stopped. Pausing when she reached the steps that led to the altar, Isobel waited for the conversation to restart. When she heard nothing, though, she had to fight the urge to turn and make sure the two men were still where she'd left them, tucked in the recess of shadows—and not standing in the aisle just behind her. Or worse, gone altogether. Off to report what they had seen.

She cast a flickering glance between the two stone angels to see if they might open their eyes, raise their swords against her. As she stared into their serene faces, though, something about their appearance struck her as strange. How each held an uncanny resemblance . . . to *her*.

Disquietude swept over Isobel, causing her skin to buzz, and she wondered if the statues' echoing features might support Reynolds's claim that Varen saw her everywhere—in everything.

She mounted the steps, and as she passed between the stone guardians, the sensation of being watched intensified. As if the number of eyes upon her had grown by two more pairs.

Though she could no longer see the angels, Isobel could sense them awakening—*feel* them turning their heads in unison to chisel stony glares into her back. If she dared to turn and look, then the two dreamworld figures would know instantly that she wasn't like them. Their mouths would fall open, they'd start screaming, and their siren cries would shatter the windows. The Nocs would come pouring through from the woodlands. Then they'd have her. They'd have her. They'd never let her go and—

Stumbling up the last step, Isobel stopped herself from slamming into the altar by grasping its cold edge. She clamped down hard and forbade her imagination to progress any further toward chaos.

As real as the stone felt beneath her fingers, as detailed as the world around her appeared, she *had* to remember that it was all still malleable, changeable. She could take control if she needed. Whisk herself to some other place or even wake up back in the gym, back in her body. But if she started to alter things now, to interfere with this palace facade that had to have come from Varen's own imagination, she would also give herself away.

Forgetting the angels, Isobel swept her thoughts clean, replacing her fears with her original purpose. Her *only* purpose. *Find Varen.*

She peered down into a rectangular pit in the center of the altar from which the white wisps of smoke arose. Several feet below, at the bottom of a narrow brick channel, a collection of glass bottles sat around a dish of burning incense cones. A slant of dim, smoke-diluted light shone into the recess through a squat archway at the very bottom.

A fireplace, Isobel thought with a scowl, realizing she was looking down the flue of a truncated chimney. And the assortment of the dried flowers in those familiar colored bottles told her whose.

Climbing onto the altar, Isobel lowered herself feetfirst into the tight space. Her sneakers knocked into the incense dish as she landed, spilling its embers and sending several bottles toppling.

Isobel slumped to squeeze out of the casket-size space and, dropping onto her hands and knees, she crawled after the largest bottle as it barreled out onto the wooden floor with a thunderlike roll.

The bottle clinked as it collided with a pair of polished men's dress shoes, dumping its sprig of flowers. With a jolt of sudden terror, Isobel looked up.

Dark-gray and neatly creased slacks accompanied the matching jacket of an empty, immobile business suit. Where there should have been a man's head, there was only the hollow circle of a starched white collar. A red tie laced an invisible throat, while silver links gleamed from stiff, white, hand-free cuffs.

Moving only when she was certain the suit would not, Isobel pushed to her feet.

As she'd suspected, she was in a reversed version of Varen's bedroom. But the jam-packed interior no longer resembled the open and orderly space as she knew it.

Varen's posters, books, DVDs, and bed were all gone.

Dusty boxes and cloth-draped furniture cluttered the room instead, while drab and milky light struggled to filter through the shuttered windows. Piled high, stacks of books wrapped in cobwebs obscured the legs of a plush velvet violet armchair that Isobel was sure she'd seen somewhere before. Not here in Varen's attic bedroom, but . . . where? She couldn't recall.

On a table nearby was an empty birdcage, its white wires eaten by rust, its door held closed by a red, heart-shaped padlock. Lining the circular bed of the cage, yellowing scraps of sheet music peeked through a mixture of mismatched skeleton keys.

An old-fashioned oil lamp, its glass casing cracked and sooty, sat next to the birdcage.

Isobel went to the table and, touching the base of the lamp, imagined it lit. In response, a tall flame sprang forth from the dried wick, sending a flush of warm amber light dancing up the peeling walls. Along with several flittering moths, the shadows fled to the four corners of the room, the farthest of which held another sheeted form — this one human in shape—its white covering untouched by the dust, as if the secret concealed beneath was the attic's most recent.

Forgetting the ghostly suit, Isobel hurried to the form, winding her way between towers of boxes, past a covered desk and a toppled chandelier.

She fell to her knees beside the figure, which lay slumped against the wall, its covered head lolled to one side, the sole of a single black boot poking out from beneath the sheet.

Isobel took one edge of the pristine fabric, but before she could tear the cover free, she caught sight of line-crackled fingers tipped by blue claws, long and curved.

The figure beneath the cloth. It wasn't Varen, as she'd feared, but Scrimshaw.

Poe's last remaining Noc.

Releasing the cloth, she fumbled to stand, hands leaping to cover her mouth, feet forcing her into a retreat. She stumbled, her heel knocking into something solid—a bowl. Ashes filled the shallow dish, which, for an instant, tottered and rattled before settling again.

Embedded in the soot, like bits of broken shell in sand, jutted a collection of mismatched porcelain shards. On the largest, Isobel saw an etching of a woman, her lash-fringed eyes open, but only just.

Silence pulsed once more, and Isobel held her breath, her attention locked not on the immobile form beneath the sheet, but on that portrait she recognized as Virginia. Poe's wife.

The shard had once occupied the place just over the heart Scrimshaw did not possess. And the last time Isobel had seen

it, it had still been intact, though much of the rest of the Noc
had been reduced to fragments.

Pinfeathers had battled and destroyed Scrimshaw in the
rose garden while trying to protect Isobel, sustaining enough
damage to splinter himself apart as well. But now someone
had painstakingly pieced the blue Noc back together.

Isobel's gaze returned to Scrimshaw's clawed hand and she
wondered why.

For what purpose? And was it possible the shard etched
with Virginia's image was being held in reserve, the final puzzle
piece that would restore the reconstructed monster to life?

Isobel didn't know. But she didn't want to find out, either.

If Scrimshaw awoke to see . . . if he discovered that she
wasn't just a dream . . .

Fighting her rising panic, Isobel searched for an exit. She
spotted the narrow door, its surface marred with ominous
scratches, and began to wind her way toward it, navigating in
backward steps in order to keep the Noc in her sights—the
tips of those indigo claws that were still poking out from the
corner of cloth she'd dared to lift.

Then, at the sound of humming, she froze.

Someone else was in the room with her—a woman.

The song, slow and soft, was one Isobel knew. Varen's lullaby.

Isobel stalled her breathing to listen, but just as quickly as
the melody had begun, it halted.

She scanned the cluttered room, her sight settling finally
on an old dressing screen unfolded in front of the window
that, in the real world, led out onto the fire escape.

Squinting, Isobel focused on one of the narrow gaps between the hinged panels.

She could see someone there, sitting on the other side.

As she inched forward, she reluctantly let Scrimshaw's draped form slide out of her view. Peeking around the screen, she found a woman seated in a cloth-covered chair.

Except, Isobel realized with grim fascination, the figure wasn't a woman at all.

With seeming disinterest, the life-size doll stared out through the slats of the shuttered window, her eyes lazy and half-lidded, curled lashes throwing long spidery shadows over her rouged cheeks.

Cobwebs swathed her narrow frame, clinging to the moth-eaten frills of her lavender gown. Frizzed wisps of ash-blond hair framed her somber, crackled-paint features, while a familiar purple rhinestone comb secured a loose bun at the base of her neck.

Isobel slipped behind the screen, floorboards whining as she drew nearer for a better look. Triggered by her motions, the brass windup key protruding from the figurine's back twitched into motion. The key unwound, twisting the cobwebs with it as it rotated, and the humming started again.

Isobel grasped the brass key and held it steady, halting the woman's voice.

She checked over her shoulder again and could just make out the edge of the boot still sticking out from the sheet. The blue claws, too.

Isobel looked back to the doll.

Sift through his darkness, Reynolds had told her.

Was that what this place was?

Crouching in front of the doll, Isobel searched her fixed features for some answer.

Madeline, Isobel thought. Varen's mother. Was this how she existed in his mind? As a cold and lifeless mannequin? A windup memory that could only repeat the same sad song over and over? Her image preserved but faded, distorted and worn down by the years of not knowing—not being able to comprehend—what had become of her?

"Why did you leave?" Isobel whispered.

As though in response, the doll's eyelids rolled up to reveal emerald irises and a glassy stare that trained itself on Isobel. The pupils shrank to pinpricks. Then, with a quiet pop, the orbs cracked. Black oil seeped out from the inner crevices of the doll's eyes, tracking dark streaks down her cheeks.

Splattering onto the floor, two blots of oil writhed and wriggled into a pair of tiny, dark brown beetles.

Isobel straightened quickly. She jumped back from the insects as they scurried toward her and then, one after the other, into a hollowed knot between floorboards.

She glanced back to the doll and saw that her cracked eyes had fallen shut.

Without a sound, the doll had lifted a porcelain finger to her ruby lips, as though calling for silence.

Somewhere in the room, something fell with a low *clunk.* A shadow skirted the ceiling, and with a splintering of glass, the light Isobel had lit winked out.

11
Noc Noc

Isobel grew still, holding her breath in the renewed darkness.

Shifting her weight slowly, to keep the floor from creaking again, she leaned toward the slim space between the wall and the screen. Peeking through, she saw that the bowl lay overturned, its contents strewn across the worn boards.

But Isobel did not see the largest of the porcelain shards, the fragment containing the etching of Virginia.

It was missing—just like the figure from beneath the collapsed white sheet.

"They call them deathwatches."

The deep, static-corroded voice—almost incomprehensible in its distortion—had come from directly beside her.

Isobel's eyes slid in the direction of the screen. Poison-tipped hooks of fear snagged her through the gut as she caught sight of a single pitch-black eye, watching her through the narrow slit between panels.

Grinning, the Noc flashed a double row of serrated teeth, an intricate network of cracks spreading into view on the visible slice of his porcelain cheek.

He inserted an indigo claw into the gap and pointed at her.

"If you listen closely," he continued, a glossy bead of black liquid racing down his curved nail, "you can hear them in the walls."

Isobel zeroed in on the droplet as it reached the very tip of the Noc's claw. Before the drop could fall, however, it wriggled to life, forming into another of the rust-colored beetles.

Tumbling onto the floor, the insect scrambled to right itself, then scurried off into the same hole as the others.

"The sound, it goes something like this . . . ," the Noc hissed, and retracting his claw, he tapped lightly against the screen.

The same noise answered from beneath, below the patch of floor right under her.

Tensing, Isobel readied herself to run. But she already knew it was too late. There was nowhere to go.

Nowhere the Noc wouldn't be able to reach first.

"Their ticking is said to herald the final moments of one who is close to death," Scrimshaw went on, his jagged grin spreading wider. "So their name, you see, is very suiting."

Growing louder, the clicking began to spread, multiplying into a cacophony that Isobel could feel through the soles of her shoes.

Dream, she thought, shifting from one foot to the other, edging away from the hole where, inside, something moved.

"There's only one problem," the Noc said, his tone dropping to a hush while the tapping noise continued to rise in volume.

Just . . . a dream.

"History has proven that I *can't* die. And since you already have, one is left to wonder what all their fuss is about."

Suddenly the ticking ceased. The floor groaned.

Silence.

Then, in a rushing surge, a torrent of tiny bodies came flooding up through the hole.

Isobel cried out. She shrank back.

Stumbling into the chair, she knocked the doll aside. The figure's head cracked against the windowsill, causing the key affixed to her back to jog into motion again.

The sound of the doll's humming, slow and stilted, arose to join the beetles' renewed clicking as her eyelids rolled open, each socket unleashing a fresh cascade of insects.

The bugs converged on Isobel's shoes, and the screech that had been building inside her at last broke free. She kicked at the gathering swarm, but quick as flames, they engulfed her legs. They scurried up her jeans and scuttled beneath the hems, onto the cuffs of her socks and then the bare skin of her ankles.

Isobel stomped to shake them free and tried to sweep the bugs clear from her in handfuls. But the insects clung to her arms and wrists, scaling her shoulders and then her neck.

She twisted and, tumbling into the screen, slammed with it to the floor.

The bang rattled the boards, rallying even more bugs from all the rotted-out knots that had not been there moments before.

A deep chuckle filled her ears as the tide of insects swept over her.

Her screams pitched higher, joining the doll's dying song and the Noc's laughter until all were eclipsed by the now-deafening sound of the ticking.

She needed to get away. Out of there. Home. She wanted to be home. To wake up and never, ever sleep again. She needed—

"Reynolds!" she managed to screech while the writhing mass enveloped her throat, scrambling up her jaw and over her chin.

Clamping her mouth shut, Isobel jerked to one side. She threw her head back, but that didn't stop the hordes of tiny bodies from hurrying over her pinched lips.

Lashing left and right, tearing at her own face, she rolled and felt the moving sheet of shells beneath her crunch like a layer of dead leaves. Everywhere, her skin prickled with the sensation of thousands of minuscule legs.

She shut her eyes just before the frenzying ranks could scramble over her lids and into her ears, obliterating the last hints of light and sound—all but their own incessant ticking.

Her screams, no longer containable, burst forth in glass-shattering tones. Sanity left her the instant the insects flooded her mouth, cutting her off before she could cry Reynolds's name again.

Tick tick tick tick tick tick.

Beneath the drone, a far-off voice repeated her name, urging her to take control, telling her again and again that she was dreaming.

Dreams . . .

They only feel real when you let them, she'd told Danny. *When you let them . . .*

Curling into herself, Isobel imagined the living sheath that encased her shriveling up and crumbling away into cinders. As she focused hard on the visual, she felt the currents of scampering legs dissipate, the weight of the attacking insects lift from her body.

All at once, the clicking inside her head ceased, and with a rattling gasp, she sat up.

Frantically brushing her arms and legs, swiping at her collar and shoulders, Isobel wiped away only dust. She coughed up grime, the choking soot coating her mouth and throat. She didn't care, though. Not so long as the beetles were gone.

She flinched, eyes darting wildly in search of her tormentor, but like the beetles, the Noc and the attic had vanished. An even deeper darkness bathed new surroundings, interrupted only by the red glow of embers emanating from a fireplace far larger and more ornate than the one through which she'd entered.

She was now in a tidy study.

Quaking uncontrollably, Isobel whimpered, raking her fingers through her hair. Breathless, she whipped her head from side to side, anticipating the next horror Scrimshaw would no doubt inflict on her at any moment.

"Shh, we're here now," spoke the distorted voice through the gloom, its tones softer than before, though no less caustic.

"Stay away," Isobel said, wrestling herself onto quivering legs.

"Hush now," the Noc said. "Hush. No need for all that. It was just a bad dream. That's all. We're here, and that means he's gone. For now."

Isobel wrapped her arms around herself tight and, though her eyes searched, she could not find the source of the voice that seemed to echo from everywhere and nowhere.

On a nearby table, she saw the same oil lamp she'd encountered in the attic. Its chimney, now clean and unbroken, guarded a minuscule blue flame. Then the lamp's skeleton-key handle twisted on its own, and the flame grew into a tall column of flickering violet fire.

The glow illuminated the same leather-bound books from the attic. Now clear of cobwebs, the tomes lined shelves that followed the walls. Thick purple curtains hung over a shuttered casement window, their folds pooling on the floor, and against one wall stood a familiar pair of ornate double doors.

The plush velvet armchair from the attic now sat facing the glimmering hearth, and suddenly Isobel remembered exactly where she'd seen it before.

Here. In this very room. The purple chamber where she had found Varen imprisoned the night of the Grim Facade.

But someone other than Varen occupied the chair now, red claws resting on one of the arms.

"Don't be angry with us," the Noc whispered, "but we had to let him have his fun. Only because we wanted to be sure. Then again, scars don't lie, do they?"

Motionless, Isobel waited to see if the claws would move,

if the seat's occupant would rise and face her. Well aware that this could be yet another illusion brought on by the treachery inherent in this ever-changing realm, she held her ground.

Still, if Scrimshaw had been pieced together again, then couldn't the same have been done for—

"Pin?" Isobel said, the single syllable quavering.

"You know how the saying goes," answered the voice, which sounded weak now, fading. "Where there's one . . ."

"There's more," Isobel breathed, her memory snatching the final line from the poem Varen had written about the Nocs, the same one she'd read in his sketchbook just moments before burning its pages.

She started forward, keeping her gaze trained on that clawed hand. But when she rounded the chair, she found the seat empty—like the crackled, hollowed limb that occupied the armrest, amputated at the bicep.

Someone snickered.

"*Please,*" Isobel said, spinning to search the shadows again. "No more tricks. No more games. If it's really you . . . then help me. Help me find him. Help me find *both* of you."

"If it's really you," the voice whispered, its nearness causing her skin to prickle, "you'll know where to look. You always do."

A hand stroked her hair, claws clicking as they grazed her shoulder.

She snapped her head to the right, but still, there was no one. Even the empty limb had vanished.

Behind her there came a quiet click followed by a low

creak, and, turning, she saw that one of the tall double doors had eased ajar.

Her gaze trailed up the slim black crack to where, positioned at the top of the door frame in an extension of its decorative molding, the back-lit bust of the chamber's Grecian warrior woman held the appearance of slumbering.

Isobel remembered that the statue hadn't been sleeping when she'd been here before, though. Nor had it so closely resembled her, with its hair no longer tightly coiled but straight, falling long to rest around bare shoulders.

"*Issssobel.*"

Feet sinking into the thick carpet, heels trailing the dusty residue of her last nightmare, Isobel approached the beckoning call that had come from the open slit between doors—and whatever new horror waited beyond.

She paused in front of the gap and, peering up at the bust one more time, drew strength from the warrior's image, from the suggestion of courage it gave.

Then, as she watched the sculpture's smooth face, a thin crimson split appeared on one alabaster cheek. Blood seeped from the wound, blazing bright.

A phantom pain emanated from Isobel's own mirroring scar.

She ignored it, though, and taking one knob in each hand, she pushed the doors apart.

12
Phantom Chased

Darkness waited for her in the long, silent hall.

Heavy chandeliers floated above untethered, their underbellies dripping shards of crystal.

The ominous, rolling presence of the smoke ceiling alerted Isobel that she was back in Varen's Gothic palace, though now she wondered if she'd ever left its boundaries.

She leaned into the hall and glanced left. A pair of violet velvet curtains framed a high wooden archway that led into a joining corridor.

Craning her neck right, toward the opposite end of the hall, she squinted through the gloom—and started. Someone was there, peeking at her from behind a matching pair of curtains midway down.

Isobel withdrew fast into the purple chamber. Waiting a beat, she risked a second glance around the jamb.

The same figure moved in time with her, the stranger's straight blond hair draping long, just like hers . . . leading Isobel to realize she wasn't viewing a long corridor at all.

It was a short hall. One that terminated in—a mirror?

Venturing into the center of the passage, she faced her reflection, frowning in confusion. Because she knew she shouldn't *have* a reflection. Not as long as she was here in astral form. Not as long as she was dreaming.

With cautious steps, Isobel started toward the image of herself. Taking in the details of her own dust-coated figure, she tilted her cheek slightly to one side to ensure that her reflection shared her scar. It did. She drifted closer before stopping a few feet away.

The image in the mirror matched her movements—her stillness—perfectly.

Until it winked.

Isobel blinked in surprise.

Smiling, her duplicate whirled—and ran.

Isobel darted after the double.

Passing through the curtains ahead, the entity skidded to a halt, opening its arms to keep balance. Following suit, Isobel staggered to a standstill in front of the mirror, unable to fight the sensation that, without meaning to, she'd performed the exact same movement.

Next, she whipped her head around to see her doppelgänger standing under the archway at the opposite end of the corridor. The specter had whipped its head around too, giving the illusion that there was another mirror at the opposite end of the hall. Then the figment grinned again and, sticking its tongue out at Isobel, dashed to the side, disappearing into the adjoining hallway.

Isobel sprinted after, recalling as she did what she'd overheard the two cloaked figures in the cathedral say about her dream-selves—that they always went to the same place. To the same person. Varen.

She sped around the corner, and up ahead, she glimpsed a fleeting whip of blond hair as her double vanished around the next bend.

Isobel rounded the bend too, to find herself in a new corridor, this one empty.

The drapes at the far end hung motionless. She slowed as she approached them, then stopped, carefully drawing back one side of the hangings.

There, at the end of the next hall, her look-alike mirrored her stance, peeking around one drape into the connecting corridor.

Confused, Isobel pulled back. Pressing her spine flush with the wall, she glanced down the passage through which she'd just come.

Nothing. There was no one. And yet . . . one of the curtains swayed.

With bewilderment, Isobel lifted an arm, extending it out into the passage.

And an arm appeared at the far turn.

Isobel withdrew. The phantom limb copied her, vanishing, the drapes rippling. She repeated the test, and keeping her arm extended this time, she stared at the copycat arm, trying to grasp what was happening.

Had she somehow become caught in a looping illusion created by her own mind? Was this dream version of herself toying with her? Could dreams do that? Or was something else at work?

She let her arm sink to her side again—and felt her

stomach plummet when the hand sticking out from the far end remained extended.

Twiddling fingers at her, the hand then swept out of sight.

At the sound of a giggle, Isobel pushed away from the wall. Resuming the chase, she dashed around the corner where she'd seen the arm, ending up not in the corridor she'd passed through moments before, but in altered surroundings. New, but utterly familiar.

Trenton's reversed north hall lay before her, its lockers and linoleum flooring still covered in the ash of last night's dream.

Facing Isobel, her double stood in the center of the debris. Its smile was gone now, though.

With its eyes closed, the dream held a single finger to its lips, offering the same warning as the doll in the attic.

The clone then turned and went to the stairwell, where Varen's boot prints trailed off. Isobel hurried to catch up as the specter shoved through the blue, push-bar doors that, in reality, led to the same room where she'd left Reynolds — and her body. Sliding through after the double, though, Isobel found herself in an enormous, mist-filled courtyard.

Ash rained from above, filtering over an assembly of statues.

Like ascending spirits, the winged angels jutted up through the stagnant white fog. Posted atop short pedestals and tall columns, under the domes of carved marble gazebos, standing alone on the ground or in pairs flanking mist-shrouded steps, some tilted their faces heavenward; others bowed their heads, as if in reverie or prayer.

All the stone maidens' eyes were shut, their expressions serene with sleep. All bore Isobel's features.

Soft as snow, the ash fell to collect in the grooves of sculpted gowns. It gathered in the folds of trailing robes, pooled in the palms of outstretched hands and on the curves of fanned seraphs' wings.

Scattered between the figures, gnarled woodland trees twisted toward the clouded gray sky like thorn bushes, their limbs dotted with the black bodies of crows.

Nocs, Isobel thought when the ghouls-in-bird-form began cawing, rankled by the presence of her and her double.

As Isobel followed her own ghost into their midst, the birds flittered and flapped. They croaked back and forth to one another, frill feathers bristling. One of the larger birds, its plumage scraggly and ragged, launched itself from its branch to cross the courtyard. Its dark shadow skimmed the fog, and glancing up, Isobel saw the bird crane its neck toward her, as if to get a better look with its single good eye.

When the bird lighted on another knotted bough, the layers of fog thinned, and Isobel was suddenly aware of a form seated on the low brick wall directly across from her. Of feathery edges of jet hair and slumped black-clad shoulders. Someone living.

Varen.

He sat with his head hanging, his attention fixated on the small object he kept turning over and over in his hand.

Another of Isobel's stone twins sat at his side. Arms stiff and shoulders hunched, she clutched the edge of the wall. Her wings tucked, the statue leaned toward him as if patiently waiting for him to take notice of her. Or for a kiss.

A wreath of ash-dusted stone flowers crowned her head, and the layers of her dress spilled onto the floor in folds that, like the statue itself, held only the appearance of softness.

While Isobel stalled at the sight of him, her ghost double sprinted straight for him, and disturbed by the sudden burst of movement, the crows in the trees began to squawk.

Their shouts of warning echoed across the courtyard, ricocheting from wall to wall.

Varen looked up. Setting eyes on Isobel's double as it closed in on him, cutting a straight path through the fog, he stood. His fist closed around the item he'd been studying, and his arms fell open.

That single gesture, so helpless, caused something inside Isobel to leap out of dormancy.

Though her heart had been restarted in a literal sense once before, jogged from a state of dead matter into a beating force of life, she had not since felt the electricity of her renewed existence. Not until that precise moment when Varen enwrapped her ghost, pulling the phantom in close as it swung its arms around his neck.

His face pinched tight with pain, though, as if he knew what would come next.

Almost the instant the two collided, Isobel's double shriveled in Varen's grip. Its limbs fell limp and its skin sucked inward, its face hollowed out, flesh contracting. Blond hair faded to scraggly gray. Now a skull, the phantom's head lolled backward, its jaw falling open as if in a silent scream.

Still Varen refused to release the double. He held tight to the bones even as they broke apart.

Transforming to ash, the entity's remains fell through his grip, cascading into the vapors that swirled in their wake.

Varen lowered his arms. He looked up, his face smudged with the gray dust of the phantasm's essence. His dull eyes, despondent, black as nothing, flicked to Isobel.

A beat passed, and she knew how this must seem to him. That a replay was about to begin.

When he began striding quickly toward her, she felt her heart stop all over again.

Isobel's terror returned, dousing the bittersweet spark that had flickered awake inside her.

Dropping open of their own accord, her arms invited him in the way his arms had her ghost.

But Isobel could sense what Varen intended to do. He'd send her away like he had last night. He'd obliterate her to nothing to prevent her from deteriorating in front of him again.

Reliving her demise over and over, seeing her image all around him, frozen in the form of these cold, unfeeling monuments locked in eternal sleep—*this* had become his fate in this horrendous realm. His existence.

This was his darkness.

His hell.

But she wasn't dead. And she wasn't ready to be sent back, either. Not yet.

Brushing aside the nagging memory of Reynolds's warning not to interact, Isobel focused her mind on doing the only thing she knew *to* do. The only thing that would hold any power at all.

More power than any words.

Shifting her thoughts, she channeled her concentration on one single objective.

To do what a mere dream could not. And change *everything*.

13
Within the Distant Aidenn

The light that she summoned came cold.

Though it didn't match the sharp blast of warm sunlight Isobel had called forth in her mind, it *did* accomplish the goal of halting Varen.

He swung toward the silver glow. Pearly like moonlight, it streamed through the surrounding windows of the courtyard's high walls, bouncing off the fog, which, though Isobel commanded it to disperse, refused.

Frowning, she clenched her fists tight at her sides.

She had to fight to keep the light there. Doing so felt like trying to maintain tightrope balance, or shoving against an invisible wall.

She didn't understand. She'd never had to strain like this before to affect something in the dreamworld.

After Reynolds had taught her how to alter her surroundings and shown her the power of lucidity in her dreams, she'd been able to take control. In the past, her battle had been in *recognizing* her power, not wielding it.

She should be able to annihilate this gathering of statues like she had the duplicates of herself in the hall last night, or the deathwatches in the attic.

But the cold memorials remained, solid and imposing.

Varen's gaze returned to her, and the sight of those two unchanging black eyes sent a spear of sorrow straight through her. The poison of that stare proved fatal to her light.

Her glow winked out. Darkness returned, and a new fear opened wide inside of her.

Varen. *He* had to be the force she'd been fighting against.

These constructs around her were of his imagination. His subconscious had to be what was holding it all in place. In his unbending belief that she was gone, he had created an immovable fortress.

The fog swelled thicker as Varen stepped forward again, closing the distance between them. Lifting a hand, he touched her cheek.

Isobel's eyelids flickered, and she waited to feel herself crumple as she had last night.

She didn't fade out, though. And neither did he.

From the trees, the crows' cawing rose in a drone. All of them rasped the same deranged call, as if urging Varen to act on his impulse, to dispense with her and deliver them all from her presence.

As the seconds ticked by, though, she began to wonder if . . . if he could be stalling.

Was it possible her attempt to prove her realness, however feeble, had achieved this small pause, this brief moment of uncertainty?

Isobel seized the chance. Placing her hand on his sleeve, she tilted her face to his and clamped down hard on both his wrist and her thoughts.

Then, as though they'd been there all along, awaiting the return of her resolve, Isobel's imagined rays of light returned. Bursting through the windows, sharper and more intense than before, the beams sliced through the ramparts like blades, shredding them. The Gothic facade of the castle evaporated, eaten through by the heat of Isobel's beckoned dawn to reveal the innumerable trees of the woodlands. Varen whipped his head away from her, looking to the eye of blinding light that bled his violet horizon gold.

As Isobel's sun rose higher, the slanted shadows of the trees and stone angels shifted, rotating in unison like a thousand synchronized clock hands.

The fog vaporized, and Isobel's heart swelled in sudden triumph. That she'd penetrated Varen's illusionary kingdom had to mean he'd lowered his guard. Enough for her to slip into a tiny crack of hope he had to be harboring somewhere within. Hope that, beyond all reason or doubt, she would find a way keep her promise.

Unconstrained, her summoned sunbeams ricocheted through the woodlands. Patches of moss sprang to life, crawling up the tree trunks. A blanket of lush grass rolled outward in every direction, forming a floor of eye-stinging green.

Without allowing her concentration to waver—even for a moment—Isobel continued to alter each element of their surroundings as it occurred to her, knowing she had to create something Varen himself would never conceive. She needed to build a dream he would know had come from *her*. The real her.

So she imagined the craggy tree limbs sprouting countless

buds, and in an explosion of pink, a million tiny blossoms burst into bloom. The sudden eruption of color sent the crows fleeing into the overcast sky, their simultaneous lift-off releasing a cascade of petals that tumbled like confetti between her and Varen.

Laced with the scent of cherry and vanilla, the flurry replaced the flecks of falling ash. More petals poured from the sky where the crows swarmed in a mass of black, their cries of shock turning to shrieks of fury.

But Isobel ignored the Nocs, and, focusing next on the statues, those lifeless forms that represented her memory—her presumed loss—she shattered them all into still more blossoms.

Pink spilled onto green, petals settling into a patchwork carpet.

High above, the Nocs drew in tighter and, circling, formed a dense whirlpool. Flapping, cawing with growing agitation, the birds focused the eye of their spinning storm directly overhead.

While Varen looked to their gathering ranks, Isobel took the opportunity to cast the sky above the ghouls—the final unturned element—a brilliant blue.

Blue azure, she thought, recalling the shade Varen had named her eyes in his final letter.

Without consciously meaning to, she'd rendered for him the world he'd wished for in that note. *Her* world, complete with the warm summer sky he'd longed for in the moments after he'd believed all was lost.

Varen's gaze dropped away from the birds, returning to her in confusion.

The flecks of pink caught in their clothes and their hair, collecting in the collar of Varen's black coat and on the cuff of the sleeve she still clutched, even though he'd long since lowered his hand from her cheek.

"How can you write me out," she whispered, "if you never made me up to begin with?"

Fear flashed in his eyes. Varen recoiled. As his arm jerked from her grip, their surroundings shifted again.

The crystal blue of Isobel's sky melted to coal-fired orange. The horizon blazed crimson. Shivering, the canopy of flowers dissolved to dust. The grass beneath them withered, and the trees crackled dead in one fell swoop.

Her spell broken, Isobel reached for Varen, unwilling to let him slip through her fingers again. But the army of Nocs chose that moment to descend. Swooping low, the birds cut between them in a fierce current of feathers and ripping talons.

Lifting her arms to shield herself, Isobel swung away from the sharp hooks that tore at her. The creatures attacked from all angles, their wings whooshing loud in her ears, rubbing out all other sound.

"Varen!" she shrieked.

An arm hooked her around the middle from behind, drawing her close.

Yanked to one side, Isobel felt herself leave the fury of attacking birds and re-enter a realm of muted noises and blurred shapes—the veil.

But how—*why* had—?

"Gluttons for punishment, aren't we?" a low, static voice whispered in her ear. "We both just keep coming back."

Looking down as the arm that held her loosened, Isobel caught sight of claws.

"Wait," she gasped, but the Noc—Pinfeathers—had already released her.

She felt a familiar tug at her midsection and flew forward. Everything blurred into one colorless smear, and with a whoosh and a snap, she rejoined her body. She opened her eyes to find herself lying on the floor in the gym, but still in the gray-white between-space of the veil.

Reynolds stood over her, his image the only clear form against the fuzzy backdrop.

Those dark eyes glared down the curved length of his rusted blade, aimed straight at her.

Through the open rift behind him, a flood of screeching black shapes—crows—rushed out to fill the ceiling.

Like blots of ink dropped into water, they began to unfurl into smoke tendrils.

Then the wisps and coils took on new shapes, pouring into an army of tall silhouettes that drew in close, encircling them both.

Staticky whispers joined into one unintelligible hiss.

"I thought I told you," Reynolds growled through gritted teeth, "*not* to engage."

14
Emergence

Isobel focused on the sharpened blade tip that hovered less than an inch from her nose.

In her periphery, she saw the dark ring of collecting figures close in tighter, their whispers growing louder. She heard one of them hiss her name.

"Leave," Reynolds snapped, "now."

She started to speak, but silver sparked as he slashed at her with the blade.

Isobel flinched away. When she opened her eyes again, she saw that the gym had returned to normal: empty, dark, and soundless.

Reynolds was gone. The Nocs, too.

She'd emerged from the veil. Now fully awake, she'd rejoined with both her physical body and with reality.

Her limbs tingled, alive with the electric sensation of pins and needles. Though her arms stung where the crows had clawed and pecked at her, her flesh bore no wounds.

The doors leading outside still hung wide before her. White sunlight streamed through. Winter's chilling breath blew over her, wafting across the parking lot, stirring a layer of tiny pink petals.

Isobel wrestled to her feet to survey the scene before her.

It had happened again. The dreamworld had met with reality—blended.

Hurrying through the doors, Isobel saw that the small blots of pink she had imagined into being covered the windshields of parked cars, the cracked asphalt, and the sidewalk, too.

She glanced toward the gym again.

She knew Reynolds was still there, fighting in the veil. Or had he fled, leading the Nocs away?

The Nocs.

Pinfeathers . . .

Could he truly be back from the dead? But, then, had he ever really been alive?

Isobel wrapped her arms around herself, over her midsection where that clawed arm had held her. She recalled how, after Varen had written her name in his sketchbook, drawing her into his story and binding her to the link he'd created, she'd been able to see the Nocs in the real world.

After Isobel had burned the sketchbook, though, she'd also severed *her* ties to the dreamworld, and that had to be why she could no longer see the ghouls. But like Varen— whose ability to project into reality broke all the rules— Pinfeathers had always been the exception. *What one can do,* Pinfeathers had cryptically told her the night he'd appeared in her living room, *so can the other.*

So why, if the Noc had been restored, could she not see him now? Had he already gone? Vanished back into the dreamworld, leaving Isobel on her own?

She switched from foot to foot, hesitating. Unsure of what to do next.

Reynolds had told her to leave, but . . . where did he expect her to go?

For an instant, she thought about trying to re-enter the veil. Knowing what waited for her on the other side, however, she dared not. Her spirit wouldn't stand a chance against all those Nocs. And she'd already jeopardized so much. She'd endangered herself and Reynolds—the only source of knowledge she had on how to break the bond between Varen and Lilith.

But she hadn't been able to help herself. She'd *had* to show Varen her true nature. Show him that, like before, what he believed was a lie. And now, now she knew for sure that he still cared for her. She'd seen it in his face the moment he'd wrapped his arms around her ghost double. Yet she hadn't done enough. Not even draining the darkness from his dead world and replacing it with light and life had been able to convince him that she'd returned for him yet again.

There was more to Varen's darkness, it was clear now, than could be sifted through from within. More than the empty suit and the doll and the lullaby and the pieces of him that she'd found in the dreamworld. More at play in all of this than just *her* involvement.

You're going to need more in there than backflips and cute tricks, Pinfeathers had said to her moments before she'd come face-to-face with Lilith for the very first time. Isobel had no doubt that the Noc had been right, like he had been about so much else, and that she would soon find herself confronting the demon once more.

When that happened, she would need Varen by her side. *On* her side.

Isobel knew that she had never been part of Lilith's original design. Even before Isobel and Varen had grown close, Lilith had preyed on Varen for a reason. Not just for his ability to create, the demon had once said, but also for his capacity to destroy.

According to Lilith, Isobel had entered Varen's life as a distraction. But when Varen's feelings for Isobel had grown stronger, protecting her from the Nocs, Lilith had been forced to switch tactics. So she used Isobel as a catalyst to ignite a dangerous fuse within Varen, and in so doing had awakened his powers, transforming him into a new link.

His darkness didn't end in the dreamworld, though. Nor did it begin there. There were pieces here, too. In the very reality Varen had so desperately sought to escape.

Varen had been drawn to the woodlands because of the peace they promised. Because unlike his life, the dreamworld was something he could control. And because Lilith had represented all that was missing for him in *this* existence.

> For the heart whose woes are legion
> 'Tis a peaceful, soothing region—

The bell dismissing lunch rang, interrupting the lines of Poe's poetry her memory had somehow retained.

Beyond the blue doors, she knew the halls were filling with students.

Isobel took a step backward, and then another, glancing toward the passing traffic on the road nearby.

There was a city bus stop two blocks away. She and her mom passed by the covered bench every day on the way to school.

Dipping a hand into her pocket, she retrieved the lunch money her mother had laid on the counter for her that morning.

It would be more than enough, she thought, to get her to the city's preservation district.

15
Images

The house loomed over her, blank-faced, ordinary.

This was not how she remembered Varen's Victorian home.

Instead the image of the reversed, cracked, slanted mansion from the dreamworld, its windows blacked out, forced its way through her memory, making *this* house seem like the strange one.

Behind her, rows of parked cars lined either side of the serene, sun-filled court. Among them, Isobel saw the champagne Lexus Varen's stepmom drove, its sparkle-flecked finish gleaming bright. Knowing this meant that Darcy had to be home, Isobel climbed the steps to the porch and lifted a fist to knock. She hesitated, though, and a full minute elapsed before she could admit to herself that she was stalling, waiting for piano music to drift from the parlor, for the amber stained-glass window of the door to bleed violet, for the knob to melt or the concrete beneath her to transform into a pit.

But the house remained silent, the doorknob as solid as the cement under her feet.

Sucking in a breath, Isobel rapped twice.

More seconds ticked by, and the urge to bolt grew strong, as if, by knocking, she had somehow triggered the countdown of a bomb.

Her fear stemmed less from the prospect of facing Darcy than it did from being this near to the house itself. Monsters, in one form or another, had shown up each time she'd entered its walls.

Thudding footsteps, heavy and fast, interrupted Isobel's thoughts. She shifted, her uneasiness escalating, because those footsteps didn't sound like they belonged to—

An enormous figure filled the stained-glass window. The door opened, and a man dressed in a spotless gray business suit—the exact twin to the one she'd seen in the dreamworld attic, complete with red tie and silver cufflinks—appraised her with a hardened glare.

"Yes," Mr. Nethers said, holding the door open by a foot, as if he needed only one half of a good reason to send it slamming home again. "What is it?"

"I—I" Isobel stammered. She hadn't expected Varen's father to be home. Not this early in the day. "Um—"

As she scanned her brain for something comprehensible to say, she couldn't help but marvel at the man's six-foot stature, his bulky shoulders and steely gaze. This, after all, was the first time she'd ever encountered Varen's father one-on-one, in person.

On the night Mr. Nethers had stormed up to his son's bedroom in a drunken temper, shouting slurred obscenities at him, she'd caught only a brief flash of the man's face from the closet where Varen had forced her to hide. Red and blotchy, knotted with fury, that face had seemed like an ogre's.

And early last month, Isobel had glimpsed Varen's father a second time through a keyhole after he had entered Bruce's shop looking for Varen. Sober but just as angry, Mr. Nethers had slammed his giant fist on the countertop, issuing threats and demanding answers of the elderly bookstore owner.

But here, up close, Mr. Nethers looked drawn and tired, sapped of his ferocity. His soot-colored hair hung loose in greasy strands around his ashen features, as if he'd run his hands through it a thousand times that morning. Heavy bags underlined his leaden, red-rimmed eyes, and their hooded dullness made her wonder if he'd already been drinking.

"How old are you?" he asked. "Aren't you supposed to be in school right now?"

Unbidden, a string of accusatory counter-questions began flipping through Isobel's head like cue cards, making it impossible for her to conjure a single excuse.

"I—I'm—"

"*Isobel.*"

Mr. Nethers swiveled his head in the direction of the soft gasp from within the house.

Over his shoulder, Isobel saw Darcy approaching. Still dressed in the black slacks and pumps from earlier, she moved toward them with purpose, her silk blouse rippling.

"Joe," Darcy said, placing a manicured hand on his shoulder, "I forgot to tell you. I went ahead and posted that ad for a housekeeper. I know you said you weren't sure, but I thought it would help to take some of the stress off."

"Her?" He squinted at Isobel, his upper lip twitching into a sneer. "She's a kid."

"Who needs an after-school job," Darcy replied.

Isobel kept quiet, eyes flitting between the two as she waited to see if Darcy's fib would convince him.

"Except it's not after school." Mr. Nethers checked his wristwatch. "Not nearly."

Darcy took the door from him. "I found the aspirin," she said. "I packed it with your lunch in the kitchen. You'd better take it with you, though, or else you might as well go ahead and take the rest of the day off."

"I can't afford to take the rest of the day off," he snapped, irritably stripping his watch from his wrist. "Especially not since, apparently, we're hiring a housekeeper." He broke away, adjusting the watch as he headed toward the back hall. "And if you've got time to post a want ad," he called as he went, "then you've got time to post a sale ad for that damn car."

"It's not mine to post," Darcy said, her voice flat, resigned.

"Post the car, Darcy."

With that, Mr. Nethers swept from the room, disappearing down the hall.

Isobel knew they had to be arguing over the Cougar, confirming her suspicions that Bruce had indeed bequeathed the car to Varen.

"Please come inside," Darcy said, stepping back, making

room for Isobel to enter. "You must be freezing out there without a coat."

Folding her arms against shivers that had nothing to do with the cold, Isobel stared past the woman, into the mouth-like doorway. Soft yellow light bathed the foyer within.

"He'll leave in just a minute," Darcy said, and the tremble in her voice made Isobel wonder what she was afraid of. Was it that her husband would find out Isobel's visit pertained to his missing son? Or maybe that Isobel would run off like she had that morning at the fountain, taking all the answers with her?

"It's . . . not him," Isobel said.

Varen's father might be imposing, and the prospect of invoking his anger had terrified her once, but she'd faced worse—far worse—since she'd first glimpsed him through that closet door.

"He'll suspect something if we stand at the door like this," Darcy warned, her breath puffing in a small cloud of white.

Isobel vacillated for half a beat longer. Then she stepped into the house.

Her gut tightened with a residual surge of fear as she ventured into the foyer, a series of images flickering through her memory, electrocuting her with the past. The free-floating chandelier. The sheet-covered furniture. The dilapidated stairs. Everything reversed. And the painting on the wall, the one of the storm-tossed—

At the sound of the door clicking shut behind her, Isobel yelped and spun around.

Darcy froze, eyes full of alarm.

"The ship," Isobel breathed, pressing a hand to her collar and wrapping the hamsa in her fist. "It's gone."

"Excuse me?" Darcy asked, head tilting.

Isobel pointed at the painting, which had shown only white-capped waves and angry black clouds. Except now the ship had returned.

Lowering her arm, Isobel frowned at the painting. She let go of the charm.

While she'd been in the dreamworld, fighting with Reynolds, she'd seen the same painting come to life. Animated seas had devoured the vessel whole.

"What time is it?" she asked Darcy, the question all but leaping out of her mouth.

"Um, around one. I think."

"Do you have a watch?" she asked, her anxiety building. "Or a clock?"

Darcy bit her bottom lip, as though refraining from voicing a question. She pointed to the ceiling. "Upstairs. In the office."

Turning, she crossed to the steps.

Isobel deliberated, shifting from foot to foot. Then she followed.

As she grabbed the banister, she took a moment to will its varnished surface to transform into a boa constrictor. The banister did not respond to her silent command, but this provided less comfort than she'd been hoping for. Especially since, in her periphery, she thought she'd seen someone standing in the parlor.

Could it be that her mind, punch-drunk from the terrors of the other side, had become conditioned to anticipate horrors at every turn?

No. She *was* awake. And now—now it was time to get a grip.

Isobel reached the second floor just as Darcy opened the closest of several doors. Whisking past her, Isobel entered a spacious office.

A pair of cream curtains flanked the room's lone window. Papers, ledgers, and notebooks littered the surface of an enormous oak desk.

While Darcy remained in the hall, presumably to listen for her husband, Isobel made a beeline for the squat, antique windup clock that sat on one corner of the desk. In reaching for it, though, she knocked over a small picture frame.

The image within made her stop cold.

Varen's smooth and serious face stared up at her.

Picking up the photo, Isobel studied the black-and-white image more closely. She could tell by the angle that Varen had snapped the photo himself. In it, he lay against a bed of brittle leaves. He held the camera above, gazing straight into the lens so that his hair fell away from his face, leaving his eyes more naked than she had ever seen them.

Varen's jade irises, Isobel knew, should have appeared pale gray in the photo. But they were black as inkwells.

Pressing her fingers to the glass, Isobel wished so badly that she could reach through the expanse of months separating this moment from the one in which Varen had taken the self-portrait. When *had* he taken it? How long after Lilith had begun to thread herself into his life? How long after she'd started to take control?

Downstairs, the front door slammed.

Ignoring the sound and the silence that followed, Isobel flipped the photo over. The soft *tick-tock* of the desk clock boomed in her ears while she pried the frame open.

Just as she'd suspected, Varen's violet writing blazed against the watermarked paper.

There was no date, though. No lines of looping poetry. Only one word.

Lost, he'd written in his beautiful and old-world hand.

Isobel shut her eyes, but the word remained, searing bright against the backs of her lids like a neon sign. She wondered where Varen's parents had found the photo. Mixed among his things?

They had to have seen the writing on the back.

Isobel assumed that the cold, stark office belonged to Mr. Nethers; how many times had he glanced at this picture of his own son and not realized that something was horribly wrong? That these eyes were not his son's? Had he even kept the photo on his desk before Varen's disappearance? Somehow, she doubted it.

Something brushed against her leg. Startled, Isobel fumbled against the desk, dropping the frame onto its surface, where it clattered apart.

Whirling, she scanned the floor.

There weren't any bugs filing out in droves. No spindly

fingers tipped in claws. No birds. Only Slipper, Varen's Siamese cat.

The creature peered up at Isobel with icy eyes, electric blue against the dark center of her face. Meowing, the feline flashed a pair of sharp white fangs, leaving Isobel to wonder if she'd been issued a plea or a threat.

"You can relax," Darcy said, shutting the door to an inch. "He's gone."

Isobel looked up from the cat, meeting the woman's gaze dead-on. "I'm not afraid of him," she replied. "Though I can tell you are."

Darcy folded her arms. "He's . . . going through a lot right now. We both are."

"I guess he was going through a lot that night the two of you came home early from that benefit party too."

Isobel swallowed hard, both awed and cowed by her own audacity.

But something about the photo of Varen had stirred anger in her. Darcy cared. That much was clear. But it was growing more and more apparent that her reach extended only so far as it was allowed.

"What were you—" Darcy started, but Isobel cut her off.

"You've probably guessed by now that I was here—there. With him in his room." Isobel flicked her eyes toward the ceiling. "We were doing homework that night you saw me drive away with him. He had put me in the closet almost as soon as he heard the front door open. He . . . was afraid too, I think."

Darcy drew a shaky breath and let it go. Folding her arms in tighter, she gripped either elbow. "I read the note."

"I figured," Isobel said, "since you knew my name."

And just like that, their conversation had jumped from one uncomfortable track to another.

Slinking between Isobel's ankles, tail unwinding from her calf, Slipper padded to sit in front of the gap in the door.

"I've never known him to say he loved anything," Darcy began again, eager, it seemed, to stamp out the awkward silence that had settled into the room. "Or anyone. Not even when talking about something like writing or drawing. Not even Slipper." She gestured loosely to the cat. "Or Bruce."

Isobel looked up, surprised.

"Varen didn't use that word," Darcy added in a murmur. "You . . . you must be very special."

Her words took Isobel aback, though they shouldn't have. After all, it was no secret to her that Varen treated his heart like a vault. He kept so much to himself—practically everything.

Of course, he'd been conditioned to. The less people knew about the things he cared for, yearned for—the less his *father* knew about them—the less likely they were to be stripped away. Or damaged by ridicule.

Keep away, Varen's exterior had always said. But the black clothing and the sunglasses and the biting sharp tongue had only been part of an elaborate defense system meant to shut everyone out. Somehow Isobel had penetrated through its boundaries. Somehow she would need to do so again.

"Varen is the special one," Isobel said, plucking the black-and-white picture from its frame.

"Is?" Darcy asked, eyes wide with sudden intensity, filled with equal parts hope and fear.

"I'm not here because of the note," Isobel began. "I'm here because I need to know . . . about Madeline."

Darcy's expression changed, hardening with suspicion. "How do you know that name?"

"Varen. He . . . told me she left."

"He *told* you that?"

"Nothing else. Not even when I asked. Why? What happened?"

"What does she have to do with this?" Darcy asked.

"You *do* know something."

"Apparently a lot less than you," Darcy said, her tone sharpening.

"I need to know what happened," Isobel said.

"And I need to know what you know about Varen's whereabouts. Where did you get that note? When did he give it to you? If you don't start talking now, I'll call the police."

"Because they've been so much help so far."

"If you know where he is —"

"*You* know where he is!" Isobel yelled. Catching herself, she lowered her voice again. "You said so yourself this morning."

Darcy stiffened. Her hands clutched her elbows tighter.

Isobel could tell she wanted to talk, but something was holding her back. It was not the same something that had held her back before, though, that night in Varen's room. Or minutes earlier, when Mr. Nethers had commanded her to post Varen's car. This time, her fear stemmed not from her husband, but from having to admit—no, *accept*—that something more was at work, something she couldn't explain or understand.

"I gave you that note today because I thought it was all over," Isobel said. "Because I thought you deserved an answer. Confirmation of what you were trying to tell me you already knew. Because I thought you actually care—"

"I *do* care," Darcy cut in. She pressed her hands to her heart. "*So much*. Joe does too. He's beside himself. This whole thing, it's tearing him apart. It's tearing *us* apart. He just doesn't—he can't—he's—"

"He's what?" Isobel asked. "What excuses him? I mean, besides you."

Darcy's mouth fell open, but Isobel didn't regret her words. Hadn't Varen once confronted Isobel with a similar inquiry when she'd dismissed Brad's behavior? Hadn't he been right?

"Never mind," Isobel said, glancing down at the picture. "Just . . . forget it. I should have known better than to come here. It's obvious that you only care about *looking* like you care."

Isobel left her place by the desk and started for the door, taking the photo with her.

"Madeline lives in Boston," Darcy blurted.

Isobel stopped short. Slipper stood, fur prickling, ready to shoot through the gap as soon as it opened wide enough.

"She could write or call," Darcy went on, and Isobel remained rooted, listening without moving. "But she doesn't. She even took on a new legal name. Joe went digging years ago. Before we got married. He doesn't know I know that. But . . . I got worried when he refused to get rid of her piano. I thought he was still holding on to the hope that she might . . . come back one day. So I went through his files. But it's clear Madeline doesn't want to be found. She left them, Isobel. She left both of them without a word. And no word since. That's . . . that's everything. I don't know any more than that."

Isobel turned her head toward Darcy, who hurried on.

"Joe won't say it, but I can tell he's starting to fear the worst. He wakes up almost every night swearing he hears footsteps in the attic—voices, too. We've both run up there countless times. But there's no one, nothing. One night, when Joe was driving home, he said he saw him by the fountain. Said Varen just appeared out of nowhere, and he had to swerve to avoid hitting him. Then he just disappeared. Like . . . like a ghost."

Isobel frowned at the story, recalling the note Mr. Nethers had left in the Cougar's glove compartment that day at Nobit's Nook. In the note, he had commanded Varen to *stop playing morbid games* and *come home now*. Isobel now understood that the note had been an attempt to coerce some solid response from Varen, some definitive evidence to prove to Mr. Nethers that he wasn't going crazy, and that his son still existed in this world. That he was, at the very least, alive.

"We were both there today, you know," Darcy went on, "at the funeral. Joe sat in the car, though, because he couldn't come to the tent. He'd been certain that Varen would be there, and when we didn't see him, he . . . well, he's running out of hope. *We* are running out of hope."

"I . . . ," Isobel started, but she didn't know what to say. Like her, Varen's parents had made Bruce's funeral their final resort. They'd had the same idea she'd had. And the same result.

But if Mr. Nethers had been there, then . . . "Why didn't you show him the note?" Isobel asked.

"I couldn't," Darcy whispered, eyes brimming. "You heard Joe tell me to post an ad for the Cougar in the paper just now." She shook her head. "He's not trying to get rid of the car. He's trying to hang on. I can tell he thinks that somehow, Varen will see the ad and come back for it. You don't know him. Joe's not going to stop until something solid comes up. Isobel, *you* are that something. So please, please, *please* tell me that piece of paper wasn't a suicide note."

Isobel drew a sharp breath, but it caught in her throat, lodged there by the utterance of that single hissing word.

By giving up the note that morning, Isobel had wanted to bring both herself and Darcy some semblance of closure. Not more despair and uncertainty. Not more pain.

True, Darcy had glimpsed the other side, but she still didn't know all that Isobel did.

Nor could she ever.

She hadn't been there. In that nightmare realm that gave as much life to the terrors and sorrows of Varen's mind as it had to those of Poe's.

"What you saw in the mirror was real," Isobel said, choosing her words carefully. "I was there with him. On the other side. And . . . *I'm* here now, aren't I?"

Aren't I? The question echoed in her head, taunting her as Slipper hunkered low before the gap in the door, her tail twitching in agitation.

Isobel's focus fell to the cat—then to the wavering shadow on the floor just outside.

"What is it?" Darcy hissed. "Who is that out there?"

Isobel pulled slowly on the doorknob.

Darting through the opening as soon as it grew wide enough, Slipper rushed out, dashing pell-mell past the form that stood waiting on the top step just outside.

16
Perils Parallel

"You know where my boy is?" Varen's father asked.

Mr. Nethers pressed his fist to the wall, barring Isobel's way, as if he thought she might follow the cat's lead and try to barrel down the stairs to escape him.

Isobel had meant it when she'd told Darcy she wasn't afraid of him, though.

Stepping out of the office, she drew nearer to Mr. Nethers. As her shadow drifted over him, she watched the dullness in his eyes sweep clear, the mask of anger fall away. A different man now stood before her from the one who had greeted her at the front door. Or the one she'd seen yelling at Varen in his room—at Bruce in the bookshop.

This man was present. Awake. Aware. Not just an empty suit.

His lips quivered as though he wanted to speak again, but he held back, waiting, it seemed, for Isobel to speak first, to tell him something that would ease his pain.

Nothing she could say held the power to accomplish such a feat.

Still, the sadness—the sheer devastation radiating from

him—felt too real to ignore, and though Isobel had wanted to hate him, she found she couldn't now.

The office door creaked behind her. She sensed Darcy watching, waiting for her cue to step in and play her practiced part of umpire.

The game to win control had already come to an end, though. And in her hand, Isobel held what felt like the final score.

She extended the photo of Mr. Nethers's son out to him.

"This photograph," Isobel said. "How closely did you look at it before you framed it?"

His big fist left the wall, and with shaking fingers, he took the picture.

As he looked down at it, tears formed in his eyes. They spilled, falling with audible pops against the stiff, glossy paper. His other hand—so strong and fierce before—quaked as it went to cover his face.

Like a crumbling mountain, Mr. Nethers sank to a sitting position on the top stair.

Darcy brushed past Isobel, a whiff of expensive-smelling perfume wafting after her. Kneeling next to her husband, she draped an arm around his shoulders, whispering words Isobel couldn't decipher.

But Varen's father said nothing. He didn't ask any more questions, and he didn't look up. He only hung his head and sobbed.

Palpable, his remorse pulsed through the air, chiseling into Isobel's own heart to strike a resonating chord there.

Regret was a feeling she had grown to know well.

Thick, heavy, suffocating—it was the one sensation that came closest to what it felt like to die.

"I'm sorry," Isobel murmured, and it wasn't until she'd uttered the words aloud that she realized why she'd done so: She wished she could tell *her* parents the same thing.

She had come here hoping to dig up the skeletons of Varen's past. But in her attempt to gain understanding, to find out why the one person who should have cared for him the most had left him, she was instead reminded how badly absence itself could hurt. How much damage it could inflict.

Isobel wondered if she could ever accuse her own mother and father of what, in essence, she'd accused the Netherses of. Of not having paid enough attention. Of not caring enough until it was too late.

No, she thought. *Never.*

And still, here she was. Missing. Gone from their lives. Again.

Staring at the hand that clutched the photo of Varen, Isobel recalled the way her own father had squeezed her shoulder the previous night, and suddenly, all she wanted was to be back in that moment.

If she could live it again, she would stand up and wrap her arms around her dad and hug him so tight. She would beg him to forgive her. She'd tell him over and over that she loved him.

The school administrators had no doubt called her mom and dad by this point, and right now, wherever her parents were, they had to be going ballistic. Were they out looking for her somewhere? Or, like Varen's parents, were they teetering on the verge of resigning themselves to the worst?

Her family had suffered through her death once.

She couldn't put them through that again. No matter what came next, she couldn't just turn her back on them and walk away, vanish into the dreamworld again without a single word— even if her only other option was to tell them everything.

And why hadn't she? Why, if they'd been listening?

"I—I have to go," Isobel murmured, the words meant more for her own ears than for Mr. and Mrs. Nethers.

Skirting past the pair, she hurried down the stairs.

Though Darcy called out to her, Isobel didn't stop.

Without looking back, she tore open the front door and rushed out into the cold.

The bus lurched to its third stop since Isobel had boarded. Its doors slid open to let riders off and on.

"Eastern Parkway and Preston," came the driver's voice over the intercom, "Eastern Parkway and Preston."

Isobel gripped her knees and thudded her heel against the floor. For the millionth time, she wished she had her phone. She also wished that there weren't so many stops between the downtown preservation district and Cherokee Park.

Most of all, Isobel wished she was home.

Once or twice, she'd thought about asking to borrow someone else's cell, deciding in the end to hold off. Another half hour and she'd be at her doorstep.

Though it was possible neither of her parents were home, Isobel still wanted to try the house first. She wanted to talk to her mom and dad in person without being overheard by a bus full of people, or having to field frantic questions about calling from a strange number. More than that, she wanted to speak to her mom and dad together.

Go home, Gwen had told her.

What had Gwen picked up on? And why hadn't Isobel listened?

Thinking back to yesterday's conversation with Danny, all that he'd divulged, she now wished she *had* followed Gwen's instructions.

No doubt this latest disappearance of hers had triggered another blowup between her mom and dad. Had they caught wind of the rumors circulating around school about Varen's return, too? Isobel wasn't certain, but, at the very least, she assumed her parents were calling off their damage-control date. And what about Danny? Was he still in school, oblivious to her being missing? Or had her parents pulled him out?

Would she ever be able to convince him not to hate her?

A fresh wave of guilt fell heavy on her shoulders, but Isobel did her best to bear the weight, telling herself she'd deal with the fallout whenever and however it came. She didn't have another choice.

She could only hope that, at this point, her parents would still want to listen. That they would believe her. That they might even understand.

"There. Sitting in the middle."

Isobel froze, ears tuning to the static voice that had spoken from several seats behind.

"That isn't her," rasped a second voice.

"It *is* her. Can't you feel it?"

Though her instinct was to turn and look, Isobel remained still, shoulders rigid, fingernails digging into her jeans.

Her eyes flitted between the other passengers.

Near the front, a businessman worked a newspaper crossword puzzle against one knee. Across from him, a woman holding a sleeping girl on her lap gazed distractedly out the window. Another woman sat with her head bowed, thumbing at her cell phone.

None of them had heard the exchange of whispers. Not that any one of them could have done a single thing to help her even if they had.

"Let's move closer."

"Patience. If it's her, she'll get off at the next stop. At the park behind her house. Watch."

Careful to keep still, to appear oblivious, Isobel checked the driver's rearview mirror for the source of the static voices, aware that she wouldn't see the creatures even if she did turn around.

But the bus mirror—her only window into the veil—was tilted in such a way that she could see just the top half of the operator's lined face.

Leaning forward, the driver ducked out of view, triggering the doors. They closed with a *clunk*, sealing her in.

The bus rumbled louder.

The Nocs. They expected her to get off at the *next* stop. If she wanted to evade them—if she even had a chance at that— she'd have to act now.

Shooting to her feet, Isobel yanked the stop cable.

At the sound of the *ding*, everyone looked up.

"Sorry," Isobel said, sliding into the aisle, legs trembling. "This . . . is my stop."

As she made her way to the front, she could feel all eyes on her—the seen and unseen.

She bowed her head, allowing her hair to fall forward enough to hide her face. When the doors rattled open again, she took hold of the metal grip bar.

Then, in the split second before swinging herself down the short set of steps and out, she did something she shouldn't have.

She risked a second glimpse into the mirror.

At the rear of the bus, a pair of blood-haired Nocs rose from their seats next to unsuspecting passengers.

Isobel dropped her head again, but as her feet met with the sidewalk outside, she knew the pair had seen—and recognized—her, too.

17

Back into the Tempest

Suppressing the urge to run, Isobel veered into an oncoming group of college kids dressed in jerseys and hoodies. They chattered loudly, sipping from paper coffee cups as she broke through their ranks.

"Excuse you," one of the girls snapped.

"Sorry," Isobel muttered without looking back.

She didn't hear the Nocs' hissing whispers anymore, but as the city bus rumbled past, she knew better than to think they were still onboard.

Keeping her steps even, casual, Isobel did her best to appear at ease, banking on the hope that, though the Nocs had spotted her in the mirror, they wouldn't immediately assume she had seen them.

Even if the charade couldn't last long, it was a better alternative to running outright. The only choice available that might buy her any time.

Time.

She'd forgotten to check the desk clock at Varen's house.

There were none on any of the nearby stores or restaurants.

Wondering what had become of Reynolds, Isobel hoped

he was there with her somewhere, waiting for the right moment to intervene as he'd always done.

After the disruption she'd caused in the dreamworld and what she'd seen in the gym, though, she knew it was not a good sign that he hadn't shown up yet. Unpredictable as he was, Reynolds wasted time about as well as he wasted words. He should have emerged by now with the next phase of whatever self-serving plan he'd concocted.

But the Nocs had caught up to her before he had.

Caught up, and caught wise, she thought, cursing herself for arousing their suspicions through the show she'd put on to try to convince Varen she was real.

Though her display hadn't been enough to persuade *him,* apparently it had done the trick for the ghouls, who must have glimpsed her in the veil before Reynolds had shocked her back into her body.

A flash of terror flared inside her with a new thought: Lilith must suspect now too.

In her desperation, had Isobel given herself away, tossing aside the one advantage Reynolds had told her she—he—*they* possessed?

Isobel pushed that worry aside for later—if there was ever going to *be* a later—and commanded herself to keep walking.

She dared not look behind her as she continued down the sidewalk, but forced herself to concentrate on her next move, coming up with some sort of plan to elude the creatures that might be—at that very moment—less than two steps away from snatching her up. Body *and* soul.

Isobel fixed her sights on the nearest building—a coffee shop that stood on the other side of a narrow parking lot, kitty-corner to the bus stop.

If she went in, she might be able to create a distraction, then slip through a rear exit. Or maybe as long as she surrounded herself with people, the Nocs would hold off on their attack.

Both hopes were long shots. She knew that as well as she knew that she'd run out of options.

As Isobel drew closer to the entrance, though, what she saw reflected in the shop's glass front windows made her stop.

Dead trees filled the tinted panes, their trunks overlapping the blazing red letters of the neon NOW BREWING sign.

Beyond the glass, customers conversed at small tables. They sipped from mugs, scribbled on notepads, and typed away at laptops. At her back, Isobel heard the swish of cars, the chirping of birds, and the high drone of a passing airplane—noises that didn't match the soundless landscape of prison-bar trees.

Black crows filled the inklike splatter of interwoven branches, watching her.

In addition to the legion of Nocs, Isobel saw herself reflected in the glass.

And standing a few yards behind, just within the boundaries of the trees—Varen.

Her heart began to slam in her chest.

Slowly she turned to face him.

But instead of the woodlands, she found pavement.

Parked cars. White houses and grassy yards. A steady stream of traffic.

New people began to gather at the bus stop. One of them, a man wearing a backpack, kept staring at his wristwatch. Frowning, he crooked his arm, bringing the timepiece to one ear.

Isobel swung toward the coffee shop again. But the woodlands had vanished, replaced by the same quiet scene she had just witnessed—cars, people, concrete, sky.

As she scanned the surface of the glass, Isobel's mind raced backward through the day in an attempt to pinpoint the last moment she could say without a doubt was *real*.

But her speeding thoughts found no stopping point.

There had been the light in her bedroom, the ash in the hall, and the ride through the cemetery. The funeral. Reynolds and then the veil. Officially, *that* was when she'd re-entered the dreamworld. But . . . had it all been part of the same unending dream?

A dark shape entered her periphery—someone standing at her shoulder. Yet her own reflection was the only one in the glass.

A reflection meant for certain that she was in reality. Or at the very least, that *she* was real, present in her body and not in astral form.

But then, hadn't the mirror image she'd encountered in the winding hallways of Varen's Gothic palace proven to have possessed a mind of its own? Could she merely be facing another double?

"They tell me this is real," Isobel heard him say, his voice achingly familiar—torturous and quieting all at once. "They tell me *you* are real."

She sensed him looking down on her. In response, Isobel began to angle into him, unable to help herself despite the string of warning commands that screamed inside her head.

Don't. Stop. Run.

But she couldn't.

The two of them were like magnets that way. As equally drawn to each other by invisible forces as they had been repelled.

She focused first on where his hair brushed his black collar, then on the hollow of his throat. His Adam's apple . . .

Triggered by the sight of him, by their sheer proximity, memories began to surface in her mind as if from another lifetime.

Her very own cobwebs . . .

She recalled that day her dad had come home from work and freaked at finding Varen in the house. Varen had left in a hurry, and helpless to stop him from leaving, Isobel had followed him out to his car. Together, the two of them had stood on her street just like this. And just like now, Isobel had wanted nothing more than for him to lean down and kiss her.

She tilted her chin up, forcing her eyes to his.

Sunglasses hid his black gaze from her view, and, in their lenses, she was again confronted with her own image, the slanted scar on her cheek more prominent than ever.

"I'm sure you would tell me the same thing," Varen went

on, his silver lip ring catching a white spark from the sun as he spoke. "You always do."

Isobel blinked, frowning. So stunned by his sudden presence at her side—so mesmerized by the sound of that low, calm voice that she hadn't been able to register the meaning of his words.

Now her brain scrambled to backtrack, to recall what it was he'd been saying.

"Try to tell me, anyway," he added, his tone going glacial, sending sharp spikes of cold fear through her.

A soft *click* drew her attention to his open palm, and she almost gasped to see her small butterfly key-chain watch perched on the tips of his fingers. Its wings were open, exposing the face of the clock inside.

Behind the small circle of glass, its three hands spun around and around, winding wildly opposite one another, a sure indication that this *was* a dream after all.

Checking the window again, though, and seeing her reflection there proved just the opposite.

"I came to show them they were wrong," Varen said, clicking the watch closed, folding his fist tight around it. "And remind myself while I'm at it."

An invisible pressure settled on Isobel's shoulders, pressing down.

Condensing, the air grew suddenly thick and heavy.

Yet in defiance of the sudden shift in gravity, pebbles and rocks, stray leaves and bits of litter quivered, then rose to hover an inch above the pavement and patches of grass.

The asphalt beneath them buzzed, sending a shiver of electricity into the soles of Isobel's shoes, causing the hairs on her arms to lift.

Varen, it was clear, hadn't come to talk. He certainly had not come to listen.

And wherever they were—whether within a dream, reality, or both—Isobel began to sense that something horrible and irreversible was about to happen.

She had only a moment. A breath's worth of time at most. She felt it.

"I love you," Isobel said. Because even if the words could not stop what was coming, they were still her first and sole defense.

"I know," Varen surprised her by saying as he turned away. "That's why you're gone."

Thunder cracked from above, calling her attention heavenward.

Spun from nothing, billows of violet-black clouds began to roll in from every direction. Fast as a time-lapse video, they converged to swallow all traces of blue. A sheet of solid shadow blanketed the parking lot and strip mall and, as darkness fell, the people gathered at the bus stop lifted baffled gazes from the floating debris to the sky.

On the street, cars halted, brakes squealing, horns blaring.

Isobel looked back to the coffee shop window, but her reflection had vanished, wiped out along with the sun's glare.

Inside, customers rose one after the other. Abandoning their floating cups, their lazily drifting pens, notepads, and other belongings, they gathered at the windows, frightened faces tilted skyward.

Colliding, the clouds began to mesh and meld, mixing in a swirl over Varen, its center following him as he strode toward the street.

The wind blasted stronger, coursing through the lot with a sudden upsurge, carrying with it dead leaves and bits of flittering trash.

Thunder boomed a second time, and as its clap echoed, the eye of the maelstrom ripped wide, opening like the maw of some enormous, toothless beast.

Blackness occupied the void within, the gaping pit marbled with white static.

"Varen, stop this!" Isobel called out to him, her voice sounding so small amid the roar of wind and thunder that she couldn't be sure if he'd heard her.

But when he halted, glancing back at her over one shoulder, she knew he had.

"You stop it," he said. "If you can."

Turning forward again, he continued toward the street while ash began to filter down around him, falling from the crevice in the sky.

Isobel latched on to his words, trying to visualize the wound in the clouds closing, but the crater only grew. With Varen's every step, the ash poured thicker.

She started forward, about to go after him, but was halted by the deafening smash of glass at her back.

Shards flew, bursting from the strip mall.

Screams rang out, and Isobel swung away, her own shriek mixing with the noise of sudden chaos while glinting slivers rained over her, tinkling as they showered the cars and the pavement.

A cacophony of alarms blared.

Lowering her arms, Isobel looked around her. Panic-stricken people darted this way and that, flying past her as they streamed out of the strip mall.

Ahead, farther than his slow steps should have carried him, Varen stood among a group of stalled vehicles in the middle of the street. The wind raged through his hair. It pulled at the hem of his long coat, causing the fabric to flutter and snap.

From the chasm came a torrent of crows. Screeching and flapping, they shot into the storm-torn sky.

The pavement crackled and shifted beneath Isobel. She skittered back, but the fissures spread quickly past her, fanning out in all directions.

The ground shook. The fractured glass rattled and slipped into the widening rifts.

The quake sent Isobel to her knees. She caught herself with her hands, bits of glass biting her palms.

Above, the crows squawked louder, their unending buzz like a swarm of locusts.

Isobel did her best to tune out their cries, the people screaming and running, the rumbling of the earth, and the ash that had begun to catch on her clothing and cling to her hair.

Focus, she told herself as she tried to conceive of some way to halt the rupturing of her surroundings, but she couldn't concentrate. Not while the trees dotting the patches of strip mall landscaping began to twist and shrivel. Not while more trees burst through the fractured blacktop, jutting upward like spikes.

Isobel pictured the lot as it had been moments before, restored, whole, holding the visual for what felt like an eternity.

When this attempt failed too, she tried picturing her and Varen somewhere else entirely, in a desert far away.

Instead of sand, the pavement beneath her dissolved into the gray dust of the dreamworld. Isobel closed her fists around the powder, crying out in frustration as the scrapes in her hands burned with pain.

Nothing was working.

She was too late. He'd become too strong. She couldn't fight against him like she had before.

Whatever this was—*wherever* this was—it felt like the end Reynolds had warned her about.

Opening his arms, Varen threw his head back.

Spears of violet lightning shot up from the ground around him, connecting with the darkness above and forming a cage.

Isobel zeroed in on Varen's illuminated form, his arms spread like the wings of the white bird on his black coat.

As the lightning fluttered in and out of view . . . so did he.

In that instant, Isobel realized that no matter what dimension they occupied, Varen was not there in physical form. He was projecting. Like he had the day of the Poe project. Like *she* had when she'd crossed through the veil.

If that was true, then this—the parking lot, the coffee shop, and the street—must be reality. Because Varen wouldn't *need* to project in the dreamworld. And if he was projecting here, then that meant the veil hadn't completely eroded. At least, not enough to allow Varen to physically rejoin his own world.

But that would also mean that she could not overpower Varen, and she would have no way of stopping this. No way of stopping *him*.

Everything would merge. Reality and dreams. Eternity— it was all headed for oblivion.

Time itself would end.

Unless . . .

Isobel pushed up onto her feet.

Even with her thoughts still spinning, slowly formulating an answer she dreaded, she started moving toward him.

Before, when the two worlds had overlapped like this, the blending had happened through a link—a role previously served by Varen's sketchbook.

According to Reynolds, that role had since been transferred to something else.

Some*one*.

Isobel sped her pace to a run, closing in.

Even as she neared him, dodging cars and entering the forest of lightning, she didn't know if her plan would work. If it could.

Over the din of the whipping winds, the cawing of the Nocs, and the crashing thunder, she screamed his name.

Like before, she hadn't expected him to hear her, to turn. But, just as he had then, he did now.

Launching herself at him, Isobel wrapped her arms around him. They fell backward together, and for one blissful instant, she held him tight.

And even as the flames conjured by her mind engulfed him, Isobel could not bring herself to let him go.

White-hot and blinding, the blaze enveloped them both.

Colliding with the pavement, Varen's figure disintegrated on impact, his form dissipating against the dusty ground that caught her fall alone.

18
Ashes, Ashes

Blood. Pain. Grit.

Opening her blackened hands, Isobel found only those three things in her grasp.

Varen was gone.

Her plan to banish him had worked.

The fire had vanished with him, snuffing out the moment he had ceased to exist in this world, and as they had before when she'd summoned them in the bookshop, the flames had left her unscathed.

Breathing out in a rush that caused the cinders beneath her to disperse, Isobel found herself wondering how it could have happened again.

Before, when she'd asked Reynolds why she had survived the summoned flames, he had told her that since the fire she'd created had been a dream, it had ceased to exist when the realms parted. He'd also told her that the underlying strength of Varen's feelings for her had provided protection.

But that protection, which once shielded her from the Nocs, had been lifted. That was why Pinfeathers had been able to scar her. And why he had. So she would know.

Could that protection have somehow been reinstated?

If so, did that mean some small part of Varen—conscious or not—still hoped she *was* real?

Isobel wasn't sure.

Rolling onto her back, she gazed up past the gray-powdered grilles and bumpers of the surrounding cars to where Varen's storm unraveled.

Bleeding white, the clouds evaporated, giving way to blue.

Sunlight burned through the cascade of ash, the remnants of which floated down to light softly upon her.

Her skin prickled, alive with the sensation of pins and needles, and Isobel blinked long and slow as the car alarms continued their frantic blaring—though now without the underscoring cries of the Nocs.

Along with Varen, the crows had receded into the dream-world, through the veil that somehow—despite its now accelerated disintegration—still managed to separate her world from his.

From somewhere far off, the howl of sirens rose, and she knew she needed to move. To get up and get out of there.

As the full weight of what she'd done came crashing over her, though, she found herself unable to lift even one limb.

She'd sent him back. Back into that world of despair. Back into his empire of shadow.

But doing so had been the only way to prevent him from bringing it all here with him.

The only way of closing the link.

Soon, she was sure, Varen would return, stronger and

more malevolent than before—bent on wreaking the havoc that would bring his darkest imaginings to life. Because even if there *was* a small part of him that *did* suspect she could be real, there was an even stronger part that had lost the capacity to trust in anything other than the nothing he'd come to know so well.

The nightmare. How would it ever end if she could not reach him?

How, when she had already gone to every length, faced each monster, risking all in the process?

His darkness remained—impenetrable. And it would stay that way as long as he refused to believe her.

To believe *in* her.

In himself.

The thought floated up through the mire of her anguish in a whisper. As her eyes traced the open sky, she knew it was true. Reynolds had been wrong to suggest that Isobel could dispel the darkness, could stop the worst from happening, by proving herself to Varen.

That power, in the end, lay with Varen alone.

Then again, at this point, maybe Reynolds—wherever he was—would see his mistake.

She doubted she would ever find out. He wasn't coming for her. That much was obvious. If her name had still been penciled in his murky agenda, he would have found her by now, before Varen had.

Soon, though, it wouldn't matter even if Reynolds did appear. The two worlds were already blending, merging as they had Halloween night. It was the reason Varen could no longer tell the difference. And why the hands of her butterfly watch had spun out of control. They would do so wherever he went. So long as *he* remained the link.

Varen must have discovered the trinket in the rose garden. After the cliff.

And he'd kept it with him. She'd seen him fiddling with it in the courtyard of statues, she realized. What had he been thinking as he held it?

Tasting ash, smelling the sharp scent of ozone, Isobel clutched at her collar. She wrapped the hamsa in one fist. The pendant could not instill her with the same strength it had that morning, though.

Muscles aching, she managed to climb onto unsteady feet and survey the damage.

Dust covered all.

Though the charcoal trees had disappeared with the storm, the buckles, rents, and pockmarks they'd made in the pavement remained.

Looking down, Isobel found herself standing in the center of a scorch mark not dissimilar to the one in the attic of the bookshop, where she'd burned Varen's sketchbook.

The shrieking sirens grew louder.

Backpedaling from the charred starburst, Isobel began to weave her way through the maze of stalled and abandoned cars.

Then she paused, turning slowly in place—because no matter which way she faced, she could not see where the blanket of ash ended, or where the preexisting trees had not twisted and gone black.

Whirling, she started running in the direction of Cherokee Park, toward the path that would take her to the home she hoped she still had.

19
Double Exposure

Only when Isobel arrived at the next bus stop, her stop, did the field of damage caused by Varen's storm reach its end.

Car horns honked as drivers steered slowly past the cop-car barricade blocking the intersection. A police officer directed traffic while pedestrians stopped to gawk at the mess and confusion, holding up camera phones and pointing.

Isobel, trying not to draw attention to herself, slowed to a jog as she hurried over the place where the layer of dust terminated, its blanketing white giving way to the curb and the painted lines of the crosswalk.

Someone shouted at her as her feet found the sidewalk, but she didn't stop, not until she arrived at the side entrance to the park—the same she'd taken that night after meeting with Varen at Nobit's Nook.

Until this moment, her plan had been to use the shortcut to get to her house. Now, though, even with the midafternoon sun blazing and the sight of people strolling within, bundled in their coats and scarves and still unaware of the chaos that had rocked the world mere blocks away, something held her at bay. An inkling that warned her against entering.

Isobel told herself she didn't have time to deliberate—or

to take the long way around. She didn't have time for inklings, warranted or not.

She needed to get home, to check on her parents and Danny, to warn them about what was coming. And to tell them she was sorry.

Pounding pavement, her feet carried her up the snaking road, past thickets of trees that flanked the narrow lane. As she rounded one bend after another, winding farther into the park, flashes from her previous nighttime run along this same stretch began to flip through her head.

Murky figures skirting through the brush. Whispers in the woods.

Something hissing her name.

Isobel shoved the memories aside. Keeping her pace up and her head down, she focused on the pavement, on putting as much of it behind her as quickly as possible.

Veined with the shadows cast by branches overhead, the road skimmed by beneath her. Her own shadow rotated this way and that, orbiting underfoot while she followed each curve.

When the lane straightened, however, her shadow, which had situated itself in front of her, grew suddenly longer with each stride.

Isobel slowed, watching her silhouette stretch then fade into a sudden darkness that, like a consuming presence, seeped in from every corner.

The nagging sensation she'd tried to brush off at the entrance returned, too intense now to dismiss. This time the foreboding brought company—that old feeling of being watched, a ghost in and of itself.

Isobel drew to a stop and tilted her head back. Gone was the white-gold sun. In its place, ragged patches of clouds blotted brightening stars from view. The darkness thickened. Night was falling—in the middle of the day.

Glancing one way and then the other, she no longer saw the pedestrians, snug in their winter wear. She didn't hear talking or footsteps or the whirring *tick* of coasting bikes.

Aside from the forestlike patches of trees, though, there wasn't anywhere any of them could have gone.

Straining her ears, she tried to detect the sound of voices, the chattering of birds. Anything at all.

She was rewarded only with the hush of the wind and the rustle of dry foliage as it scampered across her path.

Scowling at the collage of papery hand-shaped leaves, she wondered how, in the dead of winter, they had managed to retain their vibrant autumnal colors.

Whirling, she found the answer waiting at her back.

Fall trees, their boughs garbed in ember orange and flame yellow, now bordered the narrow lane. Their fiery colors drained away fast, though, siphoned off by the deepening dusk that should not have arrived for several more hours.

Isobel turned again, looking ahead.

Darkness waited on the stretch of road before her, where the canopy of limbs and leaves became an all-too-familiar tunnel.

Slap slap slap slap.

The sound of someone running up behind her, panting hard, had Isobel pivoting yet again.

A girl barreled up the road toward her, and Isobel knew her instantly—as well as she recognized the scene unfolding before her.

Fear, primal and gut-wrenching, owned the girl's expression. Clutching tight to the straps of her backpack, she kept glancing behind her, blond hair whipping this way and that as she tried to see what was chasing her through the line of trees.

Isobel had no time to dart aside before the past version of herself rushed into her—through her.

The world flickered black, and Isobel swung in the direction of her running self, aware that somehow she'd become caught in another memory. Like when Pinfeathers had shown her what had happened to Poe. But how?

Squinting through the gloom, she no longer saw her past self on the path. That specter had vanished.

In its place stood another on the road.

Even with his lean figure enswathed by shadow, she could still make out the insignia of the upside-down bird on the white patch of cloth pinned to the back of his jacket.

Turning his head, he glanced at her from over one shoulder, revealing the open pit in his porcelain cheek.

"Some say memories are merely another form of dreaming," the Noc said. "We, of course, would argue that they are, rather, another form of torture. Wouldn't you agree?"

"*Pinfeathers.*"

He angled toward her, lifting a clawed finger. "Half right," he said. "Or, pardon, do I mean right half?"

She took one cautious step in his direction; then, automatically, she took another.

"No, I don't think so," he continued. "You had your chance. Made your choice. Besides, we broke up. Remember?"

"H-how?" she said. "How did you—"

Now he aimed the claw at her, and the slight smile he wore dropped away. "The question you *should* be asking is *why*."

Isobel quickened her steps.

"*Stop,*" he said.

Her heart, already pounding, thrummed louder in her ears. A fresh surge of adrenaline coursed into her bloodstream. But she didn't heed his warning; loosed inside of her, apprehension and relief merged to create a hybrid emotion. Fear mixed with longing. Tenderness laced with trepidation. It drew her toward him.

"*I said stop,*" the Noc commanded, leveling a look of hate at her, the shadow of which she'd seen before on another face. Varen's.

She broke forward in a run, and even though it seemed as if he wanted to dissipate, to become smoke and slide out of reach, the Noc stayed rooted.

Colliding with him, Isobel wrapped her arms around his middle. She pressed her cheek—the same cheek he had scarred—flat against his chest, right over that place he'd once hollowed out in order to store her stolen ribbon.

"The rose garden," she murmured into him. "You . . . I thought you were gone for good."

"We're at least as gone as we are good," he muttered, trying, it seemed, to resist touching her. "And equally annoyed to see that, still, you don't *ever* listen."

"I'm glad you're not," she rushed on, ignoring his admonishments. "So glad. I—I need a friend."

"Ah." She heard his form creak and felt his claws stroke her hair. "I get your game. You would deliver cruelty for cruelty. Torment for torment. It won't turn out the way you think. We'll get our revenge. We always do. Even if only in our mind. Don't you forget that, cheerleader. Don't you ever forget it."

His voice, pained and bitter, as rueful as it was distorted, reverberated through his hollow frame, causing her cheek to buzz.

"I never meant to hurt you," she whispered, aware that in some sense, Pinfeathers *was* Varen. Part of his psyche, if not his soul. "Either of you."

"We *are* hurt."

"I know," Isobel murmured, tears stinging her eyes, slipping free to sear her skin and seep into his jacket. "And I'm sorry . . . so sorry."

He laughed.

The sound, acidic and humorless, unsettled her enough to make her loosen her grip on him. She started to pull away, but his hands clamped down on her shoulders. Claws digging in, he held her in place, keeping her close.

"What I mean," he said, "is that's all that's left. All we are. All we have to give."

"That's not true." Shaking her head, she clutched the lapels of his jacket, Varen's old green mechanic's jacket, which, like the pink ribbon, she had lost in the dreamworld—*to* the dreamworld. Pinfeathers must have found it. Did he want to hold on to it like he had the ribbon? To keep it because of what it represented?

Lost things found . . .

"You aren't *like* that."

"Recent history would suggest the contrary," the Noc said.

Her eyes traced over his collar, where the top two buckles of his underlying jacket lay undone. Within, an impossible network of cracks netted his chest and throat. With the exception of the large piece plating the place where his heart would have been—its jagged edges poking just above the black fabric—the jigsaw collection contained no shard bigger than a small coin.

Aware that neither Scrimshaw nor Pinfeathers could have been responsible for their own reconstruction, Isobel found herself again wondering who had performed the task.

"What happened on the cliff wasn't really you," Isobel insisted. "You're different than that. You're both different. That's why she wanted you. That's why she—"

Snatching her by the wrist, Pinfeathers swung her around fast. The trees, his broken face, the sky and the road swam by in a colorless blur.

"She wants *you*," he hissed.

One of his arms looped her waist, and the Noc pulled her snug against him. "But then," he added, pressing cold lips to her ear, "don't we all?"

Isobel held her breath. She fought against a shudder, but unlike during her initial encounters with the Noc, she had no urge to pull away from him or to try to jerk free.

He wouldn't harm her. She knew that. And though she wasn't sure how she could be so certain, it didn't change the fact that on some intrinsic level, she was.

"So she knows now," Isobel said, more to herself than to the Noc, "that I'm alive."

"As well as she knows you were never dead."

Isobel blinked. Frowning, she clutched the arm that encircled her waist.

"Wait," Pinfeathers said, speaking in a monotone, feigning disbelief, "don't tell us you bought oil from that old snake *again*. Really, cheerleader, you have *no* discernment. No ability to see things the way they really are. Otherwise, you might have seen me coming. All of this. Everyone else did."

So Reynolds *had* lied to her. About Lilith thinking she was dead. But why? Even if she hadn't fully believed him, that he was on her side, she'd wanted to. Desperately.

"What's happening?" Isobel asked. "Tell me."

"But you *know* what's happening."

She wanted to spin in his grip and face him. When she tried, though, he only squeezed her more tightly, forbidding the movement.

"Then tell me how to stop it," she pleaded. "Tell me you know how."

"First, you'd have to stop us."

"I keep trying. But he—*you* won't believe me."

"Oh, we want to," he said. "We do. But then, it would destroy what's left of us to find out we were wrong. And with the pain already too much to bear, why not just go ahead and eliminate the guesswork? And everything else along with it."

"It's not going to help, is it?" she asked, her shoulders sagging. "That's what you're saying. I can't prove *anything* to him, can I?"

"No," he said, laughing again, "but trying sure stirred the hornet's nest, now, didn't it?"

She jerked her head toward him and, in her mind, something clicked with those words.

"Oh my God," she breathed. "Reynolds. She *sent* him to find me. She *wanted* me to go into the veil. She knew I would try to make him believe. They *both* did. She knew how Varen would react. What he would do. She *knew. She*—"

"Doesn't need you anymore, FYI," Pinfeathers whispered in her ear, the drop in his voice causing her blood to freeze. "But how to get rid of you. How? How to lure you in close? How to hurt you inside *and* out? And keep you from fighting back?"

He nuzzled her neck, lips trailing to her shoulder.

"You . . . ," Isobel said, her throat constricting.

"*Us.*"

And now she had her answer as to why Pinfeathers had returned. Lilith had brought him back to use as a weapon against her. Isobel had fulfilled her purpose, igniting the fuse that would send Varen on the rampage to destroy the veil and blend the two worlds. So the demon had deployed the Noc—Isobel's lone would-be ally—as a final trap.

Hadn't the Noc himself once confessed that he had to do whatever Lilith commanded?

"But . . . ," Isobel murmured, her voice quavering, suddenly weak, "you wouldn't. I know you wouldn't. I know you."

"For your sake, my dear Isobel, I very much hope you do. Because we certainly no longer recognize ourselves."

"You're not going to hurt me," she said, her voice channeling a resolve she didn't feel. "Even if you tried, you wouldn't be able to."

"It's good to know you harbor so much faith in us," he replied. "Because it's all too far gone now, including us—*especially* us. And unfortunately for you, I'm very sorry to say, aside from *this*"—slowly his hand trailed up her body, claws snagging the fabric of her T-shirt, grazing her skin through the thin material, stopping only when his crackled palm pressed over the hamsa—"believing in the best of us— that we have a best to believe in—is the only weapon you have left."

Isobel placed a hand on his. "You don't have to do what she says. You've already proven that once. You protected me. You would do it again."

She felt his hand twitch. "What do you suppose I'm

trying to do right now?" he asked, his voice trembling. He seemed just as afraid as she did.

"You can't hurt me," Isobel said, the conviction in her voice failing. "No matter what, you won't be able to."

"I'm going to let you go," he said. "And then . . . I want you to run."

"*No.*"

"Run away. Like you did before. Like you should have done from the start."

"I won't," Isobel said, tightening her grip on him. "I *told* you. I'm not afraid of you anymore. *Either of you.*" She shut her eyes, blocking out the trees and the road and the night, hoping that would help to make her words feel true.

"Oh, don't you worry," Pinfeathers said, loosening his arm from her waist. "Whether that's really the case or not, there's still plenty left to fear."

Isobel spun before he could release her. She pressed her forehead to his chest.

"Don't do this," she breathed against him, gripping his jacket.

"*Issssobel,*" he hissed, drawing her name out as though to savor its sound.

Sharpened claws threaded into her hair. Her stomach clenched at the sensation, and when he leaned down, pressing his broken cheek to hers, she went rigid.

"You won't." She repeated it like a mantra, as if to reassure them both.

"Again . . . ," he said, stepping back from her, the movement causing the open collar of his jacket to shift. Enough to allow her a glimpse of an etching, chiseled onto the shard positioned over the center of his hollow torso, over his nonexistent heart.

Slowly he withdrew his hand, and in her periphery, Isobel saw blue claws — not red — unthread from her hair.

"Half right."

20
Twixt and Twain

Frozen in place, Isobel stood aghast as Pinfeathers continued to retreat from her, revealing more of himself the farther away he drew.

Horrible and heartrending, the truth left her wondering how she hadn't guessed it all along.

A zigzagging crack split the Noc's face in two. On the right half, the side that bore Pinfeathers's trademark crater—the side that mirrored her scar—a single black eye watched her.

On the other, a hollow socket appeared to do the same.

Her gut feeling about Pinfeathers, she now knew, had been right. He *wouldn't* harm her.

Of course, her gut had been right about another thing too. That she should never have entered the park. That something horrible awaited her within.

The very same something that had stalked her through its boundaries the last time.

Isobel's hands sprang to her lips. "What—what did she do to you?"

"Ah well," Pinfeathers said, shrugging. "Apparently, it was either this or scrapbooking. You know what they say.

Everyone needs a hobby. You should take up jogging. Now would be optimal timing, I think." He tugged at his collar with one claw, as if loosening a necktie. "I'm starting to feel a little *crowded* . . . if you catch my drift."

Though the two Nocs apparently occupied a single shell, it was becoming more and more evident with every passing second that only one Noc could hold dominion over the shared body at any given time. What had Pinfeathers said when she'd heard his voice in the purple chamber? *We're here, and that means he's gone.*

The struggle—it must be constant. But . . .

"You *can* fight him," Isobel said, inferring through his words and by the way he flinched, his head jerking suddenly to one side, that Scrimshaw was attempting to surface. To push through and take over. "Like . . . like you did in the garden," Isobel added more weakly, and now she sounded desperate even to her own ears.

Wrapping his arms around himself, Pinfeathers lowered his head. Claws digging into his biceps, he quivered with restrained energy.

"*Yes*, the garden," Pinfeathers said. "While that little scrap was *so* easily won—no contest, really—we'll have to tag-team it this time, I think. Me plus he against me and you. Two against two. What do you say, cheerleader? That way the odds are more even. Can't beat that now, can we? Ha. Well, I guess we'll soon see."

Without her telling them to, her feet began to take her in reverse.

"Don't let him through," Isobel urged. "You're strong enough. You are. Please. You—you're all I have."

"Touching." Wincing, he held up a palm. "Really. Romantic even. But save it. I think we both know that's not how you would have it. Otherwise, you might have stayed in the dream. The one I made for you. For us."

She knew he was referring to the last time the dream-world and reality had come this close. On Halloween night. Almost as soon as Isobel had crossed from the warehouse of the Grim Facade into the masquerade ball of Poe's story, she had encountered Pinfeathers. After throwing her into a mad waltz amid the masked revelers, guiding her through steps she shouldn't have known how to execute, he'd swept them both into an alternate version of reality. Appearing to her there as Varen—blond, like in the childhood picture Isobel had glimpsed in Varen's house, normal-looking right down to his blue button-up shirt and jeans—Pinfeathers had entrapped her, lulling her senses with the promise of an ideal existence.

At first Isobel's mind had accepted the lie as easily as it would have the beginnings of any pleasant dream.

But then, there'd been something off about the other people populating the classroom setting. Most of all, *everything* had been off about Varen.

One at a time, the inconsistencies and contradictions had pushed her further and further toward the truth, until she'd had no choice but to blast through the deception. And there, on the other side of the Noc's carefully constructed mirage,

Pinfeathers had been waiting for her in Varen's chair. Angry. Disappointed. And, Isobel recalled, hurt.

"Think about it," Pinfeathers said. "We'd *still* be there if you hadn't spoiled it all. If you hadn't insisted on waking up. There, in that world where your parents loved me. Where your friends accepted us. We could have graduated and gone to college together. Anywhere you wanted to go. *Every*where you wanted to go. Everything would have been the best. *I* would have been the best. The version of us that you keep hoping exists. Everything you'd ever want and more. *Any*thing you'd want. And it might have all worked out, Isobel. It might have all been okay, if only I *was* what you wanted. But . . . we both know I'm not."

Her eyes brimmed once more, burning with restrained tears because she couldn't deny any part of what he was saying. Pinfeathers might have been connected to Varen, but as much as she'd wanted to believe the opposite moments before, he *wasn't* Varen. Only a piece of him. And even though she and the creature had come this far, meeting and parting time and again as if they'd never quite disengaged from their crazed masquerade dance, Isobel still couldn't say what exactly— *who*—he really was. She doubted the Noc could either.

"I'm sorry," Isobel said, because those were the only words she could offer him.

"*You're* sorry?" He threw his head back, his laughter manic until another wave of pain caused him to double over at the waist, wiping his grin away and replacing it with a grimace.

She reached toward him, wishing there were some way to stop this. To make it all okay. To make *him* okay. To take away the pain it caused him just to be. "I don't know what to say. Please, tell me what to say."

He straightened, chin lifted. "Say that you'll keep shattering expectations. That you'll show her—and us—that you *can't* be predicted. Say that when ole Stencil Beak here gets close"—he pointed a red claw at his empty eye—"when he thinks he has you, and when I push through and hold steady, you'll prove to me that this time you *have* been listening. That you'll strike." Pulling down the fabric of his collar with one hand, he pointed at the etching of Virginia with the other. "Here. Hard as you can."

Horrified, Isobel closed the distance between them, taking hold of his arms, fingers twisting around the coarse material of Varen's jacket. "I—I can't do that."

"You'll have to," the Noc said, and though he clutched her arms in return, it was only to push her back, to hold her away from him. "If you expect to live long enough to keep your promise. And you damn well better keep it. After all, you wouldn't want to have us demolished *twice* in vain. Talk about rude. Besides, you should know better than to think you can have us both—me *and* I. Three's a crowd, remember? Selfish of you to even consider it, really. Can you let go now? You're wrinkling the duds. Might be secondhand, but, as you can see, that's part of my new loo—"

"Stop making jokes!" she screamed, shaking him. "It isn't funny."

"Who's laughing?" he asked, his voice doubling, its register dropping low. And then he did start to laugh—though Isobel knew she wasn't dealing with Pinfeathers anymore. She knew it the moment his right eye went empty, flickering out.

She swallowed hard, releasing him as, on the left, the other eye filled with a murky lens of black.

Isobel backpedaled and the Noc's laughter continued, the lower voice taking over, growing stronger. A piranha's grin, slow and devious, crawled its way up his face to reveal a double row of serrated teeth—half indigo, half red.

"Well, hello, stranger," said Scrimshaw, running a blue-clawed hand through his coarse quill-and-feather hair, its color divided down the middle like his teeth. Like his face. "I knew Pin would find you for me. He can't ever help himself. Pathetic, isn't it? Oh, by the way, so sorry for dousing the glim on you in the attic like that—but, you see, we didn't want to spoil our surprise. By the way, before we forget . . ." His grin widened, causing the cracks on the left side, his Scrimshaw side—to deepen. He spread his arms. "Surprise."

It would do her no good to run. She knew that. But that was what Pinfeathers had told her to do. And so, turning, Isobel ran.

The trees whizzed by on either side of her. Beneath her, the pavement flowed fast like a black river. She wouldn't look behind her, though. She wouldn't waste precious time like she had during that first run. Because there wasn't going to be any escape this time around. No secret guardian to slip through the veil and fight in her stead. No Pinfeathers to absorb death for her.

Scraping asphalt, her sneaker skidded on the road, bringing her to a stop as, straight ahead, a haze of black-violet smoke congealed into a humanoid shape.

Isobel wheeled away from it. She charged in the opposite direction, but Scrimshaw met her there, too, uncoiling right in front of her, re-forming fast—too fast.

Too close to try to dart away again, she swung at him, but he caught her fist in his fierce clay grip.

"Do you remember this place, my dear?" he asked, crushing her hand in his.

Isobel cried out. Her legs buckled, the pain sending her to her knees.

"Being that it *is* our place of meeting, is it poetic or trite, do you suppose, that it would also be our place of parting?"

Lifting a boot, the Noc kicked her hard in the shoulder. He released her in the same instant, sending her sprawling.

She landed with an *oomph*, all her breath expelling the moment she connected with the pavement.

Though her body screamed for air and her muscles demanded that she start running again, Isobel forced herself to lie still. With her face hidden under her splayed hair, she could only hope that the Noc would take her for unconscious, would lower his guard. . . .

If she couldn't get away, then she would have to do as Pinfeathers had told her. She would let him in close.

She could feel him drift near, sense his shadow falling over her.

"I know what you're thinking," Scrimshaw said. "That Pin-featherbrain's little plan will work—oh yes, I heard. I've been listening the whole time. Our hearing, you see, it's very acute."

Damn it, Isobel thought when he grabbed her by the ankle. She rolled onto her back as he dragged her toward him, but before she could raise her hands to try to ward him off, he knelt over her. With his red-clawed hand, he gripped her throat, holding her down.

Curling her fists, Isobel fastened her arms at her sides and waited, hoping Pinfeathers would come through, that somewhere inside, he *was* fighting.

"And just as *I* have heard you, he can hear you now. Isn't that lovely?" Scrimshaw continued, his smile reappearing as he pressed the indigo claws of his free hand into the soft flesh of her belly, preparing, she knew, to drive them through her. "So don't forget to scream really pretty for him."

Involuntarily, Isobel's thoughts drifted to the Grim Facade. To a moment so similar to this one, except there it had been Pinfeathers hovering over her. What had she done then?

"Knock-knock," Isobel said, startling herself with how calm she sounded.

Apparently, the prompt was enough to startle Scrimshaw as well. His smile fell, and he stiffened. A look of confusion flashed on his crackled face, replaced quickly by a glare of annoyance. Tilting his head at her, he blinked in that filmy-eyed, birdlike way that made her stomach turn.

"*Whoooo,*" Scrimshaw began, his cracked upper lip twitching into a sneer, "*is there?*"

Isobel uncurled a fist. If there was one thing she had learned for certain about these creatures, it was that they could not resist their own insatiable sense of curiosity.

Imagining a door at her back, she felt the ground beneath her shift.

She groped at her side, relieved when her fingers stumbled over a knob.

"The woodlands," she said, and, grabbing the knob, she twisted.

21
Head Games

Isobel let go as the door under her swung wide, dumping them both into the open air above a landscape of snarled tree limbs.

Freefalling with the Noc, she grabbed the lapels of his green jacket and jerked to one side, flipping his hollow frame under her.

The ground rushed to meet them, and she knew she had him.

They'd hit, and he'd be crushed for sure.

Just as long as he didn't—

Scrimshaw screamed in her face, the sound like metal grating rusted metal, and the Noc dissipated into smoke. Isobel fell through the swirls, crashing into the bed of ash alone, sending up plumes of dust.

She scrambled in the smog and pulled herself up. Ignoring the pain radiating through her jolted limbs, she took off, bolting headlong into the woodlands.

Legs and arms pumping, troops of charcoal trees flying past on either side, Isobel began to regret the knee-jerk choice of once again crossing the border between worlds. Another stern warning that Reynolds had once given her somehow, through the raging vat of her panic, bubbled to the surface of her consciousness.

Die here, stay here.

At least, that was the abridged version of what he'd told her in that cold Baltimore graveyard. He'd reminded her, in nearly the same breath, that perishing in the woodlands — becoming trapped here forever — had been his own fate.

And even if Reynolds *was* playing her again, positioning her like a pawn, signing her up for yet another trip to the funeral pyre, she wasn't going to take a chance on betting *that* particular bit of advice had been a lie.

"Still have that old pluck, I see," Scrimshaw bellowed after her, his voice booming from all around so that she couldn't be certain from which direction it emanated. "A few charming stunts left to pull. Well, you're bound to run out of cheek eventually."

Another door, she thought. She needed to make another door. To re-enter reality.

Staggering to a halt, panting hard, Isobel reached out. Imagining the front of her house, her street and the driveway, she grabbed for the knob that, like the one she'd made second's before, should have appeared.

Nothing. Air.

No, no. Come on. She'd *seen* Reynolds *do* this before. Why wasn't it working?

Isobel hissed a curse, spinning in place as Scrimshaw's laughter echoed around her, growing closer.

She whipped her head this way and that, scanning the

multitude of burned matchstick trees. But she didn't see his scarecrow figure anywhere amid the stalks or against the woodlands' violet back-lit glow.

"Door to door," the Noc called. "It's the only way to make a sale. Everyone knows *that*."

Trying again, Isobel pictured her bedroom door, remembering specifically that Reynolds had passed from one world to another using the exact same entry point.

In spite of her faltering hope, a familiar frame materialized before her out of the nothing. Her heart leaped, and her hand itched to try the knob—so familiar—now in her grip.

Sensing eyes on her, though—*an* eye—she stalled.

"Well, go on," came that craggy voice from mere feet behind. "What are you waiting for? Take me home. Introduce me to the folks. I'd *love* to meet them. And if I remember correctly, a little meddling bird *might* have mentioned a younger brother as well."

Her grasp on the doorknob loosened.

"Come to think of it," the Noc went on, "I may have seen him here before. Short and sort of round? A bit like a pigeon. Black ruffled feathers always in his eyes?"

Lowering her arm to her side, Isobel turned slowly.

Arms folded behind his back, crimson claws poking out on one side, blue on the other, Scrimshaw displayed a self-satisfied grin as yesterday's discussion with Danny again returned to Isobel's mind. How her little brother had mentioned he'd been having bad dreams. Nightmares about her dying . . .

Had he encountered the Nocs too? Or was Scrimshaw merely trying to goad her?

Deciding that it didn't matter either way, that it was enough to know Danny was in danger, Isobel gave up on all thought of going home.

She couldn't. Not so long as Scrimshaw remained locked on her trajectory like a heat-seeking missile.

If she was going to be free of him, if she was going to keep her family as safe as she could in the already bleeding worlds, she would have to stand her ground. She would have to fight—and defeat—Scrimshaw here, on his turf.

And maybe, Isobel thought as she reached behind her, fumbling for the doorknob again while she kept her eyes trained on the Noc, maybe her odds of achieving those ends were better in this realm, anyway, where everything was malleable.

"Change your mind?" Scrimshaw asked. "Afraid I won't make the best of first impressions?" He gestured to his chest. "It's the tattoos, isn't it?"

Clutching the knob, Isobel banished her bedroom from her mind, imagining instead someplace else entirely. Somewhere she knew for certain would not intersect with reality. A place that, because its creator had conjured it in his imagination, existed solely in the dreamworld.

Scrimshaw's gaze flitted between her and the door that must have taken on a new shape behind her. His smile waned, fading out along with the cunning crocodile gleam in his single eye. He took a halting step toward her, cocking his head to one side.

"Tell me truly, girl. Do you not ever tire of running?" he asked. "Do you never grow faint from the sickness, the pitiless pain—the *fever* that is living? From the horrible, *horrible* throbbing of your own aching heart?"

Isobel stood motionless, surprised to catch herself actually considering the question.

"No," she said at last, "at least, not nearly as tired as I get from listening to *you*."

With that, she shoved through the door, into the cathedral hall of Varen's Gothic palace.

Whirling, she ran again, steps echoing as her feet carried her fast down the long alley of columns and violet stained-glass windows.

She headed straight toward the altar, to the twin angels and their double-edged swords.

"Wake up!" she snapped at them.

Their eyes sprang open, those sapphire orbs glowing in faces that mirrored hers.

Isobel sprinted up the short set of steps. She slammed a hand on the altar, vaulted over it and, landing on her feet on the other side, twisted in time to see Scrimshaw storming down the long corridor toward her, a crazed smile contorting the entirety of his halved face.

"Break him," Isobel commanded her angels in a whisper.

The seraphs moved in unison as they swung their swords up, holding them at the ready.

"Two can play, child!" bellowed Scrimshaw, and, as he slid to a stop, he sliced his hand through the air. Instantly the feathers of the stone angels' wings shriveled, dropping away to reveal dragons' wings. Wheeling on Isobel, the pair of figures morphed into crimson-eyed gargoyles, foreheads sprouting curling rams' horns, faces elongating, noses sharpening into snarling snouts. Forked tails lashed out behind them like whips.

The statues released their swords. The blades clattered to the marble floor, and dropping onto all fours, two grotesque, doglike creatures growled and snapped in place of the seraphs.

Isobel groped through her mind for a counterattack, keeping watch on the serpentine tails that flipped and twitched as the chimeras stalked toward her, their massive stone paws cracking the marble beneath them with each stride.

Then, before she could even think about dodging the pair, they bounded forward. Leaping onto the altar, they opened toothy jaws wide, roars deafening and breath furnace-hot as they descended upon her. They might have crushed her even before they could have torn her to shreds—and would have—had Isobel not turned them to dust with a well-timed thought.

Debris rained over her, powdering her in yet another layer of grime.

"A bit like playing a game of chess, isn't it?" Scrimshaw asked, materializing on the opposite side of the altar. Leaning his elbow against the marble top, he propped his split chin in one palm. Red claws drummed the right side of his face, the Pinfeathers side. With a blue claw of his free hand, Scrimshaw drew circles in the dust of his demolished demons. "That would make it your turn."

Chess? Pawn. The words brought a sudden idea to her mind.

Swiveling on her heel, Isobel dashed to a tapestry covering the rear wall. Imagining another door behind it, picturing the first place that came to mind—the only space big enough to host her plan without overlapping the real world—she ripped the drapery free.

She visualized herself in her cheer uniform, the one with HAWKS embroidered on the top and the matching blue skirt with yellow pleats. As she shoved through the ornate double doors, her clothing morphed in compliance, her performance sneakers squeaking on the floor as she hurried into the white ballroom of Poe's Red Death masquerade story.

Quickly, though, she skidded to a halt, too arrested by what she saw to engage the next phase of her plan.

Bodies—more skeleton than flesh—lay everywhere. Mounds of them.

Still clothed in their rotting costumes, their decaying faces half-hidden beneath their garish, gore-stained guises, the courtiers and revelers lay strewn across the floor, draped over one another, a corps of corpses.

Limp forms draped the banisters and balconies, arms hanging free.

Shrunken and shriveled, the musicians sat slumped in their chairs. Their mouths hung agape, the ragtag wings of their dragonfly costumes bent and broken. Several of them still held on to their instruments with mummified grips.

The walls and flaking gold-leafed domed ceiling of the formerly grand ballroom matched the state of its inhabitants: decrepit and crumbling.

Isobel's hand rushed to cover her mouth. Fighting the urge to retch, she spun back to see Scrimshaw leaning a shoulder against the frame of the open doorway, his arms folded.

"Don't care much for the redecorating, I see," he said. "That's too bad, since you're about to join the decor." Pushing off from the jamb, he started toward her. "So thoughtful of you to have changed into a costume."

"It's not a costume," Isobel snapped, scuttling backward. "And if we are playing chess, then it's still my turn."

Smirking, the Noc paused. "By all means," he said, with an inviting wave of his hand.

Continuing to put distance between them, Isobel imagined the floor taking on a checkered pattern, like in the lunchroom at Trenton. Like on a chessboard.

The bodies from Poe's story vanished from the ground at her whim as on every square, she pictured herself exactly as she was now.

Everywhere, doubles—*pawns*—began to flicker into being. Ten squads' worth of Cheerleader Isobels.

The Noc's black eye narrowed at her. "What are you doing?" he asked, the confidence in his smile wavering.

Isobel didn't answer. Instead she slid into the crowd of doppelgängers.

"Stop!" the Noc snarled, darting after her, but she'd already commanded each of her selves to switch places.

Taking a square of her own, Isobel now became one of them.

A single face among many.

22
Checkmate

"Clever, clever," the Noc called through the hall.

Isobel held steady amid the other versions of herself and, careful to keep her focus forward, she followed Scrimshaw's movements in her periphery.

His boots tapped on the black-and-white tiles as he entered the ranks of her conjured army, his echoing footfalls the only sound in the ballroom-turned-game board.

"Well played," the Noc said, giving an appreciative nod, though he spoke through clenched teeth. "Well played, indeed. You're smarter than you look. Though still not quite smart enough, I'm afraid. For it's my turn now, and I'm sure I needn't remind you how your cunning has bought you only time."

He slid out of her sight line then, and Isobel had to fight the impulse to turn her head. Stiffening, she willed her doubles to blink and breathe in tandem with her while she scrambled to come up with her next move. She couldn't deny that Scrimshaw was right. Though the idea to multiply herself and hide among a legion of look-alikes might be enough to preserve her life now, it would not keep the Noc at bay for long. Playing defense would only delay death. Not prevent it.

But what attack could she make that he wouldn't simply turn against her, like he had the angels?

She needed Pinfeathers. Had he not yet returned because he couldn't?

"Eeny, meeny, miney, moe . . ."

Isobel flinched at the sound of the Noc's voice. He was close—and getting closer. No more than a single row behind.

"My mistress told me to pick the very *worst* one, and it is—"

She swallowed, and in her ears, the gulp sounded like an explosion. Had the other Isobels made the same noise? She didn't think so. She hadn't commanded them to, she'd been so focused on *him*. On where he might be. And where *was* he? Why had he stopped talking?

Isobel didn't hear footsteps anymore. She didn't hear the creaking of his frame. Or anything at all.

Don't move, she told herself. *Hold very still, breath normally, and whatever you do, don't—*

"*You!*"

Isobel screamed, jumping as indigo claws burst through the chest of a double standing two spaces down from her.

"Aha!" Scrimshaw shouted, and withdrawing the clawed hand that had impaled the fake Isobel, he rounded to face the real her.

Collapsing in a heap, Isobel's slain pawn became ash at the Noc's feet. Scrimshaw strode through the pile, boots dragging dust as he closed in on her.

Isobel scuttled backward again, ordering the duplicates to switch—to shuffle.

Her imagined army obeyed, moving once, then twice, some shifting places on the diagonal, some from side to side, others forward and back. They bumped the Noc, jostling him as they brushed past him like robots, taking no note of his presence among them.

Sneering, Scrimshaw shoved through the crowd, and though she would not look at him dead-on, Isobel could tell he was straining to keep his vision fixed firmly on her. She could also tell by the way his head twitched from side to side that he'd again lost her, that she'd once more become anonymous in the midst of the copies.

Roaring in anger, Scrimshaw stalked through the assembly and began slashing indiscriminately at the doubles. One after another, they became heaps of ash that showered the floor, spattering the other duplicates and, as Scrimshaw raged nearer, her, too.

Isobel racked her brain, knowing she needed to act. *Now*. As in, ten seconds ago. But how was she supposed to fight something she couldn't catch?

"Come out, come out, wherever you are," Scrimshaw lilted.

He swiped at another duplicate and then another, claws hacking through Isobel's summoned pawns, reaping them like dry wheat.

Her jaw tightened, and for a brief instant, she feared the manic thumping of her own heart would give her away.

Think. There had to be *something* she could do to end this. To end him. For good this time.

Briefly, she considered ordering her replicas to attack him all at once, but that wouldn't stop him from dissipating into smoke again. So she thought about sending a decoy running in one direction to create a distraction, but that would only lead him away. If it even worked. She needed him close, like Pinfeathers had said. Luring him to point-blank range would be her only hope of landing a hit.

And she *was* tired of running. So tired of all those things Scrimshaw had mentioned.

Threading himself through a line of doubles, the Noc drifted to within mere feet of her. She stared forward, refusing to look at him, not even as his smile returned and he homed in on her. The real her.

He crept to stand directly in front of her, and Isobel forbade her hands from twitching into fists. She kept her body rigid and her face slate, as unflinching as any statue's.

He was close enough now that she could strike at him outright. But would she have time to rear back, to prepare a punch strong enough to prevent him from shredding her as he had the others? She doubted it. As Scrimshaw tilted his head at her, eyeing her with increasing suspicion, she realized that their battle of wits was about to come to an end. And if she couldn't win a contest of the mind, she knew she had no hope of surviving one of blows.

"Forget something?" he asked her.

Isobel blinked.

He had to be bluffing, trying to get her to give herself away. It had to be a coincidence he'd found his way to her.

Any second now, he'd pass her by and go on to interrogate the next figure. *Then* she'd have her chance. She'd spring on him when his back was turned. As soon as his back was turned.

"I asked you," the Noc repeated, "if you forgot something."

He lifted a red claw, pointing to the hole in his cheek. In Pinfeather's cheek.

Oh no, she thought, terror dissolving her insides as his meaning dawned on her.

The scar. She hadn't thought to give the duplicates the marking.

Isobel wrenched away, but he proved too quick. "Checkmate!" Scrimshaw growled, his arm lashing out, fast as a whip. He caught her by the throat and she choked as he drew her forward, dragging her out from the lineup of doubles.

"Shhhhhh," the Noc hushed, pressing a red claw to his lips.

Her troops began to erode and flake away, her shining checkered tiles fading to cloudy white again while her imagined cheer uniform transformed back into her ashen street clothes.

Her cover blown, Isobel tried to jerk free, fingernails scraping at the Noc's porcelain hand.

"Oh, he's really fighting me now," Scrimshaw said. "I can feel him, fluttering about inside as if on fire. Tell me, should I let you two lovebirds bid each other a final farewell?"

Pinfeathers. He was talking about Pinfeathers.

"No, I think not," said the Noc through a gritted grin. "Never been a fan of good-byes myself. Especially the kind that have been said once already."

Isobel opened her mouth, wanting to call out to the other Noc, to beg him to push through. But Scrimshaw clenched her neck tighter, slowly crushing her windpipe.

"You should *hear* him implore me," the Noc continued. "Pleading like a child. It's *almost* painful to listen to. You really ruined him, you know. And now I have to wonder what it is—pardon, what it *was* about you that did it." The Noc tilted his head at her while he continued to strangle her, as if he really wanted to know. "What type of poison *are* you, girl?"

Poison?

Because Pinfeathers cared for her, Scrimshaw saw her as poison? As Pinfeathers's downfall? His ruin? But if she had become the biggest weakness of the leader of Varen's Nocs—then, in regard to Scrimshaw, couldn't the same be said for . . . ?

Light-headedness closed in on Isobel, stealing her ability to think. The room began to blur, and the bodies of the court-iers, still draping the balconies above, became fuzzy blobs. Scrimshaw's dual face melted into a jagged smear, and sparks flashed in the corner of her vision. But one fading glance at the creature's open collar, at the delicate, hazy image carved into his chest, and she was reminded of who the girl was. Who she had been to Poe.

Isobel tried to speak. A gasping sound escaped her, but

the Noc must have read what she'd tried to say on her lips, because for an instant, his squeezing grip faltered.

"What was that?" he demanded.

She again attempted the one-word utterance—a single name. One she knew he knew. At least as well as Pinfeathers knew *her* name.

Scrimshaw let go of Isobel's neck. He switched hands, snatching her by the shirt collar instead.

Isobel inhaled, gulping for air. Her dizziness lifted, and Scrimshaw's split face snapped into clarity.

"Speak plainly," he snapped, shaking her. "Tell me what you just said. Say it again, girl."

"Virginia," Isobel rasped, pressing fingers to his cold chest, to the engraving of Poe's young cousin and bride.

Scrimshaw's expression collapsed. Pain blended with sorrow, replacing his rage.

"Why?" he snarled, thrusting his halved face in hers. "*Why* would you dare speak that name to me? Why make hers the last you'll ever utter?"

"Because," Isobel said, her voice hoarse, ragged—almost gone. "She's standing right behind you."

23
In the Hearts of
the Most Reckless

There hadn't really been anyone there. No one at all.

But Isobel's lie that there *had* been someone—a very specific someone—proved a far better distraction than she had initially dared to hope.

Because when Scrimshaw turned his head to look, suddenly there *was* someone.

Isobel had not imagined the young woman into being. She hadn't been able to think that far ahead. Or that fast. Not with the Noc gripping her throat, squeezing the life from her.

So the phantom standing before them had to have arisen from the depths of the *Noc's* consciousness, triggered by Isobel's suggestion and, perhaps, by the underlying current of Scrimshaw's own repressed longing.

Though Isobel could recall only a few specifics regarding the appearance of Poe's wife—a handful of vague characteristics picked up during her study with Varen, retained from the one or two glimpses she'd had of her portraits—Scrimshaw, it seemed, had forgotten nothing.

Black-haired and pale in complexion, her small hands clasped in front of her, the round-faced young woman—so real, so completely lifelike—watched the Noc with large and soulful brown eyes.

Releasing the fabric of Isobel's shirt, Scrimshaw angled slowly toward the vision.

Freed, Isobel retreated from him fast, and though she expected the Noc's head to snap back in her direction and for the illusion to rupture as instantaneously as it had materialized, she was relieved when the Noc remained entranced.

"Do you remember the Valentine I've been writing for you?" Virginia asked, her voice soft and high, sweet like a songbird's. "Well, you and Mama will both be pleased to know that even though I haven't yet finished it, I *have* begun setting the lines to music. Just as you suggested."

Transfixed, Scrimshaw took two slow steps in Virginia's direction.

Isobel watched, clasping her throat where he'd gripped her, still stunned that her bluff had worked and that, somehow, she'd managed to buy back her life again. For at least another moment.

But maybe, she thought as she trained her gaze on the upside-down crow in the center of the Noc's back, another moment was all she needed.

Spinning away, Virginia strode to the piano bench that appeared only just as she sat, the skirts of her simple, cream-colored dress swishing. With girlish flair, she lifted delicate hands and placed slender fingers on an invisible keyboard.

As Virginia pressed down, a squat, rectangular piano

unfurled from the nothing and the middle chord she'd struck resounded softly, as gentle as a sigh. More notes followed, her hands wandering to and fro over the keys as if the song were one she had to find her way back to.

"Oh, and Eddie?" she went on to say. "I've hidden your name in the lyrics, so keep a sharp ear. Listen closely and tell me—either of you—if you can discover the trick."

Isobel curled her fists at her sides. Her chance, hard won, had arrived.

So why hadn't she taken it?

If she moved now, if she ran fast enough, she could slam right into him. She could shove him straight to the floor. As fractured and fragile as he was already, such a fall would surely finish the Noc.

Of course, it would finish *both* Nocs. Was *that* why she was hesitating?

And why *hadn't* Pinfeathers returned? Couldn't he do so now that Scrimshaw was distracted? Now that his guard had been lowered?

"Lenore," the Noc whispered, and as he spoke the word, the decorative molding and flaking gold paint of the once-decadent walls began to melt away, becoming plaster.

Worn wooden boards bled through the dingy ivory dance floor, seeping through like a spreading stain.

Against all inner urgings, Isobel continued to wait and watch as the room morphed around them. The walls smoothed and squeezed inward. The ceiling dropped low.

In mere seconds, the ballroom had transformed, its

macabre scenery replaced by the cramped interior of a meager and sparsely furnished sitting room.

Oblivious to the shift, Virginia played on.

Individual notes, clunky at first, tinkled forth from the instrument, whose flat back met flush with one of the four unadorned walls. Against another, orange flames crackled in a tiny fireplace.

> *"Ever with thee I wish to roam—*
> *Dearest, my life is thine.*
> *Give me a cottage for my home*
> *And a rich old cypress vine."*

As she sang, Virginia's melody evened out. The notes became more certain, as light and airy as Virginia herself.

> *"Removed from the world with its sin and care*
> *And the tattling of many tongues.*
> *Love alone shall guide us when we are there—"*

The last note, higher in register than the others, caused her voice to crack. Startled, Virginia paused.

She lifted a hand to her lips. Bringing fingers away, she frowned at the smear of crimson that blazed against her pale skin.

Blood, Isobel thought, suddenly realizing this moment was not a random dream or imagining as she'd first thought. Instead it was another memory. Like the one Pinfeathers had transported her into that morning she'd found him at the fountain.

Reynolds had testified that that memory, the one depicting Poe's death at Reynolds's own hands, had been "stolen." But if that was true (and, at this point, considering the very little she knew for sure about Reynolds, there could be no telling), then had Scrimshaw been the owner of that stored memory—as well as this one? Had both memories originated from Poe himself?

At first glance, it would seem so.

On the night before their project was due, Varen had described this moment of Poe's life to Isobel: Virginia playing the piano, singing for her husband and her mother. Then the appearance of blood—the heralding sign of consumption. Tuberculosis. Death.

"Eddie?" Virginia said, and she swiveled in her seat to look toward Scrimshaw, her face childlike in its expression of confusion and alarm.

Freeze-framing, the replay stopped there.

Isobel, startled from her reverie, channeled her focus once more to the image of the upside-down crow and steeled herself to charge the Noc.

But her feet stayed grounded, because she knew she'd waited too long.

He'd surfaced from his trance. That had to be why the scene before them had halted. Any second now, he'd turn on her and it would be over.

"Years later, she finished it," the Noc said, pointing one

blue claw at Virginia. "By then, however, she'd already been devoured from the inside out. From this day forth she lived — if indeed you could call it living — as though Death himself had taken residence within her very heart. A death as red as the blood that never ceased."

Isobel's clenched hands slackened. Maybe, she thought as she listened, she *could* still make her attack. Or rather, finish the assault she'd already unwittingly initiated.

If she aimed accurately, said just the right thing, was it possible her words could inflict more damage than her fists?

"You loved her," Isobel said.

"*Worshipped,*" Scrimshaw corrected. "But more ludicrous than that, let us not forget, she loved *me.*" He gave a short ironic laugh. "Not just him — the poet. But me as well. I, the epitome of our own penchant for self-destruction. Do you know how difficult . . . how *impossible* such a feat must have been?"

"Yes," Isobel said, pressing a hand to her own heart, certain she could feel echoes of the same pain that resonated within him. "I do."

For a long time, the Noc remained quiet. He lowered his arm to his side, and when he spoke again, his words came soft, almost too low for her to decipher.

"There are chords in the hearts of the most reckless which cannot be touched without emotion. Even with the utterly lost, to whom life and death are equally jests, there are matters of which no jest can be made."

Isobel thought she might have heard those phrases

somewhere before—or read them. Maybe in one of Poe's works, though she couldn't recall which.

"You have conquered, and I yield," the Noc went on to say, his words doubling midsentence when a second caustic voice rose to join the first. "But I'll advise you not to allow my return. Because your final play, girl, effective as it was, stands with us as too grievous an onslaught not to seek vengeance for. I grant you a reprieve, but not forgiveness. One cannot give what he does not possess for himself."

With these words, another vision shimmered into view before him, superimposing itself over the first. Similar in composition, though a hundred times more familiar, an alternate memory unfurled, causing the room to transmute yet again.

In Virginia's stead, Madeline, clad in her violet evening gown, her hair pinned with that rhinestone comb, now occupied the bench of a grand piano, the same one that sat in the parlor of Varen's house.

The built-in shelves of blacked-out picture frames materialized on the wall at the phantom's back. Decorative curtains spilled down to flank the window.

Everything looked just as it had the first time Isobel had seen the memory through the TV, on that night she'd found Pinfeathers waiting for her in her family's living room. And again, after she'd entered the reversed dreamworld version of Varen's house.

The memory. Could it have switched because . . . ?

Slowly the Noc turned in place, and Isobel had her answer.

His left eye—Scrimshaw's—had gone empty. On his right side, a black eye blinked at her once more.

"Low blow," Pinfeathers said. "But then, we told you to aim for the heart, didn't we?"

"Pinfeathers," she breathed, her shoulders sagging in relief.

"For now, yes. But while we're all here and accounted for—mostly—allow us, if you will, to tell you one other thing before we go. Before *I* go. Well, make that *two* things."

"Please," Isobel said, her eyes flickering to the memory of Madeline as she played the notes of Varen's lullaby, humming softly along. A glitch froze the scene, and then the notes and their player restarted. Distantly, Isobel wondered what it all meant, why the memories of Varen and Poe were linked to their Nocs. She knew she didn't have time to ask for an answer to that mystery, though. Not when Pinfeathers was talking about leaving. She knew him better now than to assume his plan was merely to dissipate and depart.

She sensed that they were *both* done with running.

"You can't go," she said. "Not yet. I still need your help."

"I *have* helped you," the Noc replied. "And will yet. You'll see. We were sleep-flying before you woke us up. Practicing what we've learned, crossing thresholds while trying our best not to wake you before you were ready to see us as we really are—holes and all. And what the crow has seen, the pigeon knows. Besides, you heard Fossil Face. I think you know as well as I do that it's better for the both of us—for all of us, really—if we . . . if I don't stick around. Though first I must attest that old scribble-necked codger is a great fat liar. That drawn-out bit about begging?" The Noc folded his arms. "Never happened."

Isobel shook her head. "You're making even less sense than usual."

"Item number one," the Noc said, ignoring her. He withdrew several steps, striding directly through the repeating memory of Madeline. As if the memory had been composed of smoke, the entire image disappeared, swirling away to once more reveal the interior of the white chamber. "Goodbye, cheerleader."

She started after him, alarm spurring her forward. "Wait—"

"Item number two," he said as he lifted his arms out to either side, "you should know that, as far as we can—the boy and I, that is—as much as we allow ourselves—"

"Don't." Isobel broke into a run.

"We really do—"

"Pinfeathers, stop!" she yelled.

"—love you." This he said while tilting backward, tipping toward the floor.

"No!" Isobel screamed, her cry echoing through the hall the moment before the crash sounded.

Bursting along all the refitted lines and reconstructed fissures, the Noc's doubled body exploded, several shards pinging her shoes.

Isobel collapsed to her knees, her hands leaping to grasp at the skating shards as she watched the blackness in his solitary eye snap out.

The back of his skull had caved inward. The sleeves of his jacket, Varen's jacket—*their* jacket—had flattened out along with the Noc's black clothing.

In less than a second, Pinfeathers had executed his own demise, and as far as Isobel could tell, the only part of him that had survived total annihilation was his face.

Faces.

Split down the middle, the two halves lay like masks atop the debris.

Isobel took hold of the jacket.

She pulled the garment from the rubble, causing splintered bits of Virginia's fractured portrait to tumble and scatter free, broken now for good.

"I love you, too," she whispered into the collar, hugging the jacket close. "Both of you."

24
Mummer

For a long time, Isobel continued to hold the jacket close, eyes closed.

Breathing long and slow, she detected an almost imperceptible trace of Varen's scent: dried orange peels, crushed leaves, and incense. Along with the aroma came the bitter taste of the dust of this world and, perhaps, of the Nocs, too.

She would have shuddered at that thought if she'd allowed it to linger. She might have even let herself cry.

But Isobel didn't have the luxury of indulging in either form of release. There was still so much hanging in the balance, so much piled on her shoulders. Even more than before. Because now . . . now she really *was* alone.

Pinfeathers had believed in her, though. And along with his confession of love, the Noc had suggested that somewhere deep beneath the outer layers of his consciousness, Varen shared the conviction that Isobel *would* come for him. If that hadn't been true, Pinfeathers would not have sought her out. Not if there wasn't still a chance she could turn this all around. He wouldn't have risked bringing Scrimshaw this close just to warn her about an inevitable and inescapable end. Or even to say good-bye . . .

He wouldn't have played Lilith's game that way.

And if Isobel hadn't still been a threat herself, would Lilith have needed to form such an elaborate weapon against her by recombining the Nocs?

No, Isobel thought, opening her eyes. *She wouldn't.*

Pulling herself to her feet, she looped the jacket around her shoulders. She threaded her arms through the sleeves, allowing its familiar weight to settle into place.

Even if its embrace could not warm her, the feel of its stiff yet well-worn fabric and the memories it carried still gave her comfort.

She scooped her hair, gritty from all the ash, out from beneath the collar, but paused when again that nagging sensation of being watched tingled along her spine.

Heeding its call, Isobel turned away from the wreckage of the Nocs' commingled forms.

Her heart stammered a beat, confusion rattling her.

There, standing in the center of a single remaining black tile, one of Isobel's cheerleader pawns watched her.

But . . . if the others had gone, if her concentration had fallen away from maintaining their presence, was it possible that one could linger?

As a test, Isobel sent a dismissing thought at the figure. When the doppelgänger remained, though, Isobel knew her own mind couldn't be responsible for its existence. She doubted it was one of Varen's imagined phantoms either, because, squinting at the copy, she saw that it bore a matching scar on its cheek.

That detail, more than anything, warned Isobel that something more insidious was at work.

She began walking toward the duplicate.

"You," Isobel said, but stopped when the pawn spoke in perfect unison with her.

Nails of ice pricked her skin, and this time, Isobel took a long moment to formulate the words she would speak next. Because now she had no doubt to whom she was speaking.

"I know it's you," Isobel said, and again, the double matched her words, its inflection timed exactly with Isobel's to create an eerie echo effect.

"You led me to the courtyard, to Varen, on purpose," Isobel went on, doing her best to ignore the copy's mimicking speech. "That was you in the hallway at Trenton, too, wasn't it? In that dream you told Reynolds to take me to. You were the one holding the stack of papers. Am I right?"

Going quiet, Isobel waited for a response, but it never came. The double only stared, blinking when she did.

Isobel sneered, a flash of fury igniting inside of her.

"Haven't you learned yet not to mess with me?" she asked, walking forward again, and this time the duplicate did not copy her.

Instead, as Isobel drew closer, it began to deteriorate.

Turning sallow, the entity's skin shriveled, sucking inward, clinging to the underlying framework of bone like cellophane. Its eyes welled black, sinking farther into its head with each of Isobel's approaching steps. But Isobel didn't stop, because the distortion only helped to affirm what she already knew.

"What's the matter, *Bess*?" Isobel hissed. "If I didn't know better, I'd say I was making you sick."

This had happened before when Isobel had neared Lilith while wearing the hamsa necklace. Nestled under Isobel's shirt now, it bolstered her with the same strength Gwen's presence had given her that morning at the cemetery. The charm's small and steady pressure, coupled with the obvious effect it had on the demon, helped to remind Isobel that a power greater than this monster standing before her *did* exist. It had helped her once, and would again.

"I told you before," Isobel went on, stopping three feet from the silent demon and its hollow, penetrating stare. "You won't get what you want. No matter *what* you do, how hard you try to get rid of me or to twist Varen's mind, you won't win. I'll find him because I always do. You should know by now that you can't stop me. You haven't yet. And when he wakes up from this nightmare and sees that I *am* real, we're both going to put you back into that filthy stone box you crawled out of. And that's where you're going to stay. Forever."

Now a ragged corpse, its cheerleading uniform hanging limp from an emaciated frame covered in gray, weblike flesh, the demon smiled at her.

Revealing two rows of sharp and spindly needle-teeth, that grin seemed to dare Isobel to venture a single inch nearer.

But when she stayed put, the demon slowly lifted an arm, extending a skeletal fist toward her. Through those disintegrating fingers, Isobel glimpsed something small clutched in the wraith's grip.

"Death comes for us all eventually," the double said at last, again using Isobel's own voice. "Sooner for some than others, though nearly always sooner than expected. Especially, as you just witnessed, in regards to those we hold most dear."

The demon opened its hand, those awful fingers crumpling toward the palm where there rested a small wad of what appeared to be pink construction paper.

Isobel hitched a quick breath when she recognized the crushed origami butterfly as the very same she had made at her family's kitchen table the evening before.

"And to think," Lilith said with a giggle, her voice going guttural and low, mutating to match her decomposing body, "they actually believed I was you."

With that, the entity fell apart into ash—just like all the other pawns.

Oh God, Isobel thought as she snatched for the crushed paper butterfly, rescuing it before it could float to the floor with the rest of the demon's discarded guise.

The paper felt too real in her grasp.

Her mom and dad.

Danny.

25

Disturbances

"Mom!" Isobel shouted, and as she burst through the front door of her family's home, all around, objects rose into the air.

"Dad!" she called into the solemn emptiness of her house.

Lifted from their hooks, the picture frames lining the wall floated in separate directions. To her right, the empty umbrella stand flipped end over end, drifting lazily by.

She looked behind her, through the open door she'd made in one wall of the white chamber.

The dilapidated ballroom still lay on the other side, making her uncertain whether she'd actually crossed back into reality. If there was a reality left to cross into . . .

Isobel slammed the door shut, blocking out the visual of ash and death. Almost in unison with the deafening *bang*, the floating objects hit the floor with a collective *clomp*.

A corresponding *thump* sounded from the living room, and snapping her head in the direction of the archway, Isobel scanned the space for a sign of anyone.

Miscellaneous mundane artifacts littered the floor: the TV remote, her mother's paperbacks, a cardboard drink coaster, one of her little brother's video-game controllers.

But where was Danny? Her mother and father?

Isobel's gaze locked on the mantel clock, its hands spinning around each other in endless freewheeling circles.

Running fingers through her matted locks, Isobel tried to get a handle on herself, on her surroundings. Yes, the clock was spinning, but the layout of her house wasn't reversed. So this *couldn't* be the dreamworld. Not . . . not unless she really *was* too late. Not unless the veil had already eroded and the two worlds had merged.

Then again, how *else* did she think Lilith could have crossed to this side?

Had the attack from Scrimshaw merely been a distraction? A diversion thrown at her for no other reason than to keep her occupied and away from Varen while Lilith used him to finish her plans for destruction?

No. No. It couldn't be. The butterfly had to have been a lie. Her parents and Danny, wherever they were, they had to be okay.

"Mooooom!" Isobel wailed into the house, her mind spiraling further into chaos as it flipped from one horrible conclusion to another. "Dad! Dan—!"

The sound of the front storm door opening made her whirl around in time to see the inner knob turn.

As the door swung wide, Isobel took a retreating step.

Sunlight flooded the foyer, and with it came Danny, his cheeks red from the cold, his nose rosebud pink. Taking one look at her, he dropped the cell phone he held and rushed her. The phone thudded to the floor, joining the rest of the bric-a-brac, and slamming into her, Danny wrapped his arms tight around her middle.

Automatically, Isobel's own arms wrapped him back.

"Danny, omigod," she breathed, squeezing him hard, fingers gripping the nylon fabric of his puffy winter jacket.

Relief poured through her like a drug, numbing her from head to foot as a cold breeze wafted in to cool her heated face. "You're okay. I'm so glad you're okay."

"I hate you," Danny sobbed into her shirt, and through the thin layer of fabric, Isobel could feel the sudden cascade of warm tears.

This was real, then. Wasn't it? Of course. It had to be. It *had* to be.

Glancing through the open door again, Isobel no longer saw the gruesome interior of the corpse-lined ballroom. Only her quiet street.

She'd been fooled by appearances before, though.

Keeping a tight hold on her little brother—on the boy who she hoped was, in fact, her little brother—Isobel scanned her surroundings, searching for any inconsistencies.

Across the way, squirrels darted in the branches of Mrs. Finley's oak. Familiar cars sat in equally familiar driveways. Empty trash cans waited next to mailboxes. Normality pervaded the street, the neighborhood.

And there, sitting on the front stoop, next to her backpack and winter coat, Isobel spotted the pink paper butterfly she'd made for Danny less than twenty-four hours ago, its wings as crisp as they had been the moment she'd completed the final fold.

So the demon *had* lied. But why?

Because, Isobel thought, *this* was the distraction.

The veil still existed. Lilith *hadn't* been able to traverse the barrier. Not yet. Isobel still had time. And *that* was what Lilith wanted to eliminate.

She had to go back. Right away. But first—she had to get away.

"I *knew* you were going to leave again," Danny said, his words muffled against her. "I knew you would. I should have said something. I should have told Mom and Dad."

"Danny." Placing her hands on his shoulders, she tried to push him from her, but his arms only constricted. "Where are Mom and Dad?"

"Where do you *think*?" he snapped. "They're looking for you. *Everybody's* looking for you. Including the police. They found that letter you wrote."

Letter? Oh no, Isobel thought, realizing Danny meant the Valentine confession that had all but flown out of her pen the day before in Mr. Swanson's class.

After discovering the ash in the hall that morning, she'd forgotten about the loose paper stuffed in her notebook. And she'd dropped her binder and papers in the stairwell when Reynolds showed up. Someone must have discovered her things soon after, intensifying the search for her. Surely Varen's parents had spoken up about her visit to their house by now, too.

Isobel brushed a hand against Danny's overheated face.

"You're here by yourself?" she asked. Once more, her eyes

trailed out the door, her gaze falling on the backpack she knew she'd left at school in her locker. How had it gotten here?

"I was supposed to go home with Trevor after school," Danny said, his words rushing out in one long string, "but I knew no one would be here, so I took the bus home instead. Just in case you came back. Like you did the first time. When you went to that party. But the power's out and I don't know why, and I can only get reception outside. I tried calling you and calling you, but then that stupid friend of yours came by with your stuff."

"Gwen?" Isobel asked, trying to keep up with the rapid-fire stream of information.

"You left your cell in your coat," Danny snapped, and pulling away, he shoved her. "Why would you *do* that?"

"Danny, calm down." She reached toward him again.

"Where did you go?" he demanded, ripping himself from her hands as a fresh wave of tears streamed down his reddened cheeks. "Why are you covered in that white dirt again? What's happening?"

Isobel didn't answer. She couldn't. Never before had she seen her brother this upset. Not even in that hospital waiting room in Baltimore on the day she'd flatlined, when he didn't know she was there, watching in astral form.

Maybe, Isobel thought, *reliving* someone's death was far worse than experiencing the initial death itself. Certainly that had proven true for Varen. For Poe.

"That Gwen girl told me you were in trouble." Danny shook his head, his bangs falling into tear-filled eyes. "She said not to let you go anywhere if I saw you, but how am I supposed to stop you when I know you won't listen?"

After not hearing from her again, Gwen must have gone into Isobel's locker, snagging Isobel's bag so she'd have an excuse to stop by the house without seeming suspicious. She must have found Danny sitting outside—and her worst fears confirmed. That Isobel had never come home as she'd instructed.

Why *had* Gwen been so insistent about Isobel going home, anyway, if her note to Varen hadn't been found yet?

Isobel also wondered if Gwen had seen or heard about the damage wrought on Eastern Parkway and the strip mall. Had her parents? Probably. But only Gwen would know for sure that the incident was tied directly to her.

Like Danny, her mom and dad and best friend—wherever they were—had to be going insane with worry. And now that Isobel's letter to Varen had surfaced, her parents would know that their suspicions had been right—that she had remembered everything all along.

"That's his jacket, isn't it?" Danny asked, calming at once, his voice going flat. "That guy."

"Danny, listen—"

"No!" he yelled, jerking away from her. "*You* listen! He's gonna kill you, Izzy! I saw him do it!"

Isobel's jaw dropped.

"That's what I've been seeing in the dreams!" Danny shouted, using the back of one sleeve to try to clear away the tears that wouldn't stop. "He's always there. Every time you try to go after him, he kills you. He turns you into a skeleton and you fall apart."

Danny's words brought with them a flash of recognition. She thought about Varen in the courtyard of statues. Could it be that Danny had seen—and misinterpreted—different versions of the scenario Varen had been reliving? Versions of the same scene *she* had witnessed? It sounded so. But . . . how?

"It's going to happen for real this time," Danny said. "Izzy, *please*."

"No, it's not." The words *I promise* leaped to the tip of her tongue, but Isobel held them in check. She couldn't say it. Not when she had another promise, still unfulfilled, to keep.

"Why?" Danny asked her, the sorrow and confusion in his voice making her stomach churn with shame. "Why do you care about him more than you do about us?"

"Danny, it's not like that. You don't und—"

"That phone call last night wasn't about you," he said, and for a split second, Isobel wasn't sure what he was referring to. Then she remembered the discussion they'd overheard as their father had entered through the garage door. "Dad was talking to his and mom's lawyer."

Shocked, Isobel grabbed his arm. *"What?"*

"After Baltimore, Mom told Dad she wanted a divorce," he said. "I'm not supposed to know, but I overheard them talking last night. Dad's trying to fix things. That's the real reason they were going on that stupid date, except now they're not because they're out looking for *you*!"

"I . . . ," Isobel started, but everything within her had already collapsed in on itself, suffocating anything she might have said. And what *could* she say? Nothing. Nothing at all. Because she could see by her brother's lost expression that it was all true. And they both knew it was her fault.

"Danny . . . I'm sorry."

"No," he said, taking a step away from her. "You're not. You did this all before, and now you're going to do it again."

Turning, he hurried to where he'd dropped his phone. He picked it up and, dialing, pushed out onto the front porch.

"Dad!" Isobel heard him say seconds later through a choked sob. "Dad, come home right now. She's here, but I know she's not going to stay. She's going to leave again. So come home. Please hurry."

Isobel moved to go after him but paused at the door.

She had time, she told herself, to cross into the dream-world once more. But if she was going to do that, if she was going to leave her family and Gwen behind again, then she would need to create a distraction of her own. A diversion that would lead them all away and, at the same time, keep them together. As safe as possible in this reality.

Isobel pushed through the screen door and, crouching by her backpack, dug through her coat pocket to retrieve her cell. Flipping it open, she ignored the string of texts and missed call alerts and sent a quick reply to the fifteen messages Gwen alone had sent.

MEET ME AT THE DANCE

Clamping the phone shut, she made sure Danny saw her stuff it into her bag again.

"He wants to talk to you," Danny said.

Isobel glanced at her little brother, but her focus landed on the back-lit screen he held out to her and the photograph he had assigned to their father's contact info.

Dressed in the makeshift Edgar Allan Poe costume he'd donned for Isobel and Varen's project, his fake black-comb mustache on his upper lip as askew as the spray-painted cockatoo hanging from his shoulder, their father sat at the kitchen table, a goofy, too-serious expression plastered across his made-up face. He aimed the tip of a black pen at the camera. At her.

"Isobel," she heard her father's voice buzz on the line. "Are you there? You answer me right now. Do you hear me?"

Isobel took the phone from Danny and saw the tension knotting his brow ease slightly.

"Isobel, damn it," her dad said, his voice growing louder, more frantic. "I said answer me!"

She didn't raise the phone to her ear. Instead she stared at that picture. Studying it, she took in all the details— memorizing every last one. Just in case.

"Izzy?" her father said, and now his voice came soft, almost too quiet to hear. "If you're there, for the love of God, please say something."

"I love you—Mom, too," she said. "And I'm sorry," she added before driving her thumb into the end button.

26
Crisscrossed

Isobel turned her back on her brother, unable to meet his gaze again.

Re-entering the house, she dropped his cell to the floor and, dodging the cracked picture frames that littered the foyer floor and steps, pounded up the stairs.

The eyes in the photos seemed to watch her as she passed: Danny in his Scout uniform, Isobel in last year's cheerleading portrait, all four members of her family beaming in front of the Christmas tree two Decembers ago.

Their mother and father's wedding photo . . .

The storm door slammed a second time.

"Isobel, stop!" Danny yelled, and she heard him thundering after her.

Veering down the hall, Isobel hurried into her bedroom. She shoved the door closed just as Danny reached it.

"Open the door!" he yelled, banging, twisting the knob, but she'd already locked it.

She spun to face her room, which someone had ransacked.

The contents of her dresser drawers lay strewn across the floor, and nearby, the sheet she'd thrown over her mirror sat in a heap.

Atop her cubbyhole headboard, the numbers on her digital clock flickered and jumped.

In the center of her bed, laid out like it was waiting for her, rested Isobel's tattered pink dress. The same one Gwen had bought secondhand and altered for her to wear to the Grim Facade.

But Isobel had buried the gown away in the bottom drawer of her dresser.

Seeing it exhumed from its resting place and arranged with such care across her comforter, she now doubted her father or mother could have been responsible for the raid.

But who, then?

"Dad's coming," Danny said. "He's on his way. You won't get far, so you might as well open the door."

Tuning out her brother's frantic knocking, Isobel ventured with slow steps to stand at the foot of her bed.

She remembered how Gwen had chosen the gown specifically for its hue, knowing Isobel would be the only one in such a color at the underground goth party.

In a way, the dress had been meant as a beacon, a signal that had allowed Varen to spot her easily amid the sea of black-clad bodies. To make her a light in the dark.

Gwen's plan had worked, too. Varen had found her right away.

What was more, he'd *known* her right away.

Isobel placed a hand on the dress, fingers grazing the hemline and torn tulle of its poufy underskirt.

Along with the grit and grime embedded in the material,

once pink but now pale gray, black blots of her own blood dotted the dress's lace overlay and stained the underlying skirt.

The dress had changed so much since she'd first put it on. Almost as much as she had . . .

Varen, Isobel thought. All this time, he'd been seeing different versions of her. The scar-free Party Pink Isobel, Cheerleader Isobel, Bleeding Black Dress Isobel. Dead Isobel.

But . . . what if she dared appear to him as a blended version of herself? The past and present merged together? Would that help him believe it really *was* her?

Sitting out in plain view this way, the dress seemed to suggest the idea all on its own. As if that had been the exact intention of whoever it was who had pillaged her things.

Isobel glanced at the door, which had gone quiet.

Danny, she figured, must have retreated down the stairs. Had he gone outside to try calling their parents again? Or even the police? Maybe he'd gone to retrieve her phone, like she'd wanted him to, to see what she'd texted.

Whatever the case, Isobel would be gone by the time he returned.

Quickly she shucked her clothes and donned the dress, managing somehow to zip up the back on her own.

The cool satin lining hugged close to her skin, the bodice only slightly looser than it had been on Halloween.

Pulling on Varen's jacket as a final touch, Isobel turned to face the door. She stopped, though, caught off guard by the sight of herself in her unveiled dresser mirror.

With her face smudged, her hair caked with grime, and

her dingy skirts crinkled and stained, she looked as if she'd just survived an explosion.

Well, she thought wryly, taking in the ensemble, *at least I match.*

Tearing her gaze from the mirror, she started for the door. She reached for the knob, one of her sneakers causing the floor to creak.

"He said you'd be wearing that jacket when I saw you again."

Isobel halted at the sound of her brother's voice, which came muffled through the door. Startled both by his words and by the fact that he was still there, that he must have been there the whole time, she lowered her hand.

"He said that when you had it on, that's when I would need to tell you . . ."

She frowned, somehow doubting that by "he" her brother could be referring to their father.

Moving right up to the door, Isobel pressed her hands flat to its surface and waited, but for a long while, Danny didn't say anything else. Then, just when Isobel was tempted to ask who he'd meant, he spoke again.

"Last night was the first night he ever talked."

"Who?" Isobel heard herself ask, even though she already had an inkling.

"The black bird," Danny replied.

Isobel's eyes widened, her suspicions confirmed. Her breath caught in her throat as, suddenly, it made sense how Danny had been seeing things in the dreamworld — how he'd *been seen* in the dreamworld.

What the crow has seen, the pigeon knows, Pinfeathers had told her in the moments before destroying himself.

Danny, she thought, remembering how Scrimshaw had referred to her little brother as a pigeon.

Could Pinfeathers have been taking Danny into the dreamworld, showing him Varen's nightmares about her on purpose? But . . . *why*?

"He's really real, isn't he?" Now her little brother didn't sound like himself at all. His voice had gone small and afraid. "The dreams. They weren't just dreams, were they?"

"Whatever he told you to tell me," Isobel said, "it's . . . important, okay?"

"He said that you should know it was never about you," Danny replied. "He also said that you have to 'remind us of who we are.' He said you would know what that meant. . . . Do you?"

Isobel didn't answer. Instead she waited, her eyes searching the blank white surface in front of her as if it could provide the aid Pinfeathers's cryptic message failed to offer.

She rested her forehead against the door.

No. She didn't know what, specifically, that meant. And she still didn't know why the Noc had sought out Danny instead of her. Maybe he'd had to in order to protect her from Scrimshaw.

And if Pinfeathers had taken *her* to the dreamworld instead, wouldn't her brain have interpreted things the same way Danny's had? Varen destroying her over and over?

Then she might have truly gone insane.

Maybe Pin had known Lilith's plan to use Isobel against Varen. As a means of luring him into this destructive state of mind. Into becoming this destructive force . . .

Could Pinfeathers have overheard the demon and Reynolds talking—plotting?

Isobel didn't know the answer. But the Noc never seemed to take the direct route where logic was concerned. Any logic other than his own, that is.

"Is . . . that it?" she asked. "Is that everything?"

"He said memories make better weapons than words."

Again Isobel waited. And just when she thought her brother had finished, his muffled voice spoke again.

"And . . . there was one other thing."

"What?" Isobel asked.

"He made me promise to tell you 'I told you so.'"

Isobel looked down at her feet. She tried hard not to smile, but it was either that or cry. She allowed the smile, and it came sad and small.

There was no need to wonder what Pinfeathers meant by that statement. She already knew this was his way of ensuring he got the last word. Of leaving Isobel with a final proclamation that would underscore everything he had ever tried to warn her about.

Of course, like nearly everything he ever said, that phrase could hold a double and opposite meaning. "I told you so" might have been meant to underline his promise that he would still help her. Or to provide proof of the confession that he loved her.

Maybe he'd meant the phrase in every way possible.

She would never know. Not for sure.

Isobel took hold of the doorknob.

"Izzy?" she heard her brother say, and his voice sounded farther away now, fading out, as if he were floating off.

As Isobel drew a clear image of Varen in her mind, though, she knew that, in truth, *she* was the one who was phasing out, departing into another realm.

"Yes?" she answered.

In her periphery, she saw the smaller objects in her room begin to rise and float, her scattered clothing and her "Number One Flyer" trophy.

"I love you," her brother's voice echoed, sounding now as if it were emanating from the bottom of a deep well.

The words sent a sharp pang through her, and turning the knob, Isobel ripped open the door again.

Her brother was gone, though.

In his place waited windowless stone walls, a winding spiral staircase, and far below, a bottomless well of pure darkness.

27
Amid the Mimic Rout

There was no banister. No railing. Only the looping ribbon of stairs and, at their center, the abyss.

With one guarded step, Isobel crossed out of the reality she knew into the realm she dreaded. Placing a hand to the cold stone wall to ground herself, she peered up—and found an exact replica of the descending view.

An upside-down flight of steps, like the coiling underbelly of a serpent, wound up and away forever.

Fighting a wave of vertigo along with the sense that she'd somehow been transported into an optical illusion, Isobel turned to face her room again. Her door had vanished, though, and as she stared into the grooves and cracks of the stone surface, nausea crept over her.

Swallowing, she concentrated on the solidness of the step beneath her, the sense of gravity pulling her down, holding her in place.

While she thought she could move if she didn't peer over the edge of the stairs again, she doubted she could bring herself to climb any higher than she already was. So, shifting, legs shaking, she angled herself toward the descending path. Not willing to risk losing her equilibrium a second time, she kept her focus on where the steps anchored into the wall.

Down and around, down and around. Down, down, and down.

The farther Isobel went, the deeper the black helix seemed to wind, making her wonder if she could be venturing underground.

She considered stopping to alter her surroundings, to open a wall or create another door. But would that only lead her away from what she sought? *Who* she sought?

Isobel thought of Varen's name over and over. She pictured his face. The stairwell didn't change, though. No doors appeared. And yet each time Isobel completed a revolution— or assumed she'd completed one—she kept expecting to encounter an archway or a window. Something.

But there was only rough stone, mortar, and more stairs.

Halting, she pressed her spine flush to the wall. She flicked her eyes to the inverted set of steps above and wondered why her thoughts weren't working.

Every time before, when the images in her mind had been clear, when she hadn't been battling distractions like the Nocs or Reynolds, the dreamworld had, in some form or another, always presented her with a pathway.

But even when she'd entered the dreamworld through the veil earlier that day, her thoughts, she reminded herself, had failed to take her directly to Varen. Instead they'd led her to the cluttered attic, which housed the remnants of the Varen she knew from before. The fragments of his subconscious. Pinfeathers.

True, she *had* found her way to the courtyard, to the real flesh-and-blood Varen. She knew now, though, that that had been Lilith's doing.

Like Reynolds, the demon had *wanted* Isobel to find Varen—to interact with him. Yet even though it seemed as if Reynolds and Lilith shared the goal of igniting the fuse to the bomb Varen had unwittingly become, Isobel still wasn't sure the two had the same endgame vision.

Of course, she thought, switching her gaze to the wall directly across from her, she highly doubted that *she* and Reynolds did either.

Nevertheless, at least *some* of the information Reynolds had imparted to her had to be accurate. When Reynolds had drawn her into the gym at Trenton, for instance, and attempted to explain to her that Varen could not have stayed in reality even if Isobel *had* been able to bring him home on Halloween, he'd said it was because of Varen's unbreakable ties to the dreamworld. In so many words, he'd said that Varen had become *ingrained* in this world, part and parcel of it. As lost to it as he was to the demon who had taken him.

Lilith, Reynolds had said, had a claim on Varen just as she'd had on Poe. And even if the dreamworld had yet to absorb Varen utterly, he had still become a cog in the machinery of this realm. A puzzle piece clicked into a slot fashioned to fit him perfectly.

Or, Isobel wondered, was it that Varen, being the way he was, just so happened to fit the mold? Like Poe would have.

Whatever the case, if Varen had become an element *of* this

world rather than a trapped outsider, then maybe thinking of him as a way to locate him was like pressing enter on a blank Internet search. It could only lead nowhere.

Did that mean, then, that there was *no* way to find him?

Isobel sank to sit on the step. Draping her arms on her propped knees, she let her head thud against the stone behind her, unable to accept that all her efforts had brought her *here*, to a point where her actions could only lead her in endless circles.

Combing through her memories, she considered the different ways she'd found Varen in the past.

During the masquerade party, she'd just kept searching. Pinfeathers had tried to stall her, transporting her into that fake reality. Reynolds had attempted to detour her too, but in the end, neither had succeeded in keeping her from him.

And Baltimore. After Isobel had entered the dreamworld through the tomb door in that churchyard, after she'd crossed into the rose garden, she'd been able to use the butterfly watch Danny had given her as a compass. The hands of the clock had pointed the way through the garden's maze to where she'd found Pinfeathers waiting for her in Varen's stead.

Isobel didn't have the watch now, though. She didn't have Pinfeathers, either.

Those last thoughts crashed hard over her, until with a sudden spark, Isobel realized that there was one thing she *did* have. Knowledge of the watch's whereabouts. And even if its possessor was barely a part of reality, the watch itself remained as real as ever.

Pushing herself to her feet, Isobel shifted the image in her head from Varen to the key-chain timepiece her little brother had given her last Christmas. Closing her eyes, she took care to conjure every detail exactly as she remembered it, right down to its pink flip-open wings, its silver accents, and its yellow, needle-thin second hand.

A heavy *clunk* from far below echoed through the stairwell. Isobel opened her eyes.

Edging forward, maintaining contact with the wall through her fingertips, she peered down into the corkscrew spiral where, in the center of the blackness, a distant pinprick of light glinted like a coin.

As she watched it, the glowing point began to expand, growing wider into a shaft of light that shot up past her like a flashlight beam into the nothing overhead.

She began moving again, faster now. As she twined round and round, she glanced between the sloping path in front of her and the thickening beam that pierced the center of the stairwell.

When the shaft of light widened to bathe the outer rim of the steps, there came a low boom that Isobel felt through the soles of her shoes and the palm she held pressed to the wall.

A door must have opened below. Or the floor itself . . .

Whatever shift had just occurred, Isobel hoped that it meant she'd found the way out. Or that it had found her.

Before she could venture another glance over the edge, though, she saw the light beam waver, flickering in and out as if something had passed in front of it—a large something.

Quickly she moved back a step, battling a sick sense that down was no longer the direction she wanted to go. That it never had been. She waited, though, keeping a hand cemented to the wall, senses dialing to full alert as a soft clicking noise, like stone nicking stone, rebounded up to her.

Click. Tick. Clack.

Peeking over the edge again, Isobel's stomach lurched with new terror.

Through an open porthole lay the expanse of a starless night sky.

The beam flickered again as wispy streams of clouds coasted swiftly between the unraveling hem of the tower and the source of the light—a pale-faced half-moon.

Steps loosened from the crumbling wall below, tumbling free like loose teeth from a broken jaw.

For whole seconds, Isobel could only gape in horror while the opening raced higher, climbing toward her, the spiral stairs fanning off like dominoes. Then, just before her own step could fly out from underneath her, Isobel jolted out of her shock.

Turning, she ran.

Legs burning, she fought to keep herself vertical as she darted up and up, around and around.

She stumbled, though, and, slamming onto the slabs as they loosened, scrambled forward on hands and knees. Pushing off from the steps as they flipped out from underneath her and into the sky, Isobel tilted her head back. When she caught sight of the upside-down stairs looping the walls, impulse took over. With no time to pray her plan would work, she jumped, aiming her shoulder at the wall.

Isobel connected with smooth stone, and instead of bouncing off, she rolled.

Tucking her arms in like she would for a stunt fall, Isobel flipped—until her sneakers met the set of steps that moments before had been overhead.

Gravity accompanied her on her switch, causing the world to invert with her, down becoming up and up down.

Descending once again, Isobel quickened her pace to a pell-mell run, while all around her, pieces of the upended stairwell continued to evacuate their structure, bricks and steps lifting to sail skyward, defying the gravity she'd so stupidly assumed had really been there.

Unrestricted, the moonlight illuminated her surroundings, and she could now see where the separating tunnel terminated.

Another door—this one stamped into the center of the tower's marble floor.

The wooden, glass-paned entry was one Isobel knew well. As well as she knew the solitary boy seated in the classroom within, his head hung low over a familiar desk so that the locks of his raven-black hair brushed its surface.

Isobel reached the bottom just as the last step soared upward and the final stones disconnected from the ground, ripping free of their foundation.

She flung herself onto the door, and even as the jutting shapes of the Gothic palace entered her periphery, its limitless turrets and spires spiking into the sky all around her, she dared not look away from what lay beyond the glass pane beneath her.

Tuning out the distant roar of rushing waves and the howl of whipping winds, Isobel pounded a palm against the glass, eyes locked on the boy she swore to herself that, from this point forward, she would not allow to leave her sight again.

"Varen!"

28

The Assignation

He wouldn't look up. He only kept staring at the glinting object he held between his fingers. Isobel's watch.

She banged on the glass again, ignoring her hair as it whipped in her face.

Still, Varen would not lift his head.

Isobel gripped the knob with both hands. It slipped in her grasp—locked. She pushed hard with her mind, picturing the cylinder inside turning, the latch sliding back, but the knob only rattled.

As before in the courtyard of statues, her mind was clashing with Varen's, her thoughts pitted against his. And as long as Varen refused to believe she was real, she was destined to lose the fight.

So she would just have to *make* him believe.

Isobel pounded a third time, hard enough to send a lightning-bolt crack up the center of the pane, straight through her view of him.

"Varen!" she shouted.

His eyes flicked up from the watch. Instantly the howling winds, the distant thundering waves—all of it ceased.

Isobel's hair fell limp. Her breath grew loud in her ears as roaring quiet replaced the din.

When Varen finally spoke, she saw his lips move—but his voice, calm and monotone, came from behind her.

"Call it a hunch, but I don't think he can hear you."

Isobel swung her head around.

Appearing just as he had through the glass, seated in his usual chair in a now-reversed version of Mr. Swanson's classroom, Varen stared right at her with hollow black eyes.

"At least, not over all that banging and yelling," he said.

Confused, Isobel again checked the door, which, though now upright, somehow supported her full weight as if she were still horizontal, lying curled against it.

Beyond its splintered windowpane, rows of blue lockers lined the walls of a deserted Trenton hallway.

Another instantaneous switch had occurred, bringing her inside the classroom.

Heart pounding, Isobel swiveled her head back to Varen. As she did, one of the fluorescent fixtures directly over his head clinked, flickering out.

Isobel continued to hold tight to the doorknob, as if her clutching it was the only thing keeping her vertical. Then she carefully set her feet flat to the floor, one after the other, glad the industrial tiles proved as solid as they appeared. As she slipped free of the door, the folds of her tattered dress fell to hang loose around her legs once more, and, hands shaking, Isobel loosened her death grip on the knob.

Past the rows of empty chairs, through windows lining

the back wall, the familiar landscape of the woodlands stretched as far as she could see. Now, though, a crimson sky radiated in place of the violet horizon.

"You're late," Varen said. His red-rimmed, shadow-lined eyes fell from her to the watch as he thumbed open its wings, and Isobel knew what he saw through its small window. A mixture of lies and truth.

This was a dream. *She* was a dream.

"No later than usual," Isobel murmured, striving to flash a bit of her old spunk, though her voice sounded small even to her.

She needed to keep him talking, though. To keep him calm. Contained.

But what could she say? The words—the right words— evaded her.

"Varen," Isobel began, taking a step toward him when he did not reply.

"I wanted you," he said, interrupting her before she could continue, his gaze never lifting from the watch. "From that very first day. I can tell you that now, I guess."

Isobel stopped, startled by his out-of-the-blue admission. Curious in spite of herself, she tilted her head, uncertain about what, exactly, the confession meant. Or where it had come from.

"I kept it to myself," Varen went on, "like everything else that was happening to me. But in the beginning, it was all just superficial anyway. As shallow as I'd convinced myself you were." He paused as if searching for a memory that had become distant, remote. "I meant it, you know, when I said you weren't my type."

A pained smile, involuntary, tugged at Isobel's lips and then faded. She remembered that conversation. Of course she did. How could she forget their first phone call?

"And *I* meant it, when I told you I'd be back for you," Isobel replied.

"Obviously. And that's why, now, you never . . . ever . . . go away."

Isobel kept her feet planted on the tile beneath her, fighting the impulse to go to him. She didn't dare try. Not when that was precisely what all the doubles did. Not when the long-fingered, ring-lined hands holding her butterfly watch still frightened her.

Isobel winced inwardly, recalling how the same hands that had once communicated such gentleness had also gripped her with frightening force. How they'd tossed her to the side. And let her go . . .

"It was easier to hate you," he said, snapping the watch closed with a sharp *click*. "A lot less painful, too."

Vines of longing wrapped around her heart, urging her to tell him how she'd gotten there and what was happening— to explain how all this could be possible. Words continued to fail her, though, because his candid brashness and calm indifference all served to further confirm her fears that in his mind, he was only speaking to another figment—a soulless projection of his own consciousness.

"We were better off that way," he went on, glancing up at

her again. "Well, *you* were better off. Back when I assumed you thought you were better than everyone else, which—ironically enough—allowed me to go on telling myself that you were beneath me. Back when you believed I was everything everyone said I was."

"I didn't—"

"Admit it," he said, cutting her off. "They were right about me, weren't they?" An off-putting smile touched one corner of his mouth, causing his silver lip ring to glint. "Your friends. Your boyfriend. Your dad." Just as quickly as it had appeared, his smile fell. His eyes darkened and slid to the far wall. "*My* dad."

Isobel wanted to respond, to say the right thing, but she still didn't know how to enter into the battle that was taking place before her. The one Varen was so clearly waging against himself.

It was never about you.

Pinfeathers's words rose inside of her, right along with his final message of—

"'I told you so,'" Varen said. "I bet that's what they all wish they could say to you now that you're gone. Your friends, your family—all our teachers. Hell, I wish I could tell you myself."

"You have," Isobel replied, forcing strength into her voice. "In a way. And you're telling me right now, too. But . . . I'm here to prove that you're wrong. Just like they were. *Are.*"

Varen rose from his desk, pocketing the watch, wallet chains clinking as he drew to his full height.

Isobel's heart raced faster with every step he took toward her, clumps of ash tumbling from his boots and the hem of that black coat. Her instincts screamed for her to back up, to slide behind Mr. Swanson's empty desk, if only to put something between them.

She stayed rooted, though. He stopped to stand before her, and even as her body chanted the command to run, her heart begged for her to step nearer, to enfold him in her arms.

She could risk neither.

"I've only been wrong about one thing," Varen said, shaking his head. "And that's you. Every step of the way, in fact. Whenever I was sure of one thing, you always surprised me, proving just the opposite to be true. Every. Single. Time."

Keep shattering expectations.

Another of Pinfeathers's cryptic one-liners shot to the forefront of Isobel's mind. Building on one another, each phrase offered glimmers of insight, linking with everything Varen was saying to her now. Maybe, she hoped, that meant the Noc's advice would do just what he'd said it would: reveal what she needed to do in order to penetrate—and dispel— Varen's darkness.

"Not anymore, though," he said. "And I guess that's the one perk of loving a dead girl. She never changes."

Isobel's head jerked up, and she met his onyx stare.

Loving?

With that single word, the slow-burning ember of her faith caught fire anew, and it occurred to her that she just might be able to do this, to save him. To bring them both home to a reality that still waited for them. She only had to break through. Everything she needed was here. *He* was here. Pinfeathers had spoken the truth. *It should be simple,* she thought. As easy as saying it out loud.

Maybe it would be.

"You think I'm a dream," Isobel said, "that I'm dead. But Varen, I'm not."

"You always say that," he murmured, eyes tracing her face, stopping at her lips. "Always. Just before you die."

"I won't this time," she said. "Wait and see. I'm still here, aren't I?"

"Sometimes I do it without meaning to," Varen continued, as if he hadn't heard her. "Other times, on purpose. Just to get rid of you. To get you out of my sight. Out of my head for one moment. Every time, though—and it doesn't matter where we are"—lifting a hand, he touched her cheek, his cold fingers trailing electricity in their wake—"what we're doing. I'm always the one who does it."

"Varen, *look* at me." She seized his hand and, squeezing, pressed it over her scar. "How *can* I be a dream? This scar. My dress. It's real. And your jacket, how did I get it? Remember the petals in the courtyard? The blue sky? And on the street. That was me too. I sent you back, but only because I *had* to. Because it *was* real. And Varen, *we* are real. I *am* here. For you. And . . . it's time to go home now."

"The worst is when I get close, like this," he went on, and leaning down, he brought his lips almost to hers. "When I try to kiss you."

Isobel didn't attempt to speak again. Her gaze fell to that small silver loop, and gripping his hand harder, she willed him to continue, to move in and press his lips to hers so that she could *show* him just how real she was.

"I don't try that anymore, though," he whispered, pulling back.

Though she attempted to keep his hand, Varen pried free and turned away, leaving her only the view of that horrible, white, spread-winged raven.

Pins and needles played over her skin each place he'd touched her.

"If you really believe I'm a dream, like all the others," she said, watching him as he drew to a halt at the opposite end of Mr. Swanson's desk, "then change me. Go ahead. Try."

It was a risk. She knew that. But at this point, what wasn't? Especially when she could sense she was failing. Again. Her window of time with him was closing fast. He would shut her out once more, and that would be it.

"Try," she pressed, "and you'll see it won't work. Then you'll—"

He moved quickly, snatching the black stapler from Mr. Swanson's desk. At first, Isobel thought he might throw it at her. Instead, his arm swung out, and he aimed the item straight at her—but now the stapler become something else entirely.

Varen pressed his thumb down on the hammer of the sleek handgun, cocking it. The weapon made a sharp cracking sound like the splintering of bone.

Isobel's voice, her breath, her comprehension, *everything* jarred to a halt inside her, and her renewed terror gave way to a single thought. That the black hole of the gun's barrel exactly matched the soulless centers of his eyes.

"That . . . that isn't real," Isobel whispered, lips scarcely moving.

He swiveled his arm toward the windows and fired. Isobel jolted as one deafening bang after another rang out, bullets shattering glass.

Varen returned the gun to point at her. "It's at least as real as you are."

She clamped her mouth shut, setting her jaw.

He wanted a fight, she thought. He craved contention. His self-hatred had become a drug, an addiction he needed to feed. His lone source of perverse comfort in this forsaken realm.

Isobel's soul ached for him with that notion. He had given up on himself as well as her. But knowing that also provided her with a scrap of strength—kept her from fracturing into a thousand pieces as she faced him—because at least it gave her somewhere to start.

Remind us of who we are, Pinfeathers had said.

"This . . . this isn't you," Isobel whispered, rolling the Noc's words over and over in her head and choosing her own carefully. This time there could be no going back, no try again after the game over, if he pulled that trigger. "You aren't like this."

Varen held himself as steady as he held the gun. Seconds

ticked by, each one more unbearable than the last. Then, finally, relaxing his arm, he tilted the gun upward.

But the reprieve didn't last.

"Maybe you're right," he said, nestling the muzzle of the gun under his chin. "Care to find out?"

"Varen, *stop it*," Isobel snapped, her own anger spiking, mixing with the panic she could no longer restrain. She dared not make even a slight movement toward him, though. Not now that he held them both in the thrall of his black erraticism.

"That's just it. *I can't*," he said. "I can't ever stop. Even if I wanted to. It's always *just* too late when I'm ready."

"This isn't who you really are," Isobel insisted. "I know it isn't. And so do y—"

"How?" he asked. "How do you know *anything* about me? You don't. Not anymore. Because now I've become exactly what everyone expected. The only difference is that I've decided to stop fighting it. To fit the mold, so to speak. Isn't that what we're supposed to do in life? We've all got a part to play. Someone's gotta be the bad guy."

"I *do* know you," Isobel said. "You are gentle. You're kind. You care about what's important, what's right, even when no one else does. I've seen the real you, and that person—that beautiful soul—he wouldn't hurt anyone. Please. If you let me, I *can* show you that I'm real."

"You don't have to show me," he said, his tone turning mocking. "All you have to do . . . is promise."

Once more, he switched the gun's position, leveling its

barrel at her. He squeezed one eye shut, taking aim at her head. Though he stared directly at her, his gaze would not meet hers.

"Do you promise?" he asked.

"Varen, I never meant to leave you—"

"I said!" he yelled, and her heart stalled. He lowered his voice again, his tone suddenly soft, rational. "Do you promise?"

Yes, Isobel wanted to tell him. *Yes, I promise.* But was that the right answer? *Was* there a right answer?

She didn't know what to do, what to say. Even if she could shift their surroundings again, break through the constructs of his world, it wouldn't change his mind—it hadn't before in the courtyard of angels. He'd shut down completely this time. And if he could be counted as lost to this realm, then he was even more lost to himself.

Isobel didn't know of any way to combat that. How could she reach him when he wasn't even present?

Darkness there and nothing more . . .

Taking a step forward, moving before she even knew why, Isobel brought her forehead to the mouth of the gun. The sensation, cold and hard, reminded her of the last kiss Varen had given her, delivered to the very same spot just before he'd sent her over the cliff.

"I made you a promise once," she said.

She saw the cuff of his sleeve move when she spoke, the fabric stirred by her breath, and she knew he'd felt it, because his hand, so steady before, suddenly began to quiver.

"I tried to keep it," Isobel went on. "I tried, and I failed.

So I came back. I know you didn't think that I would. I know that's why you did what you did. On the cliff. Because you didn't think it was me. That I would find you again. I guess I failed you twice. But Varen, I never gave up. No matter what it looked like to you. I never did."

The anger in his expression began to siphon off as she spoke, transmuting into sorrow. His finger eased from the trigger.

"In your note," Isobel continued, "you said we would see each other again, and I never stopped believing that. I never stopped believing in you. After you showed me what I should have known already—that there's so much more to someone than can be seen on the surface—I couldn't *ever* give up on you. But . . . what about me? I'm not everything you thought I was either, am I? You said so yourself. Just now. So what if I *am* really me and not just a figment of this place? If you thought there was a chance, even a small one, that I *could* be real, tell me, would you still pull that trigger?"

Varen cringed. Withdrawing the gun, he spun away. He tossed the weapon aside, and at once it burst into a flapping crow. The creature squawked loudly, its brash voice and frantic flittering breaking Isobel's spellbound stare as Varen moved through the now-occupied classroom chairs.

Aside from her own chair and Varen's, each desk now seated a skeleton.

Books and notepads littered the desktops in front of them. Bony fingers held pencils, while empty eye sockets stared down at papers filled with unfinished writing.

Isobel recognized the skeletons by their clothing. These were her classmates.

Even Mr. Swanson's swivel chair held a skeleton, her teacher's familiar spectacles askew on his nonexistent face.

Dumbstruck by her altered surroundings, Isobel felt her blood freeze.

She found Varen again and watched in horror as he threaded himself through one of the shattered windows. The bird, cawing, shot through another.

A peal of warning bells sounded in Isobel's head as Varen straightened into a standing position on the ledge, opening his arms wide as though he, too, could fly.

She spurred herself forward, running, knocking aside desks, causing the skeletons to slump and topple.

She caught herself on the windowsill just as Varen tilted forward.

"No!" She grabbed for him, but the hem of his long coat only grazed her fingertips, fluttering in the breeze as again, he slipped out of her reach.

29
Time Out of Time

Below, the brambly treetops resembled legions of bony hands, outstretched and waiting.

Varen had not fallen into their grips, though. He hadn't fallen at all.

Boots firmly planted on the side of Trenton's brick facade, he stood perpendicular to the building, staring toward the garden of black arms.

Strong winds lashed at him, whistling as they assailed his impervious form.

Afraid he might disappear again, Isobel hoisted herself into the window frame. Broken glass crunched under her feet as she ducked through to crouch on the sill.

Battling gales slammed into her from every direction, as if conspiring to shove her from her perch. She hung on, but when her hair fluttered in her face, she lost sight of both Varen and the drop.

Maybe that was for the best, she thought, as she straightened.

Stiffening her body, locking her muscles, she thought back to all the calculated falls she'd taken in the past, the cheerleading aerials that had, more often than not, landed her squarely on her feet.

Isobel let go of the frame. She tipped into the open air.

The wind shrieked in her ears. The world blurred in her periphery. For an instant, she careened down, straight for those grabbing branches.

Then the school's brick siding rushed up to accept the step she'd gambled, and Isobel staggered forward. Landing on one knee, she caught herself, palms splaying flat to the rough brick surface of the building's exterior. She released the breath she'd held in reserve, along with her hope that this latest gravity-bending stunt wouldn't be her last.

On either side of her, like still pools of water, the school's windows gave off a mercury sheen. Detecting movement in the pane closest to her, Isobel turned her head and caught sight of Varen's pale reflection.

She pushed to her feet, turning in time to see him stride past her, moving in the direction that, seconds before, had led up.

As though in a trance, he trained his gaze on Trenton's four-spired bell tower, his gait even and graceful in that way that had always distinguished him in the hallways of Trenton.

Opening his arms out low at his sides, he ignored the winds that battered him, initiating with that single gesture the metamorphosis that came next.

The school's red clay bricks faded to alabaster, widening into stone slabs beneath their feet.

The windows elongated, narrowing like the slit pupils of serpents' eyes. Nets of black spread across glass panes that, as though lit by fire from within, burned with the same crimson glow as the horizon.

Varen walked on. A tremor shook the building, and with the low, rumbling groan of stone on stone, a pointed steeple emerged from between the bell tower's spires. Shaped like the head of a spear, the spire's spiked point telescoped far into the sky, piercing through the screen of clouds that rushed by.

Gargoyles, their grotesque faces fixed in toothy grimaces and open-jawed snarls, slithered out from every corner. Fastening lizardlike bodies to the wall, they swung their heads in Isobel's direction, glowering at her with glowing red eyes.

At once awed and paralyzed by the quaking beneath her, the transformation happening all around them, Isobel could not bring herself to move. She only stared as Varen drew to a stop in the middle of the tower's center window.

As he halted, the pane under him widened into an enormous circle. A round pedestal rose beneath Varen's boots, elevating him by a foot, and two ebony vanes sprouted sideways from the base. While one vane remained short, the other grew long enough to reach the sets of roman numerals that emerged along the disk's perimeter.

Like helicopter blades, the vanes wound around and around, passing one another in chaotic loops. A deep, steady grinding noise accompanied their race and joined with the rumbling just before it all died out, signaling the end of the tower's transmogrification.

A clock, Isobel thought. Varen had converted Trenton's

bell tower into a clock tower. Simultaneously, he'd transported them to his Gothic palace—onto the exterior of this grand castle sanctuary he'd conjured into being.

The next time the colossal minute hand swung in front of Varen, he stepped forward to board it. With balanced, even steps, he made his way down the length of the appendage as it swept the circumference of the clock's face.

Varen stopped at the hand's spade-shaped apex, and when its point swung past Isobel, their gazes again met.

His black stare both beckoned and dared, silently asking a single question: *Are you coming?*

Then the clock hand wheeled away, breaking their connection. Varen disembarked when the spade's point reached the twelve. Continuing forward, he entered the foggy drifts of clouds that coasted by.

Isobel urged herself after him, and now her steps came more steadily. Because she thought she finally knew what it was he was doing. He was provoking her, challenging her to join him on another ledge—another cliff.

We'll get our revenge, Pinfeathers had warned her. *Don't you forget that.*

The Noc hadn't been talking about Varen's revenge on *her*, Isobel realized. He'd meant Varen's escalating need to exact vengeance on *himself*.

And what better way to do that than to deny himself any chance of escape from the prison of his own mind?

Isobel arrived at the outer rim of the clock and waited. When the minute hand swung her way, she leaped aboard, throwing her arms out to her sides for balance. But she wavered anyway, managing the ride with far less grace than Varen.

Through the pane of the clock face beneath her, massive gears twitched and spun. The low clunking of the cogs vibrated through her entire body, reminding her how much of a dream this wasn't.

She jumped when the numeral twelve entered her view and, stumbling, her momentum carried her forward into the clouds and onto the spire.

When she looked ahead, she saw that, like another grim fixture of the palace's forbidding architecture, Varen now stood at the pinnacle of the horizontal steeple. Where one more step would have sent him plunging.

The Ultima Thule, Isobel thought grimly.

"I know what you're doing," she yelled out to him over the howling winds.

He glanced back at her. Though he said nothing, he lifted an arm, opening his palm toward her.

"You're trying to prove to me—to yourself—that it can't be done," Isobel went on, stepping forward. "That you can't be saved. That you don't deserve to be."

Venturing farther out, she took care to place one foot directly in front of the other, treading the steeple's tapering point as she would a balance beam.

Varen watched her without speaking.

Isobel kept her eyes fixed on him as well.

Though she refused to look down, spindly sideways

spires spiked into her lower periphery. Somewhere past them, a swirl of movement and the distant roar of waves alerted her to the presence of the white sea.

But Isobel pushed the thought of raging waters aside and, through the strands of her whipping hair, did her best to maintain focus on Varen's outstretched arm.

One inch at a time she shuffled nearer, and when she came close enough to place her palm in his, Varen's hand clamped like a trap, fastening tight around hers.

Isobel winced, but she did not try to pull free.

"After everything," she said, "I think I finally realize that . . . if you believe you can't be saved, then of course you're right. Because I can't force you to listen. And no, as badly as I want to—and Varen, I want to, more than you'll ever know—I can't be the one who saves you. Only you can do that."

A flicker of confusion knitted his brow, and Isobel sensed it was because he was trying to banish her with his will, to cause her to disintegrate like he had done to her astral form in the mirrored hall.

"But there is one thing that I *can* do," she whispered, twisting her hand in his fierce grip so that she could thread her fingers through his. She took his other hand too, and tilted her chin to find him scowling at her, his eyes stony but uncertain.

That uncertainty was the thing she'd been waiting for.

Because she needed only the merest of cracks in his fortitude, for his guard to lower for the smallest instant, in order to play her final card.

"I can prove to you that you're worth saving."

Isobel clamped down on his hands. In the same instant, she envisioned the clock face and the rows of bloodred windows shattering in unison.

A hundred thousand shards burst upward with an ear-splitting smash.

Transforming, the tinkling splinters became a throng of origami butterflies.

A hush of pink paper wings filled the air like the whispering of a million voices, loud enough to drown out the cry of the winds, the crash of the sea.

The butterflies swept toward them, funneling around the place where she and Varen stood, flittering to create a living curtain that sealed the two of them off—blotting out the tower, the steeple, the drop, the very sky.

30
By Horror Haunted

Varen tried to wrench free, like Isobel knew he would. But she was ready.

Holding him steady, she willed her butterflies closer.

When the throng followed her silent command, swooping near enough for wings to rasp against Varen's coat and snag loose wisps of her hair, she actually smiled.

Varen looked left and right, his confusion melting into disbelief.

Taking advantage of his disorientation—the distraction she'd created—Isobel concentrated fully on banishing Varen's sideways tower. In its stead, she pictured the first place she could think of.

The butterflies dispersed to reveal an enormous room with a gallery walkway lining its upper level: the warehouse where the Grim Facade had taken place.

They stood together in the very spot she'd imagined, on that patch of dance floor where they had shared their first last kiss.

Gathering into clusters, the butterflies merged into people and things.

Caught in mid-sway, leather-clad boys and bodice-laced

girls stood all around, frozen in tableau as though, for them, time had stopped. Leaning this way and that in the fog-machine haze, the goths held wrists aloft with bracelets and studded cuffs, their masked and painted faces half-lost in shadow, half-illuminated by the eerie blue-green glow spilling from the stage.

All eyes were closed, including those of the singer, who cradled her microphone between hands gloved in lace, her face lined with false stitching like a rag doll's.

Though her lips were frozen, the girl's siren voice, far away and muffled, rebounded through the hall. The unintelligible lyrics of her song joined with the low, echoing moan of a cello.

Isobel stood as motionless as the spectral goths.

She wanted to grant Varen enough time to acclimate to their altered surroundings. To check with himself to be sure *he* had not been the one to cause the shift.

Then, unable to hold back any longer, she released his hands and, touching his cheek, drew his gaze back to her.

Varen's scowl had returned, but his anger seemed false now, just another mask meant to hide the doubt he was still too afraid to let go of.

If it was more *proof* that he needed . . .

Grasping his collar with both hands, Isobel rose onto her tiptoes. She tugged him down to meet her halfway and, pressing her lips to his, delivered the softest of kisses—a shadow of the one they had shared in this exact spot on Halloween night.

Varen tensed. He gripped her upper arms, as though bracing himself for the worst.

He did not return the kiss. But, Isobel noted, he did not try to pull away, either. And as he allowed the connection to linger . . . and linger, the cold loop of that silver ring searing her lips, Isobel decided to count it a win.

Only when the metal warmed to match her own temperature did Isobel lower herself onto her heels again, ending her kiss.

As difficult as it was for her to relinquish her hold on him, she let her hands fall to her sides.

For a long time, Varen only stared at her in that unreadable way that always left her feeling scorched from the inside out. She wanted so badly to whisper her own *I told you so*, but she held her silence, letting her persisting presence speak for her.

Memories make better weapons than words, Pinfeathers had said, and Isobel hoped that, for both her and Varen's sakes, the Noc's final scrap of wisdom would prove as true as his warnings.

Lifting his hand at last, Varen grazed hesitant fingertips along her jawline, his touch tentative and unsure, as if he were testing the realness of a polished window to see if the glass could truly be there. Or if it was all just air.

"You shouldn't be here," he murmured, and Isobel remembered that he'd uttered these same words before, in that forever-ago moment.

Was he still testing her? Waiting for her to repeat old

lines and reveal herself as yet another hallucination, another nightmare waiting to self-destruct and eradicate the remaining fragments of his sanity?

"You're right," Isobel replied, resting a hand on his sleeve. "I shouldn't. But that's why I *am* here. Because . . . neither should you."

He frowned, pain flickering across his face.

"It can't really be you," he said. "I know it can't."

"Why not?" Isobel asked, offering him a rueful smile. "I mean, don't you think it's at all romantic, the idea that love could conquer death?"

Alarm flashed in Varen's eyes. He snatched his hand away as if she'd burned him.

When he began to back away from her, Isobel knew she'd struck a chord. *The* chord?

Of course Varen would recognize the question; he'd once posed the same one to her. On that night she'd stayed late to help him clean up after Brad and the crew had trashed the ice cream parlor where he'd worked.

And maybe it was the fact that Isobel had returned Varen's own words to him, instead of repeating something he'd heard her say in the past. Or maybe the combination of all her efforts had finally compounded, cornering his convictions. Whatever the reason, Isobel could tell that Varen's room for denial had at last been obliterated.

He *knew* she wasn't a dream.

But as Varen's eyes widened, his shock morphing into terror, her burgeoning sense of relief quickly drained away.

As he continued his retreat, the singer's muddled crooning died out. The light from the stage flickered, creating a strobe effect. The phantom goths began to move, heads turning in Varen's direction. Slanted slits appeared on every cheek, oozing blood.

"That's not possible," Varen mumbled, shaking his head. "*You* are not possible."

Isobel frowned, confused by his reaction. She reached for him, but as she did, another girl's arm shot out from the crowd, snatching Varen by the sleeve. He wheeled away, jerking free, but another hand latched onto his arm.

When he looked to the girl who clutched his sleeve, instantly the figment became the bleeding and bedraggled Black Dress Isobel.

"It's time to go," Isobel heard the dark double say. "Come with us," echoed an identical voice as another duplicate stepped to his side.

Isobel started forward, but the surrounding goths shifted to block her path. She shoved against them, but they refused to budge. Varen's thoughts were taking over again, building in power to overthrow her own.

But this time Varen had lost the control he'd exhibited before.

"Varen!" Isobel shouted, trying to insert herself between the barricades of bodies that separated them.

"Don't worry, Izo," came a male voice, one Isobel had not heard for a long while, but one she knew well all the same. "I got this."

Another arm appeared, reaching out from the blanket of shadows behind Varen. Its heavy hand fell on his shoulder, and the connection sent a ripple through the scene Isobel had created, causing it all to rupture.

The goths and the doubles and the stage and the walls all dissipated to vapor. The dance floor became pavement.

A nighttime blackness took the place of flashing lights, pierced only by the single streetlamp that sprouted from the leaf-strewn parking lot.

Even in the darkness, though, Isobel could discern whose hand was tightening its grip on Varen's coat.

Dressed in his letter jacket, his frame once more hulking and rigid—strong, unlike the last time she'd seen him—Brad Borgan, Isobel's ex, made quick work of tossing Varen backward into the side of the Cougar that materialized just as Varen collided with it.

Slam!

"No!" Isobel screeched.

Varen collapsed onto hands and knees. Behind him, the words YOU'RE DEAD FREAK now blazed in reverse on the Cougar's driver's-side door.

Isobel broke forward in a run, but she wasn't fast enough to stop Brad from sending a sharp kick into Varen's side.

"Stop!" she yelled, but the faster she charged, the farther the scene withdrew, the pavement elongating in front of her.

A pair of walls rose on either side of the road as it became a familiar stretch of hallway.

Brad grabbed Varen again and, hauling him to his feet,

swung him straight into a row of blue lockers. Varen's head bounced on the metal.

With the echo of the sharp *bang*, everything shifted yet again.

The walls smoothed, turning mauve as the ceiling dropped, pitching up in the middle. The fist fastened around Varen's collar changed too, swelling in size, its sleeve cuff bleeding gray.

A slatted door materialized to block Isobel's view and her path. She skidded to a halt in front of it as, simultaneously, walls lifted on either side to seal her into the dark and narrow space of Varen's closet.

"You're never going to *wake up!*" boomed Varen's father.

Isobel shoved against the door, but it only rattled in its tracks.

She shouted to Varen that none of it was real. But a low hum like a roll of thunder rose to nullify her voice.

Helpless, Isobel could only stand and watch as a horrible scene she had witnessed once before began to replay itself.

31
Reversion

"Look't this waste—your goddamned life."

The muffled roar continued, underscoring the deep voice as it resounded through the attic.

Isobel recognized the words. Mr. Nethers had spoken them the night he'd stormed up to Varen's bedroom—the night before everything had spiraled out of control. But now the phrases were jumbled.

Did that mean Varen was reliving this moment as *he* remembered it? Or was this all just a series of snapshots? A flipbook of old wounds reopened, each with a single pinpoint stab?

Isobel shoved her fingers between the wooden slats, trying to snap them, but they refused to even bend. Through the gaps, though, she saw Mr. Nethers fling Varen away, his face splotched deep red in a furious scowl.

"What did you do?" Varen's father demanded, his voice slurring.

Varen retreated from the figure. When his back met with the wall, the room tipped, slanting downward on his end.

Teetering, Isobel threw her arms out to brace herself. She tried again to call out to Varen, if only to remind him she was close. But no sound could penetrate the pervading rumble.

None but that damning voice.

"What did you do, you screwup?" Mr. Nethers railed, even as his face began to loosen, drooping, stretching like taffy.

The figure took one stilted step toward Varen, and the movement sent several flesh-colored globs to slap the floor and those polished black shoes.

The thing that had been Mr. Nethers snapped its melting fingers once, then again before pointing to the falling drips.

"Wherts thrs merss?" it blubbered.

The rumble thundered louder now, building into a deafening roar.

"Yer judst lik yer fadther," the figure bellowed.

Varen covered his ears and squeezed his eyes shut. He opened his mouth in a noiseless scream.

The windows shattered.

Glass flew inward—then halted to float in midair.

Other objects in the room began to rise and hover with the glinting constellation of shards. Isobel's hamsa necklace rose too, the charm lifting to float in front of her.

The blending of worlds. Not again. Not now.

Isobel snatched the amulet. Clutching it tight, she rammed one shoulder against the slatted door. When it didn't give, she tried again. One final attempt sent the door flying back with a crack.

She spilled out of the closet and landed hard on the floor. Sudden stillness boomed, almost as deafening as the rumble.

As she pushed herself onto hands and knees, Isobel saw

white chalk writing beneath her. She read the words that had been scrawled over every inch of the wooden boards—the walls and ceiling, too.

In backward letters, the phrase YOU'RE DEAD FREAK repeated itself a thousand times.

Though the attic retained its downward slant, the room had again become the cramped and cluttered space in which she'd discovered Scrimshaw under the sheet, the windup doll in the corner. The same place she'd endured the deathwatches . . .

"Varen?" she said, her whisper loud as a scream in the uneasy quiet.

No answer.

Isobel climbed to her feet. She didn't see him anywhere.

Managing the sloping terrain with bent knees, she groped past the tables and draped chairs that, despite the floor's incline, hadn't budged.

She stopped when something crunched underfoot.

Amid the sooty shards of the oil lamp Scrimshaw had smashed lay the white wire birdcage, its little door open, skeleton keys strewn about like scattered bones.

Nearby, one of the keys speared the undone heart-shaped padlock, its decorative handle turning on its own, around and around, like the key affixed to the doll's spine.

The doll . . .

Isobel whipped her head in the direction of the window. Next to the fallen dressing screen, the antique chair sat in the same spot as before, though its occupant—the life-size figurine bearing Madeline's likeness—had vanished.

Through the open window, black cliffs cut a jagged line through the red horizon.

Isobel spun to face the fireplace. She scanned the room but saw no sign of the empty suit—nor any other trace of Varen's father. Only the towers of boxes, the dust-covered bric-a-brac, and, sitting in the corner where she'd found the reassembled Nocs, his head bowed, hands still plastered over his ears—Varen.

Quickly Isobel sidled between the violet armchair and the desk.

Half sidestepping, half sliding, she maneuvered down the slope, then dropped to her knees beside him.

As she did, a distant pounding rose from outside the door, growing louder. And louder. Varen lowered his hands and looked up, a sheen of sweat plastering his hair to his forehead. His eyes, sunken and bloodshot, darted to the scratch-marred door.

A quiver ran through him as the echoed banging focused into the heavy stomp of climbing footsteps.

"Ignore it," Isobel urged, clasping his face between her hands. "Pretend it's not real. That's what you told me . . . remember?"

His hollowed eyes cut to hers. "Tell me," he muttered, "how did that work out?"

The pounding ceased. The knob rattled, the door clattering in its frame.

Quiet buzzed again then, so that the soft scrape of metal on metal—the key rotating in its padlock—filled the room.

Then it, too, stopped.

Isobel heard Varen draw a breath. Felt him tense. A beat passed.

Wham!

Something enormous struck the door—hard enough to cause the wood to crack.

Isobel stood. Positioning herself in front of Varen, she opened her arms to shield him as he had shielded her the night of the Grim Facade, when he'd pulled her into the warehouse's cramped office. When whispering shadows had danced under the door.

Wham!

"Go away!" she screeched.

A third bang sent the door flinging wide.

But . . . there was nothing. No one.

Isobel glanced back to Varen, who stared past her, his gaze fixed on the empty door frame as if the horror he'd been expecting might still emerge from its dark perimeter.

"There's nothing," she whispered, returning to his side. "It's over. Please. We need to go. I can take us, but we have to—"

"You were never supposed to see," he muttered in a monotone, his eyes glazing over as they remained on the doorway.

Isobel clamped her mouth shut. Though she assumed he meant the original encounter with his father, the flesh-and-blood version of this incident, a part of her wondered if he could simply mean *everything.* All his inner terrors that had been exposed to her. All his darkest thoughts revealed. His secret fears brought to life.

His deepest desires personified . . .

"You ruined everything," Varen said. "You know that, don't you? I was going to fade out. Disappear. I *wanted* this. . . ."

Keeping quiet, Isobel glanced down at her hands knotted in her lap.

"Then our names got called together," Varen continued, "and from that point on, we were both doomed. Because being with you made me start to want something else—to buy into the hope that I could actually have it. You. I couldn't seem to get you out of my head. And by then, that was a dangerous place to be."

Isobel shifted toward him. "Here I am," she said. "I'm here. Aren't I? Aren't you?"

Rolling his head against the wall to look at her, he sent her the barest of smiles. But it did not reach his eyes.

"Why *are* you here?" he said. "You have to know I can't go with you."

Isobel's heart contracted, pain squeezing her gut. Now that she'd finally found him, now that she'd broken through, he was only confirming her greatest new fear. His voice seemed so certain, too. So resigned. And yet . . .

"You can't?" she pressed. "Or won't."

"Wherever you came from," he said, his focus returning to that open door, "you should go back. Before she comes."

Though his words confused her, they angered her even more. Isobel clenched her fists, imagining the door slamming shut. When it fell closed with a slam, she knew Varen would not try to fight her anymore, to block the dreams she imposed over his.

"You *know* where I came from," she said. "And I know about the bond. But I also know that there has to be a way to break it. And if you believe I'm me . . . that, despite everything, I came here to find you . . . then you also have to believe that we *can* break it. We'll *make* a way. Together. Do you hear me?"

Isobel's frown deepened when he said nothing. But she'd come too far to allow him to persuade her this was hopeless. That *he* was hopeless.

Concentrating, Isobel pictured the room righting itself. She felt the floor seesaw back into place, leveling out beneath them.

Next, she evaporated the layers of dust. The sheets tore themselves free like magicians' cloths and then vanished, taking the furniture with them. The writing on the walls faded out, and the boxes evaporated.

Taking care to restore Varen's bedroom to the way she remembered it, she filled in as many details as she could recall.

Varen's black-and-white Vincent Price poster unrolled on one wall. His narrow single bed emerged from another, sliding them both forward on the small throw rug that materialized beneath them.

Books flipped from the floor onto his shelves, while the collection of toppled bottles righted themselves in the fireplace. Isobel imagined their study materials laid out around them.

Last of all, as she unfolded her legs in front of her, she

conjured Varen's copy of *The Complete Works of Edgar Allan Poe*. The book appeared between her hands—open—its pages blank as she tried to recall the poem Varen had been reading to her before his father had torn into the room, interrupting the one moment that might have changed everything.

She thought the blankness of the pages might be okay, though. Her purpose was not to re-create the moment precisely—only to remind Varen that it had transpired. Or rather, to remind them both of what had *almost* transpired.

"This is when it happened," Isobel said. "Right in the middle of your reading to me."

Varen didn't move. But knowing that he was listening, she pressed on.

"I know you think I'm talking about when everything fell apart—when it all went wrong. But I'm not. . . ."

She scooted nearer to him, settling again when her shoulder met with his.

"I'm talking about the moment . . . when I fell in love. With you. Officially."

She saw his hand resting on his knee—the one bearing his onyx, V-stamped class ring—twitch.

"When you were reading, I was listening to you, but at the same time . . . not. I heard your voice. Felt it. But the thing is, you had my hand, like this."

Isobel gathered Varen's hand in hers, pressing it between her palms as he'd done. The hard corners of his ring pressed cold and sharp into her palm.

"And I remember being so torn," she continued. "Split between never wanting you to stop reading and wishing you'd shut up and kiss me." Isobel allowed herself a small laugh. "I think it must have been on your mind too."

He didn't speak, but he turned his head toward her again.

Isobel tightened her grip on his hand, and her own went numb from the connection.

"Sometimes . . ." Isobel paused, then started again. "At least once every hour of every day . . . I find myself wondering how things might have been if . . . if your parents hadn't come home early. If we *had* kissed then. Do you ever wonder the same thing? If any of this would have turned out differently?"

A beat passed in which he said nothing. Then, suddenly, Varen's hand tightened around hers. "Read me something?" he said. The sound of his voice, the question itself, startled her.

Isobel's eyes fell to the pages open in front of her as, slowly, the white space began to fill. She scanned the text as it formed, recognizing the poem by its title as one of Poe's.

She remembered Varen mentioning this piece several times, though she'd never once read it. This had to mean two things: that Varen knew at least a portion of it by heart, and that *he* was the one making it appear.

Drawing a shaking breath, Isobel did the only thing she could do. She began to read out loud. To him.

"*It was many and many a year ago,*
    In a kingdom by the sea,

> *That a maiden there lived whom you may know*
> *By the name of Annabel Lee;—"*

Varen clenched her hand tighter, but she didn't look up and she didn't stop reading.

> *"And this maiden she lived with no other thought*
> *Than to love and be loved by me.*
>
> I *was a child and she was a child*
> *In this kingdom by the sea;*
> *But we loved with a love that was more than*
>   *love—*
> *I and my Annabel Lee—*
> *With a love that the winged seraphs of Heaven*
> *Coveted her and me."*

Isobel stopped there. Because that was where the words dissipated.

She frowned, feeling the thump of her heart grow heavy while she waited. The right-hand page remained bare. Could it be that was all he recalled of the poem?

Then Varen spoke, picking up the lines from the memory that hadn't failed him, after all.

> *"But our love it was stronger by far than the love*
> *Of those who were older than we—*
> *Of many far wiser than we—*

And neither the angels in Heaven above,
Nor the demons down under the sea,
Can ever dissever my soul from the soul
Of the beautiful Annabel Lee."

He stopped there. Pulling his hand free of hers, he rose.

As he did, the boards beneath them began to loosen, softening into . . . sand?

Isobel gasped when the support at her back vanished, and she would have fallen if not for the hand that caught hers just as a surge of warm water rushed in around them.

When Varen pulled her to her feet, sunlight—blinding— broke through the dissolving walls, illuminating the crystalline waters that now enveloped her legs.

Varen drew Isobel to him, and she saw that his clothes had changed. In place of his long coat, he wore an old-fashioned charcoal waistcoat and, beneath it, a white stiff-collared shirt, sleeve cuffs rolled to the elbows.

Isobel pressed her hands to his chest, stunned and entranced by how much the timeless style seemed . . . right. Almost as if she'd always known him this way.

At her legs, she felt clinging folds of fabric much longer than her tattered pink party dress. She looked down to see that she now wore an off-the-shoulder gown the hue of white wine. Small burgundy bows held gathers of the fine material, pinning it around her in elegant drapes.

Touching her brow, her fingertips found a crown of velvet-soft flowers.

In a flash, she remembered the statue she'd found next to Varen in the courtyard and realized he'd transformed her into the living version.

A new wave surged in around them, and as it did, Varen swept her up and out of the water's path. He swung her in a slow circle as the water rolled and crashed, frothing white.

Isobel's heart swelled with the sea. She felt weightless in his arms.

Enwrapping his neck, she leaned in close, laughing as the spray of water sprinkled their skin and beaded in his dark hair like minuscule diamonds.

Pastel-yellow rays sliced through the puffy pink-and-blue-bellied clouds that gathered overhead. Straight as arrows, the light shot down to meet the glittering sea.

Perched at the zenith of a high rock, Varen's castle cut a striking outline.

No longer menacing but regal, the ivory fortress—all turrets and waving green banners—seemed to watch over them, as if awaiting their return to its grand halls.

Isobel clung closer to Varen, holding tight to him and to this moment that felt so much like a fairy tale.

Varen tilted his head toward her, his lips brushing hers as he spoke.

"'For the moon never beams, without bringing me dreams of the beautiful Annabel Lee.'"

Isobel's smile returned. Finally she got it.

The poem. He'd taken them right into the middle of

it—this ballad that felt as if it told the story of a previous life. One they'd shared together, just like this.

"'And the stars never rise, but I feel the bright eyes of the beautiful Annabel Lee.'"

As though taking command from his words, the daylight faded and the sky swirled sherbet. The sun sank into the shimmering sea, giving way to a lunar glow that swept the dreamscape in tones of deep blue and shining silver.

Tilting her head back, Isobel watched the sky fill with innumerable stars.

When she looked to Varen again, she was so startled by the sight of the two jade spheres gazing back at her that she nearly let go of him.

"Varen. You—"

"Shut up," he said, tilting his head as he leaned in, "so I can kiss you."

32
Dissever

He pressed his lips to hers.

Immediately Isobel's hands went to his face.

She held him there, too afraid he might try to pull away. Or that she'd wake up somewhere without him.

Gently, as the tide rushed out from under them, Varen set her down. But he did not break the kiss; encircling her waist, he drew her in closer.

Isobel rose onto tiptoes, bare feet sinking into the pliant sand.

With another rolling surge, the warm waves returned, swelling higher this time, past their knees.

Varen's silver lip ring teased as it caressed, lulling Isobel's mind as it beckoned the rest of her toward abandon.

Watching him through the lashes of lids that had dropped on their own, Isobel found herself locked in a bittersweet battle, torn between never wanting this moment to end and needing to look into his eyes again. To be certain she hadn't imagined the return of their polished jade hue.

She pressed her palms to his chest but could not bring herself to push him back. The fever of his kiss, the strength of the arms that held her to him—the power of the spell he'd cast over them both—won out.

Giving in, Isobel permitted her thoughts to float off without her. Her lips matched his painstaking pace, trading brush for brush and stroke for stroke.

Varen lifted both hands, hooking them under her jaw. His thumbs grazed her cheeks as he took his turn to hold her in place.

He kissed her as if doing so was the one thing that could keep him, all of this, from unraveling—again—into pande- monium.

She knew how he felt. Lost and found. Freed and captive. Calm and desperate . . .

She knew, because she felt it too.

So she let the fabricated dream continue, trying to keep the nagging truth at bay for one more moment. Then another, and another . . .

But when the water's warmth began to fade, when the current grew stronger with each sigh and heave—when the sensation of pins and needles crept into her awareness, grow- ing strong enough to drown out the sensation of his lips—she had to stop.

Isobel froze. Her eyelids lifted.

Grimacing, Varen parted the kiss that had already ended.

He pressed his forehead to hers, and Isobel relished the sensation of his hair catching in her lashes. She saw that he held his own eyes shut, clenched tight, and she knew his fear had returned.

That had to be why the water had turned cold so quickly. Why, in the passing seconds, the darkness surrounding them had grown more absolute.

Already the tide had risen to mid-thigh. But . . . he couldn't still be doubting her, could he?

"Open your eyes," Isobel urged, tucking silken bits of hair behind his ear, though the strands wouldn't stay. "Please?"

"You'll leave," he murmured, his voice hoarse with the emotion he was trying hard to keep bottled.

"Never," she said. "Nevermore," she corrected in a whisper.

She stayed silent for the next few seconds, watching him, giving him time to trust.

When Varen finally did open his eyes, he kept them fixed on her hamsa charm. She could feel him holding his breath as he grabbed her shoulders and squeezed.

Isobel ignored the pain of his fingers digging into her flesh, because she knew what he was trying to assure himself of. That when he looked up, he would not find a dead girl staring back at him.

Then his clear green gaze flicked to Isobel's, igniting a smile that sprang, involuntarily, to her lips.

"There you are," she said, taking in the sight of those twin emeralds, whose color she could detect even in the dark. "I knew I'd find you."

Varen scowled in pain as though her words had cut him. But she could feel relief, too, in the breath he exhaled as he pulled her against him.

With fierce strength, Varen's arms wound around her, and he clutched her tightly. Isobel surrendered to his hold and, laying her head to his shoulder, yielded to the rush of bliss that she could not have fought off if she tried.

But even in his embrace—on the other side of fulfilling her promise—she knew they both had to be thinking the same thing. How, as beautiful as this was, as real as it seemed, it wouldn't last. Couldn't . . .

"Please," she said, pushing back against him gently, enough to find his gaze again. "Say you'll come with me."

"Where?" he asked. But he sounded so uncertain.

"Home," she said with a nervous laugh. "Where else?"

His brow knitted in confusion. "Home," he repeated, as if the word was foreign to him. "You mean . . . heaven?"

The question, as startling as it was sobering, stole her already faltering smile.

She let her arms slip away from him.

Though it was clear that Varen now believed she was real, that he understood she'd come here to get him, it suddenly became equally clear that somehow, he still thought she was dead.

And if he was asking about heaven, did that mean he assumed they *both* were?

The memory flashes. The writing on the wall. Varen's horrified reaction after her words about conquering death— now it all made sense.

He still believed that he'd killed her. It was the only way he'd been able to reconcile Isobel's presence in the dreamworld.

"Varen, I'm . . . ," she started, but as a look of dark concern clouded his features, her voice stalled in her throat and she thought better of trying to explain.

If keeping the truth to herself meant he would follow her more readily, if it gave her a better chance of luring him out of this realm—of convincing him that, with her, he *could* leave its boundaries—would it not be better to go on letting him think she was . . . what? A spirit sent to collect him?

An angel, she corrected herself, remembering the pair of statues standing watch at the altar, the stone seraphs populating the courtyard. The bust of the helmeted warrior girl stationed above the purple chamber's doors. A *guardian* angel.

"Tell me you trust me," Isobel said, peering into his eyes again. "Do you?"

His gaze narrowed on her, and he gave no answer. She could tell he knew there was something she wasn't divulging. Something he was missing.

Another wave bowled into them, hard enough to knock Isobel off balance. Varen reached for her and held her steady. They watched the wave as it tumbled to the shore, crashing there with a low boom, hissing as it spread its way up the long bank of sand.

The tide had begun its nocturnal conquest of the beach, giving the illusion that, though she and Varen hadn't moved, they'd drifted farther out.

"Are you doing this?" Isobel asked.

"No," he said, jaw flexing, his focus still on the shore.

A beat passed before he spoke again. "It's not over . . . is it?" he asked, looking down at her.

Isobel grasped him by the sleeves.

She bit her bottom lip and dug deep for what to say, wishing she could tell him that the nightmare *had* ended, that they'd reached their forever and there wasn't anything left to be afraid of.

For one blissful instant, it had certainly felt like they had.

"Do you trust me?" she asked again.

Varen watched her with concern, brow knitted, his stare suddenly sober, searching. Slowly, he nodded.

"Then come with me," she said, taking his hand. "And don't let go."

Gathering her soaked skirts in her free hand, she tugged at Varen.

He didn't ask any more questions, and when Isobel started in the direction of the shore, he followed behind.

Black waters lapped at them, pearly pockets of white moonlight mottling the surface that seemed to lengthen as they headed toward the beach. Step after sinking step, Isobel trudged ahead, but the coast drew no closer.

Dread gripped her, but she pressed on. She squeezed Varen's hand, peering back at him once, and then again when she noticed him staring at something.

She whipped her head forward and saw what it was that had stolen his attention.

Eddies of white fizz left by the crashing waves swirled

and spun on the shore. Emerging from the froth, a slender figure lengthened upward.

Sea foam became glowing gossamer. The delicate swathes of material unfurled in folds and drapes, clinging to the specter's distinctly feminine form.

Haloed in a glow that shamed the moon stood Lilith, her beetle-black eyes watching them through the shield of her transparent shroud.

Isobel felt Varen freeze when, gliding toward them, Lilith waded into the ocean, her train of veils dragging behind her, rising to float like trails of smoke.

The demon opened ivory arms over the water, and as she did, the ocean surged up to Isobel's neck and Varen's chest.

Isobel bounced on the ball of one foot to stay afloat. Keeping the demon in her line of sight and her hand fastened to Varen's, she tried to think of somewhere to take them, some way to shift them away from *her*.

But she couldn't make a door in the water. And with the waves now swelling to her chin, threatening to swallow them both, she couldn't concentrate. She couldn't—

Isobel sank below the next wave, and this time, her foot found no purchase. Plunging deep, through the place where the sea floor had existed moments before, she released Varen in a burst of panic.

Crying out, gulping seawater, she scrambled for him, groping blindly through the murk.

Her hands passed through empty water while the current

carried her away and the sodden skirts of her heavy dress dragged her down.

She threw her arms out, kicking to propel herself up toward the swiftly rising surface.

Something soft brushed her naked shoulder. Whirling, she reached for the hand that wasn't there and found herself in the midst of countless luminous white veils. They wound around her throat like tentacles.

Unleashing a muted, bubbled scream, Isobel thrashed against the weblike material.

Her lungs, now empty, burned for air.

Yanking a fistful of veils free, she felt a faint snap at the nape of her neck.

Isobel released the wad of gauze and scoured her throat for the hamsa, nails clawing her own flesh.

Gone.

Spinning in search of the amulet, in search of Varen, she quickly lost her sense of which way led up and which led down.

Then, like a beacon, a pale face appeared in the gloom. Netted by a screen of black hair, it floated toward her.

But it was not Varen's.

This face—waxen, skeletal, hideous—belonged to a monster.

33
Yet Unbroken

A pair of wasted hands reached for her, their curved black nails like barbed hooks.

At the center of the creature's sunken eyes flashed two pinpricks of light.

Isobel flailed to get away, but with lungs pleading for air and muscles numb from exhaustion, her efforts came weaker now.

Closing in on her, the demon curled a hand almost tenderly around Isobel's bare throat, claw tips scarcely pricking the nape of her neck.

As Lilith's emaciated form coasted to a slow-motion stop, her loose ebony hair rushed around them both. Innumerable black threads intertwined with the clouds of floating veils, tickling Isobel's shoulders, blocking her surroundings from view.

Isobel saw no sign of Varen. Only inky tendrils, billows of white, and straight ahead, that pinhole gaze.

Like a spider preparing to wrap its prey, Lilith pulled her nearer.

Isobel strained in the demon's grasp, yearning for the strong, gentle grip of Varen's hand. But it never came, and she knew he'd lost her just as she'd lost him.

The demon's pale and shriveled lips peeled back to display a needle-toothed grin.

Death would come next. Isobel had no doubt. And there was no stopping it, or what would happen after.

She would become a Lost Soul, like Reynolds, bound body and spirit to this realm—to Lilith—for eternity.

Gwen had been right, and, enemy or not, Reynolds had been right too.

She'd never stood a chance.

Cold and caressing, the creature's knuckles trailed Isobel's cheek, brushing over her scar before sliding up to her temple. There, the wraith's talons wove their way into her hair, causing Isobel's crown of flowers to dislodge and drift off.

Though Isobel tried to wrench her head away, the demon tightened its grip at the back of her skull, holding her face to its own.

With lungs now threatening to explode, Isobel ceased her feeble side-to-side twists. She waited, anticipating the piercing pain of those spiked teeth, the ripping sensation of having her throat torn out. The clawed hand that would contract and crush her windpipe.

When none of those things happened—when *nothing* happened—Isobel's yearning for air became an all-consuming need, and it occurred to her that delivering a swift death was not what Lilith had in mind.

The demon wanted to watch her struggle, to drink in her final throes as she drowned slowly in its clutches.

But she'd come so far. Survived too much. Risked everything . . .

Isobel kicked her legs again, though no longer in an effort to escape. Now she hoped only to fend off the fog of unconsciousness that had begun to steal over her, lulling her toward the last bat of her eyes, since her final breath had already been taken.

Varen, she thought, her fingers wrapping the sinewy wrist of the hand that held her. Where was he?

Shhh, a woman's voice hushed in her head. *Sleep now, so you can awaken safe in your new bed. Forever and always home . . .*

Of course, Isobel thought dimly, lids drooping.

The demon's plan was to seal her away. That open tomb. Halloween. The blue marble crypt. Lilith's own vault.

Total darkness. Complete and everlasting.

The very fate Isobel had threatened the demon with in the ballroom.

Gritting her teeth, Isobel summoned one final burst of strength, attempting a second time to tear the creature's grip away.

She succeeded only in ripping more of the clinging silk.

Shhh, the voice in her head shushed. Then, out of nowhere, the same voice began to sing.

> *"Hush-a-bye my little bird*
> *Hush-a-bye my child"*

Gwen's lullaby. Isobel recognized the melody immediately.

"*I have lost a love so great
Oh, woe is me.*"

So, Isobel thought, her body slackening, *that's what the lyrics meant.*

The singing turned to humming then, one melody to another, and Gwen's lullaby morphed into Madeline's. Varen's.

Isobel's lids fell closed at last under the weight of the soothing refrain. Her arms drifted open, her body preparing to indulge in the lethal inhale it so wanted to take.

Don't you ever tire? Scrimshaw's voice echoed over the humming.

Too late to turn back now, Isobel heard Gwen say.

Good-bye, cheerleader . . .

Good-bye, Isobel thought, just as her back collided with something solid. The ocean floor?

No, she thought when she felt an arm loop around her waist—pulling her in close against a body.

The moment seemed so familiar. Like it had happened once already.

Isobel opened her eyes to slits. As her mind attempted to make sense of murky shapes, garbled sounds, and hazy colors, she wondered if it was now her turn to relive old memories.

Pinfeathers, pulling her from one side of the veil to the other . . .

Then her clouded brain registered a look of rage contorting the demonic face that still hovered inches from her own. Lilith's pitted eyes weren't fixed on her anymore, though.

They were locked instead on whatever—whoever—had taken hold of Isobel.

Isobel grabbed the hand gripping her, feeling for claws, but she found strong fingers instead.

A glint of silver sparked in the fringe of her vision.

Was that . . . ? Her arm shot out, and as soon as her fist closed around the veil-wrapped hamsa, the demon's hands unlatched from her like loosed manacles.

Recoiling, Lilith's face fractured down the center, spilling clouds of black and violet ink.

The creature opened its mouth in a soundless shriek, palms pressing to its rupturing face.

Then, before Isobel's lungs could collapse, forcing her to inhale the swirling ink, the arm encircling her wrenched to one side—transporting her.

A sharp splash crashed in her ears as she felt her body depart suddenly from the crushing ocean, hurtling through a wall of water into . . . a room?

Inhaling with a rattling gasp, lungs filling to the brink, Isobel fell, tumbling hard with her savior onto carpet.

A hand grabbed her by the shoulder, and the world swam by in a whir as she was thrown onto her back. She caught a brief glimpse of glittering crystal shards, violet flames, a rolling ceiling of smoke.

Then Varen's face, drenched and shocked, appeared over her.

Jet hair streaming, electric-green eyes wide and darting, he scoured her form, his expression lit with a mixture of panic and disbelief.

Isobel turned her head away, coughing and sputtering. Behind Varen, the wall undulated and rippled, still liquid at the point through which they'd entered until it snapped solid. As she drew in breath after breath, Isobel took in the sight of ornate gold frames everywhere, each encasing its own fractured glass.

He'd transported them into the mirrored corridor from that morning's dream.

Along with the green mechanic's jacket and her own bedraggled, sodden pink dress, Varen's usual black clothes and coat had returned.

Reflected in every splintered shard of glass, Isobel saw herself and Varen, their pale, drenched faces repeated into infinity by the cracked mirrors that bounced them from one wall to the other and back again.

"You have a reflection," Varen said between gasps, his tone accusing.

"We," Isobel wheezed as she sat up, one hand tightening around the hamsa still in her fist, the other clutching his sleeve, "need . . . to leave."

Varen's expression changed, his bafflement melding with something that just might have been hope.

"You're alive," he breathed. "We both are."

But before Isobel could answer, a crackling sound drew their attention to the frame-filled wall.

Tink went one of the glass shards as it leaped free of its mirror.

A trail of water poured from the crack.

Tick. Tack. Crack.

More shards sprang from their frames, each releasing its own stream. Trails of water flowed down the wall, soaking the carpet.

"Get up," Varen ordered as he shot to his feet and, grabbing her, pulled her after him.

Ting. Another shard flicked into the hall, this one unleashing a forceful horizontal spurt. The leaks kept coming, with more frequency now, springing to life with hiss after hiss.

Then the whole wall bowed, emitting a low groan. The legions of reflected Varens and Isobels began to warp with it, ready to buckle under the pressure of the ocean that seemed to have followed them.

The demon, Isobel was sure, would not be far behind.

Tugging her after him, Varen started down the hall at a run, hurrying them toward a gilded archway that filtered into being as they neared the end of the hall. Had he made the escape route for them? Of course, he must have. But where was he taking them?

Isobel fumbled after him on rubber legs, her feet heavy as clubs.

"Wait," she pleaded.

Pausing, Varen turned to her.

"What are you doing?" he asked as, with quivering hands, Isobel strung the hamsa's chain around his neck, trying to keep her fingers steady enough to knot the chain, since the clasp had been broken.

"There isn't ti—"

The walls at the opposite end of the hall blew out their mirrors with an earsplitting crash.

White rapids gushed into the hallway, turning it instantly into a canal.

The torrents raged toward them with a deafening roar, proving Varen's curtailed warning true: There was no time, no place, to run.

Grasping Isobel close, Varen ducked her head into him.

He swung her away from the approaching floods, shielding her with his body just before the booming waters bowled into them both.

34
Darkness and Decay

WHOOOOOOOSSSSSSSSSSHHHHHHHHH.

Cringing, Isobel clung to Varen.

But the floods did not tear them apart as she'd expected.

Instead she and Varen remained standing, unaffected by the wall of water that became something else the moment it met with their joined figures.

Ash.

Cascading past them in a billowing cloud, the dust settled across the hall with a hiss.

A tinkling sound drew Isobel's gaze upward.

Through the haze, she saw the ash-coated chandelier above them sway.

Then it fell, plummeting straight for them.

Isobel dropped her head. She held tightly to Varen, shutting her eyes in anticipation of the impact that—again—never came. She felt only the spray of dust and knew that *he* must be the reason why.

Just as he could create—the gilded door frame, the corridor, this palace, the seashore—Isobel knew that Varen could also abolish. He had to have destroyed the rapids and the falling chandelier.

With his awareness had returned his control. But was it strong enough to pit against Lilith's?

Isobel pushed back from Varen, blinking cinders from her wet lashes. She scanned his collar, where the dust had already begun to seep into his soaked clothing, turning to muck. Her fingers finding the charm she'd managed to secure there, she tucked it beneath his shirt.

Comforted by the knowledge that he was protected, that as long as the hamsa remained on his person, Lilith could not lay a hand on him, Isobel allowed her aching shoulders to sag.

She glanced up to Varen, meeting his gaze, his green eyes grave and searching.

For one heartbeat, she let herself bask in his complete return to lucidity. To himself.

But the brief flash lasted no longer than the instant it took for Varen to turn his head and look away from her. Toward the far end of the hall, from where the waves had rushed them.

Reluctantly Isobel shifted her gaze in the same direction.

Flecks of ash swirled through the devastated hall, providing the only barrier between Isobel and Varen and the white demon who, like an ivory idol, watched them from less than ten yards away.

Behind Lilith and through the ragged mouth of the wrecked hall lay an endless assemblage of trees, a hazy silver light glowing through their prison-bar trunks.

Lilith's face, unveiled, stark and whole once more, showed all the emotion of an ancient ceremonial mask. Like the walls around them—*like this entire world*—her features had become caught in a state between beauty and ruin.

Shadows nested deep within the hollows of her high cheekbones. Dark veins marbled her snowy skin, and the masses of her wild hair clung to her soaked figure in straggly strands.

Sodden veils spilled in weighty folds from her, clinging close to her narrow and gaunt frame.

The demon's eyes, no longer sunken pits but enlarged inkwells, leaked great streaks of the same violet-black substance that had spilled from her cracked skull in the depths of the ocean.

"You forget," Lilith said, a slick of glossy liquid sliding from her mouth to drape her chin and drench her pristine shrouds, staining the gossamer bright violet. "You *both* forget," she went on, her voice low and throaty, thick with the heavy fluid, "that you cannot evade what lies within your own mind. You cannot run from yourself."

Varen shifted in front of Isobel, planting himself between her and the demon, who started toward them, the tips of her taloned feet poking out from the hem of her dragging robes.

"When the light at last dies, as it *always* dies," she said, "darkness *will* devour. Be it that darkness which is your own"—pausing, Lilith locked her gaze solely on Varen, lips curling, spreading to display a jagged, stained grin—"or someone else's."

Her eyes darting, Isobel checked the cracked and dusted mirrors.

She saw her own and Varen's reflections—mere shadows beyond the filmy layer of ash.

But just as Isobel had noted once before, in the dream-world parlor of Varen's house, the demon's figure cast no reflection. Now, though, Isobel noticed something else, too.

The mirrors did not reflect the Gothic, ash-strewn hall-way where they stood, either. Instead the murky glass showed another hall, one lined with familiar lockers, their cobalt color only just discernable through the clinging grime.

Trenton?

"Darkness devours because it *must*," Lilith said, stopping at a distance, and Isobel knew it was because of the hamsa. "And so there *is* no escape."

Isobel's gaze flicked from one wall of mirrors to the other, recalling how Varen, in her dream, had transformed the north hall into *this* corridor. Did that then mean that all three of them currently occupied a space that ran parallel to that portion of school?

Raising an arm, the demon pointed one black-nailed finger at Varen. "A talisman may guard you for a time, but it can no more liberate you than can this foolish girl, who is as doomed as you."

"Don't listen," Isobel whispered against Varen's shoulder, huddling closer, her thoughts racing to formulate a plan before the demon could inflict them with her own.

"Relent now," Lilith ordered, "cast off the amulet, and I will allow her to live, to return to her world. Refuse, and her soul is as forfeit as yours."

"Varen, *think*," pleaded Isobel. "There isn't going to be a world to return to if she gets her way. And if she can't be stopped, why go to such lengths to keep us apart? To make you believe I wouldn't come? To let you go on thinking I was dead—that you had killed me?"

"You know I cannot be destroyed," Lilith called to him. "I *am* destruction. And as I am, so now are *you*. You *will* be the cause of her death."

"If the bond can't be broken," Isobel countered, her words fast and low, "then why try to barter with my life? Varen, if she *could* kill me herself, she'd do it. She's been trying this whole time. From that day we met for the project at the library, when I first read about her in your sketchbook. Ever since you started seeing me in your dreams. But she can't. Not on her own. For some reason, she can't. That's why she sent the Nocs after me. That's why she—"

"The tie that binds us *is* indissoluble," Lilith said, louder now. "You belong to me. At least"—she paused, her smile growing wide—"until death do us part."

Varen glanced over his shoulder at Isobel, and in that jade eye, she could read what he was thinking, what he was considering, and she knew it was exactly what the demon wanted.

"It isn't true," Isobel blurted, speaking faster, her own voice rising in volume. "Nothing she says is true. Varen, you *know* that."

"How else can it end?" he asked her, sorrow sweeping his grime-smeared face.

"Not like this," Isobel said, taking his hand in hers. "Not here."

With that, she whirled and began to run, hurrying toward the gilded archway through which she could see another chamber of Varen's palace—a grand foyer filled with standing candelabras, their milky tapers lit with violet flames. More candles lined the steps of the curving marble staircase within, one that wound up to an unseen floor.

"Ask yourself," Isobel heard Lilith bellow after them, her voice echoing down the corridor, "where can you go that you will not bring me?"

Isobel felt Varen's hand twitch in hers, his hold loosening. She tightened her grip as, together, the two of them shot through the doorway and into the foyer, which presented them with not just one route, but many. Too many.

Multitudes of elaborate, sprawling staircases split off in every direction. They led up and down, overlapping, endless flights of steps crisscrossing and intertwining up and away into infinity.

But stairs weren't what they needed. What they needed was a *way out*. A link back to reality.

A door.

What had Reynolds once told her?

Make a door, he'd said. *When there is no way, you must make a way.*

Isobel conjured an image of her bedroom door in her mind— an entry point she *knew* would work because it had before in the woodlands with Reynolds, and again earlier with Scrimshaw.

At her beckoning, Isobel's doorknob materialized in her grip.

Twisting the knob, she shoved, rushing through the opening and pulling Varen after her.

Her feet met with carpet. She saw her bed with its cubbyhole headboard, her ransacked dresser and messy closet.

Once inside with Varen, she released his hand and sent the door slamming shut with a bang, blocking out the grand stairwell, the armies of flickering candles, and that horrid image of Lilith standing in the gold-framed archway.

Backpedaling into the foot of her bed, Isobel frowned at the quiet that seemed somehow too intense.

Something was wrong. She felt it as a buzz—an electric charge infusing the air.

Turning, Isobel scanned the pink walls, eyes flying around her room.

Everything appeared just as she'd left it. Normal. Unreversed.

And yet, when she'd made the door just now, when she'd opened it, she had not found her things floating in midair. Instead her belongings lay strewn about, scattered across the floor where they must have fallen before, when she'd left Danny in the hallway of the real world. When she'd entered the castle turret with its spiral staircase.

It didn't make sense. Before, when a portal opened between the worlds, objects always rose.

Isobel glanced at Varen to see him staring, transfixed, into her mirror. Reflected in the glass, through the dark square of her bedroom window, beyond her white curtains and the fizzing screen of silent static were . . . the Woodlands of Weir.

Impossible. They'd crossed into reality. Hadn't they?

Isobel swung to face her bedroom clock. It read *6:17* in brilliant blue numbers that scrambled, then steadied.

No, she thought.

Returning to the door, she ripped it open to see the gold-framed archway, the foyer, and the candles all still there, the scene missing only the veil-draped, ink-smeared figure of Lilith.

Suddenly Varen was at Isobel's side. Again he took her hand.

"This way," he said, pulling her back into the foyer. Isobel followed, grateful to know that *he*, at least, had an idea of somewhere they could go.

Varen hurried forward to a descending set of steps flanked by two gilt candelabra, their pronged torches held aloft by the arms of two angels bearing Isobel's features, their sightless eyes wide open.

Rushing past the statues, Varen took the stairs fast, rattling down them with Isobel in tow.

Glancing back at the angels, Isobel saw them turn their heads to watch them go as bleeding slits opened in unison on their cheeks.

Varen swung around the curve of the staircase, then halted, causing Isobel to collide with him.

Below, she saw what had made him stop.

A plain flight of steps descended to a cramped and familiar landing, one encased by tightly set walls.

Dead ahead, dark-paned windows showed Isobel and

Varen's reflections, their images pale and filthy, only just recognizable.

They were at school, at Trenton, in the exact stairwell
where Reynolds had first appeared to Isobel that morning. In
fact, they stood in the precise spot where *he* had stood, their
forms now as disheveled and ash-dusted as his had been.

Isobel checked over her shoulder and saw only the door
leading into the deserted third-floor hallway.

And yet, though the darkened windows reflected her and
Varen, the stairway they showed was the grand and Gothic
one they'd just left.

Then, through the dim glass, Isobel saw Lilith's streaked
form turn the corner to loom at their backs.

But she *knew* Lilith couldn't have a reflection. And suddenly the truth hit her.

The windows, like the mirrors in the hall, were showing
what lay on the *other side*, on the plane parallel to whichever
world they currently occupied.

That meant that they really were in school, just as they'd
really been in Isobel's room moments ago. Somehow she and
Varen *had* re-entered reality.

The worlds were blending. The merging that had nearly
taken place on Halloween night, the collision Reynolds had
warned her about from the beginning—it was happening now.

Or had it already?

No, Isobel thought. It couldn't have. Otherwise, Lilith
wouldn't still need Varen. She wouldn't have commanded
him to remove the hamsa. The demon's work wasn't finished.

And that meant they still had time.

Taking the lead, Isobel tugged Varen after her as she charged down the stairs, past the window through which she saw Lilith pivot away from them.

Isobel didn't stop to question why the demon would not try to follow them but tore around the next corner and down again, retracing with Varen the path she'd already taken once that day.

When their feet parted from the bottom step, though, the scene before them shifted once more. They halted to find themselves at another bottom step, one belonging to an ascending staircase, its steps wide and marble.

At the top of the landing, the twin angels they had passed before watched them still, their heads craned in the same positions as if they had known the whole time that Isobel and Varen would reappear soon enough.

But if they had run in a loop, ending up on the landing they'd just departed from, wouldn't that mean . . . ?

Suddenly it dawned on Isobel why she'd seen Lilith revolve in place. Varen, it seemed, must have reached the same conclusion as well, because, yanking her forward, he started pell-mell up the steps.

Unable to keep herself from looking back, Isobel glimpsed the eerie pale light of the demon's aureole in her periphery. Then, as Varen dragged her over the last step, beyond the angels, who swiveled their heads to keep the two of them in sight, she saw through the strands of her own straggly hair the demon climbing the stairs after them, seeming to float.

They backed away, and Isobel wanted to run again. But if all the stairways were similarly looped, threaded through the fabric of reality, then what route wouldn't take them straight back to this point?

To *her*.

Looking left, Isobel saw the gold-framed arch and the hall of mirrors. Except now the hall no longer terminated in the woodlands, the place where she'd first thought to retreat. Rather, the walls faded into those of Trenton's north hall.

When Isobel looked right, she scowled to see the familiar set of blue double doors that led to the gym.

Before she could change direction and start toward them, however, Isobel's back met with something solid.

With a low and scraping *sssssskkkkkrrrrrr*, she felt that something move.

Whirling, Isobel found herself trapped in Reynolds's bleak and steady black stare, his dark form uncloaked, his sharp face unmasked.

His twin swords unsheathed.

35
Deadlocked

Reynolds elbowed Isobel, hard, and sent her sprawling.

She yelped and, skidding backward on the polished floor, slid to a halt in time to see metal flash.

One curved cutlass sparked violet-silver in the candles' glow as it whipped toward Varen, its sharpened tip halting just short of his throat.

"I could end this all right here," Reynolds said, speaking quickly as he glared at Varen down the length of the blade. "And I know that if I pledged to you the girl's safe return to her world, you would not try to stop me by bending this realm against me."

Isobel's mouth dropped open. She sat stock-still, shocked by Reynolds's sudden appearance, even more stunned by his words, their meaning only halfway soaking in before Lilith interrupted.

"*Gordon,*" came the demon's voice, sharp and full of warning. "You know what will happen should you dare."

"A variation of the same events that transpired the last time I severed your ties to their reality," Reynolds replied. "The two realms separate. Useless to you, the boy awakens as one of us, another Lost Soul for your collection. You, in the meantime, return to lying in wait, infiltrating dreams, searching out new prey through which to create a new link."

"There would be one difference *this* time," Lilith said, the talons of her feet clicking against the marble as she stepped onto the landing between the angels. "I would know the face of my enemy. And what to do with him."

Though Reynolds's blade remained at Varen's throat, his dark eyes flicked toward Lilith. "You have taken pains to make the price of my treachery quite clear, and while the threat of spending an eternity entombed holds all the horror you intend it to, you forget one thing. For some time, I have watched you from the deepest shadows of this world—those cast by your own hubris. Mired with the deceit you inflict upon yourself and others, they have hidden me well. It would not take a wise man, who has witnessed what I have, to conclude that your plans for me will change little depending on what action I take next."

"Thank goodness for your sake, then, dear Gordon," Lilith said with a laugh, a demure smile curling her lips, "that you are no more wise than you are a man."

Though Isobel couldn't be certain, she thought she saw Reynolds flinch. When he tore his gaze away, looking sharply back to Varen, she had to wonder if he did so in an effort to hide the momentary slip in his impervious demeanor.

Isobel could never tell when it came to Reynolds. But she was done with guessing, where he was concerned. She could no longer afford to wait and find out what it was that made him tick.

Taking her chance, the only one she thought she might have, Isobel pushed to her feet just as Reynolds dipped the tip of his blade beneath Varen's collar, nicking flesh as he hooked the chain of the hamsa.

In two fluid strides, Reynolds positioned himself behind Varen, guiding the sword up so that its blade looped the necklace and rested against Varen's bare, bleeding throat.

Isobel's hands rose of their own accord, knotting themselves into a single, useless ball. She held them close to her chest, where she could feel the rapid thrum of her heart.

"Your choices, limited though they are, do appear rather clear-cut, do they not?" Lilith asked Reynolds. "Yet you hesitate. And that is what betrays *you* as being the one lost to self-deception. For, despite what you have convinced yourself of, you have not *truly* decided at all in whose corner you will stand . . . have you?"

There it was again. Isobel saw it. The smallest twitch on those hawkish features.

"Whether you have been consciously aware of it or not," Lilith continued, "you have been waiting. Playing sides while biding your time to see whether the girl might achieve the upper hand, might defy your estimation of her once again and, somehow, against all odds, best me. The prospect of your release, I am certain, holds enough allure for you to indulge in such an ambitious gambit. I almost don't blame you. She *is* tenacious. But now we've arrived at the moment of truth. You stand to lose your wager, as she has yet to live up to your lofty expectations. What will you do?"

Isobel's gaze found Varen's. He watched her through the mussed strands of his ashy hair, and like so many times before, he needed only his calm jade eyes to communicate a warning to her.

Hold off, he seemed to be telling her, and it took every ounce of self-control Isobel possessed to remain planted. To do nothing. To merely watch and endure.

"What a predicament indeed," Lilith went on. "For if you kill the boy and destroy the link, it will prove quite difficult for you to honor your vow to return our dearest Isobel to her so thoughtfully preserved world. Especially since, despite your unique and enviable ability to traverse the realms, which you have managed to keep hidden from me for so long, you would not be able to do so from the place where *I* would send you. Even if you did manage the feat, you would still have me to contend with upon your inevitable return. But . . . should you do me the kind favor of removing the boy's talisman and eliminating the small barrier currently standing between me and what is rightfully mine, you would then have something to grant you immunity, wouldn't you? To purchase a small sliver of the time you have perhaps not had quite enough of." As if to illustrate her point, Lilith took a single step forward, her increasing nearness to Varen and the hamsa causing her already sunken features to tighten on her skull. Fresh strands of ink leaked from her eyes and mouth, retracing old paths.

"At the very least," Lilith continued, "procuring such a trinket *could* facilitate another friendly chat between us. Another heart-to-heart to determine whether or not you do still have any value to me, and if I am quite as transparently devious as you proclaim me to be. Kill him, though, and you ensure a sentence served in vain, since we seem to agree I will only begin again. This time without the hassle of your obstruction."

Isobel burned to move. Thinking on Lilith's words, she had to wonder why Varen continued to stand idle. Hadn't Reynolds himself admitted that Varen could turn the dreamworld against him? That he had the ability to change what was happening? So why didn't he try?

More important, Isobel thought, wavering where she stood . . . why didn't *she*?

"While it *is* truly fascinating," Lilith said, her crooked smile twisting into a sneer, "how you would all unanimously stake the fates of your souls upon one another in this manner, without even realizing you are doing so, your shared delusion that there *is* a way out, amusing as it is, tries my patience. We have reached an impasse, and one of you must now make your move so that I may know mine."

"I could kill him," Reynolds said, "and still take possession of the charm."

"No!" Isobel cried, starting forward.

Without looking away from Lilith, Reynolds pressed the blade closer to Varen's neck, and Isobel halted, sneakers squeaking.

Varen kept his eyes locked on hers, asking her again through that pointed glare to stand down. But *why*? He couldn't truly believe Reynolds was telling the truth about taking her home, could he? And even if he did, how could he allow Reynolds to end his life, to enslave him eternally to the demon Isobel had fought so hard to save him from? Hadn't he believed her when she'd promised him they would find another way?

"You would rather start an unnecessary war between us," Lilith asked, her voice softening, "one that you know you cannot win, than accept my offer of peace?"

"Can peace be made with a demon?" scoffed Reynolds.

"Oh, Gordon." Lilith sighed. "Creature of few words that you are, I doubt you would bother to ask if you thought you knew the answer. So I will respond with a question of my own. Can a weak, puerile, lovesick girl offer you better?"

When Reynolds glanced in Isobel's direction, she sent him an entreating stare.

"Reynolds, please," Isobel said, her voice small and shaking. "You told me there *was* a way. If that's true, if there *is* a way to free Varen, then there has to be a way for you—"

"*Enough*," Reynolds barked, and, hardening his expression, he returned his gaze to Lilith.

Several moments passed in which no one moved. Then . . . *click*.

The snapping of the hamsa's chain echoed loudly through the silent foyer when Reynolds jerked his sword forward, freeing the charm from Varen's neck.

Lilith laughed, her mouth stretching into a too-wide smile as, with one unceremonious shove, Reynolds sent Varen to the floor at the demon's clawed feet.

Released from her self-inflicted paralysis, Isobel scrambled to Varen's side and dropped to her knees.

Wrong, she thought as she threw her arms around him, glancing back at Reynolds to catch sight of his captured prize—the hamsa—its chain now hopelessly wrapped about the hilt of his cutlass.

Varen had been wrong to hold off. To ask her to do the same.

She'd been wrong too. Wrong ever to have believed Reynolds again. Wrong not to have acted when she'd had the chance. And wrong, especially, not to have heeded Pinfeathers's warning about him when the Noc had been right about so much else.

"Predictable, Gordon," cooed Lilith as she drifted to stand a mere foot from Isobel and Varen, those black eyes turning down on them both, "but a commendable decision, all the same."

A flash of bright white sparked from overhead. Isobel looked up to see Reynolds raise his arm.

The opal embedded in the hamsa glinted again as Reynolds reared back with his blade as if preparing to—

"Get down," Isobel heard Varen snap the second before he yanked her to the floor with him.

Singing high, Reynolds's sword sailed over their heads, spinning handle over tip as it spiraled straight toward—and then into—the center of Lilith's chest.

36

Out All

Impaled, the demon arched her back.

A beat of silence pulsed.

Then, with head thrown back, Lilith emitted a low and grating croak.

The demon grabbed for the blade, trying to wrench free the sword sunk deep in her chest. Upon contact with the metal, however, her hands shriveled and crumbled, flaking to nothing.

The croaking became a choked wail as ink bubbled up from her mouth. Spilling over in streams, dark liquid fell to splatter the floor.

Isobel flinched when she felt droplets sprinkle her face. Transfixed by the horror unfolding in front of her, though, she could not tear her gaze away. Not even as Lilith's head lolled forward, sending forth more of the black bile to pool at her taloned feet.

Isobel felt Varen shift at her side. Edging backward, he pulled her with him, away from the expanding bath of blackness.

Lifting her streaming chin, Lilith glared after them through the wild mesh of her hair, focusing her bleeding black eye sockets on Isobel.

"*You,*" Lilith gurgled, taking one jerky step after them, then another. "*Yooouuuu.*"

Varen tugged harder, sliding them both along the smooth marble.

Though Isobel heard him say her name, she couldn't shake herself from the trance induced by the depth of those two empty hollows. Her mind remained fixed on the demon, who, faltering with her next step, collapsed to the floor, soaked veils slapping the marble.

"*I will fiiinnd you,*" rasped the demon, her haggard voice dropping low, going guttural. "*Rot your heart before your own eyes.*"

Still Lilith continued to advance on them, using elbows to drag herself forward. The sound of the sword hilt scraping stone sent spikes of terror through Isobel's gut, but still she could not snap herself out of her spellbound stare. Not until a pair of white-spattered boots stepped in front of her, blocking her view.

"Go," came Reynolds's voice. "Through the blue doors. For now, the worlds blend and part at your whim. Use it to your advantage. Go somewhere safe. Somewhere hidden."

Isobel blinked up at the tall figure standing over them.

But Reynolds's piercing stare was not aimed at her. And neither was his command.

Rising, Varen brought Isobel to her feet.

"W-wait," Isobel murmured through numb lips, but Reynolds had already turned toward Lilith.

Taking Isobel's hand, Varen tugged her in the opposite direction.

"Wait," Isobel repeated, louder this time, and she wondered why neither of them seemed to have heard her. Or were they choosing not to listen?

Before Varen could drag her any farther away, Isobel snagged Reynolds's sleeve.

"Come with us," she managed to blurt when his head snapped toward her.

Reynolds glared sternly at Varen, ignoring Isobel altogether. "Keep her safe," he said. "I have bought us only time. And precious little at that."

"I said," Isobel snapped, pulling harder on his sleeve, her anger at being snubbed helping to jolt her back to her senses, "come with us."

Reynolds scowled, but when he glanced to where Isobel gripped him, the knit in his brow softened.

"I'll not be far behind," he assured her, this time meeting her gaze full on.

Isobel hesitated. Then, deciding to believe him, to trust him . . . she let go.

"*GOOORRRRDOOOOOON,*" Isobel heard the demon howl.

Isobel looked to where Lilith lay like a spider in tar, all limbs and joints. Her body, reduced to bones, crackled as she moved, her sword-pierced rib cage dripping sludge.

"Gordon is dead," Isobel heard Reynolds say in a monotone, his words echoing through the corridor as he placed the tip of his other sword beneath Lilith's putrefied chin, drawing her hollow eyes to his. "As I shall continue to wager you very soon shall be."

Isobel kept her gaze on the two figures as Varen drew her toward the blue double doors Reynolds had told them to take.

CLUNK came the sound of the push bar, loud in Isobel's ears as Varen collided with it.

He pulled her with him beyond its boundaries, and as they shot through to the other side, Isobel's eyes flickered up. Countless figures now populated the endless crisscrossing network of stairs — most of them cloaked, all of them men.

Lost Souls, Isobel thought, meeting the stare of one who, unlike the others, had channeled his focus on her instead of Lilith's writhing form.

Then the door swung shut, blocking the sight.

Music boomed, bass thumping the floor beneath the soles of their shoes like a thundering heartbeat.

Colored lights blazed. Streamers and balloons — red and pink. People everywhere.

As Isobel's vision adjusted, she slowly began to register the faces surrounding them as . . . familiar.

Boots squealing on glossed hardwood, Varen skidded to a stop, halting Isobel with him.

Though the music pounded on, those dancing nearest to them lowered their raised arms.

"Oh my God," said someone nearby, inciting the unanimous withdrawal that came next.

Bumping and jostling into one another as they retreated, Isobel and Varen's classmates formed a wide circle around the two of them.

Smiles fell. Faces paled.

And as the shock of their sudden presence rippled its way through the gymnasium, through the attendees of Trenton High's annual Valentine's Day dance, it dawned on Isobel what had just happened.

They were back.

37
Neither of Ingress or Egress

No one spoke. No one moved.

For five fleeting seconds, they all just stared.

Then from the midst of the crowd rose a sweater-sleeved arm. Its hand held aloft a cell phone. Flashing bright white, the device snapped Isobel and Varen's photo.

When a second flash sparked, Isobel whipped her head in that direction, her damp, clotted hair swinging.

A third flared right in front of her face. Then a fourth from behind.

Even over the throbbing music, Isobel could hear the digitized clicks of the cameras, the pings and chirps of phones receiving alerts.

With the rise of the discordant chimes came murmuring and pointing fingers. Isobel heard their names repeated again and again, growing louder with each utterance as the shell shock in the room began to thaw.

"Move!" a voice roared above it all, and Isobel turned, her heart thrumming.

Scanning the sea of cell phone lights, she searched for the source of that brash voice, recalling in the same instant the text she'd sent earlier before crossing into the dreamworld.

At first Isobel saw only the wide eyes of the cameras.

Then, wrestling between a pair of clinging couples, some-one broke through.

"Isobel!" Gwen shouted, throwing off the hood of the oversize black-and-white checkered sweater Isobel recognized as Mikey's.

Slung across one shoulder, Gwen wore her patchwork purse, and in one hand, her own cell glowed.

Isobel had just enough time to register the ash-smeared forms on its screen before Gwen rushed her.

Isobel released Varen's hand to catch her friend.

"I'm glad you're alive," Gwen said, her voice high, pinched with fear. "So I can *kill* you."

Though Isobel wanted to return Gwen's fierce squeeze, to tell her how relieved she was to see her, her thoughts swarmed around the photo she'd glimpsed on Gwen's cell.

Had someone texted the photo to her? Or had the snap-shots already splashed their way across the Internet and all of social media?

How many more minutes—how many more *seconds*—before those images found their way to Varen's parents? To *her* parents. To the police . . .

She and Varen couldn't afford to get caught, to be hauled off in different directions. Not now. Not without first sever-ing their ties—*Varen's* ties—to the other side. To Lilith.

Taking Gwen by the shoulders, Isobel parted their embrace.

"Gwen, listen to me. We have to—" She stopped when she noticed a flitter of shadows skirting the room.

Gwen had clearly sensed it too, because her eyes went to Varen, who stared at the ceiling.

Looking up, Isobel saw what held his attention.

A dark haze had begun to wrap the mirrored surface of the lazily spinning disco ball. Sharp faces, distorted, broken, and jagged-toothed, appeared between the smoky tendrils, causing the globe's grid of projected light to flicker again.

"Thaaat's . . . not a special effect," Gwen said, "is it?"

Snapping from his trance, Varen moved. He snatched Isobel's hand, and she, in turn, grabbed Gwen's.

In one fell swoop, the legions of cell phones winked out, screens going black.

A screech of feedback sliced through the music, its piercing shriek killing the thudding bass and vocals.

Everyone ducked their heads and covered their ears.

Pulling Isobel and Gwen after him, Varen ran toward the glowing exit sign and the double doors beneath—the only barrier between them and the parking lot, which contained, Isobel hoped, Gwen's car.

Girls in heels backpedaled from their path, shoes clattering while boys in dress shirts peeled away, everyone giving them a wide berth.

The colored lights dimmed, fluttered, and snapped out, plunging the room into darkness.

Screams rose, followed by an earsplitting crash.

Through the coarse material of Varen's mechanic's jacket, Isobel felt debris pelt her shoulders. She looked back to see Gwen's stricken face, pale pink in the red glow of the nearing exit sign, and behind her, lying in shambles on the cleared floor, the obliterated disco ball.

Though Isobel no longer saw the Nocs, she knew they were there. All around them. All around everyone.

Suddenly the blazing fluorescents burst on; someone must have tried the main lights. One after the other, each fixture burst with a loud *pop*. Showers of sparks and glass rained down into the renewed darkness.

"—got a gun!" Isobel heard someone shout as people hit the floor all around her, covering their heads. Covering one another.

No, she thought. *No no no.*

"Isobel?!"

Her head swung toward the panicked cry.

"Isobel!" boomed the voice a second time, and as the emergency lights kicked on, Isobel saw him. Her father.

His head bobbed above the others, his gaze darting through the confusion before homing in on her.

Then her dad started running, dodging through the groups and around the couples as they scrambled past him, all of them hurrying in the opposite direction. Trying to get away.

Close behind him, Isobel spotted Principal Finch's bald head. Mr. Nott's glinting glasses and salt-and-pepper hair, too.

Even from a distance and with so many people dashing back and forth between them, Isobel could still mark the change that overtook her father's expression the moment he laid eyes on Varen.

Rage. Hate. Fury.

Terror.

"Isobel!" her dad shouted again, the sheer panic written across his face causing a landslide to take place inside of her. But even as she ached to stop, to run to her dad and throw herself into his protective arms, she kept her hold on Varen's hand and allowed him to pull her to the doors.

As she moved, she kept eye contact with her dad, doing her best to project a silent apology. For this. For everything. And whatever happened next.

But then another man rushed between them into the center of the room, blocking Isobel's view of her father. It was the police officer Isobel had seen that morning, the one who was assigned to Varen's missing-person case. Detective Scott.

Gun drawn and held low to his side, he halted atop the emblem of Henry the Hawk.

"LMPD," he shouted at them. *"FREEZE!"*

CLUNK came the sound of the door's push bar, and, yanking hard, Varen pulled Isobel and Gwen past him, through to the other side.

Isobel staggered out into the open, but the soles of her shoes did not meet with hard pavement.

Ash, soft and silent, absorbed her steps.

Trees and darkness greeted her instead of cars and street-lamps.

Swinging back toward the school, Isobel saw no door, no gym, no cop. Only the familiar black chasm she'd encountered before when she'd crossed through the veil.

"What just happened?" Gwen panted beside her. "What's going on? Where are w—?"

Hundreds of coils of violet smoke poured through the black opening, whisking in every direction.

Taking on their bird forms, the Nocs screeched. Caws filling the air, they began to circle around the three of them. Then they morphed yet again, from crows to smoke, before solidifying into ghouls.

"Run," Varen commanded, as pair after pair of buckle-lined boots landed in the dust, sending up plumes of white.

38
Shrapnel

Clutching Gwen's hand again, Isobel turned to go, but she found their way barred on every front as more and more Nocs landed in the dust.

Wafting high, the unsettled ash became smog, its haze thick enough to obscure the emerging figures and turn them to silhouettes.

Though Varen had told them to run, short of creating another door, there was nowhere to go. And what door *could* deliver them from these creatures, whose attachment to Varen enabled them to follow him anywhere?

At least here in the dreamworld, Isobel reasoned, she could *see* her assailants.

Hissing and whispering, the Nocs inched closer, their bodies clinking and clattering as they jostled one another. But as they bared their claws, drawing tighter, Isobel began to note a difference in their demeanor.

In her past encounters with the Nocs, they had always laughed and jeered among themselves, sharing in some mutual and heinous mirth.

Pinfeathers, in particular, had displayed a penchant for an especially dark brand of humor. His malevolent glee, Isobel recalled, had been interrupted only by intense emotions like fear or rage.

Or love . . .

Of course, Isobel didn't have to guess which emotions had triggered the shift in *these* Nocs, not one of which smiled or snickered.

Instead they sneered and glowered, their sharp, broken faces fixed in glares of hatred.

We are *hurt,* Pinfeathers had said to her in the park. And only now, as the creatures stared past her, *through* her, to their source—Varen—was she able to fully comprehend what the leader of Varen's Nocs had meant.

Isobel would not be able to fight these Nocs, let alone defeat them, like she had with Scrimshaw. There were too many to fend off with blows or dreamworld tricks, and despite her track record of landing lucky punches, Isobel knew she was unequipped for this battle.

"What *are* they?" Gwen asked, her voice trembling as hard as her hand in Isobel's. "Please tell me this isn't real."

"They can't hurt you or me," Isobel said. Huddling nearer to Gwen, she hoped her words—the only remotely comforting ones she could think to offer—were indeed still true.

Varen opened his arms wide and splayed both hands, as if that might somehow force the creatures to retreat.

The action only drew them nearer.

Gwen clung to her harder as Isobel fought a rising tide of helplessness. Then her racing thoughts latched on to what she'd just told Gwen. About their being protected.

"Varen," Isobel said, pressing her back flush to his. "The Nocs. They couldn't harm me before. Even when they tried. None of them could. Because of you. Because they come *from* you, and in your mind, you wouldn't *let* them. Because you cared for me. About me."

"Don't take this the wrong way," he said, "but if you have a point—"

"They can't get to you unless you let them. Like you wouldn't let them get to me."

"*Weak,*" whispered one of the snarling Nocs.

"*Worthless,*" snapped another.

"Surprising as you may find it," Varen replied, his voice as doleful as it was dry, "I somehow doubt they share the same affinity for me."

Isobel's heart stammered a beat at this response and she scowled, arrested by how much Varen had just sounded like . . .

Breaking free from Gwen, Isobel rushed to stand in front of him. Though she saw no sign of Pinfeathers's presence, no evidence that the Noc could have somehow rejoined with Varen, she now found herself wondering if the two had ever truly been separate to begin with.

"Don't you see?" she said, gripping him by the arms. "That's what I'm trying to tell you."

"*Screwup,*" came another hiss.

"*Waste.*"

"Ignore them," Isobel urged. "Tune them out. Focus on me. On what I know you know in *here.*" She pressed a hand against his chest—his heart.

"I can't fight them." He shook his head without looking at her. "And I can't send them away with a thought. Believe me, I've tried."

"You don't have to fight," Isobel said. "Not when they only have as much power as you give them. These things answer to *you*. To your deepest thoughts. Your unconscious desires. Please, say you understand."

"I'm afraid I do," she heard him mutter, his eyes at last shifting to hers.

"I need you," Isobel said through gritted teeth. "She is losing and she knows it. Why else would she send them?"

"Oh, I don't know," he said. "Trouble letting go?"

"*Hey.*" She gave him a stiff shake. "You are *mine*. So don't you dare let her win. Do you hear me?"

"If anything will help," he said with a sad smile, touching her cheek, her scar, "that might."

Panic clenched a cold fist around Isobel's heart. She started to speak again, to remind him once more how much she loved him. But she didn't get the chance.

The Nocs converged on him.

Cut off and thrown back, Isobel plowed into Gwen, who caught her and held her tightly.

"*Varen!*" Isobel screeched, struggling to free herself as the Nocs tore into their prey.

39
Redoubled

Though Isobel continued to fight against Gwen, her actions grew weaker with every passing second, enabling Gwen to pull her away from the carnage that, by this time, had already accomplished the worst.

Dying as quickly as it had begun, the chaos of noise and movement, of shrieking and slashing, subsided to nothing.

Stillness took the place of the mayhem and, not daring to breathe or blink, Isobel ceased her struggles.

Gwen's grip on her eased. They both remained in place, staring into the clouds of white that had risen thick enough to hide the onslaught—and now, its outcome.

The curtain of soot thinned. Hours seemed to pass while Isobel scanned the haze, searching for something—*anything*—to make sense of.

She stiffened when, from nowhere, more dark forms emerged in her periphery.

Reluctantly Isobel broke her gaze from the dissipating fog, her eyes catching those of the towering figure who now stood beside her.

Confused by his sudden presence, Isobel frowned, trying to place the stranger's sallow face, his rigid features.

She'd seen him before, she thought dimly. He'd seen her, too.

In the Gothic cathedral of Varen's palace.

This man had been one of the two shrouded figures standing in the shadows, whispering about her. The man who had removed his hood. One of the Lost Souls?

"Isobel, who are these people?" Gwen asked.

Tearing her gaze from the man's black stare, Isobel glanced all around to see that the forest now held as many shrouded forms as it did trees.

Robed and hooded, grim-faced and onyx-eyed, each held a weapon at the ready, their assortment of arms ranging from swords to axes to spiked clubs, maces, and even scythes.

How long had they been there? Where had they come from, and why were they—

Crash!

Isobel and Gwen started in unison. The noise, like the shattering of porcelain plates, was one Isobel knew well.

The same sound—that of a shattering Noc—came yet again, louder than before, closer.

Then, as though he'd been thrown, a Noc flew out of the mist. Striking a tree, his hollow body exploded on impact.

A second Noc stumbled from the smog, and, choosing that moment to move, the Lost Soul beside Isobel rushed forward. Seizing the creature by the throat with an enormous hand, he knelt and quickly slammed the Noc down, smashing him to pieces against the ashen ground.

From the clearing vapors, violet smoke spirals shot into the air, zooming in every direction.

Dust mixed with smoke. Snarling faces appeared in the gloom.

Re-forming, the Nocs diverted their attacks to the Lost Souls as they dashed into battle.

A myriad of clashes and clangs, shouts and screeches, crashes and splintering noises rose, building into a crescendo.

Charging straight ahead, Isobel ran headlong into the heart of the riot.

"Isobel!" Gwen cried. "Wait!"

Though Gwen caught her by the arm, Isobel didn't slow down. Not until she spotted two silhouettes standing opposite each other in the densest portion of the mist.

One of the figures, gangly and long-limbed, belonged to that of a Noc. The other, Isobel saw with a surge of relief, belonged to Varen.

He stood tall, alert, whole, and, aside from a few scrapes and a deep gash that marred the center of his right cheek, unscathed.

The Noc opposite him sought to change that, though, and he lashed out as Varen raised his arms to shield himself. But he couldn't block the claws from raking clean across his body.

Reeling from the blow, Varen staggered backward.

Isobel halted with a gasp, and when Gwen crashed into her from behind, she fell to her knees in the dust. She looked on helplessly as Varen curled into himself.

As the battle between the countless dreamworld ghouls

and Lost Souls continued to rage all around them, both Isobel and the Noc watched Varen, waiting and hoping, she knew, for opposite outcomes.

Slowly Varen lowered his arms.

Then he raised his head and straightened.

Isobel saw no blood—no more, at least—and she tasted relief a second time. Varen had listened. He'd heard her, and had been able to protect *himself* from the Noc this time.

The Noc's face contorted with fury.

"You *asked* for this!" growled the monster.

"I've changed my mind," Varen said.

"*Turncoat!*" roared the Noc.

"Your name," Varen replied with a stiff shake of his head, blood trailing to his chin, "not mine."

The Noc's glower deepened, and for an instant, Isobel was sure he would attack again. The creature held off, though, seeming to deliberate. And then, without warning, his expression shifted from malice to delight.

"Our name is always the same," said the ghoul, grinning widely as he aimed a curved red claw at Varen, "whether or not you care to admit it."

As the Noc spoke, his outstretched hand began to change, claws receding, porcelain shell morphing into pale flesh. "*We* are the same," the monster added, his voice shedding its caustic tone for a more familiar one.

A duplicate to the long coat Varen wore unfurled over the Noc's figure. His dark, bloodstained feather-and-quill hair went soft and black.

"No," Isobel muttered, and slamming hands into the ash, she pushed herself onto her feet.

Then she broke into a run, arms pumping at her sides.

But the creature had already completed his conversion, taking on the same shape that Pinfeathers, too, had shown the ability to adopt—one that mimicked Varen's exactly. Right down to his crimson-smeared cheek, his ashy clothes, his lip ring and dirt-caked boots. Even his cool stare of derision.

"You should know by now," Isobel heard the Noc shout as she closed in on them, his voice a perfect match to Varen's, "that, try as you might, you can *never* escape the things that lie within. No matter how strong your cheering section."

"Watch out!" Isobel screamed as the doppelgänger dove at him.

But her warning came too late.

The two Varens collided.

Falling into the ash, they rolled away, one over the other, until it was impossible to tell them apart.

40
Dual

The grappling doubles flipped to a halt as they tumbled into a clearing.

Isobel dodged through the trees after them.

"You don't control me anymore," she heard the victor growl as he slammed the other one hard into the dirt.

"And you don't control me," grunted the grounded Varen before inserting a knee between them, kicking his opponent with enough force to send him wheeling backward.

Seizing her chance, Isobel dashed into the clearing. She lurched to a halt between them and threw her arms wide, as if that could keep them separated.

To her right, the Varen who had been flung back regained his balance. At her left, the other duplicate climbed from the ash to his feet.

"Varen, whichever is you, just stop!" Isobel whipped her head back and forth, addressing them both. "Don't you see that he *wants* you to fight? That *she* wants you to?"

Ignoring her, the doubles started toward each other again—toward her—and Isobel knew her Varen wasn't listening. Not anymore. That left her with only one other option, and though she doubted she could appeal to the Noc, she knew she had to try.

"I said stop!" Isobel shouted. "*Both* of you. You'll destroy each other."

"Isobel, move," said the Varen to her right.

"No!" she shouted, her gaze snapping toward him.

"Do what he says," came the duplicate voice to her left.

Taking in their identical glowers, their replicated stances, Isobel tried to comprehend why the real Varen, whichever he was, would *choose* to enter this battle that was so obviously a trap. Especially when there was so much at stake, and so little time left.

She didn't have a sure answer to her question, but one thing was certain: As long as she stood in the way, as long as she kept herself between them, neither would attack the other.

"Which one of you is which?" Isobel demanded. "Tell me."

"He's the monster," said the Varen on her right.

"Don't listen to him," replied the Varen to her left. "He is."

Isobel's panic mounted as she looked from one to the other. No matter how fast her thoughts spun, she couldn't think of a single way to defuse the situation. No more than she could conceive of a way to tell them apart. What was worse, she felt the tension between them building, poised to boil over regardless of what she did or said. And though the Noc had not been able to harm Varen moments ago, Isobel worried that the ghoul's new appearance had changed the rules again.

With the rest of the Nocs preoccupied with the Lost Souls, and with Varen's internal strength renewed to at least some degree, *this* Noc—the new front-runner who seemed eager to claim Pinfeathers's place—must have sensed he was losing. Losing both Lilith's fight, and his own grip on his host and source. Morphing into Varen's form, Isobel guessed, had been the ghoul's final resort, his last-ditch effort to shatter Varen's resolve.

The Noc's plan was working, too. Isobel could tell by the way each Varen glared straight through her, as if she was made of glass.

She'd seen this look on Varen's face before. Only a little while ago, in the dreamworld version of Mr. Swanson's classroom. When Varen had leveled the gun at her.

It was the same glare of hatred she'd seen that day at Trenton, when she'd found Brad hovering over Varen, threatening him for writing his number on her hand. For talking to her.

The same look of dark recklessness he'd worn after the explosive encounter with his father, when he'd taken off in the Cougar with Isobel in the passenger seat.

Ripping through the streets with total abandon, tearing around corners and through lights, revving the engine, Varen had not cared in that moment about what might happen to either of them. He hadn't stopped or slowed down, even when she'd begged him to. Not until Isobel had compared his behavior to Brad's.

But now there was no mirror to hold up to him.

Not when he faced one already.

He hates himself, Gwen had told Isobel that morning at the cemetery, and even then, Isobel had known she was right. Now here she was again, caught in the middle of a cross fire. Because, in Varen's mind, he was no longer fighting down the shadow of his darker side.

He was fighting that darker side itself.

Just then Gwen came sprinting into the clearing. In the split second it took Isobel to glance her way, the double to her right grabbed Isobel.

"Don't cheerleaders belong on the sidelines?" he hissed in her ear before tossing her aside.

Hurrying to meet her, Gwen caught her before she could fall.

Well, Isobel thought, clinging to her friend as she steadied herself, *at least now I know.*

Or thought she knew.

No sooner did Isobel look back to the duplicates than they rejoined their scuffle. Again they clashed, and again she lost track of the imposter. "Which—?" Gwen asked between winded gasps for air.

"I don't know!" Isobel exclaimed.

Long coats flapped as the two Varens swung in place until, with a well-timed shove, one Varen sent the other skidding away.

The thrown Varen, who managed to stay on his feet, crouched, his boots skating over ground that became something else beneath his sliding soles—a patch of marble. The smooth surface unfurled beneath its conjurer, rushing fast as brush fire to consume and replace the dust underneath them.

Curved stone walls rose from the circular perimeter of the new floor, sealing the four of them into a rounded, roofless room.

An arena, Isobel realized, an instant before tall, black, spiked iron gates shot up in front of her and Gwen, cutting them off from the fighting ring.

Armored stone angels materialized along the other side of the gates, each offering forth a range of different weapons. Wings unfurled and orb eyes open, the angels held the air of spectators, each again bearing Isobel's likeness.

Grabbing the iron bars, Isobel pulled herself close to the gate.

"Varen!" she shouted to the duplicate who approached the carved sentinel closest to her. "You *can* stop this. You can make it all go away. You can—"

"What do you think I'm doing?" he asked without looking at her, taking a sword and dagger set from the angel with two quick scrapes of metal on stone.

Renewed terror jabbed Isobel's gut when she saw the Varen on the opposite side of the arena draw a spear from the grip of another statue. Tightening her hold on the bars, she imagined the barrier disintegrating to dust.

But the cold, unwavering metal refused to comply with her silent command.

Varen's mind was made up. His conviction that he would enter this match was too strong for her to dispel. And unlike when they had been in the courtyard of statues, there was no window of doubt that Isobel could infiltrate with her own dreams.

At least, not through her strength alone.

"Gwen," Isobel said, pushing back from the bars to face her friend. "Listen, I know you don't understand what's happening, but I need your help. Please, we *have* to stop them."

"How?" Gwen asked, her expression stricken with fear and shock.

"With your thoughts," Isobel said. "*Our* thoughts together. They're both holding all of this in place, but if we concentrate at the same time, we might be able to make the gates vanish. If I can get in there, Gwen, if I can get between them again, I *can* make them stop."

Though Isobel could tell that her friend didn't grasp everything she'd said, she was grateful to see Gwen give a stiff nod of solidarity.

Gwen approached the gates, her hands wrapping the bars. Isobel did the same.

Beyond the gates, the Varens rushed each other.

The sword slashed down. *Snick* came the sound of the blade clashing with the spear's wooden shaft. Recoiling, Sword Varen swung again. Spear Varen ducked, then straightened. He sidestepped and leaned this way and that, evading the sword at every pass until, finally, its wielder landed the first strike.

Blood gushed from the spear bearer's arm. The only color in this dull, grayscale world, it splashed vibrant and bright onto the marble.

Isobel gripped the bars harder, willing the iron to loosen.

"Think about the gate disappearing," she told Gwen. "Picture the parts we're holding dissolving away."

In the corner of her vision, Isobel saw Gwen's hands tighten, her knuckles paling to white. Yet the bars remained solid, and even though Isobel knew she'd be able to concentrate better if she closed her eyes, she couldn't bring herself to shut out the fight.

Quick shuffles allowed Sword Varen to evade the repeated jabs of his enemy's spear. Again and again, he crossed his two blades in front of him to deflect its pointed tip. But Spear Varen eluded the sword swipes with equal ease, his guard obviously raised after being clipped.

Clacks and clangs echoed through the arena as each Varen matched the other strike for strike.

Just as Isobel had been able to do things in the dreamworld without knowing how—like keeping up with Pinfeathers's mad masquerade waltz and Reynolds's frenzied sword-fighting lesson during their skirmish near the cliffs— so too, it seemed, was the real Varen able to keep pace with his counterpart.

It wasn't long, however, before one landed another strike.

Spear Varen feinted once, then twice, before penetrating his foe's defenses. With an upward flick of his weapon, he caught Sword Varen across the chest. The spear's spiked tip sent an arc of crimson over the floor, and the appearance of fresh blood made Isobel feel even more helpless; that *both* Varens bled told her that the Noc had taken care to construct a veneer that was internal as well as external.

"Isobel, nothing's happening," she heard Gwen say. And it wasn't. Because Isobel wasn't focusing. How could she?

Snap, clack, crack — clang!

Isobel gasped as the dagger fell from Sword Varen's hand. Armed now with only a single blade, he staggered away from his assailant, trailing blood.

Spear Varen flipped his weapon into a better grip and, advancing on his target again, unleashed a string of onslaughts that forced Sword Varen all the way to the gates. There they crashed together, Spear Varen squeezing Sword Varen into the iron bars.

Isobel heard one of them hiss something to the other, though she couldn't decipher what was said or which had spoken.

Then, with an angry growl, Sword Varen sent Spear Varen tumbling backward. Now, as the doubles re-entered the center of the arena, it was Spear Varen who retreated, struggling to deflect the ceaseless string of swipes and slashes.

A whip-fast swing of the sword knocked the spear aside. Moving in, Sword Varen grasped its shaft, holding it and its wielder steady with one hand. Then he coiled his blade-bearing arm, preparing to send it down on his opponent's exposed neck in a killing blow.

"Stop!" Isobel screeched, and her cry caused Sword Varen to hesitate. Long enough for Spear Varen to reclaim his weapon and break away.

"I thought you said we had to concentrate!" Gwen snapped.

Tensing, Isobel forced herself to shut her eyes.

The clanging of weapons, scuffle of steps, and snapping of coats resumed, the mixture of sounds screaming louder and louder in her ears.

Isobel tried to push the echoing clamor aside, to concentrate on the pressure of Gwen's shoulder against hers. She allowed the sensation to transport her back in time, to that moment at the burial site when she'd found the hidden reserves of her own strength. Again she pictured the bars dissolving.

"It's working," Isobel said when, to her surprise, she felt the iron loosen. "Don't stop."

She squeezed her fists and felt the brittle metal give. Opening her eyes, Isobel pushed forward and, wasting no time, burst through the gate as it crumpled apart like dry, rotted cloth.

Isobel hurried past the angels, who turned their focuses on her, bleeding scars opening on their cheeks.

She dashed into the arena, the soles of her shoes clapping against the marble just as, tripped by the end of the spear, Sword Varen went sprawling.

His blade leaped from his grip as he fell, and with a shriek, it glided to a stop at Isobel's feet.

She bent to retrieve the sword, clutching its heavy hilt.

When she looked up, however, she saw Spear Varen raise his weapon high and aim the tip for the heart of his rival.

"Do you really win if you know she won't make it out of here alive?" the felled Varen asked between heavy breaths, his chest bloody and heaving.

Spear Varen held off, his own breaths coming fast, his white-knuckled hands quivering.

"Go ahead," said the floored double. "End it. You should know better than anybody that I'm telling the truth when I say I want you to."

At these words, Isobel released the sword, realizing it would do her no good.

No weapon would. And no words would either.

She'd been wrong to tell Gwen she held the power to stop this. To stop them.

She couldn't.

Because this was not her fight. Like the angels, she was on the outside. A spectator left with no choice but to watch.

Isobel rose slowly to stand, leaving the sword where it lay.

"Strike," said the Varen on the floor.

"First, tell me why you say she'll die," snapped the standing Varen.

"I think at this point, you and I both know that it's going to be either her or us," Sword Varen responded, never once breaking gazes with his double. "You only hesitate now because you know it's true. How else can it end? I think we both understand that whichever one of us—you or I, I mean—gets to walk away from *this* little scrap will also determine who survives in the end. Her or us. So why not seal the deal now? After all, isn't control all you've ever *really* wanted?"

"You're telling the truth," said Spear Varen, his grip on the wooden shaft loosening as he lowered the weapon, "aren't you?"

"Wouldn't you be the first to know?" the double replied.

Isobel tried to keep up with the dizzying exchange, her eyes darting between the two as, stepping back, the standing Varen allowed the felled Varen to rise. Still, she could not tell them apart, and in that moment, even though knowing wouldn't have helped her at all, she despised herself for it.

The Varen with the spear extended his weapon to his opponent, who accepted it with an odd gentleness.

Isobel shook her head, already sensing what would come next.

"Please don't," she said, more to herself than to either of them because, even if she'd screamed it, she doubted they would have heard.

"I suppose this way we both win," said the now unarmed Varen, a small ironic smile tugging at his lips.

"I suppose so," replied the new victor before shoving the forfeiter to the floor and jamming the spear straight through his heart.

41
Relics

Isobel flinched when she heard the smash. And again when the conquering Varen jerked the spear free.

Tossing his weapon aside, he glared down at his defeated enemy, the empty-eyed Noc who, even in his half-shattered state, had retained Varen's likeness.

The ghoul's cracked face even held on to that last ghost of a smile, as if he'd found something amusing in his own demise.

Maybe, Isobel thought, the creature's continued disguise had been meant as a punch line. One more Grim Facade . . .

Breaking his gaze on the Noc, Varen turned toward her.

Isobel wavered in place.

Then, without her command, her feet carried her forward in a run. Under her shoes, the floor went soft, returning to ash.

Like crumbling sand castles, the angels collapsed with a unanimous *whoosh.*

The curved stone walls went next, causing new dust clouds to rise and blot out the surrounding woodlands, enclosing her with the boy who wrapped her in his arms the moment she reached him.

"Oh *God*," she breathed against his bloodied chest.

"I'm sorry," Varen whispered as he pulled her closer, squeezing her hard. "I had to."

He meant the fight, she was sure, though Isobel still wasn't certain why he'd felt obliged to risk everything—including his own soul—in order to engage in the battle.

She wondered, too, why the conclusion to their war had been so strange and abrupt. Scowling, she tried to replay their last words in her mind. To make sense of them . . .

"You said . . . one of us was bound to die," Isobel murmured. She pressed her ear to his ripped, stained shirt, listening to the frantic rhythm of a heart that was very much intact.

Then she peered over at the shell of a body sprawled in the dust. The Noc's eyes—vacant, hollow holes—seemed to watch her. But though Isobel waited, the creature's form still looked like Varen's, refusing to return to its monstrous state.

"I think one of us just did," Varen replied.

Isobel forced herself to look away from the Noc. Closing her eyes, she buried her face against Varen.

But even as she breathed in that nearly faded essence of old incense and dried orange peels, burned leaves and worn leather—an aroma now tainted by the coppery tang of blood and the mordant smell of ash—she feared she might awaken any moment to find that none of this had really happened.

Tricks and turns, twists and illusions—these were the elements that defined this world.

Here, time was a lie.

Faces perceived as false proved real and real faces false.

A dream could be as tangible as reality, and things that seemed real as ephemeral as a dream.

As she considered the sheer infiniteness of this realm and its limitless capacity for treachery, Isobel now had to wonder which category *she* fell into.

Was it possible that Varen and this whole horrible, confusing day were all the workings of her imagination? A toxic balm her mind had produced to soothe itself?

Or could it be that, unbeknownst to herself or Varen, she really was just another product of *his* imagination? A dream version of herself that, like the Nocs, had grown a cognizance of its own?

A dream within a dream within a dream within a dream...

Maybe she really *was* dead. Had she ever truly reawakened on that cold hospital table in Baltimore?

Insanity, she thought, as she opened her eyes to the relentless rain of ash.

This place, wherever it was—*whatever* it was—equated to insanity.

Fighting a strange dizziness, Isobel drew back from Varen. Delving into the pockets of his coat, she searched frantically until she found the trinket she sought: her pink butterfly watch.

Fingers trembling, she flicked open its wings.

Nothing. The hands revealed nothing because they neither spun nor ticked but stood frozen, stalled by the bit of ocean water trapped behind the watch's cracked glass face.

"Don't," Varen said and, closing his hand over hers, snapped the watch shut. "Don't start doubting now. Or we're all lost."

Isobel looked up at him, and a wave of gratitude washed over her.

Because, even as desolate and fleeting as this moment felt, it was still a blip in time in which they were together. Not only aware but awake. Alive.

This time, she had needed Varen to remind *her*.

His warm fingers tipped her chin up to him, and he leaned down.

Relaxing her hand, Isobel let go of the ruined watch, allowing it to fall into the bed of ash at their feet.

Varen kissed her then, and Isobel's hand, now free, went to grip the nape of his neck, holding him there.

"Hey!"

Isobel's eyelids fluttered at the sound of Gwen's voice. She turned her head toward its source, breaking the kiss, abashed at how, lost in the aftermath of this madness, she'd almost forgotten Gwen was there.

Through the thinning murk, she saw her friend's narrow frame hurrying toward them, her frightened face now as smeared and dirty as theirs.

"Glad you two have the wherewithal to swap spit at a time like this, but I'm going to need for one of you tell me if *that* is something we need to be worried about."

Though Gwen pointed, she didn't need to.

Above, a throng of crows flooded the sky. As they grew in number, the mixture of flapping wings and hoarse caws rose in volume.

"Tell me there's a way out of here," Gwen said. "Because something tells *me* we need to go. *Now.*"

Isobel felt Varen step away from her side, but she didn't turn to follow him.

Instead, she kept her gaze on the heavens, watching the horde of black birds swirl beyond the scraggly branches of the woodland trees. But these crows did not congregate into a vortex as Isobel expected them to. As they had done before . . .

Shrieking, their cries of "*Tekeli-li*" filling the air, they fled.

Though Isobel didn't know what it meant, she had heard the Nocs screech the same strange string of syllables before.

They had done so when Isobel stood at the threshold of the reversed BEWARE OF BESS door, with Lilith on the other side. And they had dispersed in a similar flurry as soon as Isobel laid her hand on the tarnished knob.

Isobel had also heard the cry from Scrimshaw, during the memory of Poe's death. The blue-haired Noc had hissed it before dissolving to smoke. Seconds later the white veils and equally white face had drifted through the open vat of black in the ceiling above Poe's bed.

"Gwen's right," Isobel said, looking from the escaping flocks to Varen. "We need to—"

She stopped when she saw that he'd already made a door.

In his hand, Varen held the knob to an entrance Isobel had never seen before.

Tall, wooden, and nondescript, the portal gave Isobel little clue as to where it led. But when Varen opened the door, revealing a narrow set of descending stairs encased by peeling walls, she told herself it didn't matter.

For the moment, the only thing that did was getting out. Away.

Varen glanced back at her, waiting, and Isobel snatched Gwen's hand.

"*Tekeli-li!*" the birds continued to scream as Isobel pulled her friend toward the opening.

"What *is* that?" asked Gwen, her hand strangling Isobel's. "What are they saying?"

"It means 'Beware the White One,'" answered a voice from behind, its unmistakable tone causing Isobel to halt a foot from Varen and the open portal.

Through the haze, she focused on the familiar figure now striding toward them from the line of trees.

Isobel almost smiled to see Reynolds clad once more in his wide-brimmed hat and black cloak, his two swords drawn point-down at either side. He lacked only his concealing white scarf.

But slung low around his waist like the sash of a military sergeant, Reynolds wore a new garment in its stead.

Isobel's ribbon.

Despite its muted pink, the tattered and bloodstained satin lent him an added air of authority. But most important, her ribbon's presence on his person squelched the last of Isobel's lingering doubts about his allegiance.

For Reynolds must have saved the sash from the ragged waves and kept it safe all this time. Just as he'd saved her.

Then, and now again. She knew he wouldn't have bothered with the sash if she'd been expendable to him—if he'd only saved her to use her later. If he hadn't cared.

The ribbon might not answer *all* of Isobel's questions regarding Reynolds, but it did answer the most important one of all.

He was on their side.

Her side.

As he had been the entire time.

42
Unbinding

"Izzy, get back!" Dropping Isobel's hand, Gwen leaped in front of her.

Isobel blinked in shock as Gwen delved into her purse and retrieved a small metal canister.

"*One* step," Gwen growled at Reynolds, leveling the container right at him, "gets you an instant face improvement. I got a ten-foot stream on this thing and two million Scoville heat units that will make you wish you were dead . . . er."

Isobel squinted at the canister. Was that . . . ?

"It's called *covering*," Gwen snapped at Isobel from over her shoulder. "Now would you *go*? Both of you. I'm right behind you."

So Gwen *hadn't* been joking about the pepper spray.

Isobel smirked, unable to help herself.

Unperturbed, Reynolds carefully sheathed his cutlasses one after the other.

"That's right, Barbossa, pack 'em up," barked Gwen as she shifted skittishly from foot to foot. "Now . . . just turn and walk away. Back to whatever sad, subterranean, pipe-organ-playing underworld existence you decided to take a vacation from."

"Gwen . . ." Stepping forward, Isobel placed a hand on her friend's trembling wrist. "It's okay. He's okay."

Gwen frowned, eyes flitting from Reynolds to Isobel and back again.

"What do you mean 'okay'?" she asked. "This is the guy you tackled linebacker style. The same freak who fractured my arm."

"He's a friend," Isobel said, and though Gwen remained tense, she allowed Isobel to push her pepper-wielding arm down. "I promise."

Slipping past Gwen, Isobel approached Reynolds.

His arms folded, his expression as impassive as ever—though perhaps a bit more acerbic than usual—he seemed to be waiting for her to stop and dutifully listen to whatever foreboding message he had come to impart.

Hadn't he learned *anything* about her?

Isobel charged forward and plowed into him, flinging her arms around his middle.

Reynolds went rigid in her embrace. Lifting his own arms, he held them up and out of the way, as if she were some sort of parasite that had latched on to him.

But Isobel only squeezed him tighter, not caring if he didn't like being liked. She breathed in deeply that decaying, cloying essence of dead roses and, despite its pungency, found the sharp scent oddly comforting.

Like Reynolds himself.

"Thank you," she said.

Reynolds remained silent as a moment of either tolerance

or indecision elapsed. Then, grasping Isobel by the shoulders, his sturdy gloved hands pushed her back.

"You may yet curse me when you learn how very much now depends entirely upon you," he said. "On the both of you."

With that, Reynolds released Isobel and stalked to the entryway, where he took the door from Varen.

"Right," Isobel muttered to herself as she swept a lock of matted hair from her eyes. "What was I thinking? Hugs are so last year."

"Go," Reynolds said, nodding them toward the door frame before glancing behind at the silent forest, now void of all movement and figures. "All of you." Thunder rolled in the distance, and Reynolds tilted his head back, glaring into the emptied sky. "She is coming."

Varen passed through the doorway first, but he paused two steps down to peer at Isobel.

Ushering Gwen ahead of her, Isobel entered the dark space, the wooden steps creaking and moaning beneath them.

Gwen craned her neck to glare back at Reynolds, who, after taking one last scan of the horizon, ducked in after them and shut the door.

Ahead, Varen reached the bottom of the narrow stairs, trailing white boot prints as he swiftly disappeared around a corner.

Isobel moved to follow him, but Reynolds caught her arm.

"Let him go," he said. "We must talk."

Isobel looked to Gwen, issuing a silent plea. Gwen frowned, eyes oozing suspicion as they flicked to Reynolds.

"Gwen, please," Isobel said.

Gwen stared unflinchingly at Reynolds for another long beat. Then Isobel felt Gwen's hand bump her own, passing over the tube of pepper spray. Isobel accepted the cool cylinder as she fought another smile.

Breaking her sharp glare at last, Gwen turned and rattled down the steps after Varen.

As Isobel watched her friend go, she had only a second to wonder what this place was—where Varen had vanished to in such a rush and why. Because when Reynolds spoke again, his words drew her focus entirely back to him.

"I have lied to you but once, Isobel," he said.

Isobel waited a beat before speaking.

"You're talking about today," she said, her voice a monotone. "In the gym. When you told me Lilith thought I was dead."

"Her discovery of my identity, that I was the one Lost Soul who could freely enter your world, made it necessary, in the beginning, for me to agree to her demands. To follow her plan. I could not, after all, have aided you from a tomb."

"Hold that thought," Isobel said, flashing a palm. "More on that in a second. But before we pass Go and collect two hundred here, let's just back up one space." He tilted his head at her, but Isobel hurried on. "So, putting aside the fact that I'm kind of over it now, because I have to be, I *am* curious how the whole 'Varen is safe at home' thing doesn't qualify in your book as a lie."

"That night I carried you through the park," Reynolds said, referring to Halloween, "I told you the boy was home. I said nothing of his safety."

"Oh," Isobel said, pointing at him. "I see what you did there. Neat trick omitting the truth. That's not lying at all."

"Would you truly rather berate me again than learn how your freedom may be won?"

Isobel's cool skepticism faltered. Suddenly she understood what Reynolds was trying to convey in his archaic, roundabout manner. This was his way of telling her that there *was* a way. That the bait he'd used to lure her through the veil, to entice her into trusting him again, hadn't just been lip service. Poe really must have attempted to break his connection to the dreamworld. To Lilith.

"You said Edgar tried to get away," she murmured, speaking fast. "You said he tried to break the bond but that he got caught before he cou—"

"And that is why you must now listen very carefully." Reynolds unknotted Isobel's ribbon from his waist. "For far more depends upon what happens next than just your soul or the boy's."

Reynolds extended the graying pink satin to her and she took it gingerly, surprised to find it had somehow retained its original silkiness. Her eyes searched Reynolds's, and in the shadow cast by the wide brim of his fedora, the lines on his face seemed deeper than before.

"Should you fail to do what Edgar could not," Reynolds went on, "those who inhabit this world, as well as those from my own realm, will suffer the wrath of the demon whose rage we have, in your name, dared to provoke."

Isobel's eyes widened. "*M-my* name?"

"That is why I stayed behind," he said. "To rally them. I knew they would join me only after witnessing for themselves the magnitude of your power. What you are capable of."

"*Me?*" Isobel blurted. "I—you were the one who—"

"You lived, Isobel," said Reynolds, cutting her off again. "You survived the fire you created when you destroyed the link. Then you died at that hospital and, through sheer self-will, returned to life. Not only that, but you live on. And until you dared to confront me in that churchyard, until I saw you brazenly face death and damnation upon that cliff—all for the sake of another—I had forgotten that a power greater than darkness did, indeed, exist. I had forgotten, as well, what it meant to possess a soul."

"Okay," Isobel said, clenching the ribbon tighter in her fist, "I don't know what's freaking me out more. You admitting you might have one emotion more than none at all, or the news flash that I'm supposed to save the world plus your parallel dimension buddies."

"You're afraid," Reynolds said with a nod. "And that is good. For the worst of her fury, I vow to you, she holds in reserve for you."

"See? Right there," Isobel said. "Just . . . stop saying stuff like that."

"When Edgar was captured," Reynolds said, "when he was pulled back into the woodlands, he'd been in transit on this side, in reality. Traveling between cities. He was trying to complete the ultimate objective of a quest that he believed would save him."

Isobel looked down to the ribbon in her hand, thinking back to what Varen had said about Poe's final days during their project presentation.

Poe, Isobel remembered, had disappeared after leaving Richmond. He'd been on his way to New York, where he was to meet with Muddy, Virginia's mother—his aunt. Poe's plan had been to collect Muddy and bring her to live with him at his new home in Richmond. But he never made it that far. Richmond was the last place that anyone who knew him personally had seen him.

"The objective of his quest?" Isobel murmured, shaking her head. "I don't understand."

"His ultimate goal was to return to his place of departure," said Reynolds. "To the city of Richmond. Where he was to wed."

Isobel's head snapped up.

"Oh my God," she said, remembering at once Poe's bizarre string of courtships and engagements during the last year of his life. His pursuits, she recalled, had begun with a widow who, though she had initially agreed to marry him, had ultimately called off the engagement.

Poe's final engagement had been to a woman named Elmira—a childhood sweetheart who lived in Richmond.

"He was trying to turn back midtrip," Isobel murmured, "to get to Elmira. But why?"

"His plan was to override the bond with another," Reynolds said. "To create a new soul tie. One strong enough to supersede the dark union he had already made. One of love. It was a gamble. But given the lengths to which Lilith went to retrieve him before the union could occur—"

"Are you saying what I think you're saying?" Isobel asked.

"In essence, I am saying that you have something Edgar did not."

"Spit it out."

He nodded to the ribbon in her hand. "You possess a bond already. Perhaps you need only declare it. Name it. Or . . . perhaps only *he* does."

"Isobel!"

Her brain spinning and numb, swimming as much with information as with shock, Isobel turned her head to find Gwen standing at the base of the stairs.

"We have a problem," Gwen said, lifting a framed photograph.

With a stab of panic, Isobel took in the three figures posing in the portrait. She and Gwen had seen the same photo earlier that day. Propped next to an open grave and a flag-draped coffin.

Of course Varen would come here, Isobel thought as she fumbled down the steps, a sick sensation twisting her gut.

This place—this *house*—it was Bruce's.

43
The Heart Whose
Woes Are Legion

Dropping the pepper spray but keeping the ribbon, Isobel flew past Gwen. Then, swinging around the corner she'd seen Varen turn, she tore down the cramped hallway, a collage of hanging photos blurring by in her periphery.

That must be where Gwen had snagged the portrait, Isobel thought as she skidded to a halt at the end of the hall. Glancing right, she peered into the adjoining corridor.

A grim-faced grandfather clock seemed to watch her from the shadows. Behind its glass door, a tarnished silver pendulum swayed to and fro, its quiet ticking the only sound in an otherwise absolute silence.

The clock's stationary hour hand pointed to the roman numeral nine, the filigreed minute hand hovering over the six. Below the clock's face, someone had stuck a yellow sticky note that read AUCTION in bold black marker.

Aside from the clock, there were only doors. Two on either side, all of them open.

Isobel crept down the hall with slow steps, the ancient floorboards creaking underfoot. As she passed each doorway, she peered into the room beyond.

Her first right led to a study full of boxes and stacked

furniture. More sticky notes labeled everything with one of three words: GOODWILL, AUCTION, and DUMPSTER.

Next, on the left, came an empty bathroom with dingy tile flooring, its walls peeling floral paper. The following right opened into a cleaned-out closet, its metal rack cleared of everything except for a black garment bag marked with yet another sticky note—this one bearing Varen's name.

At the top of the partially unzipped bag, Isobel spied a gray suit jacket and a striped tie. She thought they might be the same clothes that Bruce's son, Grey, had been wearing in the photograph.

Isobel pressed on, and finally, glancing into the last room on the left, she found Varen.

He stood with his back to her, staring down at the stripped and dismantled remains of a four-poster bed, its headboard propped against the wall.

The white raven still emblazoned between the shoulders of Varen's coat reminded Isobel, painfully, of how far the nightmare was from being over. How Varen's ties to Lilith still existed.

And though Reynolds had pointed the way, though he'd handed Isobel the ribbon and helped to bring them here, to this moment of all or nothing—how could she tell Varen that everything would be okay when his pain never ended? When the "nothing" part was all he knew?

When in coming home, back to reality, he had found no home to come to.

What good were her words and promises now?

"You knew?" he asked, his voice quiet, disconcertingly calm.

"I—I didn't get a chance to tell you," Isobel stammered. "I wanted to, but . . . Varen, I'm so sorry."

"How long?"

Isobel fidgeted with the ribbon, uncertain of what, exactly, he was asking her.

"How long has he been gone?" Varen snapped, louder this time.

"The funeral was today," Isobel said. "This morning. Gwen and I were both there. I went because I—"

"*Goddamn it,*" he said, snatching a small lamp from a nearby nightstand and sending a cascade of empty orange medicine bottles to the floor. He slung the lamp at the far wall, where it smashed and fell.

Isobel flinched. She watched the lamp's fractured bulb sputter before dying out.

Suddenly the objects in the room—books and boxes, a trash can, the medicine bottles—shifted. They rose together and hovered in place.

Tensing, Isobel checked the grandfather clock, the hands of which had started to spin.

"Varen," she began, but she stopped, her words catching at the sound of a woman's humming.

It was the melody from Varen's lullaby, the heartrending song Madeline had written for him when he was a child. When he'd still been *her* child.

Then the humming dissolved, becoming laughter, low and insidious.

An electric charge filled the air, causing the hairs on the nape of Isobel's neck to stand at attention. And yet she couldn't bring herself to look back in the direction she'd come from—toward the end of the hall where the building laughter rebounded.

Instead she kept her gaze fixed on Varen as he slowly turned to face the door.

Black once more, his eyes stared straight through her.

44
White-Robed Forms

Radiating fury, Varen stalked toward Isobel.

As he moved, the doorway that stood between them expanded, its rectangular arch rounding as it transformed to stone. Then Varen walked right past her, across the wide threshold and into the hall, where his continuing steps triggered more change.

Like a crawling frost, cracked stone spread out from beneath his boots. Plaster and drywall faded into rough gray brick. While the emerging walls of Varen's palace absorbed the doorways on Isobel's right, the entries on her left morphed into more Gothic arches, and the passageway before her took the form of a cloister.

Through the open arcade, Isobel saw that Varen had returned them to the courtyard of statues.

Or was it that he'd brought the courtyard of statues to them?

But then, this was not the same courtyard she'd encountered before. Not only were there no angels among the gathering of fog-enveloped white forms—no sets of wings, neither tucked nor unfurled—she saw no faces, either.

None fully decipherable . . .

Draping stone shrouds covered the statues' heads, spilling long down their feminine bodies in clinging sculpted folds.

Lilith's laughter echoed all around, trailing off into the eerie garden.

Another trap, Isobel thought. The demon's final play.

And Varen, with his mind now firmly set on revenge, was about to walk straight into it.

"Varen, wait," Isobel called after him.

To her surprise—and perhaps to his as well—Varen halted at the corner of the cloister.

"She's right," Isobel said.

Varen turned his head slightly toward her. The gesture, though small, suggested that at least he was listening.

Fixing her eyes on that white raven, Isobel held her ribbon—*their* ribbon—closer.

"Darkness *will* win," she said. "It has to. So long as you try to fight fire with fire."

Half-shielded by his tousled, ashen hair, his eyes flicked in her direction.

"Sometimes," he said, speaking in that quiet and contained way that always frightened her, "fire is the only way to fight. But then . . . you knew that already."

With that, Varen rounded the corner, passing out of her sight.

Isobel's chest contracted with fear.

Fire. Isobel had been referring to Varen's obvious plan to fight Lilith with anger, to pit his own capacity for darkness against the demon's.

But the fire *he* meant was Isobel's chosen tool to banish

him from the strip mall parking lot earlier that day. And to sever the original link—to destroy Varen's sketchbook.

Now that Varen knew *he* was the link, would he try something similar?

Immediately Isobel's thoughts circled back to Varen's duel with the doppelgänger Noc. To what had been said between the two. They had reached some sort of agreement— or rather, Varen had come to an understanding with himself.

He'd devised a deadly contract.

Then he had tried to soothe Isobel's fears with a distract- ing explanation, with a kiss.

Had that kiss been meant as a good-bye?

Panic seized her at that thought, spurring Isobel to charge around the bend after him. But she halted suddenly when she found herself back in Bruce's house, in that dimly lit hall sandwiched between the stairs and the wall.

All the photos now hung askew, their glass panes cracked and splintered.

Dead ahead, she saw Varen cross through the front door, which hung wide, exiting not into Bruce's yard but to the courtyard and its shrouded, mist-wrapped forms.

But before she could follow him through to the other side, Isobel spotted something—some*one*—lying on the stairs.

"Gwen!" Grabbing the banister, Isobel swung down to kneel next to her.

Unconscious but breathing, her chest rising with small, shallow intakes, Gwen lay on her side, head propped on one arm as if someone had positioned her that way. A red welt swelled near her temple, and in one hand, her fingers curled loosely around the canister of pepper spray.

Isobel glanced behind her, to the top of the staircase and the hall, but she saw no sign of Reynolds.

She pushed off from the steps and whirled for the open door. Barreling through it, she ran headlong into the drifts of fog and down a winding path after Varen, whose form she no longer saw.

45

Nameless Here for Evermore

"Varen!" Isobel shouted.

"*Varen,*" a hushed voice echoed back.

Isobel turned in a circle, shoes scuffling stone.

Marble faces peered down at her from every direction, their features half-lost behind carved veils that perfectly mimicked the sheerness of gossamer. Now, even through the stone shrouds, she could make out their solemn expressions — their lidded eyes that, though closed, still seemed to see.

Looking behind her, Isobel also saw that along with the door to Bruce's, the walkway had vanished, its curving path now populated with more enswathed figures.

One of the statues moved, swiveling its head her way.

With a jump, Isobel backpedaled and stumbled straight into another.

Laughter, deep and throaty, filled the courtyard, growing louder and louder until the voice swept down on Isobel — and right into her.

Isobel shrieked as the shrill cackling invaded her head. Her hands leaped to cover her ears, dropping the ribbon. She squeezed her eyes shut, but she couldn't block out the laughter as it spiked into a skull-shattering scream.

Legs giving out, Isobel collapsed. Her knees slammed hard onto cold stone, and, doubling over, she fought the urge to be sick.

Then, departing as suddenly as it had descended, the demon's voice ceased and fled her mind. Its reverberation clapped through the newly quieted courtyard.

Trembling, gasping for air as well as for the return of her senses, Isobel lowered her quaking hands. She kept her head bowed, opening her eyes again only when she felt something warm trickle from her nose.

Three blots of crimson fell to splatter the smooth rectangular slab on which she now knelt. There, letters formed, creating trenches for the blood droplets.

Through the matted dreads of her hair, Isobel read the carved words.

ISOBEL LANLEY

BELOVED DAUGHTER, DEVOTED SISTER,

CHERISHED FRIEND

LIVED FOR LOVE, YET PERISHED BY ITS HAND

"Carries a certain Poe-etic ring to it, does it not?" asked a low feminine voice.

A soft shifting followed by a quiet drag of fabric sounded loud in Isobel's ringing ears. Then pooling folds of white and violet-stained gossamer entered her view. Poking through the puddled hem, curved black talons clicked to a stop atop Isobel's engraved name.

"Pun intended," Lilith said, "as our wayward Pinfeathers might have suggested were he here. Had you not incited him to self-annihilation, I mean. But then, you *do* possess a certain knack for impelling lovesick wretches to ruin, don't you? I suppose you and I have that much in common."

"I am *nothing* like you," Isobel growled. Slamming her palms flat against the slab, she pushed to her feet and lunged at the figure in front of her. Instead of digging into soft veils and flesh, though, her fingers clashed with hard marble.

Another statue.

As though mocking her, the figure smiled serenely at Isobel from behind its pall.

"You *do* like your epitaph, do you not?" Lilith asked, her voice now emanating from a separate corner of the courtyard.

Isobel shoved away from the frozen effigy. Whirling, she scoured the endless multitude of veiled forms.

"I'd rather hoped you would," the same voice called, issuing from yet another direction. "Given that it is the prize you've been fighting so hard to obtain. A sorrowful ending to a mournful tale whose greatest tragedy is that it happened to conclude with *your* name instead of mine."

"Where are you?" Isobel yelled. She twirled in place, and in a kaleidoscope of muted faces, statues wheeled around her. "If you think you can end this, if you want to kill me, then come out! Stop hiding like a *coward*."

"You seem upset," Lilith said. "Don't care much for having your own tricks turned against you, do you?"

Isobel rotated again and again. She began to slow, though,

when she noticed that none of the statues appeared to hold the same position as before. But when she stopped, the courtyard only spun faster, continuing its rotation without her.

Isobel teetered. Her feet tangling in her ribbon, she fell onto the cold slab bearing her name.

Her surroundings whizzed by in a blur—a merry-go-round of phantoms that halted only when a familiar mausoleum slid into view directly across from Isobel.

Mist, thick and rolling, enshrouded the tomb she recognized as Lilith's.

Its decorative wrought-iron and blue stained-glass door hung wide open, revealing a rectangle of pure black.

Above the void, etched over the archway, Isobel saw a name she knew but had not noticed there before. Not until now.

LIGEIA

"Enough with games, though," Lilith said, her sultry voice resounding now from within the tomb. "You called. And now, here I am."

For an instant, the cavity of pitch darkness remained undisturbed. Then, like a dead thing floating up from black waters, the demon's hollowed white face and emaciated form emerged to stand in the door frame.

Lilith's sheer shroud, tattered and stained, hung from her in strips and shreds. Her tangled, dripping hair fell long over her shoulders, its ends still soaked in inky muck.

A pit oozed in the center of the demon's ivory chest, where Reynolds's hamsa-strung blade had impaled her. Only lightly smeared now with the violet-black substance she'd nearly dissolved into, Lilith's pale, papery lips entertained a renewed smile.

"Lilith," Isobel said, spitting the name from between her teeth as she scooped up her ribbon again. "Ligeia. Lenore. Emily. Lilo and Stitch. Which *is* it?"

"'Ulalume—Ulalume,'" Lilith replied, her voice going sweet and soft, making the syllables sound like a song. "'Tis the vault of thy lost Ulalume.'"

As the demon crossed out of the barrier of darkness, her aura of cold ethereal light burned suddenly bright, its glow evaporating the stains from her figure.

Black veins faded from hands that became delicate again as they took up the veils that still clung to her shoulders. Lilith drew the gauzy fabric over her face, and like a bride approaching the altar, she strode toward Isobel.

Her heart rate speeding, Isobel flicked her eyes between the approaching creature and the shifting letters above the tomb.

The name LIGEIA melted away, and bleeding through the stone, new letters emerged to spell ULALUME.

"'Then my heart it grew ashen and sober,'" hissed the demon, her thin lips blossoming to bloodred fullness, her face and figure regaining their former beauty. "'As the leaves that were crisped and sere—as the leaves that were withering and sere.'"

Keeping hold of her ribbon, Isobel drew to her feet. She took several retreating steps until her spine collided with one of the statues, leaving her nowhere to go.

The demon drifted nearer still, her radiance blazing to an ultraviolet shine and her skin to an eye-stinging white.

"'And I cried—"It was surely October on *this* very night of last year, that I journeyed—I journeyed down here!—that I brought a dread burden down here—on this night of all nights in the year,"'" Lilith continued, reciting lines from one of Poe's poems. The same poem, Isobel knew, whose title matched the name now written on the demon's tomb. The poem Scrimshaw had recited to her the first time she'd found herself within the walls of the blue marble crypt.

The same poem Varen had read to Isobel in his room.

It was the one work of Poe's that mentioned the woodlands by name.

"That poem," Isobel said. "Poe wrote it trying to seal you back up, didn't he?"

"And we see how well *that* worked," Lilith replied, coming to a stop in front of Isobel. "But while we're on the subject, and if you don't mind my asking, would you do me the favor of refreshing my memory?"

Isobel gasped when she felt the statue behind her snatch her wrist, immobilizing the hand that held her pink ribbon. A yelp of shock rose in her throat as bony fingers dug into her flesh, but her cry caught there, dying the moment the effigy swung her around to face it.

In place of another of Lilith's stone idols, a skeleton

leered down at her from within the shadows of a heavy hood.

Behind a sculpted pall of its own, the skull grinned at Isobel and, looping an arm around her waist, jerked her snugly against its robed body. Then, as though they'd been caught in a fervid dance, the statue threw her low into a dip and, holding her there, refroze.

Isobel whimpered in the skeleton's solidified grip, recognizing all too well where she had seen it before.

This was the Red Death. The same nightmare figure that had collapsed the grave over Isobel when she'd fallen there, trying to rescue Brad.

"I seem to recall you mentioning something earlier about . . . putting me in my place?" Lilith said, her glowing figure sliding into Isobel's periphery, her serene and lovely face half-obscured by the tails of the ribbon still hanging from Isobel's clenched fist.

At the rumbling sound of stone grating on stone, Isobel twisted in the skeleton's hold to peer down over her shoulder.

Beneath her, the long slab bearing her epitaph had slid free, unveiling a pit that reached far into the earth.

Tightly packed walls of red dirt formed a deep grave that terminated in an open pine box.

Isobel ceased her struggle in the skeleton statue's crushing grip, aware that if it were to let go of her now, she would fall into the tomb's waiting mouth—straight into that coffin.

But as she forced herself to look into the face of the skull, a new thought hit her, ignited by the changing inscription on the tomb. Lilith had once admitted to having many names.

"Bess," Isobel hissed between haggard breaths, remembering the name the demon had hidden behind when seeking Varen—when dipping into his dreams and luring him deeper and deeper into this world. *Her* world. "That's short for Elizabeth, isn't it?"

Lilith appeared on Isobel's other side, where she offered a grin—and a glimpse of razor teeth.

"'I don't know what to write,' scribbled the boy, his thoughts winding around and around, always circling back to the cheerleader who had stolen his heart and replaced the lure of his darkest dreams." As Lilith spoke, her voice dropped, phasing from a woman's to that of a beast's. "'I can't think. I can't think. Isobel. Isobel. Isobel. . . .'"

Isobel winced at hearing the final desperate lines Varen had scrawled into his sketchbook.

He had written those words in place of an ending to the story he'd been crafting at Lilith's bidding—the story meant to bridge the worlds, to allow Lilith into their reality.

Except now it was Varen himself who had taken on that role. And by choice, no less—even if he didn't see it that way. Even if he didn't fully realize what it was he was doing.

What—Isobel was beginning to dread—might have been done already . . .

In targeting Varen, Isobel realized with a gut-wrenching pang of failure, Lilith had indeed found the perfect tool to work through. A gifted yet bent spirit. A cracked soul ready to break and spill forth the poison it had absorbed, the darkness it had learned to survive on for so long.

But, in following Reynolds's orders to enter the veil, in taking the bait that had led her to incite Varen to destruction, hadn't she allowed the demon to use her own pain and longing against her, too?

So, Isobel supposed, both she *and* Varen had been guilty of walking into the demon's well-laid snares. But maybe, she thought, just maybe, the two of them had inadvertently laid one of their own. . . .

"That story," Isobel said, turning her head to stare into Lilith's hungry eyes. "It isn't over. Elizabeth never got her ending, did she? Her fate was never decided."

"And you think *you* would like to finish it?" Lilith asked with a laugh, stepping in close. "Brave. Smart, too. But you can't." The demon's smile grew into a wide grin, one of triumph and bloodlust. "You burned that book, silly. Or don't you remember?"

"Burned or not," came a voice from behind the demon, "*I'm* still here."

Sliding out from between a pair of statues, Varen stepped into view.

"That means the story still exists," he said, his black glare driving into Lilith. "And this isn't how it ends."

46
In a Mad Rushing Descent as of the Soul into Hades

"*There* you are," Lilith said, her attention shifting from Isobel to Varen. "I was curious how far you would allow things to progress. How long it would take you to scrape together the remnants of a piteous courage that, until now, had yet to show itself."

"Varen," Isobel called, straining in the skeleton's grip to twist toward him. "Listen to me. The link, it *can* be broken. It is already. *Our* bond—it's stronger. Do you hear me? The ribbon. *Look.*" Isobel swiveled her wrist, waving the sash. "It's here in my hand. Please. All you have to do is take it."

"Tell me," Lilith said as she strode toward Varen, her long white train dragging after her. "How do you like *my* new sculpture? My own version of *Death and the Maiden.* I made it for you, you know. Thought it would appeal to your tastes. Those grim sensibilities that first drew you to me."

Varen neither blinked nor flinched as the demon approached him. And despite Isobel's instructions, her pleas, he didn't look her way, either.

"You're speechless, I see," Lilith went on, "but I assume you must approve, since you've yet to make a single alteration."

Isobel frowned, eyes falling to the skeletal hand that wrapped around her wrist, and that no thought of her own could loosen.

Was Lilith just goading them again, or could it be true that Varen was *allowing* this?

If he held the power to set Isobel free with a thought, why wasn't he using it?

For that matter, if he was capable of setting them *both* free with one simple action, as Reynolds had told her, then what was stopping him?

"Varen?" she called to him again, but when he once more failed to meet her gaze, she had no choice but to consider what Lilith had said. How she knew he'd been there the whole time.

Suddenly Isobel wondered if Varen had given her the slip on purpose. Could he have been using her as bait? As a means to lure Lilith into this confrontation?

With new wounds so fresh and deep, and a spirit consumed once more by hatred, would he now trade everything—including her—for a chance to exact revenge?

Though Isobel didn't want to believe the doubts casting thick shadows over her sinking heart, the fact that Varen had yet to acknowledge her in any way only served to stoke the embers of her growing uncertainty.

"Varen, please," Isobel pleaded. "Just . . . come take the ribbon and it'll be over. She won't be able to touch us ever again."

"Hear how she *entreats* you," cooed Lilith as she wound

her way around Varen to stand at his back. "How *gratifying* that must be."

The skeleton statue moved again, and twirling Isobel to face the open grave, it wrenched her arm in its socket. She cried out in pain, her knees buckling. But the statue's sinewy stone arm caught her before she could tip forward into the grave. Pulling her snug once more, the Red Death refroze, holding Isobel's ribbon hand aloft as though they had simply entered a new step in their waltz.

"Come now," Lilith said, speaking into Varen's ear, eyeing Isobel over his shoulder, "she simply must know what this means to you before I send her off to bed. Think back to *how much* you craved the merest of glances from her in the beginning, how badly you longed for one touch, let alone an outright petition for your love. And you hid it so well from her. From everyone but me, that is. You do remember *why*, don't you?"

As Lilith spoke, Isobel could see the rigidness in Varen's shoulders increase, the dullness in his eyes deepen.

"Would that she could see all those dreams of her you could not help," Lilith continued. "But then again, in a way I suppose she already has, hasn't she? I dare say Pinfeathers saw to that. Funny, though, how that creature—your own dreams run rampant—so quickly became her nightmare."

"He scared me, Varen, yes, but I loved him too, okay?" Isobel called to him. "She'll trick you again if you let her. She'll trick us both into doing what she wants. Don't you see that she must have known the whole time about Bruce?"

"Don't you see that she must have known the whole time about Bruce?" repeated the demon, her onyx eyes flicking to Isobel as she spoke into Varen's ear.

Isobel shook her head. "I would have *told* you," she said. "I wanted to. But I had to get you home first. I had to get you *out* of here. Varen, please!"

"Well, go on," Lilith said, waving a delicate hand toward Isobel. "You have my blessing. Collect your token. Declare your fidelity to another. Send me away, if that's what you want. Be warned, though, that should you accept her terms, unlike mine, they last only as long as her love for you. And when that expires, as it inevitably will, I will return for you. Lay waste to whatever remains of your craven soul."

Varen shifted from foot to foot, his gaze at last trailing to Isobel.

"Then again," whispered Lilith, "you *could* take your stand against me now. Vanquish me however you choose. Finish my story, send me to *hell* if you wish."

"You belong there," Varen said.

"So *say* it," Lilith hissed. "You must already know how it ends." Looping an arm around him, the demon pressed a palm over his heart and grasped a fistful of his shirt. "In here."

Seconds passed and nothing happened. Varen seemed to deliberate, his eyes on Isobel. But Isobel had already decided she would not beg him again. It had become clear that Varen would now believe—and do—whatever he wanted.

Finally he slipped free of Lilith's grasp, his steps carrying him toward Isobel. He stopped at the foot of the open grave, the toes of his boots poking over the edge.

"I'm sorry," he said, "but I'm not who you think I am."

Isobel gaped at him, the hand that held the ribbon slackening with her shock.

"But don't feel bad," he added, his expression cold. "No matter what, you could never have stopped this."

With that, he turned to face Lilith again. He raised an arm and extended his hand toward the demon, palm open.

A surge of winds swept out from behind Isobel, flying in from nowhere to course through the courtyard.

The gales rushed strong past Varen, causing his hair and coat to flutter. As they surged between the statues, the currents of air rose in a chorus of whistles. They clashed with Lilith and lifted her veils and hair into a frenzy.

All around, the shrouds of the other statues began to unravel, peeling away as they turned to fabric. Curling under and over, fluttering like white flags, the loosed veils then vaporized, dissipating into smoke.

Beneath Isobel, the stone floor began to erode into pressed dirt mottled with dead grass.

She watched Varen shut his fist and curl his arm in. Suddenly the howling bluster switched courses. Lilith's veils redirected themselves, flowing now toward Varen instead of away.

The shift in the harsh air current scrambled Isobel's hair, blocking her view.

Then the statue's hold on her faltered. Slipping free of its grip, she fell—not into the awaiting pit, but onto a hard patch of frozen turf.

Isobel's ribbon flew out of her hand, up and up. Craning her neck skyward, she watched the once-pink sash sail toward the ceiling of gray that, with a crack of thunder, tore suddenly open.

Through the atmosphere's ripped seam burned a host of faraway stars.

Her ribbon danced toward the rift and then beyond it, disappearing behind the clouds.

Isobel's breath left her in a rush as she looked to Lilith, whose shroud had begun to funnel and twist, cocooning the demon's form as it bound her arms together.

The glowing veils merged and lengthened and, like wool being spun into thread, wound into a single strand.

The long, oscillating tendril slithered through the air, inching its way closer to Varen, whose focus was zeroed in on the thread as if pulling it toward him with his eyes.

A silver cord, Isobel realized the moment the luminous string connected with Varen's chest, its glow intensifying as it shot straight into him.

Throwing her head back, Lilith began to laugh once more.

"Foolish boy!" she bellowed as Varen drew her nearer and nearer. "Have you forgotten that you and I are *already* one? Destined for the same inexorable fate?"

Isobel clutched the grass beneath her, staring on in horror and grim fascination as Varen took the demon's awful face in his hands and drew her to him.

"No," she heard him say as he leaned down slowly, closing the distance between them. "But I think you have."

He kissed Lilith through her veil then, and as he did, the winds ceased their raging.

Isobel felt a coldness steal over her even as she watched Lilith fold in on herself, her brilliance dying as the last of her light and essence caved into Varen, leaving his hands empty.

Silence screamed.

For a moment, nothing happened.

Then, staggering in place, Varen lifted a trembling hand to his chest.

He glanced back toward Isobel as a long streak of thick black liquid spilled over his bottom lip.

"*Oh,*" Isobel uttered, climbing quickly to her feet.

She stopped, though, when she realized that Varen wasn't looking at her.

A sharp scrape of metal sent a warning chill up Isobel's spine. Turning her head fast, she saw Reynolds duck out from behind Lilith's disintegrating tomb, the walls of which had begun to collapse into ash.

Reynolds held a single blade at the ready, those black coined-size holes fixed on Varen.

As I am, so now are you.

Lilith's words from the hall of mirrors clanged through Isobel's head, and suddenly she knew Reynolds's and Varen's ultimate intent—the plan the two of them had apparently made without her.

To end the demon by ending Varen.

Isobel gave herself no time to think. No time to process what was happening as her surroundings began to peel away faster and faster, allowing patches of another world to show through. *Her* world, she realized, as flashes of blue and red light sparked in her periphery.

Sirens wailed, warped and distant—but getting closer.

Reynolds moved toward her with a purposeful, even stride.

"No," she said as she ran to meet him. To stop him.

Somewhere behind her, tires screeched and car doors slammed. Men shouted, their voices muffled and indiscernible.

"Please!" she gasped as she crashed into Reynolds, hands latching onto his arm and pushing it down. "There has to be another way."

To her surprise, Reynolds lowered the sword at her behest.

"I am sorry, my sweet friend," he said, his gaze shifting to meet hers.

Isobel stopped, arrested by the deadness in Reynolds's eyes, how it now seemed more absolute than ever before.

Why, if he had decided against making his attack, would he still apologize?

"You! Drop your weapon!" a man shouted, his voice now clear and sharp in Isobel's ears.

"Varen, you do what he says!" screamed another, and this time, the voice was one Isobel knew.

But . . . what was Mr. Nethers doing here? How had Varen's father find them? And why was he yelling for Varen to—?

Isobel's eyes grew wide as she realized, with a sudden gut punch of horror, that Reynolds hadn't intended to harm anyone.

He'd only been distracting her.

Whirling, she saw Varen turn to face the dark street now lined with police vehicles, leaving her, again, with only the view of that horrible, white, spread-winged raven.

In one hand, Varen held a black object. Lifting an arm, he aimed it toward the spinning lights and the silhouettes who, huddled behind their car doors, raised their own in response.

Isobel broke forward, terror shredding her insides.

Reynolds caught her, though. Pulling her back, he wrapped her tightly in his strong arms.

But his hold on Isobel lasted for only a second.

Because, when the sharp bang of a gun rang clear and loud through the street, Reynolds's arms—like Lilith's tomb, Varen's palace, and the rest of the wreckage left in the wake of the departing dreamworld—transformed into dust.

Varen's imagined handgun followed suit, his black coat as well. Both dreamworld remnants crumbled to ash.

Then Isobel's ribbon fell from the sky, tumbling to the dirt only half an instant ahead of Varen.

47
Nepenthe

The grave still looked fresh a week and a half after the funeral.

Hands clasped in front of her, Isobel's eyes traced the welt of earth. Over the next few months, the mound would sink and heal over with grass, blending in with the surrounding turf until the only evidence left that anything lay beneath would be the smooth black granite marker.

The stone shouldn't have looked so new, she thought, with its clean-cut edges and glossy surface, its numbers and letters cut so rigidly deep.

Actually, everything about the monument struck her as too utilitarian, too unfeeling for the grave's tenant. Except for the epitaph, which appeared below the standard information of name and dates, its lines written in looping, scrolling cursive.

SOUL OF STORMS AND FRIEND OF FEW,

O CAPTAIN, MY CAPTAIN,

FOREVER SHALL I MISS YOU.

Though touching and beautiful in their own right, the words—which she had not allowed herself to read until now—affected her less than the knowledge of who had penned them.

Isobel drew in a long breath and released it with a shuddering sigh. But that couldn't stop the heat that rushed to her cheeks, the tears that stung her eyes and fell despite her efforts to hold them in.

Before leaving the house to come here, she'd promised herself she would not cry. But she hadn't accounted for how real everything would feel after seeing the stone. So real that for the first time since all this began, she didn't have to fight the impulse to check a watch or clock to see if it really was.

The crisscrossed flowers piled atop the hill of brown earth helped attest to the grave's authenticity too, the carnations and roses drooping their heads as if sharing in the sorrow.

When fresh, the flowers had been colored cream and yellow, pristine and bright. Isobel found it both ironic and fitting that their petals now resembled aged parchment. And while February's dying breaths had apparently held enough chill to preserve the half-wilted flowers for this long, they hadn't been able to prevent the heavy odor that overcame all blooms at the onset of rot.

Of course, the scent was one Isobel knew well, and so it was possible, she mused, that she was simply more attuned to it.

Now, the moldering smell carried her mind backward through time, transporting her to the moments she'd spent locked in the arms of a friend she both loved and hated. Moments that had proved to be Reynolds's last.

Had he planned it that way?

Oh, who knew. . . .

Wherever Reynolds was, though—and she had to believe he was *somewhere*—Isobel knew he would be glad about being there. Freed, along with the other Lost Souls. For dying, she knew—dying for good—*had* been part of the plan.

His and Varen's.

Maybe she would see Reynolds again one day. Then again, maybe not, she thought, squinting when a spark of sunlight lit the gravestone's polished surface, causing the name chiseled there to blend out of sight.

"Hey," came a voice to her left, followed by a familiar clank of bracelets. "You okay?"

Having been so lost in her thoughts, Isobel hadn't heard anyone come up behind her.

"Yeah," she said, responding too quickly. "No," she amended, lifting a hand to cover her face as more hot tears streamed forth.

Stupid, stupid. She so should have known better than to wear makeup.

"Here," Gwen said, plunging a hand into her patchwork purse and retrieving a wad of tissues, which she handed to Isobel. "They're clean, just a little crumby. Graham cracker mishap."

"Thanks," Isobel said, and, swallowing, forced the upsurge of emotion back down. Though she blotted her face, she knew by the streaks of black on the tissue that the damage had been done. "So much for waterproof. . . ."

"You *do* know they make that stuff out of bat poop, don't you?"

"I do now." Isobel sighed.

"Where's Blondie?" Gwen asked.

"Should be here any minute. Where's Mikey?"

"Told him to wait in the car," Gwen said, jerking her head over one shoulder. "He still doesn't know . . . the details. Really, though, I was there and *I* still don't know the details. At any rate, I thought it would be better that way. Keep 'em in the dark for the time being. Given everything that . . . well . . . you know."

Isobel nodded again. "I know."

Glancing up, she met Gwen's gaze full-on for the first time. Gently she brushed aside her friend's bangs, eyeing the fading welt Reynolds had dealt her when he'd knocked her out cold. Though Isobel had caught hell from Gwen about the whole episode, not to mention a nice long tirade about being gullible, she had to admit she was glad Reynolds had made the executive decision to put Gwen out for the count. Otherwise, they might not both be standing here now.

"What did you tell Mikey about your head?" Isobel asked.

"Same thing I tell everybody else. That he shoulda seen the other guy."

Isobel grinned in spite of herself, but her smile fell at the sound of a slamming car door. She whirled around.

Gwen's gaze followed hers to the tall and lean blond figure now striding toward them through the yard of stones, a small plastic-wrapped bouquet in one hand.

"I don't care what color he dyes it." Scrounging through her purse again, Gwen drew out what—after a double take—Isobel saw was a sleeve of chocolate cookies. "I mean, you can take the blond out of the goth, but you can't take the goth out of the blond," Gwen went on, biting down on one of the cookies. "Mark my words, these Dark Knight tendencies will prevail through the years. He'll probably sleep in the closet, too. Upside down, arms crossed. But the good news is that the two of you are going to have some damn beautiful golden-haired babies."

"Appropriate," Varen said as he drew to a stop beside Isobel.

"You know what they say," Gwen said with a shrug, stuffing the rest of the cookie into her mouth. "Two uglies make a pretty."

Isobel's smile returned. Her eyes lifted to Varen's, and after a beat, he offered her a subdued smile of his own.

He looked so very different this way. The same and yet . . . not. It would be a long while before Isobel got used to seeing him with his hair shortened to half its previous length, dyed its natural color—only a shade lighter than her own—and styled with a shorter swoop that didn't obscure his gaze. But she thought his eyes, green and bright, looked somehow warmer now than when his hair had been black.

"Should you really be driving this soon?" Gwen asked. She aimed a thumb at the Cougar, which Varen had left parked to one side of the winding road, beneath the drooping branches of a naked willow tree. "I mean, I get that there wasn't any bone or muscle damage, but I thought the doc told you the sling was supposed to stay on for at least two weeks. I just sustained a fracture, and I had to wear mine fo—"

Varen's eyes slid toward Gwen.

"Right," she said, holding up a palm. "Outlaw don't need no sling. I smell what you're steppin' in."

Turning back to Isobel, Varen brushed a thumb across her cheek, over her scar, his touch causing her eyelids to flutter.

"I still attest it's a good look," he said.

Oh crap. He meant the mascara.

Flushing, Isobel bowed her head and fiddled with the tissue wad, sending a rain of graham cracker crumbs onto the dirt mound.

Having known how hard this would be for Varen—his first visit to Bruce's grave and, consequently, the last time she and he would be together before the next school year—Isobel had wanted so badly to be strong. She'd been relying on the old cheerleader trick of fake-it-till-you-make-it, but tears or not, she should have known better than to think Varen wouldn't see through her facade. Weren't they done with masks, anyway?

Isobel heard the clink of his wallet chains as he shifted to stand in front of her, his ash-free combat boots sliding into view. Tucking his fingers under her chin, Varen lifted her face to his. With his other hand, he took the tissues from her and dabbed gently beneath her eyes.

"Good look," he said, "but . . . not you."

"No, no," Gwen said after a beat, and stuffing the cookie sleeve under one arm, she snatched the tissues from Varen and inserted herself between them. "Not like that. Look. You gotta lick it first."

"Gwen!" Isobel squealed, yanking her head to one side and batting away the now saliva-swathed tissues. "Gross!"

"Yet effective," Gwen said. "Potent as paint thinner."

"You were dropped as a child, weren't you?" Varen asked her.

"Maybe once or twice," Gwen said, "but at least I wasn't raised by highly literate vampires who, every night just before bed, fed me a steady diet of dark sarcasm and gothic horror fiction."

"Every *morning* before bed," Varen corrected. Stepping forward, he moved toward the headstone. "We slept during the day."

"Right," Gwen joked, but even Isobel heard the hitch in her friend's voice.

Varen crouched in front of the stone, resting one hand on top of it as quiet settled among the three of them. Birds twittered in the trees, and somewhere far away, cars swooshed by.

Isobel watched Varen as she tried again to suppress the surge of sorrow that flooded her system. But waves of emotion washed through her at the sight of that upside-down crow spread over his back, safety-pinned to the hunter green mechanic's jacket that, for a time, had been hers.

After placing the bouquet at the base of the marker— three red roses for the three buried family members—Varen stayed low, staring down at the place where polished granite met dirt.

"It's beautiful, you know," Isobel said at last, when he didn't rise. "The epitaph. Bruce, he . . . he would have liked it."

Varen nodded, though he still did not rise or look back. Just hung his head.

More quiet. More birds. *Swoooosh. Swooooosh.*

"O Captain, my Captain," Gwen said, brightening suddenly and snapping her fingers. "I know that from somewhere. Wait—don't tell me. I got this. Eeehhh—Walt Disney."

Slowly, very slowly, Varen rose. He turned his head with equal deliberateness to send a penetrating stare over his shoulder at Gwen. Minus the shreds of inky locks that had caged his face before, the look was the same one Varen had given Isobel on many occasions. Most notably when they'd met in the library that first time to study for their project. And again in the attic of Bruce's bookshop.

"Whitman," Varen said. "Walt *Whitman.*"

"Oh yeah," Gwen said, plastic rustling as she dug for another cookie. "The guy from *Breaking Bad.* I knew that. Anybody want a Thin Mint?"

Varen shut his eyes.

He remained that way for what must have been an entire minute.

Then, without warning, tears escaped his lowered lids, rushing fast down his cheeks and over his own scar—that still-healing patch of torn skin dealt to him by the Nocs.

"Aaaand . . . looks like my work here is done," Gwen said.

"Think I'll go try to chat up the Warden while you two . . . catch up. See if I can get m'self off the naughty list, since he's in a pardoning mood."

Gwen didn't wait for permission but quickly walked away, hurrying toward where Isobel's father stood beside the sedan.

Without looking, Isobel knew her dad had to be pacing, arms folded, scowl firmly in place. Blood pressure high, forehead vein well pronounced.

She didn't care. The deal was this. And this . . . this was important.

"I'm sorry," Varen said, at last reopening his eyes.

"Me too." Sidling next to him, she took the hand of his good arm and squeezed. "Does your shoulder still hurt bad?"

"Everything hurts bad."

Angling toward him, Isobel slid her arms under his jacket and around his middle. Laying her head against his chest, she listened to the steady thud of his heart.

"Your hair," she said. "I've decided that . . . I really like it."

"Your shrink friend's suggestion."

"Dr. Robinson?" Isobel asked.

"When I told her how Bruce and I first met, she thought it would be a good way to pay homage since . . . since I didn't get to say good-bye. To mark his passing. And to . . . distance myself from . . . me."

Curious, Isobel leaned back and peered up at him.

"How *did* you and Bruce first meet?"

A thinner version of Varen's smile returned. "Before

freshman year, I used to sneak into Nobit's Nook all the time. Sometimes I could hide between the shelves, but whenever he caught me reading, he'd always kick me out. I used to think it was because of the way I dressed, but . . ."

"But . . . ?" Isobel prompted.

Varen shook his head. "He never said why, until one day I challenged him on it. He got mad and started yelling. Something about having enough ghosts to deal with already."

Understanding dawned on Isobel, giving her already well-wrung heart another small twist. "He kicked you out because you reminded him too much of Grey."

When Varen didn't reply, Isobel knew to take his silence as confirmation.

"What . . . happened to Grey?" she asked after a beat.

"He never told me and I never asked," Varen said, his expression darkening. "I didn't go looking for information, either, because . . . well, he wasn't asking *me* questions. I guess we both just sort of preferred it that way. It was like we had our own unspoken agreement. But at the start of last year, before I found out about his diagnosis, he asked me to start organizing the bookshop, and weeding through some stuff, I found pictures."

"You do look a little like him," Isobel said, shifting her eyes to the tombstone planted at the left of Bruce's—Grey's grave. "Now especially."

"Intentional," he said. "Given that the things he left me were . . . all Grey's."

"The car," Isobel said.

"The car."

"And . . . the suit?"

"You saw that?" Varen asked, but he didn't wait for her to answer. "Graduation. In his will, he stated it was his wish for me to wear it under my robes when I walked. Because . . . Grey never got to."

"Theeeen," Isobel said, drawing out the syllable, "that just means you'll have to walk."

He actually laughed, one short half chuckle that he tried to hide by brushing at his face with the back of his sleeve. "Yeah, if your dad doesn't call out a hit on me in the meantime."

Isobel glanced reluctantly in the direction of the sedan, where Gwen stood next to her dad, both of them leaning against the car. Arms folded and frame tense, Isobel's dad watched her and Varen with his circulating-buzzard face on, ignoring Gwen's repeated elbow nudges and cookie offerings.

"Don't worry about him," Isobel said, raising a hand to touch Varen's hair, which still felt silken between her fingers. "I have a feeling that as long as I play by his rules this time around, he might mellow out sooner rather than later."

"On that note," Varen said as he caught her hand and lowered it between them, turning it palm up, "since those rules happen to include that you're suspended from seeing me until I go back to school, and since Robinson wants me to wait until the fall to return, I figured I'd better ask you now."

"Ask me?"

"To prom," he said, and he placed something small and hard in the center of her hand. His silver class ring.

Isobel's eyes widened, but her fingers closed around the token, and she fluttered her gaze up to his. "Junior prom . . . or senior?"

"I'll go with you to both," he replied, "if your dad will make an exception. But you certainly picked a strange place to ask me."

He'd said it so seriously that she had to smile. "So . . . I guess this means we're official."

"I'm pretty sure Gwen is Instagramming this as we speak."

Isobel glanced over to Gwen and her father again. True to Varen's report, Gwen had moved away from the sedan and was now holding up her cell. To Isobel's surprise, she saw her father looming over her friend's shoulder, squinting at the smartphone screen—probably because it magnified her and Varen. What they were doing . . .

Blushing and wondering what the hashtag on *that* one would be, Isobel peered up at Varen again.

"Want to give them something to talk about?" he asked, pressing a warm palm to her cheek.

"Always," she said.

With that, Varen leaned down, and in that way of his that always caused everything else to blur away, he kissed her.

48
Dreams No Mortal Ever Dared to Dream

Tick tick tick tick tick tick—

Isobel bolted upright, her body flinging itself into motion before her brain could so much as register the source of its fear, or command her eyes to open.

Gasping, scrambling to free herself from her heavy comforter, she skittered back and slammed spine-first into her cubbyhole headboard, causing its contents to rattle. Frantic, she swiped at her arms and legs, brushing and slapping.

Her thrashing subsided as, slowly, she realized she was at home. In bed. Alone.

Isobel froze. Holding her breath, she listened hard, eyes darting across the tranquil blue darkness of her room.

Her open curtains hung stationary. Beyond her window, bits of snow gathered on the sill. And in the distance, she could just see the topmost limbs of Mrs. Finley's oak.

There were no deathwatches clambering up her body, no ink-faced monsters or fragmented ghouls gathered in shadowy corners or lurking in her open closet. No grim palace halls visible through the frame of her uncovered dresser mirror . . .

The ticking sound continued, though, the soft noise

audible even over the hammering of her heart, the rushing of her blood.

Tick tick tick tick tick tick . . .

Resonating louder in one ear than the other, the sound drew Isobel's attention to her left, down to the open brass pocket watch that sat on the splayed, gold-rimmed pages of a familiar book.

Isobel didn't need to read the tome's cover to know its title. And she didn't need to see the name AUGUSTUS inscribed on the inside of the watch's little hinged door to know who the timepiece belonged to either.

But . . . if Reynolds was gone, how had the watch gotten here?

Tick tick tick tick tick tick tick . . .

Scooting to sit on the edge of her bed, Isobel plucked up the watch by its long chain. She brought it close and, catching it with her other hand, held it steady, following the movement of its spindly black second hand as it ticked along one space at a time, past the stationary hour and minute hands that pointed to midnight.

Frowning, Isobel leaned over and switched on her bedside lamp. She scanned her room again, searching for any evidence that might point to someone's having been there.

There was nothing, though, and eventually her gaze wandered back to the book, which had been left open at page 119—a title page of mostly white space.

When Isobel caught sight of the name stamped in the middle, though, her frown deepened. Palming the watch, she took the book and drew it into her lap.

THE NARRATIVE

OF

ARTHUR GORDON PYM

OF NANTUCKET

COMPRISING THE DETAILS OF A MUTINY

AND ATROCIOUS BUTCHERY

ON BOARD THE AMERICAN BRIG *GRAMPUS*,

ON HER WAY TO THE SOUTH SEAS,

IN THE MONTH OF JUNE, 1827.

"*Gordon,*" Isobel whispered, tracing the middle name of the story's protagonist with her fingers.

Next, her fingertips trailed to the ship's name, which she'd also seen before. *Grampus.* Hadn't that been the name written across the storm-tossed ship in the animated painting that had hung in Varen's dreamworld house?

Hurriedly, Isobel flipped to the next page, to the place where the story began. She skimmed the first few lines.

> *My name is Arthur Gordon Pym. My father*
> *was a respectable trader in sea-stores at*
> *Nantucket, where I was born. My maternal*
> *grandfather was an attorney in good practice.*
> *He was fortunate in everything, and had*
> *speculated very successfully in stocks of the*
> *Edgarton New-Bank, as it was formerly called.*
> *By these and other means he had managed to*

lay by a tolerable sum of money. He was more attached to myself, I believe, than to any other person in the world, and I expected to inherit the most of his property at his death.

Baffled, Isobel narrowed her eyes on the tightly packed blocks of text while her mind went on autopilot, deep-sea diving for something Reynolds had once said to her. About his having had a family . . .

Like you, I had a mother and father. And a grandfather, with whom I was particularly close.

"Arthur Gordon Pym," Isobel muttered, speaking into the book. "By . . . Edgar Allan Poe."

She'd said the names aloud for a reason. Now that she had, it did not elude her that they carried such similar-sounding beats. Quickly another memory resurfaced—of a time when Reynolds had mentioned his friendship with Poe. Two sides of the same creepy coin, Reynolds had said.

Well, Isobel thought, flipping back to the title page and its lines about mutiny and the Southern seas—at least that explained the whole pirate sword thing.

Curious, she hooked a finger to catch the next segment of pages, preparing to flip straight to the end and read the last paragraph, when a low *click* from somewhere downstairs made her look up.

Her door frame stood empty. Dark. Quiet.

Then: *eeEEEEEeee.*

Isobel recognized the sound of the front door opening.

She grew still, listening for several more seconds. When she heard nothing else, she closed the book, set it aside, and, clenching her fist tight around the watch, reached with her free hand to pick up her bedside lamp.

Her fingers stopped just short of wrapping around the lamp's middle.

Deciding this time to forgo her usual impulse of grabbing the first useless, weapon-esque thing she saw, she rose and padded barefoot to the door.

Peering out into the hall and over the banister, Isobel saw that the front door hung halfway open.

Bits of snow fluttered in with a rolling fog of cold mist.

Sparing a quick glance to the cracked door of her brother's darkened room, Isobel slid out into the hall.

She stood overlooking the foyer, watching the gales of cold air waft in. Though she thought for a moment about calling for her dad, she decided against it.

Then she noticed that the outer storm door, which should have prevented the inflow of snow and air . . . was missing.

Tick tick tick tick tick tick, came the sound of the mantel clock in the living room.

The noise prompted Isobel to check the pocket watch again, but it continued to tick normally.

She slipped to the stairs and then down, the middle step creaking as she passed the collage of family photos, most of which had been repaired and rehung.

Edging around the banister, she took the door and,

opening it all the way, peered out into the familiar cemetery that had taken the place of her front yard.

To her right, perched atop its short cement stoop, its four faces aglow with floodlights, Poe's gravestone monument stood tall and sturdy. As if it and all the other tombs had always been there. Just another collection of quaint lawn ornaments.

Snow dusted the headstones and the narrow walkway, which ran between the house-shaped sepulchres.

Leading away from the threshold on which Isobel stood, a single set of boot prints dotted the trail. They ran past Poe's monument and between two rows of short, low-lying tombs. There the footprints disappeared, fading into the patch of darkness that waited beyond.

Even though her breath clouded in front of her, Isobel felt no coldness in the air.

She deliberated for a moment, but then, stepping outside, found that the fleecy snow held no frigid sting.

Isobel drifted forward through the silent cemetery. Following the trail of prints, she made her way down the path, glancing back only once to make sure her house was still there, that the door leading to her foyer remained open. It did.

Aware that despite what the pocket watch was telling her, she must be dreaming, Isobel bore onward. She paused when she reached the end of the narrow alley between tombs and, glancing right, saw that a quiet sidewalk waited beyond the tall Greene Street gates.

To her left, the footprints continued on, winding past the

closed entrance to the catacombs and hooking around the corner of Westminster Hall.

Sure, now, of where the prints must lead—and to *whom*—Isobel let go of her need to stay within sight of her house. She rounded the bend, and from there made her way quickly up the narrow, uneven brick trail that would take her to Poe's original burial spot.

He stood just where she knew she would find him, hovering over the stone marker while bits of white gathered on the wide brim of his hat.

A low breeze brushed past Isobel and swept around Reynolds, stirring the bottom edge of his cloak and the tails of his white scarf.

Her bare feet leaving the trail, Isobel moved toward him over the hardened earth. Reynolds did not glance her way as she approached but kept his gaze squarely on the marker's chiseled raven. Even as Isobel joined him at his side, he didn't turn to her or speak.

"Let me guess," Isobel said. She dropped her voice low, scrunching her face into her best Reynolds scowl. *"Do not be alarmed. This is a dream."*

To her utter shock, her impersonation actually got a smile out of him. Though she could not see his mouth for the scarf, the smirk was wide enough that it reached his eyes, causing them to crinkle at the corners.

And his eyes themselves—Isobel had to lean forward when she noticed their color. That they had a color. Wait. Were they . . . *blue*?

Unable to help herself, Isobel placed a hand on his arm. Finally, prompted by her touch, he turned his head her way.

Blue indeed, she saw. Blue, with rims of dark gray that encircled the bright starbursts of his irises.

"Yet your watch would advise you otherwise," he replied, and, lifting a gloved hand, he pinched the scarf and drew it down from his face.

"*My* watch?" Isobel asked, her voice trailing off as she marveled at his complexion.

Though Reynolds wouldn't have walked away from a "best tan" contest with any sort of honorable mention, let alone an award, she thought his pallor had been greatly reduced. Less dead mushroom and more basement recluse.

"I am of the mind you would have more use for it now than I."

That last bit hit her brain as mumbo jumbo. She shook her head, clearing their conversation to begin a new one that, hopefully, she would be able to follow.

"Hold up. I'm a little lost," she said, folding her arms against the cold she didn't feel. She glanced behind her toward the Greene Street gates. "Are we in the dream-world?"

"Tell me, what do your instincts suggest?"

Isobel glowered at him. "My instincts suggest that *you*, at least, are the real deal, given that only you would answer a straightforward question with a cryptic, open-ended one of your own."

"Since I am, according to you, being predictable, you

won't then mind my repeating old lines about not being long on time."

Isobel's hands went to her hips. "Is that why you're all dressed up? Got a Monster's Ball to attend? Or a meeting for the Literal Literary Characters of America?"

"Something like that," he said, another slight smile touching his lips—its appearance all but rattling Isobel's entire world. Because Reynolds smiled only *never*.

"I thought," he went on, ignoring Isobel's dumbfounded stare, "that, given your undeniable knack for traversing untraversable barriers, not to mention your penchant for making your point clear through brute force, it would be wisest to arrange a meeting with you now. Save us both trouble in the long run, in the event you had any lingering queries or grievances you wished to voice. And, I suppose . . . because I thought it only proper that I tell you good-bye."

Isobel refolded her arms, scrunching them in tighter than before as she shifted her weight to one foot.

"So I know you didn't just call *me* a bully," she said, rattling off words before she even knew what they would be. "I mean, you're the one flipping around swords, stabbing people like you've got nothing better to do. And on that note, PS slash FYI, strolling out of tombs and getting nerds all excited and your dumb masked face printed up in national magazines is *not* the best way to make good on your whole 'should you seek me again I will not be found' wannabe badass spiel."

She was rambling and she knew it. And she was stalling,

too. Despite all the crap between the two of them, Isobel wasn't ready yet to tell Reynolds good-bye.

"Do you suppose they will miss me this year?" Reynolds— Pym—Gordon—*whoever* asked after allowing a block of silence to pass.

Isobel trained her focus on her feet and the collecting blanket of snow beneath them.

"I'm going to pull a *you*, do the question-for-a-question thing and ask if that means you are, in fact, going somewhere other than the woodlands. Because I was kinda thinking I wasn't going to see you ever again. And now you're here, but you say that you're going for good this time."

"Thanks to you, Isobel, the woodlands, as far as I know, are no more."

Isobel's head jerked up. "She really is gone?"

"I can only assume that Lilith died when the boy did, and that her soul passed on from his body. Presumably, to wherever demons go."

"The policeman's bullet . . . it only went through his shoulder," Isobel said. "Right through him. But the paramedics said they thought the shock caused his heart to stop. They had no other explanation for it. They thought he was dead. Well, he *was* dead. Until . . . until they brought him back."

"Varen's act was one of self-sacrifice. Of love," Reynolds replied, and his words gave her pause. Not due so much to their meaning, but because she was certain she had never heard Reynolds refer to Varen directly by name. Never until now.

"Lilith would have found his heart an uninhabitable place," Reynolds continued. "They were locked in battle even after they had become one, and it is quite possible that Lilith herself—unable to withstand such torture—was the one responsible for stopping his heartbeat, simultaneously bringing about her own demise. Whatever the case, his death—brief as it was—caused the last slip in her tenuous grip. On the boy. On her pitiful existence. On her reign and her very kingdom, as well. On me . . . Now you and the boy have both tasted death, it seems, and in so doing, you have delivered the demon's. And I believe you have granted me mine."

Reynolds stopped there, and Isobel let his explanation settle over her along with the returning quiet. Glancing at the gravestone, her eyes traced its grooves and lettering—the raven carved there in profile.

Death, she reminded herself, was what Reynolds had wanted. His desire, even if he had given up hope of ever achieving it, had been to pass on. He'd been in limbo so long, halfway living and halfway dead—all the way lost. But though Isobel knew she should be happy for him, she found that particular emotion hard to summon just at this moment. So she pressed on to her next question instead.

"He . . . Varen . . . said that when the paramedics were working on him, he heard me calling. He said there was darkness everywhere and that he was alone. But then my voice appeared as a bright light. He followed it until he . . . woke up."

Reynolds's gaze trailed after hers to Poe's old gravestone.

"For that," he said after a beat, "I have no explanation. Except, perhaps, for this: that whatever force the demon could not survive is the same that has allowed my soul to return to you in this moment. The same that allowed the boy's soul to rejoin with his body—the same that returned him, whole, to you. The same that has empowered you along the way, guiding you better than *I* could have. For look at us now."

He smiled at her again, only smaller and more bittersweet this time.

Isobel hadn't been able to prevent herself from touching his arm moments ago, or from tackling him in this same graveyard less than a month ago, or even from stabbing him through the foot on the terrace in the dreamworld. And now she could not prevent the tears that surged forth from her eyes, falling down her face in two unstoppable streams.

Slamming into him hard, she actually sobbed out loud, straight into his waistcoat.

"Why didn't you *tell* me?" she wailed. "Why didn't you tell me right from the start what was going on? That you had to pretend to be on Lilith's side? That she knew I was alive? That she *wanted* me to try to show Varen I was real, so that he would re-enter reality and bring the dreamworld with him? You could have. You didn't *have* to play her game."

"You remember when we fought?" Reynolds asked. "When the demon summoned me by name? I'd stepped out to kill you on her orders."

Isobel nodded, recalling how Reynolds had tried to coach

her even then, guiding her through the sword fight on the terrace overlooking the cliffs where Varen had stood.

"It was not by accident that she called on me to dispatch you in that moment," he said, his husky voice rumbling through her. "At that point, she suspected I was the Lost Soul who had been helping you all along, and the one who had ended Edgar's life. Our fight and its outcome, I knew, would only confirm her suspicions. But I also understood that before exacting any revenge on me, she would take my ability to enter your world into consideration.

"After I returned you to that hospital, I knew that since you lived, she would try to use you again. But in order to do that, she would need me. And Isobel, if I was to be of any use at all—if I was to keep my promise to Edgar, to supply you or your world with any aid—I had to accept the demon's offer to play the part of your guide. I had to deliver her lie to you—that she thought you dead, that you would be facing an unsuspecting enemy. And I had to let *her* believe I was aiding you only as a means to complete *her* goals.

"Even if I'd told you the truth, you would not have believed me—whether or not you would admit it now. It would only have made you more wary than you already were. You would have asked more questions. You would have waited to act. I also knew that, regardless of my commands, you would interact with the boy the moment you set eyes on him. Why do you suppose I was so adamant against it? I used your mistrust of me to both of our advantages, knowing that you would take your chance when you saw it. When you saw him. The sooner the better, was my feeling. You are welcome, by the way."

"Oh, yes, *thanks*," Isobel quipped. "Good to know *I'm* the predictable one here."

"I only predicted what I hoped would be true," he replied. "My wager, as the demon called it—believing the best of you. Believing *in* you."

"Oh, you are *so* lucky this is a dream," Isobel mumbled into him. "Because if I really *was* here, I'd totally barf on you right now."

"I am . . . touched," he said.

But really, *she* was touched. Wrapping her arms around him, she squeezed him hard.

As un-Reynolds as his words had been, she thought that he must have meant them. And if he was getting mushy, if there really were no more ominous tidings for him to bring, no more secret suicide missions to send her on, then . . . then this really must be good-bye.

She still wasn't ready for him to go, though. Not yet. But without the threat of worlds colliding or demons seeking to consume reality, all she had left to keep him there were questions.

"Your ability," Isobel murmured. "Crossing between worlds. You can do that because of Poe?" Hitching a breath, she realized Reynolds's scent, that essence of decaying roses, was gone now. Further evidence that he was slipping away. That he would depart forever, when the time came. And it was coming.

"Yes," Reynolds replied, and Isobel shut her eyes when she felt his palm against her back. "I could cross between worlds because of the power granted to me by Edgar's writing."

"Through that story," Isobel sniffled, her voice muffled against him as she kept her face stupidly smashed to his chest, now if only to see how long he would tolerate it.

"My book, the only novel Edgar ever wrote, was meant as an experiment," Reynolds explained. "Edgar's idea was to take my story, which I told to him over the course of many dreams, and adapt it to fit a real location in your world. He would then publish the piece in increments, touting it as a nonfictional account. In so doing, he hoped to create a link that would allow me to cross physically into your reality and become a part of it. His plan worked, and might have saved me from my imprisonment in the dreamworld had he not been working on another piece at the same time. A story called 'Ligeia,' inspired by another dreamworld entity. The Nocs were unleashed from his soul, and I perished by the hand of Scrimshaw. Edgar, who wed shortly after, never knew of my demise; unbeknownst to him, his union with Virginia had severed his ties to the dreamworld. It was only after she died that Lilith again pursued him."

"She went after him again," Isobel said, "and pulled him into the dreamworld."

"I found him there. When he discovered what had become of me, that I was now bound to the woodlands forever as a Lost Soul, his remorse was deep. We reconciled, and after exchanging clothing, I agreed to both play the part of his decoy, and to use the ability he'd granted me to help him return to his reality—your reality."

Isobel pulled back from Reynolds, and taking up the edge of his heavy cloak, she ran her fingers along the material. "That's why they found him wearing someone else's clothes," Isobel said. "This . . . this is *his* cloak, isn't it?"

Reynolds didn't answer, but he didn't have to.

"You knew what Varen would do, didn't you?" Isobel asked. "You knew what he'd decided. That he needed to die in order for the worlds to separate again?"

Silence again.

"Typical," Isobel said. "I should have known, but, whatever. As long as you're *not* answering my questions like you said you would, can you at least tell me what happens now? Where you'll go?"

"Presumably," he replied, "wherever Lost Souls go when they are found. But you needn't worry. I will not be alone. See for yourself."

He extended an arm toward Greene Street.

"Who said I was w—" Isobel's words halted, evaporating out of her mouth at the sight of who stood beyond the gates.

No. Flipping. Way.

Stern-faced but not unkind, there stood a man in a top hat and a black comb moustache.

Touching the brim of the hat, Edgar Allan Poe bowed his head at her very slightly.

Isobel, unsure of what else to do, gave a small, shell-shocked wave.

She jumped when Reynolds brushed past her, making his way toward the gate.

Though she wanted to call after him, to dash forward and catch his hand, she let him go.

Reynolds opened the gate, and with a low groan, it swung in toward him. As he stepped through, he unclasped his cloak and unfurled it from around his shoulders, extending it to Poe, who, without pause, drew it around his own.

The two men clasped hands, shaking fiercely.

Poe turned to go then. But Reynolds, pausing, glanced back at Isobel.

He touched the brim of his own hat, giving her the signal.

The salute of the one true Poe Toaster.

The real deal indeed.

49
Only This and Nothing More

Isobel's eyes opened on their own. Above, her bedroom light blazed bright, stinging her eyes.

She breathed in fast and deep, her chest rising quickly as the final images of her dream flipped through her head. Desperately, her mind groped for them before they could turn to vapor, sorting them and storing them in an effort to preserve every last detail, every shared word. Poe standing beyond the gate, nodding to her as if she were an old acquaintance. As if she and he had somehow known each other the whole time . . .

Isobel shifted to get out of bed but stopped when she saw her father.

Seated in a chair at her bedside, Isobel's dad watched her with folded arms, his gaze steady. His eyes red-rimmed and tired.

"Hey," he said.

"Hey," Isobel replied, her voice raspy with sleep. She started to sit up but paused again when she heard a soft clink and felt something hard in her palm.

Glancing down, Isobel opened her hand to find Reynolds's watch.

"Oh," she said, sitting up quickly.

"You . . . you were talking in your sleep," her dad said.

"Um." Isobel wrapped the watch tight in her fist again. "Just . . . weird dreams."

"Bad?" he asked, eyebrows arching.

Isobel shook her head. "Good."

He nodded. Then, after a beat, he gestured to the watch. "What's that?"

"Uh . . . it's a pocket watch . . . thingie."

"Oh yeah?" her dad said through a small chuckle. "Mind if I have a look?"

"Sure," she said, offering him the timepiece.

"Humph," her dad murmured as he turned the watch over and over between his fingers. "I don't think I've ever seen one like this. Where'd you get it?"

"Friend gave it to me," Isobel murmured, scooting back to prop herself against her headboard in a movement that felt eerily like déjà vu.

Her dad clicked open the watch's little door. "Who's Augustus?" he asked.

"I'm . . . still not sure."

"Well, this is nice, but it looks ancient," her dad observed. "Hard to believe it still works."

Glancing over her shoulder, Isobel checked her digital clock.

The numbers 6:45 blared in neon blue. But the strong smell of garlic and simmering tomato sauce wafting from the hall, combined with her father's presence in her room and his mostly calm demeanor, told Isobel it wasn't morning and she wasn't running late for school.

Then she remembered that after getting home from her first day back at cheer practice, she'd come upstairs and, thinking she would just rest her eyes for a moment, curled up in bed.

Something about going back into that gym, about rejoining the ranks of the squad and reconnecting with Nikki and Stevie—not to mention picking up the slack after her short hiatus—had sapped Isobel's energy far more than she'd anticipated. And maybe she'd fallen asleep so easily because, for the first time in a long time, she'd felt safe in letting go, in allowing herself to fall under and dream. . . .

"Dinner's just about ready," her dad said, interrupting her thoughts. "Spaghetti and garlic bread."

She nodded. "That sounds good."

"Dooo . . . you wanna go out for ice cream afterward?" he asked.

Isobel pursed her lips. "Depends," she said as she drew her knees to her chest. Resting her chin on them, she wrapped her arms around her legs. "Is . . . Mom coming?"

Her dad's smile came tight, but genuine. He nodded. "Danny, too."

"Then . . . yeah," Isobel said. "Count me in."

"Great." Isobel's dad stood and set her pocket watch gently on the open Poe book.

"Doing some light reading?" he asked, tilting his head at its pages.

Isobel shrugged. "Just flipping through."

"Okay," he said. "Then I'll see you downstairs in about five?"

"Yeah, I'll . . . be right there."

Isobel's dad tucked his hands into his pockets. Without saying anything else, he went to the door. He paused there, though, and after several seconds turned to face her again.

"Hey," he said, withdrawing something pink from his pocket—Isobel's cell. "Want to invite your friend?"

She gave him a small smile, marveling at how Gwen had been able to do it again.

Never in her life would Isobel understand that girl's odd way with people, her crazy ability to weasel into favor just as easily as she fell out of it—if not more so.

"He likes ice cream, doesn't he?" her dad asked as he tossed the phone onto her bed.

Isobel's mouth popped open wide.

Seconds flew by as she tried to catch up with what he'd just said, to wrap her mind around his meaning. Then she scrambled for her cell, finding her wits and her voice in the same instant.

"Yeah," she said. "Actually, he does."

Epilogue
Boston, Massachusetts
Sweet Surrender Dessert Café
December 21
Two Years Later

"How do you know she'll be home?" Isobel asked.

Breaking her stare on the condominium complex across the street from where they sat, Isobel clutched her oversize coffee mug between both hands.

"I don't," Varen replied, before taking another bite of the slice of German chocolate cake that he and Isobel (mostly Isobel) had all but destroyed.

A small, sad smile touched Isobel's lips, and, lifting her mug, she watched Varen from over its rim. Then, deciding she didn't want the last sips of her mocha, she set the cup down again.

"Are you worried?" she asked.

"No," Varen said, his voice carrying that low monotone drone that coated his words whenever he wanted to sound like he didn't care. "She probably won't know who I am anyway."

"It's your birthday," Isobel said. Reaching across the table, she placed a hand over his. "Who else would you be?"

His fingers caught hers, and his jade eyes flicked up. "You tell me, cheerleader."

An infinitesimal smirk teased one corner of his mouth.

That sly half smile, combined with the faint scar that still marred his cheek, caused her heart to stammer a beat.

Every so often, he had moments like these. Flashes when that other side—that other self—showed through. Though they often caught her off guard, they no longer scared her.

Quite the opposite . . .

"I know we're here now," Isobel said, giving his hand a squeeze. "But . . . you *can* still change your mind if you want to. Whatever you decide, I'm right there with you. You know that, don't you?"

Varen leaned back in his chair. He peered out the window toward the condo complex.

"I do," he said. "And whatever happens next, this is all extra, you know. The part after the ending."

"After the *happy* ending," Isobel corrected. "The afterword!" she added, perking up in her seat.

"Epilogue," Varen said.

"Wait," she said, suppressing a smile, "I thought that's what the talking was called."

"Dialogue," Varen replied, affecting a stern glower as he played along. Folding his green-jacketed arms on the table, he hooked the handle of his mug with a finger and lifted his coffee—black—to his lips.

Isobel tried hard not to laugh. The moment felt like one relived from the past, a throwback to those first days. But when Varen lost his seriousness before he could take a sip, smiling in spite of his efforts to keep a straight face, Isobel grinned too.

When the bells on the café door rang, Isobel's gaze strayed over Varen's safety-pin-studded shoulder. But her smile fell fast when she took in the pair who had just entered from the street.

Varen's expression sobered with hers. Setting his coffee cup in its saucer, he twisted to look at the young girl and her mother.

Varen's mother.

"Here to pick up the German chocolate," Madeline said after approaching the counter. "You're holding it under the name Alexander."

Isobel drew in a sharp breath, recognizing Varen's middle name.

As if sensing Varen's penetrating gaze, the girl, who couldn't have been much younger than Danny, turned her head to stare at him, blond braids flying.

"Veronica," Madeline said, nudging the girl as the clerk disappeared into the back room. "It's not polite to stare."

Quickly Varen turned toward Isobel again, his face white.

Tense in her seat, Isobel switched her focus between the woman—who after accepting a white cake box from the returning clerk, took her receipt—and Varen, who, mouth slightly agape, lip ring glinting in the late-afternoon sun, gripped the edge of the table.

"Do you want me to—" Isobel asked in a small whisper, but she stopped when, shutting his eyes, Varen shook his head once.

"Thank you," Madeline said then, ushering the girl ahead of her and leading her through the door.

The bells jangled a second time as the pair left, heading across the street.

Varen reopened his eyes and watched them the entire way, until they disappeared behind the tall brick walls girdling the condominiums.

Isobel sat silent, watching Varen intently, bracing herself for whatever his reaction would be.

"We could still catch them," she whispered.

Varen looked away from the window and back to his mug. His brow knitted. He blinked slowly, jaw flexing. Then, at last, he spoke.

"There's a beach," he said, his voice half breath, "about an hour away. A cape, actually. Probably more rock than sand. And I know it's cold, but do you want to go? Just to walk." He nodded to the cake before finally looking up at her. "I'm finished. If . . . if you are."

She tilted her head at him. "You mean you want to—"

"Make out at sunset?" he interrupted. "Yeah. I kind of do."

Varen's smile returned, though different from before. Sadder now, but . . . peaceful, as well. Satisfied, maybe.

"Weeell," Isobel said. "In *that* case, yes, I do. And . . . yeah. I'm finished too."

Acknowledgments

Crafting the final book in a trilogy has been, for me, both rewarding and challenging—a journey full of twists and turns that weren't always restricted to just those unfolding on the page. As a result, I have needed a great deal of support throughout the writing of this last volume of the Nevermore story, and I owe much gratitude to many people.

First, I'd like to thank my family and, in particular, my mom, who has always been my biggest supporter regarding any of my creative endeavors. Thanks, Mom, you're my hero and my best friend. Thanks also to my three brothers—Daniel Miller, Michael Creagh, and Thomas Creagh—who have not only inspired me (and many of Danny's antics) but have cheered me up and cheered me on. Thanks as well to their families and to all of my extended family for all your encouragement.

I would also like to extend a heartfelt thank-you to my agent, Tracey Adams, and also to Josh Adams and all the folks at Adams Literary. I appreciate your guidance as well as your encouragement and enthusiasm for this project.

Many thanks go to my editor Namrata Tripathi, who helped shape the entirety of Isobel and Varen's story and who pushed me to dig deeper with this book. Thank you also for taking a shine to these characters from the beginning, and for helping me to hone my skills as a writer and a storyteller.

An enormous thank-you goes to my other editor, Emma Ledbetter, whose extra time and attention to this last volume has proven invaluable. Thank you as well for your encouragement, for asking the right questions and then asking again. Thanks in addition for doing so much polishing and for working so closely with me on the little stuff (especially the little stuff!) as well as the big stuff and for being so kind and patient. You've been incredible.

In addition to my editors, I am indebted to my entire team at Atheneum, who have put tremendous effort into each of the Nevermore books, providing everything from the most gorgeous covers to mad ninja copyediting skills, not to mention all those touches that have prepared my work for the shelf.

To my critique group, Bill Wolfe, Katie McGarry, Colette Ballard, Kurt Hampe, and Bethany Griffin: Where would I be without you guys? Thank you for your advice, your input, and for your honest thoughts regarding my work and this project. Thank you all for the laughs and for putting up with (and sometimes joining *in* with) the strangeness that is me. Thanks for being my friends as well as my colleagues. Every time we meet, I walk away a better writer. For that, I don't think I could ever thank any of you enough.

Special thanks go to Kurt Hampe, who helped reshape and spiff up the first portion of *Oblivion*. Another big ol', extra-large slice of special thanks goes to my good buddy Bill Wolfe, who read, reread, and offered notes on every scrap of this novel. Thanks for telling me to keep on keepin' on, for meeting with me for coffee shop writing time, and for offering vital insight on my plotting for world domination. Er, I mean for this story. (Halloween Movie.) My good friend April Joye Cannon is deserving of a great deal of special thanks as well. How many times did you read how many drafts? I lost count. Thanks for lending me your eyes and your thoughts, your talent for problem solving and for snappy dialogue, too. I am beyond lucky to have you in my corner.

Thank you to: Nick Passafiume, for reading each draft, for offering your insight and your encouragement. To Jeannine Noe for our many phone calls and in-person chats (most about the same thing, I know) and for being my sounding board and my friend. To Collyn Justus for meeting me to write, for helping me to craft the perfect pirate name, for letting me bounce ideas off you, and for sharing your lovely smile. To Jackie Adams Marrs, for our plot chats, replotting chats, and for letting me help with the Lightning McQueen cake.

I am also grateful to Cecy Grisham King for our Fourth of July discussion and a subsequent coffee shop conversation. I'm not sure if you remember what you told me, but I do. And always will.

During the writing of this novel, a certain Joe King taught me both how to fish and how to golf. Thanks, Joe, for the invite. It meant more than you know, and you were totally right. About the fishing, the golfing, *and* about the importance of taking a break.

And that brings me to David Grisham. Thanks for the good times and the laughter. Thanks for hashing out the tough scenes with me and for taking me to fly that kite.

In addition to perhaps more chocolate than was necessary, this book has been made possible by bucket loads of coffee. Quite a bit of that coffee (well, most of it, actually) was provided by the lovely folks at the various Louisville Heine Brothers' locations. I'd like to say thank you to the wonderful baristas for putting up with me, for preparing excellent coffee, and for resisting the urge to run or hide behind the counter whenever you saw me park my car. (Holly, I'm still chagrined about that orange juice episode, you know. I think I must have had my South Pole elf shoes on that day.)

Along with lots of coffee, a great deal of research has gone into the construction of the Nevermore novels. It has been a joy and pleasure to research the life and works of the American legend, Edgar Allan Poe. As strange as it may sound, I have often caught myself fancying that I really do know the man. While conducting research, I have met several folks who have not only shared my affinity for Mr. Poe and his contributions to American literature, but who have also helped provide me with the information I needed to represent Eddie in an accurate and respectful way. Thank you to the Poe Society of Baltimore and to Mark Redfield, Jeff Jerome, and the city of Baltimore.

I am appreciative not only for the personal help you have given to me, but for your tireless work toward keeping Poe's legacy alive, for preserving his memory, and for sharing your knowledge of his life and writings with the world and with each new generation.

Much of my research has also brought me repeatedly to the familiar doors of the Louisville Free Public Library, and I would like to express my gratitude to my friends at each of the different branches. I appreciate your continued support of my writing endeavors, and each time I walk into any location, you all make me feel so special. Extra thanks are due here to Peter Howard for your help with locating information and translations regarding Yiddish lullabies and for being so kind as to do a bit of digging on my behalf.

To Michael Steinmacher, another incredible librarian and friend: Thank you for your continued interest in my career, your enthusiasm for my work, and inviting (and re-inviting!) me to speak at Barr Memorial Library. You're the best, Commissioner.

Books are written and books are printed, but before they truly live, they must be read. Without my readership, I might still be a writer, but I would not be an author. Thank you to all of you who have read any one of my novels. Your support and enthusiasm for my work and these characters brings me such joy. I appreciate as well all the booksellers who have hand-sold my novels and the librarians who have personally placed my work in the hands of readers. I could receive no higher compliment.

Writing is often a joyful act for me, yet sometimes it is difficult. I have quick easy days and I have slow tough ones. But every day during the writing of this book and every day before and since, I know I have had guidance from above. So I will end with thanking God, my writing companion and the source of all my inspiration. Thank you for bringing me and these characters who I love full circle.